The new Zebra Re̶g̶_____ on the cover is a photogra̶_____zy." The fashionable regenc̶_____d with a satin or velvet riband a̶_____ fragrant nosegay. Usually made of gold or silver, tuzzy-muzzies varied in design from the elegantly simple to the exquisitely ornate. The Zebra Regency Romance tuzzy-muzzy is made of alabaster with a silver filigree edging.

A DANGEROUS DESIRE

Philip tightened his grip on her hand and drew her closer. His face a scarce two inches from hers, he said caressingly, "You're a baggage, Meg. A temptress who can drive a man nigh out of his head."

Whether it was the moon weaving its magic, or the sweet scent of the lilacs clouding Meg's judgment, she leaned toward Philip. His mouth brushed hers but briefly, and yet the thrill of the butterfly touch heated her blood.

Quickly, she pulled away from him. She was four-and-twenty years old and, Lord help her, a virgin—not a natural state for a woman her age. She must guard against the singing in her blood, the racing of her pulse, the foolish yearning to feel his mouth on hers once more.

She had no illusions. She knew what Philip wanted, what every man wanted from an actress when he found her desirable. As though to confirm this, he smiled at her and in his eyes was that certain look that drove warmth into her face and made her pulse beat ever faster. . . .

THE BEST OF REGENCY ROMANCES

AN IMPROPER COMPANION   (2691, $3.95)
by Karla Hocker

At the closing of Miss Venable's Seminary for Young Ladies school, mistress Kate Elliott welcomed the invitation to be Liza Ashcroft's chaperone for the Season at Bath. Little did she know that Miss Ashcroft's father, the handsome widower Damien Ashcroft would also enter her life. And not as a passive bystander or dutiful dad.

WAGER ON LOVE   (2693, $2.95)
by Prudence Martin

Only a rogue like Nicholas Ruxart would choose a bride on the basis of a careless wager. And only a rakehell like Nicholas would then fall in love with his betrothed's grey-eyed sister! The cynical viscount had always thought one blushing miss would suit as well as another, but the unattainable Jane Sommers soon proved him wrong.

LOVE AND FOLLY   (2715, $3.95)
by Sheila Simonson

To the dismay of her more sensible twin Margaret, Lady Jean proceeded to fall hopelessly in love with the silver-tongued, seditious poet, Owen Davies—and catapult her entire family into social ruin . . . Margaret was used to gentlemen falling in love with vivacious Jean rather than with her—even the handsome Johnny Dyott whom she secretly adored. And when Jean's foolishness led her into the arms of the notorious Owen Davies, Margaret knew she could count on Dyott to avert scandal. What she didn't know, however was that her sweet sensibility was exerting a charm all its own.

Available wherever paperbacks are sold, or order direct from the Publisher. Send cover price plus 50¢ per copy for mailing and handling to Zebra Books, Dept. 3377, 475 Park Avenue South, New York, N.Y. 10016. Residents of New York, New Jersey and Pennsylvania must include sales tax. DO NOT SEND CASH.

A Scandalous Lady
KARLA HOCKER

ZEBRA BOOKS
KENSINGTON PUBLISHING CORP.

To Carin Cohen Ritter

ZEBRA BOOKS

are published by

Kensington Publishing Corp.
475 Park Avenue South
New York, NY 10016

Copyright © 1991 by Karla Hocker

All rights reserved. No part of this book may be reproduced in any form or by any means without the prior written consent of the Publisher, excepting brief quotes used in reviews.

First printing: April, 1991

Printed in the United States of America

Chapter One

"Bravo! Bravissimo!"

"Meg! Meg! Our Meg!"

Applause and chanting rose to a crescendo as the curtain dropped, isolating the new darling of the London stage from her enthusiastic admirers.

Faint from the heat, the smell of grease paint, perfume, and sweat, dizzy with the success of the performance, Meg Fletcher clutched an armful of flowers to her breast as she squeezed past stagehands and flats of scenery. The narrow corridor leading to the main dressing rooms was lit by a single lantern, but Meg was familiar with every uneven floor board; she could have found her way in the dark.

She still heard the crowd clamoring for their Meg, but she never went back after she had taken a bow and blown kisses to the audience from the pit to the highest gallery. Shutting the dressing room door on the noise and bustle, Meg thrust the flowers into a vase before seating herself in front of the mirror. Of course, she had a dresser at her disposal, a competent woman perfectly willing to assist with the removal of makeup and the changing of gowns and costumes. But after a show, Meg wanted to be alone.

She liked to relax in solitude, to slowly let go of the emotions she had captured and stored for her part in the play. She liked to look into the gilt-framed mirror and

5

imagine that, in bygone years, the glass had reflected the faces of Sarah Siddons and Dora Jordan while they played at the Drury Lane. It was impossible, of course. When the theater burned down in '09, every stick of furnishing had most likely burned with it. But it was an inspiring thought. Mrs. Siddons and Mrs. Jordan had each been a queen of the theater in her own right, the one as a tragic actress, the other as a comedienne.

Someday . . .

Meg sighed, satisfaction at her achievements mingling with the longing for "someday." She let her gaze wander to the flowers delivered backstage during the performance: red roses, as usual, from Lord Ipswich; pink roses from Mr. Selwyn; and, for the third time that week, white lilacs, her favorites. Again, without a card.

Despite herself, Meg grew curious about the sender. Who knew of, or shared, her liking for the fragrance of lilacs?

Her attention was caught by a gigantic bouquet of mixed flowers. The handwriting on the attached note drew a smile to her lips. Impatiently, she broke the seal.

Meg, love. Congratulations! was written in a sprawling masculine fist. A feminine hand had added, *I'm mad with envy that you realized your dream before I did mine! Stephen and I arrived in town this evening—too tired to attend the performance, but will do so tomorrow. Come and take lunch with us! Love, Maryann.*

Stephen and Lady Maryann Fant. Without them, Meg would not yet have realized her dream.

Two years ago, she had been a dancer at the Drury Lane with nary a chance of a speaking part. Each time she auditioned, she was defeated by the speech pattern acquired during her growing years in London's back alleys.

She had also, on occasion, helped out at the Bow Street Court where her father was employed as a runner. On that particular occasion two years ago, Sir Nathaniel Conant, the chief magistrate, had assigned her to assist

6

Stephen Fant while he gathered the evidence to convict Lady Maryann's betrothed of white slavery. In the end, it had been Lady Maryann herself who helped Stephen get the proof, but she and Stephen had shown their appreciation of Meg's willingness to serve as a decoy by arranging for much-needed voice and elocution lessons.

With the transformation of her speech, Meg had immediately been offered small parts at the Drury Lane. And at the start of the theater season this past September, Meg Fletcher had suddenly, due to an indisposition of Miss Kelly, risen from understudy and walk-on to the position of leading lady in *The Country Girl*.

As Peggy, Meg had won the public's heart. They had adored her as Rosalind in *As You Like It*, and now, a scant eight months after her debut, they worshipped her as Viola in *Twelfth Night*. Meg's shapely figure and long, elegant legs were admirably suited to the saucy "breeches parts" and stirred the blood of every male in the audience while flashing emerald eyes and long, riotous curls the color of burnished copper, which she refused to hide under a wig, drew admiration from even the most strait-laced of females.

Rousing herself from her reverie, Meg changed hurriedly. She wished—not for the first time—that she were not required to put in an appearance in the Green Room. But, despite the successes of Mr. Kean's and her own performances, Drury Lane was in dire financial straits. It would not do to alienate those patrons who deemed it their right to mingle with the actors and actresses after the play.

Gathering her hair, Meg tied it at the nape of her neck with a velvet ribbon. As she was about to leave the dressing room, her eyes fell on the white lilacs. She hesitated only briefly before reaching for a pair of scissors and snipping off a fragrant spray of blooms. She always wore simply cut gowns with long sleeves and a high neckline to the theater. The only variation she allowed herself was in the material and the shade of gray she wore. On

7

this night, her gown was of silver-gray poplin, and the spray of white lilac pinned to the shoulder added a touch of elegance.

Her long, graceful stride took her quickly, yet without obvious haste, to the Green Room. She never stayed long, and on this night, her appearance would be even briefer than usual. The sooner she got home to her bed, the sooner she could rise to see Maryann and Stephen.

Meg stopped in the doorway. Already, the Green Room was crowded with gentlemen, young and old, bloods and dandies, fashionable noblemen and ordinary citizens. And it would fill even more after the pantomime, when the dancers joined the actors and actresses who had performed in the play.

Surely, no one but Lord Ipswich and Mr. Selwyn would miss her if she slipped away this one time. By now, the bucks and blades and would-be rakehells knew that Meg Fletcher, although perfectly willing to share a laugh and a glass of wine after the performance, did not accept invitations to intimate suppers, or any other tempting offers.

"Miss Fletcher."

The deep, quiet voice broke through the hubbub of chatter and laughter and caught Meg in mid-turn, poised for flight. She swallowed an expletive acquired during her years in Seven Dials and faced the speaker with the famed Meg Fletcher smile firmly in place.

He was tall. Very tall even for Meg, who stood nose-to-nose with most gentlemen of her acquaintance. Tall and dark. But not handsome. His features were too harsh to invite comparison to a Greek or Roman god.

"Philip Rutland, ma'am." His eyes never leaving her face, he sketched a bow. "I'm delighted that my flowers have found favor with you."

Meg, who hardly knew a blush and had not faltered under a man's stare since she was knee-high, felt a treacherous warmth steal into her cheeks under that look. It was a look of undisguised admiration and, at the same

8

time, one of cool appraisal.

She touched the spray of lilac pinned to the shoulder of her gown. "These?" she stammered like the veriest bread-and-butter miss. "Thank you very much. They are lovely. I've always liked white lilacs."

For a moment longer he observed her—as though weighing his next move, his next words. A smile lit his face, softening it, and she saw that his eyes, which at first had looked a dark, muddy brown, were in fact hazel with a green circle around the irises.

"Miss Fletcher, will you do me the honor of supping with me?"

The invitation was all the impetus needed to restore Meg to her normal poised, detached self. An intimate supper, no doubt in one of the private chambers at the Clarendon where, for a consideration, the obliging waiter would hand over the room key to Mr. Philip Rutland! How predictable. And how disappointing. For some reason, she had expected better of this tall, dark gentleman who sent white lilacs.

But worse—and less comprehensible—was the temptation to accept the invitation.

"I am sorry, Mr. Rutland." For once, Meg did not have to feign regret for politeness' sake. "I have an early appointment tomorrow, and I'm afraid I cannot afford to stay up late. In fact, I was about to leave when you spoke to me."

He bowed. "Perhaps I will be luckier when I return to town next month."

"Perhaps. But, as you know, in little over a fortnight the theater will close for the summer."

"I shall find a way to see you and renew my invitation."

Their eyes met, and she read in his the conviction that her answer would be yes when he invited her the next time. His self-confidence, rather than irritating, pleased and excited her. But Meg would not admit this to any man—leave alone one as cocksure as Mr. Rutland.

"Good-bye, Mr. Rutland." She held out her hand. Knowing that he would not find it easy to locate her once the theater closed, she gave him a mischievous look. "And good luck. Next time."

A corner of his mouth twitched. "Thank you, Miss Fletcher."

His handshake was firm and brief. "I shall accompany you to your carriage," he said in a tone that brooked no objection. "Or will you need a hackney?"

"A hackney," Meg told him and stepped out into the corridor, where she promptly collided with a skinny youth about to hurtle himself into the Green Room.

A strong arm caught her around the shoulders, saving her from a painful knock against the doorjamb. With his free hand, Philip Rutland steadied the youth, who looked as though he were about to collapse from exhaustion.

Now that Meg could see the boy clearly, she recognized beneath a shock of lank, untidy hair the sharp features of her father's latest protégé. Jigger was a pickpocket Fletcher had captured and, instead of turning the young culprit over to the Bow Street magistrate, had employed at the Fighting Cock, the tavern he had bought for his retirement.

Meg's insides twisted. There was only one reason why Jigger would come to the Drury Lane. Something had happened to her father. Something bad.

Above the pounding of her heart and the talk and laughter in the Green Room, she barely heard Philip Rutland admonishing the lad to be more careful the next time he planned to enter a room.

"Jigger!" Meg grasped the boy's arm. "What happened? For heaven's sake, speak!"

"Yer pa!" he choked out. "He's been 'urt mortal bad. Stabbed."

The arm around her shoulders tightened, and Meg realized that she was shaking.

But her voice was firm. "Where is he? At home? Has the physician been sent for?"

10

"Aye, an' Sir Nathaniel, too." Jigger gasped for breath. "Two runners brung yer pa to the Fightin' Cock on a door, an' Mrs. Bellamy says ye must come right quick, Miss Meg. T'old leech, Dr. Walters, wants ter bleed 'im, but Mrs. Bellamy says 'e lost more'n enough of the claret already."

Meg hurried to the side entrance of the theater. Jigger set up a shout for a hackney while they were still in the building, and before she knew it, Philip Rutland had assisted her into a musty-smelling old coach.

"Shall I go with you?" he asked as Jigger climbed upon the box beside the jarvey.

"No!"

Meg looked at Rutland, surprised and irritated. Surely he wouldn't pursue her to the Fighting Cock where her father lay gravely injured. But in his gaze she read none of the signs of a man bent on seduction; she saw only compassion.

Mollified, she said, "I thank you for the offer and for your concern, Mr. Rutland, but I'd rather go alone."

He nodded and shut the door. The coach started to roll, and her view of him, standing motionless at the curb, his gaze on the hackney, was soon cut off by encroaching darkness.

Philip Rutland, Earl of Stanbrook, did not return to the Green Room of the Drury Lane. When the lumbering vehicle carrying Meg Fletcher rolled out of sight, he turned toward the fashionable part of town.

From the tail of his eye, he caught a movement in the light by the theater door. A dark shape, the figure of a man, narrow and tall, stepped out into the street. There was something furtive, stealthy, about him, and Philip instinctively braced himself for an attack. He would not be the first to be set upon in these unsavory streets around the theater.

But the man turned away, scuttling in the direction the

11

hackney had taken. He was probably an admirer of Meg Fletcher, disappointed that he hadn't been able to speak to her.

With a shrug, Philip continued on his way to St. James's. St. James's and Seven Dials—both in London, yet poles apart. There was no doubt in his mind that Miss Fletcher was a product of that thieves' den, that most notorious of the London stews—Seven Dials. Jigger's directions to the jarvey had been explicit.

But even though Miss Fletcher still called the Fighting Cock tavern her home, she was undoubtedly destined for better things—a small house on the fringe of a fashionable district, where he could visit her at his leisure. And her own carriage and pair.

Philip smiled, remembering their brief exchange in the doorway of the Green Room. She was a superb actress, the saucy wench who had captivated him on his first visit to the Drury Lane four nights ago with her shapely, breeches-clad legs, with her pert smile and flashing eyes. She had almost convinced him with that plain gray gown, the girlishly tied hair, the blush and stammer, that she was in fact a demure young lady.

But the speech and manner of a lady were assumed. Miss Fletcher had clawed her way out of the stews, and there was only one way a girl from Seven Dials could have achieved that end—a liaison with a gentleman of the *ton*. And when she wished him luck for the next time they would meet, Philip had known that Meg Fletcher was his for the taking.

So she wanted to play coy, pretend she wasn't a bit of muslin to be won over with a supper invitation. It suited him well. When he was done with his duty visit to Cousin Richard, he would return to town and spend time "courting" the beautiful Miss Fletcher.

Her father should be well by then. Or dead, in which case he'd have to be careful. He wouldn't want to take advantage of her grief. And that she would grieve, Philip did not doubt. She had been badly shaken when the boy blurted out her father's injury. She was a woman of feeling, this Meg Fletcher.

Soon to be his Meg.

"Where is he?" Several paces ahead of Jigger, Meg ran across the dark courtyard of the Fighting Cock. She tore open the narrow back door. "Where, Jigger?"

"In the taproom. Leastways, 'e was there when I come after ye."

Skirts flying, Meg rushed to the front of the tavern. The long room smelling of ale and rum, of boiled mutton and cabbage, was empty.

"Pa? Pa!"

Fear gripped her. It lacked an hour till closing time, yet not a single customer lingered in the popular taproom of the Fighting Cock.

She looked around wildly, as though she might discover her father at the serving counter or in the dim corner by the fireplace where he was wont to drink his mug of ale in the company of cronies. She even searched under the big trestle table where she had known men to sleep off the effects of Blue Ruin. Anything, *anything*, would be better than the growing conviction that he was dead and had been taken off in the mortuary cart.

She turned to speak to Jigger, but he had slunk off somewhere.

"Jigger! Mrs. Bellamy! Where the deuce is everyone?"

"Here now, Miss Meg. Calm yerself."

Meg gave a start. Above the drum of her pulse and the hammering of her heart, she had not heard the approach of Mrs. Bellamy, the cook.

"Where is Pa?" Meg rounded on the plump woman. "If they've taken him— If Dr. Walters has—"

She broke off. If she were too late, there was nothing she could do. In the Dials, death came as quickly and as easily as the beginning of life. She had known it since she was a little girl, but she had never accepted it. Not when her brothers and sisters died one by one, not when her mother died.

Mrs. Bellamy screwed her face into the stern visage she assumed when she was fretted.

"Come now, Miss Meg," she said sharply. "Think of yer pa. He's upstairs, and what *he'll* be thinkin' when he hears yer screechin' is more than I can say. That old leech is with him, an' I'm mightily worried—"

But Meg heard no more. Her father was alive. That was all she wanted to know.

Skirts hiked above her knees, she flew up the stairs. At the end of the long, candle-lit corridor, the door to her father's room stood open. She heard his voice, shockingly feeble and thin, as he told the physician to put away his knife and leeches.

"Pa."

She entered slowly, her eyes on the burly man lying atop the counterpane of the four-poster bed. He was still dressed in the white shirt and dark breeches he wore when he was on duty as a Bow Street runner, but someone had removed his Belcher kerchief, the frock coat, checkered weskit, and boots. A wide blood-stained bandage was wrapped tightly around his middle, and as Meg watched, the stain deepened and spread.

Fletcher's sunken eyes lit up. "Meg, luvvie. Ye've come."

"Of course I came."

Ignoring the physician's mutters of protest, she hugged her father, careful not to touch the wound. "Did you think I'd celebrate in the Green Room while you're hurt? Resign yourself, sir, for I intend to bully and scold you until you're better."

Weakly, Fletcher shook his head. "Nay, luv. They got me right an' proper. In the gut."

Dr. Walters cleared his throat. "Three punctures in the vicinity of the stomach, Miss Meg. Unless I bleed your father, I'll not be responsible should he develop a fever."

"Won't have time for a fever, you old fool," Fletcher muttered. He clasped Meg's hand. "Send him away, daughter. There's things that must be said afore I die."

Meg had seen death too often not to recognize the signs in her father's waxen skin, the sunken cheeks and eyes. Her throat tight with unshed tears, she said, "I think my father has bled enough. We had best give in to his wishes, Dr. Walters."

The physician puffed out his chest, but under Meg's steady gaze his bluster evaporated. "I'll be taking my leave then, Miss Meg. Send for me if you need me."

Snatching up his leather case of instruments and the jar of leeches, he departed, stomping down the stairs and hollering for Mrs. Bellamy. No doubt, to talk her into dishing out one of her plain but well-cooked dinners.

Still holding her father's hand, Meg sat down on the edge of the bed. Her chest, her throat, hurt terribly. But she would not break down and cry. Not now.

"What is it, Pa?" she asked softly. "What must be said?"

"First of all, luv, I want yer promise not to drape yerself in sackcloth and ashes when I'm gone. Mourning is done in the heart, not with a show of black weeds."

"All right, Pa. That's an easy enough promise. But surely that's not why you wanted me to send Dr. Walters away."

A spark of the old spirit kindled in her father's eye. "Nay, lass. I also want yer promise to sell the Fighting Cock."

"Pa, no!"

"Hush, lass. I knew ye'd raise ruckus over this one. An' I know why. 'Twas here ye had a room of yer own for the first time, an' clean sheets as often as ye wanted them. But ye can have the same in a genteel lodging house for ladies. And ye can have a lady companion, too."

Meg chuckled at the thought. "Pa, I don't need a companion. I'm no lady, no matter how well I dress or speak like one."

"Meg," Fletcher said weakly but succinctly. "Ye're a lady born. Ye're Megan Carswell, daughter of a baronet. Sir Richard Carswell of Carswell Hall."

Chapter Two

Megan Carswell.

Like fireworks, the name exploded in Meg's brain. But it meant nothing. Could mean nothing. She was Meg Fletcher. Daughter of Rosemary and Samuel Fletcher. Pa was delirious. Yes, that was it. 'Twas the fever speaking.

But when she met her father's gaze, she knew he was as rational as ever.

She tightened her grip on his hand. "Pa! Are you saying that I'm not your daughter? That I am—"

That I am some baronet's bastard? She had wanted to ask. But in the end, she could not bring herself to say the word with all its implications about her mother.

There was no need to say it. Fletcher could read her face all too well.

"Nay, luv. Not bastard. Ye're Sir Richard's legitimate daughter."

It was no easier to accept. If her mother was married to this Sir Richard, why had she lived in Seven Dials, one of London's most squalid slums?

"Pa, was Mother a widow, then? Left without tuppence to her name and shunned by the family?"

Fletcher opened his mouth, but before he could speak, hurried footsteps rang on the stairs, in the corridor. Then the dapper form of Sir Nathaniel Conant, the Bow Street magistrate, appeared in the door.

17

"Fletcher, my dear fellow!"

Stepping close to the bed, Sir Nathaniel nodded to Meg, but his attention stayed riveted on the man who had worked for him and his predecessors for more than a quarter century.

He asked no questions, but after a glance at the blood-stained bandage, said simply, "Tell me what I can do for you, Fletcher."

The wounded man drew a rasping breath. "Listen to what I must say to Meg, sir. It could be she might need a witness to a dying man's last words."

A trickle of blood appeared at the corner of Fletcher's mouth.

Meg said pleadingly, "Don't talk anymore, Pa. Save your strength."

His fingers curled around hers, then slackened. "Be a good lass and don't interrupt. Just listen while I tell about yer ma."

And Meg listened as Fletcher told the story of Rosemary, the glover's daughter, who had on her seventeenth birthday married a baronet, Sir Richard Carswell, thirty years her senior. He told the sorry tale as Rosemary had reported it to him, and Meg listened with astonishment, even incredulity, and slowly mounting anger.

She learned how her mother had arrived at Carswell Hall, shy and unsure of herself but eager to do right and learn to be Lady Carswell. How Alvina Elmore, Sir Richard's widowed sister who kept house for him, made it clear from the beginning that she despised Rosemary, believed her to be a harpy who had trapped the middle-aged Sir Richard into matrimony.

When Rosemary conceived almost immediately, Alvina was furious. She had expected that her son would be Sir Richard's heir. The estate was unentailed, and although the title must eventually go to a distant cousin of the male line, Stewart Elmore could have inherited the property and Sir Richard's not inconsiderable fortune—

18

if it hadn't been for Rosemary and the children she might bear.

Alvina caused no end of trouble between Rosemary and Sir Richard, going so far as to tell her brother that his young wife had seen and still was seeing men on the sly—the curate, a groom from a neighboring estate, an itinerant peddlar.

Sir Richard, proudly anticipating the birth of his son and heir, at first refused to believe his sister, but the seed of doubt and mistrust must have taken hold. Over the months, he became noticeably colder toward Rosemary. And when she was delivered of a girl whose blue eyes and black hair had nothing in common with the green-eyed, red-haired Carswells or Rosemary's pale blond beauty, he banished her and the babe to the dower house.

A coughing spell brought Fletcher's narrative to a halt, and Meg exhaled sharply. She felt as though she'd been holding her breath since her pa started to speak. The story—her mother's story—seemed incredible. Not that she doubted the basic truth of the strange tale. Yet, if she had not known that the only reading her pa allowed himself was that of the *Hue and Cry*, a publication of crimes and matters pertaining to diverse police courts, and the crime pages in *The Times* and the *Morning Post*, she would have suspected him of embellishing the story with details from Mrs. Ratcliffe's gothic novels.

But it was Rosemary who had devoured gothic novels.

Again, Meg noticed blood at the corner of Fletcher's mouth. Gently, she wiped it away. She wanted to tell him to stop talking, that it didn't matter what had happened all those years ago. But she knew him too well, knew that look of determination on his face, and she forced herself to keep quiet.

"She was young, yer ma. Not yet eighteen. Her lying-in time hadn't been easy for her, and then that husband o' hers rejected her . . . and you." He drew a ragged breath. "And there was that sister-in-law. 'Twas too

19

much for yer ma. She left. Bundled you in a blanket one night an' ran away."

"Mother left her husband? Are you sure it was not he who sent her away?"

"Nay, luv. She ran away."

Meg could not believe it. A woman who left her husband carried the same stigma as a woman whose husband divorced her. Only someone driven by desperation and possessed of courage would take such a step. It was impossible to imagine her timid mother leaving the safety of a home in the middle of the night.

"Don't blame her, luv. She was scared."

"I understand, Pa."

But Meg didn't. Not really. What had Rosemary been afraid of? Hadn't she ever tried to convince her husband of her loyalty? Hadn't Sir Richard ever tried to learn whether Alvina had spoken the truth?

"She came back to London, to the glover's shop," said Fletcher. "But a scarce month later it burned down—"

"Yes, I know," Meg interrupted. "Mother told me that was how Grandfather Melton died. But I didn't know that we were living with him at the time."

"Aye. That's where I found ye, an' I started taking care of ye."

"*Very* good care."

Meg looked at him with love in her eyes. She could say no more. Despite the training and lessons, she could not control her voice. Instead, she bent and kissed her father on the forehead.

"Lass," he whispered, his strength waning. "Be careful. I never quite believed yer ma told me the full story. She said she'd run away because the baronet didn't love her no more and that Elmore woman, her sister-in-law, was a mean piece. But there must've been more to it. I disremember that I ever saw Rosemary more scared than when she spoke of Carswell Hall."

Remembering her mother's sensitivity, her timidity, and her love of gothic novels, Meg doubted there had

20

been more to her mother's fear. She shook her head, and a long strand of hair escaped from the ribbon at the nape of her neck and caught in the spray of lilac she still wore, the sweet scent of the tiny blooms soothing her. Whether she believed her mother had exaggerated the situation or not, she would not argue with her pa. So she only said, "Mother was often scared. And if Sir Richard rejected her because at birth my hair wasn't the Carswell red and he believed himself cuckolded, that would have been enough—"

"Sir Richard should see ye now," whispered Fletcher, his eyes on Meg's fiery hair. "Go to him, lass. Carswell Hall, somewhere none too far from Ascot. Shouldn't be hard to find."

All feelings revolted at the thought of seeking out the man who had abandoned his seventeen-year-old wife and infant daughter. And abandonment it was. For, surely, had he tried to locate them he would easily have found them while they lived above the glover's shop.

"I have no desire to see Sir Richard," she told Fletcher. "*You* are my father, and that's all I care about."

He seemed not to have heard her.

"Meg, listen to me," he said urgently. "I suspicion someone already discovered who ye really are. Someone who's afeared ye'll be recognized by others as well. Someone who means ye harm."

"Pa!" she said, incredulous. "If you're referring to the attack on me, that's pure nonsense, and you know it! *Anyone* might have been set upon by those two thugs."

"Was ye ever attacked in Seven Dials before?" Fletcher demanded weakly.

When she shook her head, he asked, "And the coach that almost ran ye down in Piccadilly? The confections—marchpanes or whatever—sent to the Drury Lane and made ye ill? None o' that happened until *after* yer face became known as that o' the old queen. I reckon it all has to do with why Rosemary ran away. She was scared, was yer ma."

21

Not once had Meg regarded the incidents as personal threats, and she did not now. Her mother had been afraid of nearly everything, be it the distant roll of thunder or a half-starved pup following her from the butcher's shop. And Fletcher . . . well, he put too much importance into her mother's fears and was, in turn, afraid for his daughter's safety. It was, therefore, not surprising that he was suspicious. After all, suspicion was ingrained in a Bow Street runner's nature.

All she could do now was try to soothe him. "Pa, please don't fret. Nothing will happen to me. I can take care of myself."

"That ye can. I showed ye how, didn't I?"

Meg nodded, not trusting herself to speak without bursting into the tears evoked by memories of her father's careful instructions while he took his small daughter into the crowds of Bartholomew Fair or the Covent Garden markets, and later, when she started to assist him in his work as a Bow Street runner. Tears must wait, for he was trying to speak once more.

"Mayhap I should have told ye sooner. Rosemary . . . she made me promise not to tell. Not you, or anyone. She was afraid. But ye have the right to know . . . the right to the name . . . the inheritance."

"Please don't say any more, Pa. You must rest."

"Later, luv."

Despite the protest, he remained quiet while she wiped his brow and moistened the dry lips. Then, with a supreme effort, Fletcher turned his face to Sir Nathaniel, who had stood by the bed, not once interrupting or intruding himself into the talk between father and daughter.

"I did right, didn't I? To break the promise?"

"Aye, Fletcher. You did what you had to do. And if Meg needs me, I'll be there to confirm what you told her."

"And give her protection if need be?"

The magistrate nodded. "Aye," he said soothingly.

"I'll give her protection."

Fletcher sighed with relief. A look of satisfaction crossed his face and he was content to lie quietly, his gaze once more on Meg.

"I love you, Pa."

He did not speak, but his look told her that he had heard and was pleased. Not long afterward, he closed his eyes for the last time.

Meg wept, briefly, bitterly. Then, while Sir Nathaniel awkwardly patted her shoulder, she dried her tears. Her father wouldn't want her to weep.

Drawing on the strength and courage Fletcher had carefully cultivated in his daughter, she went downstairs to assure Mrs. Bellamy, Sam the tapster, the maid, the ostler, and Jigger that they need not worry about the future. If and when she sold the Fighting Cock, she'd make it a condition that they would be kept on.

Fletcher would have expected it of her.

"I think you ought to seek out Sir Richard Carswell."

Seated in her own charming sitting room at Fant House in Curzon Street, Lady Maryann Fant poured tea for Meg and herself. When her friend did not reply, she wrinkled her brow. "Meg, aren't you at all curious?"

"Curious? No." Meg's voice was deceptively soft. "But I am angry enough to confront this Sir Richard and tell him what I think of him."

"I often had words with my father. There's nothing wrong with that. It's much worse to run away from difficulties or problems."

Meg ignored the implication that Sir Richard was her father. She did not acknowledge him as such.

"Running away— That shot, I take it, is aimed as much at my mother as it is at me?"

Maryann's pixie face was as bland as she could make it. She said nothing, merely handed Meg a cup of tea.

Sipping the fragrant brew, Meg let her thoughts stray

to the night Fletcher had told her the truth about her mother and herself—the night he died.

Yes, she admitted, her mother had chosen to run away, literally and figuratively. But the same could not be said of her; she simply was not interested in the man whose seed had given her life. The man who had not bothered to go after his young wife when he must have known that she was ill-equipped to care for herself and a babe-in-arms.

No, her father was and always would be Fletcher, who had taken in Rosemary Carswell and her infant daughter. Who, even though he could not legally marry her, had given Rosemary the protection of his name and had loved little Meg; cherished her the more when his own children one by one fell victim to the fever rampant in the Dials.

Yet Fletcher, too, had urged her to seek out Sir Richard Carswell—as had Sir Nathaniel before he left the tavern.

"Meg?"

Maryann's voice, hesitant and laced with concern, penetrated her thoughts. She smiled at this dearest of friends, who, notified by Sir Nathaniel, had come with Stephen to the Fighting Cock in the middle of the night and had offered comfort and support. Maryann had wanted to take her immediately to Fant House, but Meg had refused to leave before the funeral. That had been four days ago.

"Meg, I didn't mean to upset you. But I think it only right and proper that you hear Sir Richard's side of the story as well."

"If I'm to listen to him, really listen, I had better wait until I feel less angry."

"You may not have much time. He was—what? Seven-and-forty when he married your mother?"

"Yes." Bitterness crept into Meg's voice. "You'd think an experienced man like that would know how to handle a young bride."

"Perhaps. But he's over seventy now—if he's still alive. It's imperative that you contact him. There's your inheritance to consider. Why should you have to work when you could live a life of leisure?"

Meg laughed, a rich, deep-throated laugh that filled the small sitting room. "And that from you, Maryann? You, who worked harder than any woman I know, growing flowers to take to market just so you could earn the money to start a botanical garden."

"That's different." Maryann's slight figure stiffened. "When Stephen received his compensation from the War Office, he offered me all the money I could want."

"But the botanical garden is *your* dream." Meg was glad to change the topic. Too many people were trying to persuade her to see Sir Richard. But if there was one thing Meg Fletcher did not like, it was being prodded into doing something she didn't want to do.

She gave Maryann a challenging look. "Confess! You feel you must pay for the garden yourself."

Maryann smiled a little sheepishly. "Yes. At least," she amended, "I want to have sufficient funds to start the landscaping. I did let Stephen purchase the plot of land."

"What a concession."

Excitement shone in Maryann's clear gray eyes. "I want you to see it, Meg! It's nothing but rubble now. Collapsed houses, the burnt-out shell of a small church, and heaps of rubbish, but—"

She paused, giving Meg a shrewd look. "But I shan't allow you to distract me into talking about my botanical garden. Back to you and your work. You can't tell me that acting isn't exhausting."

"Yes. But I adore it."

"And it is *your* dream come true."

Meg nodded, believing her friend had acknowledged the futility of further arguments. However, she had reckoned without Maryann's tenacity.

"Now that you've achieved what you set out to do, you could—"

"I haven't achieved it yet," Meg cut in. "I've played only comedy so far."

"*Only?* I've read the papers. The critics say you're as good as, or better than, Mrs. Jordan was in her prime. Better than Kitty Clive. What more do you want, Meg?"

"I want to be likened to Sarah Siddons as well."

"Play tragedy?" Maryann was finally diverted from her original subject. "My mother went to see Mrs. Siddons in all of her plays. She says the ladies would cry when she played Isabella and faint when she performed as Lady Macbeth. Mrs. Siddons was, no doubt, a great actress, but I believe it was due in part to her being suited so well with her brother, John Kemble."

Meg shook her head. "She was great even before Kemble ever played a major part on the London stage. But I want to be greater. Greater than Sarah Siddons and Dolly Jordan combined. And I want to play beside Edmund Kean."

"Then you will."

"Your confidence overwhelms me. You have seen me in but one role—"

"And we'll see you in more." Stephen Fant, entering his wife's sitting room, gave Meg a cheerful grin. "We plan to be here in September when the theater reopens."

"Stephen!" Lady Maryann whirled across the room, into her husband's waiting arms. "You're early. I didn't think you'd return before afternoon. Shall I ring for another cup?"

"No, my love. After spending hours in the company of solicitors and barristers, I stand in need of something stronger than tea."

"And?" asked Meg. "Will Fant Court be restored to your sister-in-law?"

"I am more hopeful now that I've met the solicitors in person."

From a small cabinet, Stephen removed a decanter and glass and poured a generous measure of cognac before taking a seat on the chaise longue beside his wife.

26

"But even if we came to an agreement tomorrow," he said, "it would still take time. The courts are notoriously slow, and I can only be glad that I bought back this house when I had the chance, instead of waiting on a court settlement."

"Yes, indeed. Having lived in the house four days, I'm already in love with it. I would not have wanted to wait, either."

Meg let her gaze roam over the Adam's mantel and lofty ceiling, the delicate Queen Anne furniture, the soft rugs, the paintings. Two years ago, Viscount Tammadge, Lady Maryann's erstwhile betrothed, had won this lovely house and Fant Court in Sussex from Stephen's older brother in a game of piquet. But Tammadge had cheated, and when Richard Fant challenged him, the viscount threatened the safety of Richard's wife and young children. In a fit of depression, Richard had written a letter begging Stephen to look after his family and had shot himself.

A glimpse of Stephen's set face and Maryann's somber looks told Meg that they, too, were remembering. She searched her mind for a topic that would lighten the suddenly gloomy atmosphere, but before she could speak she saw Stephen place an arm around Maryann's waist.

He looked deeply into his wife's eyes. "Besides, my love," he murmured, "I always knew we'd need a house in London when you were ready to design your botanical gardens."

A smile, at once secretive and adoring, curved Maryann's mouth. She nestled deeper into the shelter of Stephen's arm.

Watching the couple, Meg felt the way a homeless waif would feel when, standing outside in the cold and dark of winter, he caught a glimpse, through a window, of brightly burning lamps and a warm hearth. A rare twinge of envy plagued her.

It was obvious that Stephen and Maryann were as

deeply in love after two years of marriage as they had been when Meg first knew them. It was also obvious that Lady Maryann had matured into a wise woman—one who knew better than to point out to her beloved that it was pride as well as the wish to please her that had made him retrieve the house which had belonged to his family for generations.

Stephen bent his head to kiss Maryann's brow, and all of a sudden Meg saw, instead of Stephen's gold-streaked brown hair brushing against Maryann's short honey-brown curls, a head of dark, almost black hair next to flowing copper-colored tresses. Hazel eyes ringed with green looked at her with the warmth Stephen bestowed on Maryann.

Disturbed and not a little startled, Meg pressed a hand to her burning face. Only an aberration of a confused mind could conjure the picture of Philip Rutland and herself while seeing Stephen with Maryann.

Or was it due to the white lilacs delivered to her dressing room night after night even though Philip Rutland had not come to the Green Room again?

Stephen, as in the old days, still noticed things he wasn't supposed to see. A twinkle in his eye, he looked at her.

"You are blushing, Meg. Do we shock you? It's not at all *comme il faut* for a married couple to live in each other's pocket, is it?"

"Don't let me disturb you."

Relieved that at least he didn't know about Philip Rutland, Meg rose. To divert Stephen further, she broke into the speech pattern of years past.

"If ye don't mind, Stevie love, I'll just run along an' change. There's a rehearsal for *Othello* this afternoon, an' I've a fancy ter lie on Desdemona's bed afore Mr. Kean arrives at the theater."

Maryann laughed, but Stephen asked quietly, "Still dreaming, Meg?"

"I aim to be Desdemona to Mr. Kean's Othello before the next season is over."

Meg started toward the door.

"Good luck, Megan Carswell," said Stephen.

She swung around. "Don't call me that. Meg Fletcher served me well for twenty-four years. It'll do for the rest of my life."

"Surely not," said Maryann. "You'll marry and take your husband's name."

"It's unlikely I'll marry. Who but an actor would accept a wife on the stage?" Meg flashed her bright smile. "And I haven't met an actor yet *I* would accept as a husband."

She walked on.

In the doorway she hesitated, then said without looking at Stephen and Maryann, "I received flowers last night after the performance. From my 'admiring cousin' Stewart Elmore."

Chapter Three

Again, there were flowers from her "admiring cousin."

It was rather uncanny. How did he know her when she herself had learned her true name only a sennight ago? And if he knew of her, why had he waited until now to approach her?

Meg rubbed her bare arms. Despite the oppressive atmosphere in the theater dressing room, she felt cold. Without Fletcher, she was alone in the world. And yet she had family somewhere. Stewart Elmore, a cousin. Alvina Elmore, an aunt.

My cousin Stewart. My aunt . . . She had never known what it was like to have relatives.

Annoyed with herself, Meg scrambled into a gown of pearl-gray silk, twisted and pinned her long hair in a careless knot at the base of her neck. She would not think about the Elmores. Inevitably, such thoughts led to Sir Richard Carswell, the man she wanted to put totally from her mind.

Her gaze strayed to a tall vase filled with white lilacs . . . from Philip Rutland. A week had passed since he had approached her in the doorway of the Green Room and asked her to supper. He'd be out of town for a while, he had told her, but every night after the performance she had found a fresh bouquet of lilacs in the dressing room.

She lifted the lilacs from the vase, the whole armful of fragrant blooms.

"I'll take you home," she murmured. "You may give me foolish notions, but at least they aren't foolish notions about a family I have no desire to know."

Stopping in the Green Room for her usual perfunctory visit, she accepted a glass of wine from an elderly admirer and listened politely to Lord Ipswich's remonstration that she had never taken his roses home.

She bestowed her brightest smile on Ipswich. "I am so sorry. But, you see, roses give me the sniffles."

"My apologies," he stammered. The usually loquacious young man was at a loss for words. "I never dreamed . . . I did not know . . ."

"No, how could you? It is an unusual complaint, is it not? And now, if you'll excuse me, I must be on my way."

Meg slipped away before he could say more, tempting her to tell another bouncer. She had almost made her escape from the room when a half dozen boisterous young gentlemen and two of the female dancers pushed in front of her, blocking the doorway. With growing impatience, Meg waited for them to decide which of the young blades should take the ladies to supper.

"Megan Carswell?"

The speaker stood behind her. He had a nice voice. A little light, perhaps, but filled with warmth.

"Megan— Miss Fletcher, would you grant me a few minutes of your time?"

She wanted to walk away—the path to the door was now clear. She wanted to turn around and look at him, put a face to the voice. She did neither, merely stood quite still, breathing the sweet scent of the lilacs in her arms.

Her cousin. He could be no other. Yet she hesitated to face him. He was the son of Alvina Elmore, who had so intimidated her young sister-in-law that she had run away from Carswell Hall rather than try to convince her

32

husband of her loyalty.

Again Meg wondered why her cousin had chosen this particular time—just after she learned her mother's story from Fletcher—to approach her.

Slowly, she turned.

He was not much taller than she, well-built though not as broad in the shoulder as Philip Rutland, who had a week ago stood in almost the same spot. His features were pleasant, and he had a boyish smile that made it difficult to guess his age. He might be five years older than she, or ten. She had expected his hair to be the color of her own—a rich copper. But it was merely reddish-blond.

"You must be Stewart Elmore."

Laugh lines crinkled the corners of his eyes. "And you are my little cousin Megan."

"Not so little." Meg resisted the urge to smile back at him. She would not be influenced by his friendly manner. "Junoesque is the term generally applied to me."

"Stately, regal, beautiful Juno. The Roman goddess of marriage. Yes, junoesque suits you, and yet it does not describe you totally. I have seen you on the stage. You are also graceful, swift, lithe, the way I picture Diana."

"If you've seen me in the play, you also know that I am pert and scandalous."

"Ah, those breeches," he said, admiration warring with reproof in his voice.

"How did you know I am Megan Carswell?"

If he was taken aback by the abrupt question, he did not show it. He looked around the crowded room filled with gentlemen of all shapes and ages, with actors, actresses, and dancers, some of them still in their paints and costume. With the consumption of wine the volume of talk and laughter had risen until the Green Room resembled nothing so much as a market place filled with vendors and buyers trying to outshout each other.

"Shall we go somewhere a little more quiet? I have a carriage waiting at the King Street entrance."

33

Meg thought immediately of Fant House, the cozy parlor on the first floor Maryann had told her to regard as her private domain. Nodding to Stewart Elmore, she led the way outside.

Several loiterers lounged around the theater door. One of the men, a tall, cadaverous-looking fellow, jostled her with his elbow. Muttering something that might have been an apology, he stepped back into the shadow of the door. Before Meg could open her reticule and search for a coin—the man had looked half starved—Stewart clasped her arm and propelled her down the steps. She was annoyed and started to tell him so when she saw his carriage.

She widened her eyes at the sight of the sleek vehicle, its body painted maroon, window and door frames and the wheels picked out in black. It was a gentleman's carriage, elegant and expensive. The coachman in a black coat and maroon breeches had his hands full keeping the horses still—a pair of blacks, which even Meg's inexperienced eyes recognized as Thoroughbreds.

Elmore opened the door and held out his hand to assist her. "What direction shall I give my coachman?"

Meg looked at him. Like the carriage, his evening clothes were elegant and expensive. A diamond glittered in the folds of his cravat, and a gold ring with a large ruby gleamed on the fourth finger of his outstretched hand. Suddenly, perversely, she changed her mind about going to Fant House.

Ignoring the hand and his question, she stepped close to the box and instructed the driver how to reach the Fighting Cock.

She was silent during the drive. Her mind buzzed with questions, but she wasn't certain she wanted to ask them. Every question she'd pose, every answer she'd receive, would bring her closer to the Elmores—and to Sir Richard Carswell. She did not want to know about Sir Richard, but she could not deny that she was curious about Stewart Elmore. Her kin.

And she did want to know how he had found her. And why.

She gave him a covert look as he sat opposite her, as silent and seemingly lost in thought as she had been. His face was turned to the window. She didn't think there was anything to be seen in the dark, narrow alleys they traversed. Perhaps he sensed that she needed this time to collect her thoughts and did not wish to impinge on her privacy by staring at her.

But he did stare when they alighted from the carriage in the cobbled yard of the Fighting Cock and she led him to the back entrance.

"What is this, Megan?" he asked, incredulous. "A tavern?"

"You heard me instruct your coachman. Why are you so surprised?"

"I thought an inn, perhaps. Some fashionable hostelry . . ."

A look of distaste crossed his face when she ushered him through the noisy, crowded taproom into the small chamber where two years ago she had played cards with gentlemen out on a night of slumming. It was now used as a coffee room and, as she had hoped, it was empty.

"This is my home, Mr. Elmore. The Fighting Cock tavern in Seven Dials."

"You *live* here?"

Glancing about her, she tried to see the place through his eyes, the worn and scrubbed floorboards, the narrow, uncurtained windows, the whitewashed walls enlivened by a few not-very-good drawings she had bought from a struggling artist. She started to laugh. How spoilt he was. How naive.

"You should have seen the Fighting Cock two years ago. The upstairs was presentable. Down here, it was a different story. Walls dark gray, not with paint but with mildew and grime. You couldn't see the floor beneath the accumulated dirt and rubbish. And the smell of the place—" She wrinkled her nose. "Pure Seven

Dials stench."

He looked horrified, but whatever he might have said remained unspoken as Mrs. Bellamy, followed by Sam, the tapster, bustled into the chamber. Disapproval was writ all over the cook's pink-cheeked, round face.

"An' what can I do for ye, Miss Meg?" she inquired, stiffly formal. "Would ye like Sam ter fetch a hackney to take ye back to Curzon Street?"

"No, Mrs. Bellamy. Sam may fetch a bottle of the claret Pa set aside for special occasions. And *two* glasses."

A duchess could not have spoken with more authority, and after a moment Mrs. Bellamy, who was not known to be easily intimidated and had bested more than one belligerent patron of the Fighting Cock, dropped into a curtsy.

"Aye, Miss Meg. But ye won't stay long, will ye? It ain't seemly now that yer pa is gone."

"I shan't."

Fully aware that the older woman had only her welfare at heart, Meg went to her. Giving the plump shoulders a quick squeeze, she handed Mrs. Bellamy the lilacs.

"For you," she said, and was surprised and dismayed by a pang of regret and the unworthy thought that she should have brought Lord Ipswich's roses instead. "Flowers will cheer up your kitchen."

"Thank 'ee, luv." The pink of Mrs. Bellamy's face deepened in pleasure. Nose buried in the delicate white blooms, she trundled off.

Meg invited Stewart Elmore to sit down in one of the booths, and by the time she had squeezed into the bench across the bleached-oak table and had arranged her silk skirts, Sam arrived with the claret and glasses.

Without a word, but casting several searching looks at Elmore, the tapster poured. He must have been reassured by what he saw of Meg's companion. His seamed face relaxed, and he made no attempt to linger. But neither did he shut the door when he left.

Elmore toyed with his glass. "I see that you are surrounded by would-be protectors. That is good, but I promise you, Megan, I mean you no harm."

"Please call me Meg."

Watching him, she took a sip of wine. No, she didn't think he meant her any harm. His face was open. His eyes would always mirror his sentiments, and she could see no animosity, only interest and a hint of puzzlement.

Yet, unbidden, her father's warning came to mind. Fletcher had told her to be careful, and when he had recounted Rosemary's story, he had mentioned that Alvina's son would inherit Sir Richard's wealth if the baronet remained childless.

It would be only reasonable, she supposed, if, during the twenty-four years since Rosemary's flight from Carswell Hall, Stewart had indeed come to consider himself the heir.

"Stewart, how did you find me, or even know me?"

A grin, puckish and endearing, lit his face. "Simply seeing you is knowing you. Megan, you are the spit 'n image of Lydia Carswell, my—*our*—great-aunt. Her portrait hangs in the chamber still referred to as Lydia's room at Carswell Hall, and if I believed in the supernatural I'd think you were her ghost."

She decided to overlook that he had once again called her Megan.

"So you saw me on the stage and recognized me."

"Actually, it was my mother who first saw you. She doesn't often visit London, but about six months ago she decided she needed a new wardrobe. If she had stayed at Fenton's Hotel, as is her habit, she'd never have gone to see a play. But this time she accepted an invitation from one of her old friends. And Mrs. Wordsworth persuaded her to attend a performance of *The Country Girl*."

"Why didn't your mother approach me?"

"She was in shock. You see, she had searched for you and your mother all those years ago and had been told that you died in a fire at a haberdasher's or hatter's establishment or some such."

"My grandfather's glover's shop burned down. But Mother and I escaped."

He smiled warmly. "Thank goodness."

Again, Meg had to suppress the urge to smile back. He was really very nice, and if she must have a cousin, she'd as soon have someone like him. But, until she knew the whole story, it might be best to stay aloof.

"And so she asked you to seek me out. Why did it take you six months to do so?"

Stewart tugged at his cravat as though it had become too tight all of a sudden.

"Actually, Mother does not know I planned to speak to you."

Meg raised a brow but said nothing. She wasn't about to betray her ever-growing curiosity.

"I don't think she would have told me about you if she hadn't been shaken," Stewart said finally. "It just slipped out before she could stop herself. And then she asked me not to say a word to my uncle—your father. He was in rather queer stirrups at the time, and Mother said she'd tell him herself when he was better."

Stewart raised his glass and seemed totally absorbed in sampling the claret.

"And did she?" Meg could not resist asking.

"No." He finished the wine. Refilling his glass, he said, "Mother is rather high in the instep. She did not approve when her brother married the daughter of a . . . a glover, was it?"

Meg nodded. This was not news to her. It was what Rosemary had told Fletcher, only phrased more politely. In Rosemary's words, Alvina had *hated* her.

"And so," said Stewart, the puckish look once more in evidence, "when I realized Mother had no intention of telling Uncle about you, I decided to take matters into my own hands and to invite you to Carswell Hall."

"And will you go?" Maryann asked excitedly when

Meg finished her account of the meeting with Stewart Elmore.

"I don't know. Perhaps."

"What sort of an answer is that?" Maryann's eyes snapped indignantly. "You have never shown indecision before. For you, it is always either, or. Win or lose. Black or white. Yes or no."

The two ladies sat in the parlor at Fant House, where Meg had originally planned to take Stewart Elmore. When she had returned from the Fighting Cock, she had found Maryann waiting up for her and, incidentally, for Stephen, who had been asked to dine with his former commander, the Duke of Wellington.

Meg slid her legs off the loveseat and started pacing. This was unusual for her; more often than not it was the quicksilver Lady Maryann who trod a path on the carpet when she was upset, excited, or flustered.

"Are you worried that Stewart Elmore may not have the authority to invite you?" asked Maryann.

"He said he's always inviting people to Carswell Hall and Sir Richard has never voiced any objections."

"But perhaps you fear that Sir Richard may object to *you?*"

Meg shook her head with such vigor that the pins in her hair loosened and several strands escaped to frame her face.

"No. Stewart assured me that since his last stroke Sir Richard has spoken repeatedly of the past, of Mother and me. He believes Sir Richard may actually be pleased to know I'm alive."

"Then why won't you go?"

"Of course I'll go," Meg said rather grumpily.

She had made up her mind the moment the invitation left Stewart's mouth. She was intrigued and curious and wanted to see Carswell Hall, the place of her birth. But there was the small matter of a supper invitation. Philip Rutland had said he'd be back in town next month. June. Supper in the Piazza, she had decided, would be quite acceptable.

"*Twelfth Night* ends tomorrow," said Meg, hardly noticing that she was thinking aloud. "I shan't be needed for *Othello.*"

"Not this time. It'll be a different story next season."

"Yes, indeed." For a moment, Meg allowed herself to dream. Edmund Kean was quite willing to let her try out for a tragic role in September. And once he had seen her . . .

She said, "If I leave for Carswell Hall Friday morning, I can spend a full week or longer and still return during the first days of June."

"The summer months in London are a bore. Everyone is in the country. The heat, the stench . . . If Stephen and I did not have work to do, we'd not be here either. Why would you want to return so soon?"

"Why?" Meg thought of Philip Rutland saying in his deep voice, "I shall find a way to see you and renew my invitation." Surely it would be most unkind to put a damper on his self-confidence.

She flashed a smile at Maryann. "I have an engagement in town—sometime in early June. And you did offer me hospitality for as long as I wanted it, didn't you?"

"Fant House is your home. But tell me about the engagement." Maryann bounced in her chair. "It must be a man who has you rushing back to town. Is he handsome? Exciting?"

Laughing, Meg shook her head and pointed out that a carriage had stopped in front of the house, a strategy that had Lady Maryann fly to the window in the hopes of seeing her husband return from Apsley House. Which, to Maryann's delight and to Meg's relief, he did. Meg wasn't quite ready yet to speak of Philip Rutland—not even to Lady Maryann.

Upon being introduced to Lady Maryann and Stephen

Fant on the following day, Stewart Elmore declared himself delighted to convey Meg to Carswell Hall. He had executed his commissions in town and was prepared to leave on Friday morning as Meg wished. But a delay occurred when he arrived at Fant House in his elegant maroon-and-black carriage with a second vehicle trailing behind.

"Coming down, I traveled with my valet," he said, bowing to Meg and Lady Maryann, who had accompanied her friend outside at the first sound of carriage wheels. "But what with your maid and your luggage, Megan, it'd be a tight squeeze. I thought it best to hire a coach for the servants."

"You are very thoughtful." Meg's eyes danced with laughter. "Unfortunately, it's a wasted effort. You see, I don't have a maid. And my luggage is contained in one large cloak bag."

"No maid?"

She saw that he was shocked and felt a stab of irritation.

"What did you expect, Stewart? That I lived at the Fighting Cock waited on by maids and footmen? That I had a nanny and a governess during my childhood in the back slums?"

"No, of course not. Megan, I beg your pardon if I offended. It's just that my mother would be horrified if you were to travel without a maid."

"Your mother, the high stickler," said Meg, still cross. "But I'm sure Alvina will understand. After all, once Sir Richard cast my mother off, she had no means to provide for me as befitting a Carswell. Thus I grew up a Fletcher. And Meg Fletcher has no need or desire for a maid."

"Megan—"

"And I wish you'd call me Meg. It's been my name for as long as I can remember, and I've become quite attached to it."

"Now, Meg, behave yourself," Lady Maryann said imperiously. "Whatever happened all those years ago is not Mr. Elmore's fault. He could have been no more than a toddler."

"I was eight, ma'am." Stewart gave Lady Maryann a grateful look. "I wanted Megan for my little sister. Sulked for days when Mama told me it was impossible. And when Rosemary left with the babe—" He shrugged. "But that is neither here nor there. Megan, if you have no maid, then, I suppose, we'll leave without one."

"Take my Jane," said Maryann. "I shan't miss her for a week or two."

"Absolutely not."

Meg had regained her composure. In fact, she knew it was silly to lose her calm because she felt insulted on Fletcher's behalf when Stewart showed distaste or dismay at the things anyone with a grain of common sense would take for granted. Fletcher himself would have laughed it off.

She smiled at Stewart. "I shan't take a maid, but what if I took a groom along? Would that satisfy your mother's sense of propriety?"

He looked doubtful, but said, "Do whatever you wish, Megan. I'll make it all right with Mother."

While they all trooped inside so that she might dash off a note to Mrs. Bellamy requiring her to dispatch Jigger with all haste, the thought flitted through Meg's mind that Philip Rutland would not have been as acquiescent as Stewart. And although she admitted that she would not have let Stewart—or Mr. Rutland—dictate what she must do, she would have liked her cousin better had he shown some backbone.

Jigger took his time making an appearance at Fant House. Meg suspected that, since Fletcher wasn't there to keep an eye on the youth, he had gone off on some nefarious business or other and Sam the tapster had to search for him in some disreputable cockpit or in the Covent Garden markets.

Meanwhile, her luggage was loaded into the boot of the second carriage and she discovered that Maryann had instructed Jane to pack *all* of the gowns she had left behind.

"As though I were planning to stay a month or longer," Meg grumbled, but she gave no order to have the trunk unloaded again.

Finally, close to noon, Jigger arrived, carrying a knapsack and a loosely tied bundle. Stewart paled visibly at the sight of the unprepossessing youth.

"Your . . . groom?"

Although sorely tempted to tell him that Jigger was a pickpocket—reformed, it was to be hoped—Meg only nodded. Stewart muttered something about the fellow being very young, but without further ado consigned Jigger into the care of his valet. He assisted Meg into his own carriage and, climbing in himself, gave the order to be off.

The coach was comfortable and well sprung. Meg, who hadn't been outside London—at least, that she could remember—enjoyed the undulating countryside, the green meadows and fields, the quiet villages and farmsteads. When she got tired of looking out the window, Stewart talked to her of Carswell Hall, of the vast holdings he was managing for his uncle, and of Sir Richard, who had suffered a second stroke two months earlier but had recovered amazingly well.

Stewart warned her she wouldn't be the only guest. A distant cousin had honored Sir Richard with one of his rare visits but was expected to leave shortly.

Meg did not mind. She hoped Sir Richard's cousin would stay awhile. In fact, she wouldn't object to a house full of guests. The more the merrier, and the less attention would necessarily be paid to her while she explored the place of her birth.

They stopped for a late luncheon at a very smart posting house, and if she hadn't enjoyed herself so much and lingered over coffee and strawberries grown in the hostelry's own hothouses, they might have arrived at Carswell Hall while it was still light enough to appreciate

43

the first view of the old Elizabethan manor.

As it was, she had to take Stewart's word for it that Carswell Hall was a very beautiful and impressive house set in well-tended grounds. She could see only a long, low, shadowy building, a lighted window here and there, and the stark, battlemented top of a square tower reaching into the night sky at either end of the house.

It was a daunting view—one that had undoubtedly served to intimidate her mother. Had it also spurred her imagination and made her see the disapproving sister-in-law in a light more wicked than was warranted?

When the carriage drew to a halt, Stewart helped Meg down and ushered her immediately up a set of wide, shallow steps covered by a porch and leading to a carved double door. Someone had apparently been on the watch for their approach; both wings of the door were flung wide open before Stewart could wield the knocker.

Blinking at the bright light inside, Meg entered the Great Hall Stewart had described to her. And the first person she saw standing at the foot of the central staircase was Philip Rutland.

Chapter Four

His Meg!

A multitude of emotions surged in Philip, not the least of which was a quick stab of anger at what he immediately perceived as Stewart's effrontery. Snatching Meg Fletcher from beneath his nose, the blackguard! Not that Stewart had known anything of Philip's plans for the delectable actress. Nonetheless, it was galling to see them standing side-by-side just inside the front door, Stewart's hand cupped possessively around Miss Fletcher's elbow.

None of those thoughts showed in Philip's face as he started to walk toward them. In fact, his resentment was forgotten as soon as he saw the flash of joy in Miss Fletcher's brilliant eyes, the warm smile curving her mouth as she looked at him. He realized that by far the strongest of his mixed feelings was pleasure—the pleasure of seeing her, of knowing that she was as captivating as he remembered, and that he need not wait another week before starting his "courtship" of her.

Only, what was she doing here? He was not intimately acquainted with Stewart or the customs prevailing at Carswell Hall, but he would not have believed it possible that young Elmore was at liberty to bring an out-and-out dasher into his uncle's house.

"Mr. Rutland." Her voice, too, reflected the joy he had seen in her eyes. "I had no notion I'd find you at

45

Carswell Hall."

"A duty visit, Miss Fletcher. But what brings *you* into Berkshire? I assumed you fixed at the Drury Lane for another fortnight at least."

"What's this?" demanded Stewart. "You two know each other?"

"Yes, indeed. Mr. Rutland has honored me with several offerings of white lilacs delivered to the Drury Lane."

Stewart's eyes narrowed as he looked from one to the other. "Mr. Rutland, eh? In that case, Megan, allow me to present to you a cousin, albeit a distant one. Philip Rutland, the Earl of Stanbrook."

Miss Fletcher's smile flickered, then faded. Obviously, she did not appreciate that plain Mr. Rutland had turned out to be a lord.

"I'm delighted," she said frostily.

Philip bowed. It would have given him great satisfaction to draw Stewart's cork. However, a lady was present—if a somewhat scandalous one—and he would concentrate instead on assuring Miss Fletcher that he had harbored no ulterior motives when he did not correct her addressing him as Mr. Rutland.

"Miss Fletcher, we did not have much time that night. Lest you think—"

"My dear Philip." Grinning broadly and without apology, Stewart interrupted him. "Pray allow me to present to you Miss Megan Carswell, Uncle Richard's long-lost daughter."

Philip was getting very irritated with Stewart. Bringing Miss Fletcher to Carswell Hall was one thing. It was certainly stupid, but trying to pull off a blatant hoax was worse than stupid. It was idiotic. Young Elmore must have not one, but several screws loose in his haft.

He measured Stewart with a scathing look before turning back to Miss Fletcher. "And how is your father? I hope he is recovered by now?"

A shadow of sadness crossed her face, and he knew the

46

answer to his question before she spoke.

"Pa died shortly after I got to the Fighting Cock."

"I am sorry. Pray accept my condolences."

"Thank you."

He held out his hand and with only a very slight hesitancy, she placed her hand in his. The contact was brief, but Philip felt reassured that she would not carry a grudge about the blunder with his name.

"Miss Fletcher, I know you must be devastated by the loss. Is there aught I can do?"

Stewart said, "Philip, I don't think you quite understand the situation."

"I understand only too well," he replied coldly. "And as soon as possible, you shall know exactly how I feel about a man who takes advantage of a young lady's grief."

"What in tarnation are you talking about?"

"If you don't know, I shall be glad to explain it to you." Philip gave him a meaningful look. "Later, when we are alone."

A rich, deep-throated laugh from Miss Fletcher drew his attention. It was a lovely sound, even though she was obviously laughing at him. After a moment's consideration he perceived the irony of the situation.

His mouth twitched. "Pistols at dawn?" he murmured. "You are quite right, Miss Fletcher. It is ridiculous, and I promise I'll go easy on my bacon-brained cousin. But I doubt you wish to be kept standing in the hall after a long carriage ride. Stewart, shouldn't you call Mrs. Sutton to prepare a chamber for Miss Fletcher?"

Stewart snapped his fingers at the footman who, hand still on the doorknob, stood gaping at Meg in silent wonder.

"James! Stop goggling. Take Miss Carswell up to Miss Lydia's room and tell Mrs. Sutton to send a maid to her."

James sprang to attention at the same moment as the door opened again to admit Stewart's valet holding a traveling bag and one end of a large trunk, and the skinny youth who had brought the bad tidings of Miss Fletcher's father hefting the other end of the trunk. Before Philip could so much as bow to his Meg, the footman whisked her upstairs, valet, trunk, and skinny youth following in their wake.

Slowly, Philip turned to face his cousin.

"And now," he said softly, "will you kindly explain why you offered Miss Fletcher *carte blanche* while she's in mourning for her father? And what the deuce do you mean by foisting her on this household as your uncle's long-lost daughter?"

Stewart looked taken aback. "But I did no such thing! I offered no *carte blanche*. Dash it, Philip! Who d'you take me for? She *is* Uncle's daughter. She is Megan Carswell. Rosemary's child."

"The devil you say."

Philip took a step closer to young Elmore. "Your mother told me the story a year or two ago. She was quite emphatic. Rosemary's daughter was not Cousin Richard's child. And they are both dead."

A slow grin spread on Stewart's face, and Philip found it difficult to decide whether his cousin looked merely mischievous or whether there was a hint of malice in the crooked mouth.

"My dear Philip, had you been here six months ago when Mother returned from London—where, for your information, she saw Meg Fletcher at the Drury Lane—you might have heard her confirm just as emphatically that the girl is Megan Carswell. And if you had shown a little more interest in the Carswells and their possessions, you would know about the painting in the chamber referred to as Lydia's room. It's a portrait of Lydia Carswell, Uncle's aunt. And Megan might be her twin."

News of her identity must have spread like wildfire, Meg reflected wryly, when the housekeeper arrived accompanied by a young maid whose eyes almost popped from her head in an effort to compare the portrait of Miss Lydia Carswell to the flesh-and-blood Megan Carswell.

The housekeeper, after one hard look at Meg's hair, concealed her curiosity well. Bustling about, tugging at the already immaculately straight counterpane, running a finger over gleaming surfaces, she said, "I hope you'll find everything to your liking, miss. There's a hip bath in the dressing room, but I doubt you'll have time for more'n a quick wash. The family gathers in the salon in half an hour. Dinner is in one hour."

"Rather late, isn't it?" Under the little maid's unblinking stare, Meg started brushing her hair. "I always believed that dinner in the country is served quite early."

"Not at Carswell Hall. Mrs. Elmore sees to it that we're fashionable as the rest o' the world."

Meg suppressed a smile. The "rest o' the world" excluded such masses as the bourgeoisie and simple folk like Fletcher and herself who were accustomed to eating their dinner in the middle of the day.

"But this night, o' couse," said Mrs. Sutton, "when Mr. Stewart wasn't here at seven-thirty when they usually meet in the salon to drink a glass o' sherry, Mrs. Elmore had dinner set back another hour."

Meg carefully pinned her hair. "I take it, then, that we were expected. Mr. Stewart sent a note from London?"

"*Mr. Stewart* was expected, miss." The housekeeper tapped the serving girl on the shoulder. "Here, now, Elspeth! What are you gapin' at? Run along and check there's towels for miss and a fresh cake o' soap."

When the maid had disappeared in the dressing room, Mrs. Sutton said, "She's a bit slow, our Elspeth. But she's willin' and cheerful, and if you're patient with her, she'll make a decent enough lady's maid."

In the mirror, Meg met the housekeeper's shrewd look. The woman did not address her as Miss Carswell or Miss Megan—she'd want Sir Richard to confirm the visitor's status first. On the other hand, she was as polite and obliging as she knew how, so she wouldn't find herself on the wrong end of "miss's" favor if she were accepted as the long-lost daughter.

"Thank you, Mrs. Sutton. I'll be glad of Elspeth's assistance in the morning. And, perhaps, if she could come for me in half an hour to show me the salon? For now, though, I'd like to be alone."

"Very well, miss."

The two women left, and Meg finally allowed herself to study the portrait that hung on the wall behind the four-poster bed. Lydia Carswell—her great-aunt.

According to what Stewart had told her about Lydia, the young lady could have been no older than seventeen or eighteen when she was painted. But the elaborate, puffed-out hair style of the previous century and the light dusting of powder, which by no means subdued the glow of burnished copper, made her appear the same age as Meg.

In fact, looking at the painting was like looking into a mirror after dressing for a costume ball. The eyes, the straight, slender nose, the dazzling smile, the lower front tooth that stubbornly and capriciously refused to grow in line with the others, the flawless white skin, and even the way the hair sprang back from the wide forehead—everything was identical to the features that made up Meg Fletcher.

Megan Carswell.

She was still looking up at the portrait when she heard a faint knock followed immediately by the sound of the door opening.

She turned, surprised that Elspeth should have returned so soon, and faced a tall, spare-framed lady elegantly gowned in powder-blue silk, her gray hair curled and meticulously coiffed. A faint smile stretched the thin-lipped mouth but did not reflect in the expressionless gray-green eyes which, set in a pale, blanched-looking face, measuring Meg from the top of her head to her feet.

"Welcome to Carswell Hall, Megan. I am Alvina Elmore." She paused, her mouth trembling as though she had trouble keeping the smile in place, then added in the flat voice that matched the look in her eyes, "Your aunt."

The woman who hated my mother so much she told lies about her, who turned Sir Richard against his wife and child.

"Good evening, Mrs. Elmore," Meg said calmly. Now that she was here at Carswell Hall, she would keep personal feelings under control. She'd reserve judgment until she had heard Sir Richard's side of Rosemary's story—and, perhaps, Alvina's as well. "If you've come to guide me to the salon, I'm afraid you are too early. As you see, I have yet to change my gown."

Alvina waved dismissively. "A maid or one of the footmen will fetch you at eight-thirty. I came by to greet you and—and to explain why I did not speak to you when I saw you in London. I know Stewart told you about my visit to the theater."

Two spots of red appeared high on Alvina's cheeks, startling on the blanched skin, and the look in her eyes was feverish. The older woman was wrestling with a burning anger, Meg realized, and she wondered whether her wrath was directed at Rosemary's daughter or at her own son for talking about the visit to the Drury Lane.

"You are under no obligation to explain anything, ma'am. But if you wish to do so, I'd appreciate hearing all you can tell me about my mother."

"There's no time to go into that now," Alvina said curtly. "But I do want you to know that I intended to call on you. However, when I arrived at my friend's house after the performance, word awaited me that my brother's health had taken a turn for the worse. Naturally, I returned forthwith to Carswell Hall."

"Naturally."

It was not quite the way Stewart had told it, Meg thought wryly. She was inclined to believe his version.

51

"I hope," she said, "Sir Richard has recovered?"

A breath of pink touched the pale face and mingled with the red blotches.

"He is not as stout as I should wish," Alvina said stiffly. "But he is well enough to join the family at the dinner table. Except," she added with a flash of humor that seemed out of character, "when he wants to annoy me. Then he stays in his rooms and creates a great upheaval in the household by ordering every available maid and footman to wait on him while the rest of us must fend for ourselves in the dining room."

"And will Sir Richard stay in his rooms tonight?"

The gray-green eyes met Meg's emerald ones without a flicker. "No. Your father will dine with us."

"Have you told him about me?"

The thin lips tightened.

"Our Cousin Philip," Alvina said with a touch of bitterness, "has taken it upon himself to prepare your father for the shock of meeting you."

Philip . . . Involuntarily, Meg smiled, remembering his reaction when Stewart introduced her as Sir Richard's long-lost daughter. It appeared that Philip Rutland had realized his mistake.

She became aware that Alvina was staring at her and quickly assumed a more dignified mien.

"Thank you for stopping by," she said in her best duchess manner. "I shall make all haste to change out of my traveling gown and join you in the salon."

Alvina knew she had been dismissed, and although Meg half expected some snubbing reply, the older woman merely inclined her head and left, closing the door with a very final-sounding click.

Meg took a deep breath and with suddenly shaking knees walked to one of three dainty, satin-covered chairs by the window. Hands pressed against her face, she sat down.

Alvina Elmore, the woman who caused the rift between Sir Richard and my mother.

Like the actress she was, Meg had taken on the role of a young woman reserving judgment. But now that she was alone and no longer needed to act a role, her true feelings came through. She admitted that she had, the moment she looked into Alvina's cold eyes, conceived an instant dislike for the lady.

Rosemary had been convinced that Alvina hated her and had done her as much harm as lay within her power. Meg could well believe it—had, in fact, never doubted that part of her mother's story. But now, having met Alvina, she could understand how the sensitive Rosemary had come to be afraid. There was something about Alvina, about those gray-green eyes, so oddly expressionless and at the same time as cold as ice, that could make one shiver.

Trying to recall her aunt's expression when she entered the room, Meg found it impossible to tell how Alvina had felt when first setting eyes on her niece—except that despite the words of welcome she was not filled with joy over Meg's sudden arrival.

Feeling cold all of a sudden, Meg hugged her arms to her chest. She caught her gloomy reflection in the mirror above the dressing table and chuckled. She looked like a tragedy queen in the best Sarah Siddons tradition—which was, of course, monstrously good news for her stage career, but not desirable for her private life.

She should smile and be happy. It wasn't such a bad lot to spend a week in the country, to breathe air untainted with smoke or the stench of open sewers, to walk on soft grass instead of filthy cobbles. And if some people she'd have to put up with were less than congenial, there was Philip Rutland, whom, she admitted, she had been most eager to see again. And still was eager to see, even though he was an earl.

She rose, smiling, stretching like a cat, then stooped and pulled from her trunk an emerald silk gown. Slipping out of her traveling dress, she gave silent thanks to Lady Maryann for ordering the trunk packed. The gray poplin

53

which Meg herself had placed in the cloak bag would not have done justice to this night's grand occasion—dinner in the company of an earl, no less.

And, she added as an afterthought, in the company of the man who had let her mother go without the slightest attempt to detain her.

When Elspeth knocked five minutes later, Meg was ready to face not only Alvina and the as-yet-unknown man who had fathered her, or Philip Rutland, Earl of Stanbrook, but the devil himself. She was as confident and self-assured as only Meg Fletcher could be.

"The main rooms on the ground floor are easy to find," Elspeth offered shyly. "As long as ye don't take the wrong turn. You'll want to turn right from your room. See? Then you'll get to the main stairs."

"And if I turned left?"

"Why, then, after another turn or two, you'd end up in the east tower, Miss Megan. An' ye don't want to go there. It ain't safe."

Descending the stairs, Meg caught sight of Philip Rutland pacing the marble-tiled floor of the Great Hall.

"You need not accompany me farther, Elspeth. Lord Stanbrook will take me to the salon."

The maid fell back. "Shall I unpack for ye, Miss Megan?"

Meg was about to decline when Philip looked up. As once before at the Drury Lane, she witnessed the slow smile that transformed his harsh features. Indeed, he was a fascinating man, and the time she'd have to spend unpacking after dinner could be better spent in his company. There was something, after all, in having a personal maid.

"Thank you, Elspeth. That would be very kind."

While the girl retreated upstairs, Meg continued her descent.

"My lord, I have dismissed my maid and am therefore at your mercy. Will you kindly give me your guidance to the salon?"

He assisted her down the last steps. "What if I don't? You said yourself you're at my mercy."

Standing beside him, she noted the devilish glint in his eyes and liked very much what she saw.

"I fear, my lord, I shall have to set up a great screech."

"Meg, I swear you *will* be screaming before long if you keep my-lording me."

"You called me Meg instead of Megan. For that I am eternally grateful. But what shall I call you? I'm afraid Mr. Rutland will serve no longer."

"Philip will do nicely."

She gave him a mischievous look. "I may be an actress, sir. But I am *not* fast."

"I beg your pardon. The alternative is Stanbrook."

"Stanbrook," she repeated, tasting the word. "Yes, Stanbrook will do. And now, shall we go to the salon? I wouldn't want to incur Mrs. Elmore's displeasure by being tardy."

"Alvina will have to wait. There are one or two points we must clear up between us. And then I am to take you to Cousin Richard. He wants to speak to you alone before dinner."

Meg thought a moment, then said, "Yes, I believe it is best if I see Sir Richard first without Mrs. Elmore's rather intimidating presence."

"Sir Richard? Mrs. Elmore? What is this formality, Meg? Are you not Cousin Richard's daughter after all?"

She shrugged. "He may have fathered me, but I am not certain I'll acknowledge the relationship."

"You're splitting hairs. You are his daughter, which makes matters rather awkward."

"What matters?"

He took her arm. "Let's start walking. Cousin Richard occupies a suite of rooms in the tower wing, and it'll take a moment to get there."

Diverted, she said, "It cannot be the same tower Elspeth warned me about. It's unsafe, she told me."

"That's the east tower. Cousin Richard's quarters consist of the two downstairs chambers of the west tower and the adjacent rooms in the main section of the house. The whole is called the tower wing, and it is closed off from the rest of the building by an imposing set of double doors."

"Why would one tower be safe, and not the other?"

"Something to do with the dungeons under the east tower, I believe. They're about to cave in or something," Philip replied without much interest. "Meg, we must speak about us. Do you remember that I promised I'd find a way to see you again and renew my invitation to supper?"

"I remember. Also that you were cocksure I'd accept."

His mouth twitched. "Wouldn't you?"

"You'll hardly know until you invite me, will you?"

"But that's just it. Now that I know you're a Carswell and therefore related to me—no matter how distantly—I can hardly take you to supper at the Clarendon."

"I *knew* it!"

Her vehemence surprised Meg as much as it did Philip. He stopped in his stride.

"What did you know?"

"The Clarendon with its obliging waiters and locked doors! Dash it, Stanbrook! I had hoped you'd come up with something less predictable."

A dangerous light entered his eyes. "So I'm predictable," he said softly. "And how many of your admirers have taken you to the Clarendon?"

None had, or, rather, she had allowed no one to take her there. She glowered at him. "That, my lord, is none of your dashed business. Please take me to Sir Richard now."

For a moment longer he looked at her.

"Yes," he said with a sigh. "You are a Carswell. Not only do you have the red hair but also the temper to go with it. We shall continue our conversation when you're in a better humor."

Meg did not dignify this with an answer. Matching his

stride step by step, her back straight, her head held high, she walked beside him as they traversed a long, dimly lit corridor, turned a corner and followed a somewhat wider passage to the double doors he had mentioned. She was highly incensed with the Earl of Stanbrook, and if her stomach fluttered in anticipation of this first meeting with the man who had fathered her, she remained quite unaware of it.

Philip knocked and almost immediately they were admitted by a stooped, white-haired man dressed in the knee breeches and frock coat of a generation ago.

"Marsden, I've brought your master's daughter. He is expecting her."

"Yes, my lord. Come right in. Sir Richard is in his study."

They entered a chamber lit with a multitude of candles in wall sconces and a many-faceted chandelier. Close to a blazing log fire Sir Richard Carswell, Bart., sat in a wing-backed chair, one leg propped on a cushioned stool.

Meg saw instantly whence she had her tall stature, the proud tilt of her head. Across the ten paces or so that separated them, she stared into a pair of eyes the same color and brilliance as her own.

"Well, come in. Come in!" Sir Richard's voice held an irascible note. "Now that you're here, you may as well take a close-up look at me."

Chapter Five

Slowly, Meg walked across the thick rugs. She sat down in a chair facing Sir Richard and looked around for Philip. But he had left. She had wanted to speak to the old gentleman alone, yet, paradoxically, she felt deserted.

"Stanbrook tells me you're my daughter."

She focused on the baronet. For an instant, the bitterness she had harbored toward him since she had learned her mother's story filled her mind to the exclusion of all else and reflected in her eyes. Sir Richard flinched a little under that look, but did not try to evade it.

"It appears that way, sir."

"And . . . Rosemary? Where is she?"

"She died eleven years ago."

The old man seemed to shrink. He lowered his head, his chin resting on the folds of his cravat, and Meg saw a streak of flaming copper in the silver-gray hair.

She wondered if his hair had already started to turn gray when her mother first knew him. Wondered how Rosemary had felt about him, this man old enough to be her father, and whom she had taken as husband. And what Sir Richard had felt for Rosemary, the young girl, a tradesman's daughter, whom he had made Lady Carswell.

Disconcerting questions, unwelcome and irrelevant. Irrelevant because the answers, if she were to receive any, would no longer matter.

And yet she wondered. Had he loved Rosemary? Had he hoped, since his daughter was alive, that his wife, too, might still be living in London? She stared at the bent head and felt beneath the bitterness a stirring of pity.

"Didn't Lord Stanbrook or Stewart tell you, sir?"

"Stewart told me nothing at all." Sir Richard straightened. "Didn't even come to see me. No doubt, he ran to hide behind his mama's skirts, afraid I'd ask him questions he might not wish to answer. Like, how the devil he suddenly found you when you were supposed to have died twenty-odd years ago."

"Twenty-four," she said mechanically.

Just how much, or how little, had Philip told Sir Richard? How much had Stewart told Philip? She'd make it her business to find out, but she would certainly not enlighten the old man about matters that did not concern her directly.

Sir Richard reached for the sherry decanter on a table beside his chair and with a shaking hand poured two glasses of the dark amber wine.

"Damned stroke," he muttered, shooting a fierce look at her. "Affected my right arm and leg."

"Do you want some help?"

"No, I don't," he said irritably. "I'm not an invalid with one foot in the grave."

Meg looked at him with grudging respect. A proud, obstinate man. Wouldn't use his left arm, or accept assistance. Quite possibly she had inherited more than stature, hair and eye color from Sir Richard.

She accepted the glass he handed her but didn't drink immediately. Instead, she studied the man opposite her, the aged face with the jutting chin and beaked nose, with deep vertical grooves beside the mouth—grooves that might have been carved by pain or by perpetual ill-temper. She looked at his hands, long and squared-off at the fingertips, knuckles and wrist bones enlarged by arthritis or gout.

"Gal, I know I said you should take a close-up look.

But must you stare as though you were examining a horse's points?"

"I'm afraid I don't know the first thing about horses. What are their points?"

"*Not* know about— No, you wouldn't, would you?" He frowned. "Stanbrook said you live in a tavern in Seven Dials, and you are—you're an actress."

"Yes." She met his look squarely, daring him to say something derogatory about her profession.

Sir Richard swallowed a mouthful of sherry. "If Rosemary died when you were but a girl, who raised you?"

"My father did."

He gave a start, spilling some of his wine. With a violent gesture, he rubbed a handkerchief over the stain on his silk breeches, then drained the glass.

Watching him, Meg wished there were more satisfaction in scoring a point. Not that she was suddenly brimming with affection for this man who had abandoned her mother, but something in her refused to let her enjoy the small victory.

"Samuel Fletcher raised me as his daughter, sir." She spoke evenly, calmly. She wanted him to know what had happened to her and Rosemary, but she did not want to see him flinch again. "And Mother was known as his wife."

Sir Richard poured more sherry, looked at Meg's untouched glass, and replaced the stopper on the decanter.

"He is good to you, this Samuel Fletcher?"

"He *was* good to me. Fletcher died just over a sennight ago."

The old man remained silent, and after a moment Meg said, "He was a Bow Street runner, tried to apprehend a thief and was knifed by cutthroats who wanted the thief's loot. I was able to see him before he died, and he told me that my name is Megan Carswell and that I was born at Carswell Hall."

"He told you, eh? A sennight ago." Sir Richard nodded

61

as if in answer to an unspoken question. "So that's it."

Something in his voice set up her hackles. "That's what, sir?"

"I wondered why, if you didn't perish in the fire Alvina told me about, you hadn't come sooner to claim your inheritance. But you didn't know."

Anger flared, burning hot. "I claim nothing save the right to tell you to your face that you treated my mother abominably."

An answering spark of ire glowed in his eyes but died instantly. Sir Richard suddenly looked weary and ill.

Meg rose, her anger doused as quickly as it had flared. But now, there was no feeling left in her at all. Not even pity.

"Shall I ring for Marsden?"

"No." He reached beneath his chair and pulled out a stout cane. "It's late. I want my dinner."

Alvina Elmore occupied the place of hostess at the foot of the table and Sir Richard sat at the head. Meg was seated on his right, which placed her next to Stewart and across from Philip. The four-course meal, excellently prepared and efficiently served, should have been a wonderful experience, but Meg was too perturbed to relax and enjoy the succulent dishes and various wines.

She should not have lost her temper with Sir Richard. Since she was prepared to fight her dislike for Alvina and keep an open mind regarding the role the baronet's sister had played in Rosemary's disastrous marriage, she must, in all fairness, listen to Sir Richard without prejudice. He was an old man, obviously not in the best of health although he would never admit to feebleness. No matter how well Philip had prepared him, it must have been a shock seeing the daughter he had denied at birth and, later on, believed dead.

He had not shown distress when she entered his study—had, in fact, accepted her almost too readily. But, on the other hand, she had no way of knowing how he had reacted when Philip broke the news about her.

She glanced across the table at Philip Rutland, Earl of Stanbrook, the other man who had aroused her ire that night. He was watching her with an oddly intent look in his eyes. Was he, as Sir Richard had phrased it, examining the horse's points?

Somehow, he did not appear to be studying her physical points. He did not even notice her frown. But, surely, he knew that it was rude to stare?

So much for the manners of an earl. She decided then and there not to lose any sleep over quarreling with him, and most definitely would she not apologize.

"Megan."

She turned to Alvina Elmore, whose mouth stretched in a thin smile that did nothing to hide the coldness of her eyes.

"Yes, ma'am?"

"You must let me know how we can entertain you. Unfortunately, I have no previous experience in that regard." The corners of Alvina's mouth turned down disdainfully. "You are the first actress to stay at Carswell Hall."

Meg picked up her glass and took a sip of wine. Had Alvina treated Rosemary thus, openly showing her contempt for the young bride? She remembered her mother, shy and timid to the point of shrinking from the least show of unkindness or severity. Uncertain of herself and her new role, she must have been terrified of Alvina and suffered horribly under her sister-in-law's barbs.

But Meg was not easily terrified. When she looked at Alvina again, the famed Meg Fletcher smile was firmly in place.

"Mrs. Elmore, have you ever entertained or hoped to entertain a duchess?"

A thin gray eyebrow rose. "Why, yes. Years ago, the Duchess of Devonshire stayed a few days. The races at Ascot, you know. But why . . . what does it have to do with entertaining you?"

"Treat me as you treated the duchess, and you shouldn't have anything to worry about."

Angry red spots appeared high on Alvina's cheekbones. She sent Meg a poisonous look, quickly hidden by lowered eyelids.

Sir Richard chuckled, a rough, rasping sound as though his throat was unused to the exercise. And Philip, Meg was quick to note, tried unsuccessfully to suppress an appreciative grin.

"I don't believe my question warrants an outbreak of levity," Alvina said icily. "You *are* an actress, Megan. Not a duchess."

"Megan was only teasing you, Mother," Stewart said coaxingly.

He turned to Meg. "Weren't you?"

She choked back a denial when she saw the plea in his eyes. Dash it! What was the matter with him? Or with her for acquiescing to the unspoken entreaty? She owed Stewart nothing, especially not consideration for Alvina's feelings.

She shrugged. "Yes, of course I was only joking. I did not come to be entertained. I merely want to look around, to explore the house and grounds. In a day or so I shall return to London and trouble you no more."

"You planned to stay a week," Stewart reminded her.

Drat the fellow! But she was too aware of Philip's intent look to bother with Stewart. So Stanbrook cared about her reply, did he? Well, she had cared enough about his presence to dress in the flattering green silk Maryann had had the foresight to pack. But the grand occasion she had pictured this dinner to be had turned out a most desultory affair. She'd have had more pleasure eating one of Mrs. Bellamy's plain suppers in the taproom of the Fighting Cock.

"Well, Meg?" Philip said quietly. "A week is not very long to get to know someone. Won't you give us a chance?"

She felt a treacherous warmth steal into her face under his scrutiny. A pox on the man! His words held a double meaning. Or did they? No matter how foolish of her, she wished they did.

"Why not?" Again, she shrugged. "As you said, a week is not very long, and I shan't be needed at the theater until September."

"You won't regret it," he said casually, but there was nothing casual about the gleam in the green-ringed eyes.

Dinner seemed more pleasant after the exchange. And if there was none of the easy conversation or friendly banter she had witnessed at Fant House—no matter whether Stephen and Maryann dined alone or in company—Meg did not complain. She had too much to think about to miss mere conversation.

She mulled over Philip's words. "A week is not very long to get to know someone. Won't you give us a chance?" If he had spoken of himself and her, she was foolish to give it another thought. Philip would be contemplating an affair, which was not a step she intended to take. And yet she did not stop thinking about his words.

After dinner, Sir Richard did not linger in the dining room. Bidding Stewart and Philip to enjoy their port, he rose and left with the two ladies.

"You may come to see me in the morning," he said to Meg. "At nine o'clock."

"Very well, sir."

She watched until he turned the corner to the long hallway leading to the tower wing. His gait was slow but, despite a slight stiffness of the right leg, stately. His back and shoulders were as straight as those of a younger man. He was proud and stubborn, was Sir Richard Carswell.

As was Meg. She had always been stubborn, and Fletcher had instilled in her an undauntable pride in herself, in her own worth. Also, a strong sense of right and wrong. Tomorrow, she would speak to Sir Richard again. No matter what he said then, she would *not* lose her temper.

Alvina ushered her into the salon and, while they waited for Philip and Stewart, made it her business to instruct Meg in the intricate rules of etiquette governing the *ton*—all the while setting dainty stitches in a piece of embroidery.

It was totally unbecoming in a young lady to show sarcasm to her elders, she said in a tone possibly meant to be polite but coming across as smug and condescending. Only hurly-burly girls with no breeding allowed themselves to betray such a lack of manners. And neither did a well-brought-up young lady shrug.

Meg listened to the sermon with half an ear while giving the salon a thorough inspection. She had a thick skin; none of Alvina's barbs would find a target. She could enjoy the moment of leisure and truly study the beautiful furnishings. Wherever she had been before— the Great Hall, her own chamber, Sir Richard's study, the dining room—she had been too preoccupied to spare more than a cursory glance for the luxurious rugs, the chairs covered in velvet or brocade, the gleaming wood paneling with its bosses and fancy scrollwork. No doubt about it, Carswell Hall was very beautiful.

Had she been fourteen instead of four-and-twenty, she might have resented growing up in London's back alleys instead of this beautiful house. As it was, she knew that her upbringing had shaped her into the person she was, and she liked who she was—a fighter, a woman who surmounted obstacles and battled adverse conditions to reach her goal: to be the greatest actress England had ever boasted.

Not many women had goals—beyond marriage—or fought to achieve those goals. And among the upper-class ladies, Meg knew of only one whose determination matched her own: Lady Maryann Fant. Maryann and she had recognized each other as kindred spirits. Despite their disparate stations in life, they had become friends.

She heard men's voices in the hallway: Stewart's light tones and Philip's deep, resonant ones. Her heart beat a little faster at the thought of Philip, and it occurred to her that, had she been raised at Carswell Hall, she would be an eligible *parti* even for the Earl of Stanbrook, whereas Meg Fletcher, the actress, could look only for a flirtation or a brief affair.

Common sense instantly asserted itself. She had wanted to be an actress for as long as she could remember. If she had lived at Carswell Hall, no doubt she would have run away at fifteen or sixteen to join a group of traveling players. She would have been Megan Carswell, the actress, still ineligible for marriage to a peer.

Besides, she had a notion Stanbrook was a man who kept his distance from eligible young ladies, else he would not have escaped matrimony so long.

The door opened to admit the two gentlemen just as Alvina fired off several questions. Did Meg play the pianoforte? Or paint? Or embroider?

Laughter bubbled in Meg. Alvina was painfully obvious in trying to put her to the blush, but she might have saved herself the trouble. Meg blushed only when the Earl of Stanbrook looked at her a certain way.

"No, Mrs. Elmore. Those pastimes have no value in Seven Dials. However, I am no mean needlewoman. I started sewing my own garments when I was six."

Alvina dismissed plain sewing as worthless. "A young lady *must* know how to embroider," she persisted. From a small basket, she extracted a magnifying lens and inspected her work. "How else will she occupy her time in the evenings?"

Stewart looked as though he wished he had stayed in the dining room with the port, but Philip, a lazy smile curving his mouth, watched Meg with interest.

Thus put on her mettle, she rose and curtsied to Alvina. "I pity the young lady who has no option but to embroider on such a lovely evening. *I* should much rather go for a stroll in the moonlight."

The emerald silk of her gown swirled about her ankles as she spun to face Philip.

"My lord, would you care to accompany me?"

"With pleasure."

His eyes laughed at her. He proffered his arm, then nodded to Alvina and Stewart. "I know you'll excuse us. And please don't wait if we're not back in time for tea."

"Scandalous," Alvina was heard to mutter just before Philip closed the door.

"I wonder what is so scandalous?" Philip guided Meg into the passage leading to the east wing. "That we are going for a walk? Or that we may not return for tea?"

"Must you ask?" She chuckled softly. "It's I, the actress, the scarlet woman, casting out lures to a gentleman. Could anything be more scandalous?"

"Certainly nothing could be more delightful."

"Oh, well said! You do have manners after all."

Startled, he asked, "Why would you think I have none?"

"The way you stared at me during dinner. It was quite rude, you know."

"I was not staring. I was contemplating."

"Contemplating what?"

He only grinned and opened a door. "This is the music room. Its most agreeable feature by far is a set of French doors opening into the gardens. If you stay close to me, I promise to guide you without knocking you into a harp or the pianoforte."

"I suppose it would be too much trouble to light a candle or a lamp?"

He slipped an arm around her waist. "Let us say it would not be in my best interest."

The warmth of his hand penetrated the thin silk of her gown. It was a most agreeable sensation, and she could not be angry with him for taking a liberty.

Thrown off guard by the pleasant effect of his closeness, she exclaimed, "How this takes me back! I haven't walked with a man's arm around me since Tom Easterwood squired me to the Ice Fair."

"The Ice Fair? That was six years ago."

She heard the note of astonishment in his voice and gave herself a mental shake, telling herself that no one could be expected to believe an actress led a retired life. Still, it hurt, and she was irritated that she had made the foolish admission in the first place. As though she hadn't learned over the years that disclosures about her private life served only to pique a gentleman's interest and to stoke his ardor if he was set on pursuit.

Wanting to rectify the *faux pas*, she said lightly, "Was it that long ago? No doubt, I'm confusing the incident with another occasion."

In the dark, she sensed his eyes on her and was glad that it was impossible for him to see the tell-tale blush flaming in her cheeks.

His arm tightened as he steered her around the dark bulk of the pianoforte. "No doubt you do mistake the occasion," he said, his tone matching hers in lightness. "But just in case you don't, let me ask what you expected of a man called Tom Easterwood? The Toms I know are all slowtops."

"Are they?" Her love of mischief prompted her to add, "And what about the Philips you know?"

"I only recall one at present," he said gravely, but she could well imagine a glint in his eye. "And he's top-of-the-trees, up to every move on the board. He wouldn't have stopped embracing you after the Ice Fair."

What an absurd conversation to hold with the man whose object it was to make her his next mistress!

Laughter tickled her throat, but she suppressed it. Instead, she produced a disdainful sniff, regretting only that Alvina Elmore wasn't there to witness the unladylike act.

"I don't doubt *you* sneak an arm around a lady's waist as often as you can! But to do poor Tom justice, he married that spring, and I cannot believe his wife would have let him walk with me again."

"Did you break his heart, and he married to conceal his hurt and wounded pride?"

This was true to some extent, but Meg shook her head. "Oh, no. He decided he did not wish to waste his time on a stubborn girl like me, whose first thought in the morning and last thought at night was to get accepted at one of the theaters."

"In fact, he was a looby."

The dry comment pleased her, even though she recognized that knowing always what to say to flatter a woman would be part and parcel of a gentleman's practiced charm.

They had reached the French doors and Philip let go of her to open one of the wings. A familiar sweet scent enveloped her.

"Lilacs!"

She stepped outside. After the dark of the music room, the moonlit garden seemed as bright as day, and before her, as far as she could see, stretched a border of lilac bushes. White lilacs, and lilacs in various shades of blue and red.

"How beautiful. Can we explore?"

His hand cupped her elbow. "Some other time. This path leads to a gazebo, but we shan't walk that far. There's a bench close by, the ideal place to sit and talk."

"Talk?" She remembered their earlier conversation and his admission that he had planned to invite her to the Clarendon, that famous—or infamous—place of seduction. "Are you quite sure that is all you want to do?"

"Outrageous girl!" He laughed, but Meg thought it was not a totally joyful sound. "It is all I must do."

She did not understand but merely gave him a sidelong look and said nothing.

Within a short while they reached the bench, a pretty but cold and uncomfortable-looking marble affair. Philip removed his coat and spread it on the seat.

"Your grace, pray accept my humble services."

She sat down. "Now that is what I call outrageous."

"What? My sacrifice of an excellent coat?"

"No. That you reminded me of my naughtiness toward

Alvina. Do you think she'll ever forgive me for demanding I be treated like a duchess?"

"Forget Alvina." He sat down beside her. Capturing one of her hands, he held it loosely. "Meg, what am I going to do about you?"

Her eyes widened. "I thought you had decided that when you first met me in the Green Room."

"Surely you don't believe I'd seduce you under your father's roof?"

Savoring the sweet night air, the warmth of his touch, and not intending to let him seduce her, no matter when or where, she said absently, "Wouldn't you?"

"Dash it, Meg! I'm not a cad!"

"I beg your pardon." She was careful not to let him see her smile. How stuffy and illogical men became when they felt their precious honor questioned. Yet a man wouldn't think twice about a woman's honor, unless she was his wife, sister, or mother. "I did not mean to imply you're a cad. I merely took you for a rake and a libertine."

He acknowledged the sally with a reluctant laugh. "Even a libertine or a rake has certain standards. And I want you to know that I went to great trouble convincing your father that you're a *respectable* actress."

"Ah! That rather did put a spoke in your wheel, didn't it?"

He stared at her hard. "Meg!" he said accusingly. "I believe you're enjoying this."

Her ready laughter bubbled. "How can I not enjoy myself? You came to the theater, convinced you need only crook your little finger to have me do your bidding. And, confess, when you believed I had accepted Stewart's protection, you had no doubt I could easily be wooed from him."

He raised a haughty brow. "Are you trying to tell me I could not have won you from Stewart?"

"I am trying to tell you, my lord, that you're too cocksure by half."

71

"Oh, ho," he said softly. "We are back to my lord and a crushing tone. Could it be that her grace fears for her pride?"

"Stanbrook, if I promise not to call you my lord again, will you cease calling me your grace?"

"*Do* you promise?"

"Most reluctantly, since I know it teases you."

"No more than your grace vexes you."

She raised her right hand. "I vow and declare not to use my lord—unless you aggravate me."

Chuckling, he tightened his grip on her hand and drew her closer. His face a scarce two inches from hers, he said caressingly, "You're a baggage, Meg. A temptress who can drive a man nigh out of his head."

Whether it was the moon weaving her magic, or the sweet scent of the lilacs clouding Meg's judgment, she leaned toward Philip. His mouth brushed hers but briefly, and yet the thrill of the butterfly touch heated her blood.

Quickly, she pulled away from him. She was four-and-twenty years old and, God help her, a virgin—not a natural state for a woman her age. She must guard against the singing in her blood, the racing of her pulse, the foolish yearning to feel his mouth on hers once more.

She had no illusions. She knew what Philip wanted, what every man wanted from an actress when he found her desirable. As though to confirm this, he smiled at her and in his eyes was that certain look that drove warmth into her face and made her pulse beat faster.

"Tell me," she said, determinedly brisk, "how did Sir Richard react when you assured him that I am a *respectable* actress?"

Chapter Six

The gleam in Philip's eyes died. He looked at her and said nothing for a moment, then heaved an exaggerated sigh. "I suppose you expect me to thank you for stopping me from making a fool of myself."

"I doubt you've ever made a fool of yourself. How would you have done so tonight?"

"Never you mind."

He rose, looming above her, Meg thought, like the villain in one of the more ribald comedies.

"You want to know about Cousin Richard," he said, his voice sounding harsh to her ears. "Rest assured, the old man was pleased to hear his daughter is alive. So pathetically pleased, he swallowed everything I told him about you."

All of a sudden, Meg felt chilled.

"For instance?"

Philip gestured impatiently. "You already know. I convinced him—and *how* I did is immaterial—that you're totally respectable."

"And that, of course, is a lie," she said, her voice hollow.

Gravel crunched beneath Philip's shoes as he took a step away from her and stared in the direction where the gazebo must be. She could see only his profile, the proud nose, the chin that was just a bit too strong, the mouth that had touched hers so gently a moment ago tightening as though about to pronounce a judgment.

"I have no fault to find with you," he said. "On the contrary. You delight me."

"Thank you," she said drily.

He gave no sign that he had heard, nor did he turn. "But, dash it, Meg! I cannot help but feel that Cousin Richard deserves—"

For once, he seemed at a loss for words, and with quiet dignity Meg finished the thought for him. "He deserves someone a little more respectable than an actress as a daughter."

Philip looked at her over his shoulder, wary, alert, as though he sensed something amiss.

As indeed it was. Disappointment, sadness, and anger warred in her breast. My lord Stanbrook was barely acquainted with her. How could he presume to know anything about her or decide that she was the wrong sort of daughter for Sir Richard!

She fought her surging emotions, tried to put herself in Philip's skin, to think as he would think. . . .

Megan Carswell is Meg Fletcher, the actress. She was a dancer before that. Is there such a thing as a respectable actress or opera dancer? he'd be asking himself. *Mrs. Siddons, of course, but that was some time ago. And her contemporary, Mrs. Jordan, caused scandal enough for the both of them. And then there was Kitty Clive. . . .*

No, she should not blame Philip for believing her less than respectable. And yet, she did. She wanted him to know instinctively that she was different from other actresses and dancers.

"What did Stewart tell you?" she asked, determined not to show how much he had hurt her.

"That first Alvina, then he, attended a performance at the Drury Lane and instantly recognized you as a Carswell. Something to do with a portrait hanging in one of the rooms."

"Yes," she said, "the likeness is uncanny. I'm surprised *you* did not remark on it when you met me in London."

"Never saw the painting in my life, or heard of it until Stewart mentioned it."

She knitted her brow. "You really are not a very close relation, are you?"

Philip turned to face her fully. "My grandfather was the younger brother of Cousin Richard's grandfather. I don't know how remote that makes our relationship, but, believe me, it's distant enough that under ordinary circumstances I wouldn't visit Carswell Hall at all."

"But you do visit."

"I came here for the first time four years ago when your father sent for me after his first stroke. Since, I've visited about once a twelvemonth or so. You see, I happen to be the last male descended directly from a male Carswell."

She stared at him, more puzzled than before. "But your name is Rutland."

"That's because my grandfather—that younger Carswell—took the name Rutland when he married."

Philip resumed his seat beside her. Stretching his long legs and crossing them at the ankles, he said, "I suppose it's rather confusing, but the Stanbrook title is one that may be passed on through a female."

"I never heard of that."

"It's more common with a Scottish peerage, but it is possible in England also. In our family, it happened only twice in nine generations, the last time when my grandmother alone survived of seven children. Her father, too, died young, and she became the Countess of Stanbrook at age fifteen. When she married my grandfather, Philip Carswell, part of the agreement was that he assume the Rutland name."

"I see."

Wishing she had brought a shawl, Meg hugged her arms to her breast. But perhaps it was not the night air that made her shiver. Some might say it was a goose

75

walking over her grave.

She looked at Philip. "Then *you* are the distant cousin who is heir to the baronetcy."

"I am indeed. Also, as matters stand, heir to one half of Cousin Richard's properties. And Stewart will inherit the other half."

"Only one half for Stewart? What irony!"

He frowned. "Why?"

"According to what Pa told me, it was Alvina's determination to preserve the Carswell inheritance for Stewart that inspired her to break up Sir Richard's marriage to my mother and to convince him that I was not his child. Does Alvina know you'll share Carswell Hall with her son?"

"She does. And it galls her no end. At times, I don't know what irks her more—that Cousin Richard made over a part of the estate to me, or that the baronetcy goes to me, which, in effect, means it'll be defunct upon Cousin Richard's death."

"Yes, I suppose so, since you're an earl and would always go by that title," she said, her mind awhirl with all she had learned. "That, I daresay, explains Alvina's dislike of you."

"So you've already caught on that she does not cherish me."

For a while, they sat in silence, then Philip leaned toward her. "Meg, are you truly Cousin Richard's daughter?"

She caught her breath. "Do you doubt it?"

"No." He sounded weary. "I'm merely reluctant to accept it."

Taken aback, she stared at him. Unbidden, Fletcher's warning to be careful came to mind. Meg dismissed it. She was *not* a heroine in a gothic novel in which every conversation, every comment, held sinister overtones, but before she could ask Philip for an explanation of his strange remark, footsteps approached on the graveled path.

"Megan? Philip?"

Stewart Elmore came rapidly closer.

"Ah, there you are. I feared I might have to search as far as the gazebo."

"Hello, Stewart," Philip drawled. "Escaped your mother's vigilance?"

"Alas, no. I've been sent to fetch you. The tea tray is waiting."

There was no further occasion to speak privately with Philip. Alvina saw to that. When tea was drunk, she rose, saying, "Come along, Megan. I'll show you where the bedroom candles are kept and I'll take you upstairs. We cannot have you getting lost, can we?"

Meg could only thank her, bid the gentlemen a good night, and trail in Alvina's wake as the older woman sailed majestically from the salon.

Armed with candles, which Alvina picked up from a table in the Great Hall and lit on the low-burning flame of an oil lamp kept for that purpose on the same table, they ascended the stairs. When they reached Meg's chamber, Alvina stopped.

"I understand you did not bring a maid, and Mrs. Sutton assigned Elspeth to look after you."

"Yes, Mrs. Sutton was very kind."

Alvina's mouth primmed. "I'll just make certain you have everything you need."

Meg did not want Alvina in her bedroom or in the dressing room, perhaps assessing her personal belongings while ostensibly checking the soap and towel supplies. Hand on the knob, determined to quarrel with the older woman if she persisted, she stood in front of the door.

"Thank you, but it is quite unnecessary. Mrs. Sutton took care of everything."

To insist would be an admission that the housekeeper under her supervision was incompetent, and Alvina knew it.

She inclined her head. "If there's anything you need, my rooms are at the end of the corridor. You and I are on our own here in the east wing. Stewart occupies the chambers of the west tower on this floor."

Prompted by her penchant for mischief, Meg asked, "And where does Lord Stanbrook have his room?"

Again, Alvina tightened her mouth, conveying utter disapproval of the question. "We passed Philip's chamber. It is at the head of the stairs."

"Thank you, Mrs. Elmore. Good night."

Alvina started to walk off. She had taken no more than three or four steps when she turned around.

"It is customary in our circles to address the sister of one's father as Aunt. Perhaps you will remember that in future, Megan?"

Meg widened her eyes. "I did not think you'd welcome such familiarity."

Twice before, she had witnessed the reddening of Alvina's pale skin and had known it was caused by suppressed anger. But this time, something besides anger lurked in those cold eyes. If it weren't nonsensical, Meg would have called it fear.

"Why?" Alvina asked sharply. "If it's on account of something Rosemary told you, I beg you to remember that she was . . . distraught . . . In fact, she was . . . ill when she left my brother in that clandestine manner. Whatever she said, you should take with a grain of salt."

Her mother ill? Distraught? Meg's heart thumped painfully. She had known women who, after giving birth, fell into a strange lethargy, weeping constantly and barely recognizing family or friends. Surely, if her mother had been like that during the early days, Fletcher would not have been impressed by the story she told him. Within the limits of Meg's memory, and it stretched back to the birth of her first sibling when she was only three, her mother had always been loving and sunny-tempered.

"Are you saying my mother was mentally ill?"

78

"No," Alvina said hastily.

Too hastily—as though she realized she had gone too far, thought Meg.

"Your mother was weakened. You were a very large baby and Rosemary was slight, not built for easy birthing. Also, I suspect, she still suffered from a fever when she left."

"You *suspect?*" Meg's eyes blazed. "Didn't anyone send for a physician or *someone* competent enough to know for certain? Who looked after my mother while she was recovering?"

Alvina gave Meg a high-nosed stare. "Nanny Grimshaw did. She took care of both you and your mother."

"Is she still around? Can I speak with her?" Meg asked. Perhaps she had finally found a source of unbiased information.

"You can speak with her," Alvina said with a certain amount of grim satisfaction. "Nanny is retired. Lives in one of the estate cottages not far from here. Anyone can direct you."

"Thank you." Meg smiled with genuine warmth. "And now I shan't keep you any longer. I know you must be tired."

Alvina responded with a slight relaxing of her set features and, muttering a good-night, went off to her own rooms.

It was not until Meg slipped between the lavender-scented sheets of the four-poster bed that she wondered about the tone of satisfaction that had crept into Alvina's voice when she spoke of Nanny Grimshaw, the readiness with which she had disclosed the old woman's whereabouts. It would have been more in character if Alvina had tried to stop her from seeing the woman who had looked after Sir Richard's wife and the baby all those years ago.

Or had she done the lady an injustice? Was Alvina, perhaps, not the "mean piece" Fletcher had labeled her?

Meg grimaced ruefully. Recalling the few encounters

she'd had with Alvina, she decided that something other than goodwill had prompted her aunt to be so forthcoming.

She settled for sleep. And then, just as she was about to doze off, the conversation at the dinner table when she had agreed to stay the full week popped into her mind. At the time, she had been so intent on Philip's reaction that she had not once looked at Sir Richard. Now, she had not the slightest notion how he felt about her presence in the house.

Philip had assured her the baronet was pleased to know his daughter was alive, but that did not necessarily mean he'd be pleased to have her stay awhile. Perhaps Sir Richard had asked her to see him in the morning so he might send her packing. Her presence might be an embarrassment, a disagreeable reminder of the past.

Any doubts Meg harbored about Sir Richard's plans were laid to rest when she joined him in his study shortly after nine o'clock. Once again, a fire was blazing in the hearth and the old gentleman was seated as close as possible to the warmth, his right leg propped on the footstool. Upon his insistence, Meg took the chair she had occupied the previous night.

"I had Marsden put up a fire screen," Sir Richard pointed out rather gruffly. "I need the warmth. Suffer from a touch of the gout every now and then. But you don't, do you?"

"No, sir." Meg kept a straight face. "Not yet."

For a moment it looked as though he would actually smile, but almost immediately he assumed an expression of ill-temper. It was as if he believed a smile equal to a display of bad manners.

"Want you to be comfortable," he said, his voice even gruffer than before. "Otherwise you may decide after all not to stay the week."

Excitement surged in Meg. She had not realized until

now just how much she would have minded if Sir Richard had not wanted her to stay.

"Thank you. And you won't object to my exploring a bit?"

His eyes darkened—perhaps in distress, perhaps in anger. It was impossible to tell with Sir Richard. But when he spoke, it was in the mildest tone she had heard him use.

"No need to ask permission, gal. Explore as much as you want. Stay as long as you want. In fact—" Sir Richard paused. "In fact, I want you to consider making Carswell Hall your home. All I'd ask in return is that you talk to me once in a while."

Nothing could have taken her more by surprise than his offer. She stared at him, and once again, as on the previous night, she felt a stirring of pity. He sounded and looked so . . . humble! The way she saw him now, he did not at all conform to the picture she had of him: cold, arrogant, overbearing. She still believed that his behavior toward her mother was unforgivable, and yet she was not immune to the appeal of loneliness and to the unhappiness she sensed in him.

"I'm afraid it would be rather awkward for me if I took up permanent residence here," she told him gently. "It is too far from London, from the Drury Lane Theatre. But I was hoping we could talk while I'm visiting. I shall answer any questions you may have. And, perhaps, you will answer my questions as well?"

"Yes." His head dropped and his voice was barely audible. "Yes, I'll answer your questions."

"Are you tired?"

He jerked his head up. "No, of course not. Fire away. What do you want to know?"

Meg voiced the first thought that came to mind. "Did you love my mother when you married her?"

Sir Richard was silent for a long time. There was a faraway look in his eyes, and Meg began to wonder if he had changed his mind about answering her questions. Or, perhaps, he had forgotten that she was there.

"Sir Richard?"

He blinked, focusing on her.

"Aye," he said heavily. "I loved Rosemary. Loved her more than anyone or anything."

Meg was silenced by his sincerity, the pain behind the words. She had a thousand-and-one questions for him, yet she could not bring herself to ask a single one.

An apologetic cough drew her attention to the door. Marsden had entered quietly, bearing a glass on a small silver tray.

"Pardon me, sir. It's time for your cordial and your rest."

"Damn you, Marsden," Sir Richard muttered weakly. "Damn you and your mother-hen ways."

The valet gave Meg a significant look. "If you were planning a walk, this is the best time of the day, Miss Megan."

"Indeed." Correctly interpreting Marsden's appeal, Meg rose. "With your permission, Sir Richard, I'd like to cut some lilacs for my room, and that's best done before the sun is high."

Slowly, the baronet raised his face until his eyes met hers.

"Lilacs," he murmured. "Your mother liked 'em, too."

The look of sadness on Sir Richard's face stayed with Meg as she traversed the gloomy passages that took her back to the Great Hall, then into the part of the house where Philip had shown her the French doors opening from the music room. Even when she stepped out into bright sunshine and sweet-scented air, she could not banish the image of the sick old man in the stuffy, over-heated room.

But, at least, the study and, in fact, all of Carswell Hall were appointed with every luxury and comfort money could buy.

She thought of her mother, Fletcher, her little

brothers and sisters, and herself in two small rooms on the fourth floor of a cold gray stone building in a narrow alley where the sun never penetrated. But they had been happy, the seven of them. Until death struck and took the little ones, then Rosemary.

Meg remembered how she had railed against fate, but Fletcher had soon put an end to that. "We was happy together," he had said sternly. "That's all what counts. Don't ever let bitterness spoil yer memories of those good times with yer ma and yer brothers and sisters."

Fletcher . . . her pa . . . how kind and how wise he had been. She wondered what he would have made of the residents at Carswell Hall.

Tears pricked her eyelids. She blinked hastily. Fletcher would be embarrassed if he knew she was turning into a watering pot at the mere thought of him. He would order her to stop thinking of the companionship lost to her and remember instead the good times they had been lucky enough to enjoy.

Deep in thought, she walked along the path bordered by the lilac hedge. She had quite forgotten that she wanted to cut some of the blooms for her chamber.

Sir Richard had confirmed that he loved her mother. What, then, had gone wrong?

Fletcher, too, had loved her mother, and he had made Rosemary proud to be his wife and content, despite their poverty. Contrary to Meg, who had no intention of ever being dependent on anyone, Rosemary had been just as dependent on Fletcher's strength and superiority as, no doubt, she had been on Sir Richard's. And yet, Sir Richard, who was in a better position than Fletcher to indulge and support a wife, had lost her.

Meg had planned to stay only a week, but now, with Sir Richard's offer . . . If it would take all summer, she could stay to find out what happened to make a timid young woman burdened with a two-week-old infant run away from a life of ease and luxury.

She stopped. Using a hand to shade her eyes, she

looked around. To her right was the lilac hedge, beyond which, she suspected, lay the wide lawns Stewart had mentioned, the stables, and the carriage drive upon which they had approached the house.

To her left lay the gardens, divided by formal hedges, narrow flagged paths, and wider graveled walks—gardens with flowers and shrubs that would have made Lady Maryann sigh with longing and envy.

And straight ahead, Meg saw a round wooden structure painted white, with a domed roof circled by tiny cupolas. The gazebo. A very fancy gazebo—it even had windows all around, reflecting the sun. It was a miniature fairy-tale castle, a stark contrast to the gloomy silhouette of the main house as she had seen it on her arrival.

But when she turned to look at the Elizabethan manor, its appearance was not at all gloomy. She could see most of the east wing with the mullioned windows framed by neatly trimmed creepers, the crenellated top of the east tower extending above the chimneys and steep gables of the roof. The sun cast a golden glow on the stone of the tower walls, and Meg laughed at herself and her fanciful mind that had perceived the tower as daunting the previous night.

She walked on, drawn once again by the fairy-tale appearance of the garden house. Presently, she heard the gurgle of water, smelled damp earth and lush growth. She hastened her steps. Surely, she wasn't mistaken. Surely, there was a brook behind the gazebo.

The only body of water Meg had known was the Thames, with its murky, evil-smelling banks, with its ships and ferries. But she had never seen a brook with clear water that rippled and invited the beholder to take off shoes and stockings to wade in its coolness, heels sinking into sand, toes digging into pebbles or stubbing against an unsuspected rock.

The attraction of the gazebo faded as Meg hurried on. And there, before she had walked twenty paces past the white structure, she saw the brook shaded by weeping willows.

Meg broke into a run. Shoes and stockings came off as though she had practiced the art since childhood. Still running, the skirt of her sprigged muslin gown hitched high, she entered the water.

A laugh of pure joy rose in her throat. Feeling the cool wetness, the tug of water against her ankles and calves, was the most delicious experience she'd had in a long while.

Except . . .

She came to an abrupt stop as her laugh was echoed from the opposite side of the brook and her gaze was drawn to the man watching her, laughter still in his eyes and reflected in the curve of his mouth.

. . . except for the brief touch of that very same mouth on hers.

Chapter Seven

"Hello, Stanbrook."

Meg wondered how the sight of him could fill her with such warmth. Their previous encounters should have taught her to stay cool and detached. Then, nothing he'd say could hurt or anger her.

"Enjoying the pleasures of rural life?" he asked, amusement in his voice. He stepped onto a boulder protruding from the swiftly running water. "I have a mind to join you."

"In those boots?"

"Of course not. I'd follow your example." His gaze lingered on the inches of bare legs exposed by her raised skirts.

Her cheeks flamed—very much to her chagrin and annoyance. How ridiculous! He had seen her on the stage, and she certainly felt no embarrassment during a play when a gentleman ogled the length of her britches-clad legs. This sudden shyness was totally out of character. She could only blame it on Alvina's sermon the night before.

Meg dropped the hem of her gown—too low, she realized when she felt the wet muslin press against her calves.

"Drat!" She shot Philip a look of irritation. "See what you made me do? If you cannot behave yourself, you really should not watch a lady wading."

"But I did nothing," he protested.

"*Nothing?!*" With more force than was warranted, she wrung out the lower part of her skirts. "What about that *leer* at my legs? Is that the way a gentleman behaves?"

"It wasn't a leer. It was a look of pure admiration."

"Ha!"

"And besides, a lady does not mention her legs to a gentleman."

"You sound like Alvina," she said crossly; then her sense of the ridiculous won the upper hand. She turned dancing eyes on him. "She will certainly have something to say to me when I get back with a dripping gown."

"We mustn't let that happen." He held out a hand. "Come here. I know a secluded spot where we can sit in the sun until your skirts are dry."

"Trust you to know a secluded spot," she muttered under her breath.

"Did you say something, Meg?"

His eyes mocked, but not unkindly. Most certainly he had heard her or, at least, had a very good notion of what she'd said. Meg decided the wisest course would be to ignore him—a more difficult feat than she would have believed possible.

She had thought him very elegant in the dark evening clothes he had worn at the theater and the previous night at dinner. But in a coat of corbeau superfine, fawn-colored pantaloons tucked into Hessian boots, he looked impressive—and also hard to resist with his arm stretched toward her in an imperious manner.

Still she hung back. "I'd better dry off on this side, where I left my shoes and stockings. I'll only get wet again when I need to retrieve them."

"There's a bridge a little way off. It may look flimsy, but it's perfectly safe. I used it myself."

No other argument came to mind. And if it did, the look on his face told her, he'd find a counterargument.

She waded toward him, gripped his hand, and let him

help her onto the bank.

"Shall I carry you? The ground is rough, I'm afraid."

Meg gave him a startled look. He was quite serious and not, as she had first believed, teasing or trying to be flirtatious.

She burst out laughing. "Stanbrook, you're as bad as Stewart when he assumed I'd have a maid! How do you think I grew up in the Dials? Hosed and shod, like a pampered little lady?"

For the first time since she met him, she saw him disconcerted, even embarrassed, if his heightened color was any indication of his feelings.

"I beg your pardon. How foolish of me. For a moment, there, I forgot that you haven't always lived at Carswell Hall."

"Are you saying that I fit into this—" She looked around, and with a sweeping gesture of her hand indicated the well-tended gardens and the gazebo on the opposite side of the brook. "Into this fairy-tale setting?"

"Yes." He sounded odd—puzzled, perhaps, or astonished. "I suppose that's what I mean. You fit in . . . you look at home. And not only out here, but also inside, in those long, paneled rooms with their Aubusson rugs, their velvets and brocades."

"Thank you." Dipping into a curtsy, she darted a sidelong glance at him. "An actress always appreciates a favorable critique."

He laughed, the strange mood broken. "You're a minx. You know very well I did not imply that you are acting a part."

Did she know it? Not half as confident as Philip seemed to think her, Meg tugged at her skirts, trying to keep the wet fabric away from her skin.

Philip watched impatiently. "We had best be going if you want to have that gown dry before luncheon."

They walked along the brook, bending low every now and again under dipping willow branches. The grass felt soft against Meg's bare feet, and if she hit a rough spot

89

once in a while, she did not mind. It was clean, sunbaked earth she touched, not a piece of refuse.

Wildflowers bloomed in abundance, some a deep-golden yellow, which, she assumed, were buttercups. Other plants looked as if they sprouted tiny blue stars.

She picked one. "What are these?"

"Forget-me-nots." Philip gave her one of those slow smiles that softened his features and put a gleam in his eyes. "When you leave at the end of next week, I'll present you with a posy."

"Will you? But I may be staying awhile."

"Good. I'll be glad of your company."

"Oh?" She made her voice casual. "Something Stewart said gave me the impression your visit here was nearing its end."

"I planned to leave mid-week, but Cousin Richard asked me to stay on."

She did not try to hide her pleasure. "Capital! I was not looking forward to spending the evenings embroidering with Alvina."

His mouth twitched. "Careful, Meg. I might take that as an invitation for further walks in the moonlight."

"Pray keep in mind what I said about your being too cocksure by half."

"I certainly will. But it won't stop me from hoping for another invitation."

This was an occasion to give him a set-down. Instead, she felt a most inappropriate smile tugging at her mouth. Suppressing it sternly, she walked a little faster.

They left the shaded bank and turned into a meadow. Ahead, the ruins of an ancient stone building poked above the tall grass.

"A chapel," said Philip, sensing her unspoken question. "One of the many destroyed by Cromwell's men."

"Is this where I dry my gown? In the chapel?"

"Scruples, Meg? Unnecessary. The ruin has long served as a favorite picnic spot for neighboring families.

90

And you need not fear danger, either. The walls are stout enough. Come, I'll help you up."

Gripping her waist, he lifted her onto a smooth section of wall, then swung himself up beside her.

"I want to explain something I said last night, Meg. Or, rather, something I did *not* say because I did not quite know how to put it into words. And then, you—"

"I finished the thought for you," she interrupted, wriggling to get comfortable on the hard stone. "That Sir Richard deserves someone more respectable than an actress for a daughter."

"Yes, that's what you said, and it came close enough to what I meant to say that I let it go."

With great care, Meg adjusted the folds of her sprigged muslin, exposing as much of the wet hem as possible to the sun. She did not want to look at Philip, did not want him to witness the hurt, which was worse this second time than it had been the previous night.

"Then I don't see what else there is to explain." Her voice was cool, with a hint of boredom, a credit to the excellent teacher Stephen and Maryann had provided. "Your sentiments are perfectly clear to me."

"You are a pea-goose," he said softly.

Startled, she faced him. The words were a reproof, but the delivery made them a caress.

"Meg, I'm not bringing this up to add insult to injury. Of course you understood perfectly. But that was yesterday. During the night, I had time aplenty to think about you and our encounters. This morning merely confirmed my suspicion."

"Your suspicion of what?"

"That you are really a very respectable young lady."

The acknowledgment made her feel vulnerable, defenseless. And why that should be was a mystery to her. After all, Philip had done no more than finally accept the truth.

"I am." She gave him a high-nosed stare, the kind of look Alvina had turned on her. "But hardly anyone will believe it of an actress."

"And although I am generally held to be a good judge of character, I fell into that same trap. I judged you by your profession." His face was serious, his look apologetic. "Pray forgive my boorishness, my arrogance in thinking I knew you when I had made no effort to get acquainted with the woman behind the actress."

Her eyes widened. An apology from Stanbrook! It was as unexpected as it was uplifting. Vulnerability was forgotten. She felt like jumping up and dancing atop the crumbling walls of the former chapel, but it was not something a proper lady would do. And thus, she merely smiled at him and did not mind that he could see the blush of pleasure that undoubtedly tinted her cheeks.

"There's nothing to forgive, Stanbrook. After all, it's a common enough mistake you made."

"Thank you. You are very generous." As he looked at her, an answering smile lit his eyes, then his whole face. "I like you, Meg. You're frank. Without pretense. You may rake a fellow over the coals for leering, but you also show him when you're pleased."

"Oh, well." Imp mischief raised its cheeky little head. "I cannot, after all, act every moment of my life."

"I am glad to know it," he said drily.

A thought occurred to her. "What about Sir Richard? The sad fact remains that an actress-daughter, respectable or not, cannot be to his credit. His friends, his neighbors, what will they say?"

"He won't care a straw for anyone's opinion. Meg, I don't know what he said to you, but I swear it was with unalloyed pleasure that Cousin Richard greeted the news of your existence."

She thought of Sir Richard's request that she regard Carswell Hall as her home, and could not doubt Philip's assurance.

"He's lonely, isn't he? I wonder why he did not make more of an effort to find Mother and me."

Philip's expression was guarded. "I know only what

Alvina told me a year or two ago."

"Whatever she told you, I doubt it is true!"

"I daresay it isn't." Philip drew up one booted foot, resting it on the opposite knee. "However, the point now is that Cousin Richard has acknowledged you as his daughter. Has it occurred to you that he may want you to live at Carswell Hall?"

"He did say something to that effect."

"And would you do it, Meg? Would you give up acting to be a daughter to a sick old man?"

"Give up acting!"

Meg slid off the wall. She paced a few steps to control her surging emotions, then faced Philip.

"How can you ask? He believed Alvina's lies about my mother, that she was seeing other men. He denied her the right to live in the house because I happened to be born with black hair and blue eyes. Didn't he know a baby's first hair falls out and frequently grows back in a different color? Didn't he know most infants are born with blue eyes?"

"I wouldn't be surprised," Philip said quietly. "I didn't know it either. You see, most of us poor males are totally ignorant about infants until a wife presents us with one. And even then, I shouldn't doubt, a great many gentlemen keep their distance from the nursery—at least until the little mite can stand on its own two feet."

Meg stared at him. It seemed utterly impossible that he spoke the truth. She remembered Fletcher cradling the newborn child in his arms each time her mother gave birth. Even Jigger—not one of the brightest youths Meg knew—was well acquainted with a newborn's appearance and needs. He was the oldest of nine children, and since his father was transported two years ago, when his mother expected Number Nine, Jigger had been the sole provider for the family.

But, then, in the back slums of London one did not have the luxury of a nursery and a nanny, of a study or drawing room, where a father could retreat when the

93

latest addition to the family tested its lungs.

"I suppose it is possible that Sir Richard did not know," Meg acknowledged, adding wryly, "I did not take into account that there are some aspects of life a man born and raised in the slums knows far better than a gentleman educated at Oxford or Cambridge."

"Indeed. We all make a mistake once in a while, or draw the wrong conclusion."

She met and held his steady look.

"Stanbrook, your mistake and mine are hardly of the same order as Sir Richard's was."

"Speak to him." Philip jumped lightly to the ground. "Are you ready to go back?"

"Yes." The hem of her gown was still damp, but it would dry as well, or better, while she walked. And since she had already made up her mind to question Sir Richard about the past, there was no point in pursuing further speculation on the matter with Philip.

He led the way to the bridge, which turned out to be nothing more than narrow wooden planks resting on three beams spanning the water. After the crossing, while they followed the brook in the direction of the gazebo, Philip told her of his own estates some twenty-five miles to the southwest, in the county of Wiltshire, and of the castle where he grew up.

Meg was fascinated and asked a great many questions about Stanbrook Castle, which was, in part, even older than Carswell Hall. It seemd no time at all had passed before they reached the spot where she had discarded her footwear.

Belatedly, Meg realized she had a problem on her hands. She frowned at the white silk stockings, the kid leather slippers with their ribbons that tied around the ankles. Had a lady ever been in such a predicament? How the dickens was she supposed to pull on her stockings with Philip standing nearby?

"May I offer my assistance, Meg?"

She had no need to look at him to know that he was

enjoying her dilemma. The laughter in his voice was unmistakable.

"I don't doubt you have ample experience," she said with some asperity. "But I'm perfectly capable of dressing myself. Is the gazebo unlocked?"

"I don't know. We'll find out."

He picked up her shoes and stockings and strode off, leaving Meg no choice but to follow in his wake.

"Too cocksure by half," she muttered.

A chuckle confirmed what she had already suspected—that his hearing was very sharp indeed.

Philip went up the three steps leading to the gazebo door. He turned the handle, and the door swung open.

"Unlocked. And, as was to be expected, everything in excellent order. No creaking or sticking doors. Not even a speck of dust on the floor," he said, bowing Meg inside. "Our cousin Stewart has his faults, but negligence is not one of them."

"He looks after the estate, doesn't he? At least, that's what I believe he told me when we drove down from London."

"He does, and has done so very competently, I must add, for a number of years."

"It seems a shame, then, he won't inherit all of it. I gather from what you told me about the Stanbrook lands that you're not in need of more property."

Philip looked at her strangely. She was certain he was about to refute her argument when he turned away.

Setting her slippers and stockings onto a cushioned bench, he said, "I shall stand guard outside. Call if you require assistance."

"I'm quite sure I shan't . . . require assistance or call. In fact, there's no need for you to wait. I know the way back from here."

"I don't mind waiting."

He strode out, shutting the door behind him.

Debating whether to let him stew for at least half an hour or whether to climb out one of the windows at the back and sneak past him, Meg sat down on the bench. She sighed and picked up a stocking. Neither of the two possibilities was as appealing as spending a few moments longer in his company. Besides, a lady would not dream of climbing out a window.

Efficiently dealing with garters and ribbon ties, she pondered her situation at Carswell Hall and the adjustments it called for. Not that she had set out from London with the firm intention to suit her behavior to the environment! And neither, she reminded herself, had she ever really misbehaved except when a play demanded it. But when she found herself in Philip's company, she, who had never been self-conscious, was aware that she suffered from a certain lack of social graces.

Pride would not allow her to dwell on the depressing realization. What, after all, were social graces but a display of affectations? She had poise and a certain flair, and those natural attributes were worth more than a thousand-and-one taught accomplishments.

She rose, shook her crumpled and still slightly damp skirts, and walked out into the bright sunshine.

As expected, Philip was waiting within a short distance of the gazebo. With him was Stewart.

Both men turned at her approach, Stewart giving her a somewhat harassed smile and a nod, and Philip looking distinctly put out.

"I am sorry, Meg," he said. "I will not be able to escort you after all. Stewart tells me I'm wanted in the stables."

She felt a pang of disappointment. "That's quite all right. I told you I can find my way. I'll simply follow the lilacs. In fact," she said, remembering, "that's why I came out. To cut lilacs for my room. Do you have a pocketknife, Stanbrook?"

"Yes, but Stewart had best cut the stems for you. This is a very sharp clasp knife."

Stewart, looking more harassed than before, accepted the knife.

"Philip, I should go with you to—" He broke off as the

carved ivory handle caught his attention and he stared at the distinctive design.

"This is Uncle Richard's knife!"

"No, but he has one like it. Our grandfathers had the knives made, and if you look closely at the carving, you'll see the initials P.C.—Philip Carswell, my grandfather. Cousin Richard's knife should be marked with the initials R.C.—Richard Carswell, *his* grandfather."

Philip strode off. He had not taken half a dozen steps when he stopped and turned to face them once more.

"Meg, before you make other plans— Will you come riding with me this afternoon?"

"Oh." She looked at him in consternation. "I'm sure I'd enjoy that very much, but I'm afraid I don't ride."

"You don't? Yet you brought your groom. At least, that's what Stewart said."

"Well, yes. You see, Stewart was horrified that I did not have a maid. And so, to pacify him and his mother, I suggested we take Jigger."

Philip gave a shout of laughter. "Meg, you're a pure delight! You bring a groom because you don't have a maid, yet you don't know how to ride."

"No, I don't. But, then, it doesn't matter. Jigger isn't a real groom, either. In fact, I don't know if he can distinguish one end of a horse from the other."

All amusement was wiped from Philip's face. Eyes narrowed, he took a step closer to Meg.

"He's not a groom?" he asked in a dangerously soft voice. "When Stewart told me that *your* groom, over the protest of *my* groom, took out one of *my* horses, I intended to give Jigger a dressing-down he wouldn't forget. But if I find that in his stupidity he damaged my horse, I'll wring his scrawny neck."

Speechless and motionless, Meg stared after him as he spun on his heel and rushed off. Only when he left the graveled walk and thrust through the lilac hedge did she recover sufficiently to shout, "Don't you dare lay a hand on *my* groom!"

Stewart touched her shoulder. "He won't, you know. Wring his neck. By the time he reaches the stables, he'll have calmed down."

Meg grimaced ruefully. "I'm sure you're correct. Jigger is but a stripling, and if I know anything of Stanbrook it's that he wouldn't mill down a featherweight. But have you ever seen such temper?"

If Stewart was surprised at her use of boxing terms, he did not show it.

"Yes. Many a time have I seen Uncle Richard fire up. Not so much these past four years, though, after the strokes." A grin spread on Stewart's face. "And then, of course, I've witnessed your flying into a pelter."

She smiled back at him. "That's different. At least, Sir Richard and I have the excuse of red hair."

"And Philip has the excuse of being on edge."

"Why? What's wrong?"

"Nothing is wrong, precisely. Rumor has it that he's about to pop the question. I'm surprised he agreed to stay on here when everyone expects him at Lyndon Court."

"Pop the question?" Meg repeated numbly as though she had never before heard the phrase.

"Yes. He's expected to propose marriage to Squire Lyndon's daughter. Young Evalina."

Evalina, thought Meg. Evalina Rutland, Countess of Stanbrook. The names had a certain flair, a sound of rightness.

Then why did she feel as if she had swallowed something noxious?

"Haven't seen Evalina since she went off to be educated in some fancy school in Switzerland," said Stewart. "But I understand she's a diamond of the first water. And very proper and refined. Just the sort Philip would want for his countess."

Chapter Eight

"I'm sure Miss Lyndon will make a wonderful countess," Meg agreed in a hollow voice.

Why must it occur to her once more that, had she grown up at Carswell Hall, she'd make a wonderful countess herself? As she had told Maryann, it was unlikely she'd marry. No man but an actor would accept a wife on the stage, and she was quite resigned to end her days a spinster.

But must I end them a virgin?

The thought was so fleeting she had to recall it in order to see its significance, to acknowledge that she was contemplating a step she had never, before she met Philip, considered taking.

There was no outrage in her, no embarrassment—a woman raised in the Dials knew only acceptance where a lady of the *ton* would react, or, at least, give a very good imitation of reacting, with horror. No, Meg was merely puzzled.

Why now? Why consider an *affaire* just when Philip finally admitted that she was a respectable young woman, not a scarlet lady of the stage? Why—after all these years of struggle to maintain her integrity?

Her mother, raised in the rooms over the glover's shop at the corner of Oxford and North Audley Streets and taught to consider herself a cut above the women living in the back alleys, had insisted virginity was a girl's most valuable possession. In the Dials, however, virginity was a cheap commodity, and Meg had set no great store by her mother's notion. But neither had she seen any reason to give up what was hers by right in exchange for something commonly known as a quick roll 'n tumble.

She had always been fastidious, and the mere thought of a man's grimy hands on her body had made her shudder. Even Tom Easterwood, who was a clerk in one of the East India offices and almost as fastidious as she, had not been permitted any liberties save for holding her hand or putting an arm around her waist.

No, Meg had not been tempted to follow the example of childhood friends or fellow actresses. Until now, it seemed.

Nonsense!

She gave herself a brisk mental shake. Philip Rutland, Earl of Stanbrook, might pay her flattering attention; he might be a charming and attractive rake; but she had met rakes twice as charming and attractive as he. Yet, she had not succumbed. And for good reason.

She knew two or three women who were quite happy and content to be a nobleman's mistress. They lived in fine houses, were waited on by maids and footmen, and had their own carriages. But more often than not she had witnessed a girl's misery and downfall when her lover tired of her. Meg was too cognizant of life's pitfalls to tumble into that particular one.

Now, if she loved Stanbrook and he loved her . . . that would be a different matter altogether. Meg was a firm believer in the power of love—perhaps because her mother, who had attended a small Bloomsbury academy, had taught her to write and read. Armed with knowledge of the written word, Meg had spent many hours in Mr. Finney's musty pawnshop at the corner of Portugal Street and Clement's Lane where she had discovered a treasure trove of books.

Mr. Finney was not above fencing stolen goods. In

fact, he made most of his profits that way. It enabled him to give as much as a half crown to some desperate man or woman with nothing to pawn but a useless book—useless, that was, to anyone but Mr. Finney and Meg. The old pawnbroker had welcomed Meg and had fed her growling tummy with bits of fruit and bread, and her romantic imagination by letting her read anything he had at hand.

Love always played a part in the works Meg best liked to read—love strong enough to inspire men and women to great courage or even sacrifice. But those were stories, fairy tales for adults, and they had nothing to do with her and Stanbrook.

Philip was not the man to fall in love with an actress, respectable or not. He would cherish a young lady like Evalina Lyndon, a *proper* lady, a simpering miss whom Meg would dislike on sight. A *proper* lady, to whom Philip was about to propose marriage. And above all things considered, Meg would *not* play second fiddle to another woman.

"Megan?" Stewart said anxiously. "Are you unwell?"

She realized that she was gritting her teeth.

"No, I'm quite all right," she said with a shaky laugh. "I was thinking about something, and the longer I thought about it the less sense it made."

And, indeed, it made no sense at all. As she started down the lilac-bordered path, pointing out the blooms she wanted Stewart to cut, her mind stayed preoccupied. She had reasoned like Meg Fletcher, she realized, convinced that nothing but a dishonorable proposal could come her way. But here she was Megan Carswell, a lady, even if she did practice a rather scandalous profession. Under the circumstances, Philip would no more offer her a slip on the shoulder than she would consent to be his *chère amie*.

Nothing made sense, especially not that fleeting thought that she need not end her days a virgin. Which proved, Meg concluded, that despite her self-confidence she was just as much out of her depth among members of

101

the *ton* as her timid mother had been. A lowering realization, one it was best to forget.

When she had gathered an armful of lilacs, she thanked Stewart and told him she'd walk the last stretch to the house on her own.

"I know you really wanted to go to the stables with Philip. If you hurry, you may still be in time to avert disaster."

Once again, his eyes held the harassed look she had noticed when he was talking with Philip. "I don't anticipate disaster, but I must speak to my head groom. He's in charge. He should never have allowed that boy of yours to touch the property of a guest."

"Pray don't be too harsh on Jigger. Once he understands the stable code, he'll not make such a mistake again. He was probably bored. Couldn't you assign him some chores to do?"

"Megan, this isn't the first complaint I've had about Jigger this morning. I shudder contemplating how many I'll have had by nightfall. No, it's my belief he isn't suited to the stables at all."

"Then let him work in the gardens."

"They are my mother's domain. She'd have my head if he dug up flowers instead of weeds. Come to think of it, she'd have *his* head first."

Meg sighed. "My next suggestion was to have been the kitchen. That's where he helped out at the Fighting Cock, and Mrs. Bellamy swears he's a born cook. But the kitchen, of course, is your mother's domain, too."

The puckish grin she had seen once or twice lit Stewart's face.

"The kitchen! An excellent notion. If you can talk Mrs. Sutton into convincing Cook that she needs an assistant, Mother wouldn't dare object. Uncle Richard likes his food, and he has forbidden her to meddle or in any way to upset Cook, because any interference results in charred meats and soggy pastries."

Meg blew him a kiss. "Thank you, Stewart."

"My pleasure. Megan, I want you to know—"

She looked at him expectantly, but, giving her a rueful look, he shook his head.

"Some other time. You need to get those flowers into water, and I must see what's happening in the stables. I do hope Jigger didn't damage Philip's horse. It's one of a matched pair. Devilish hard to replace."

"One of a pair? Are you telling me Jigger rode a carriage horse?"

"He did, the ignorant little bugger."

Choking on a giggle, Meg turned and fled, but her amusement was short-lived. Poor Jigger. He had probably never sat a horse in his life. It was to be hoped the beast hadn't damaged *him*.

She hesitated. Should she try to find the stables? But Stewart would be there. And Philip. No matter what he had threatened to do to Jigger, if the boy had been thrown, Philip would make certain that he was all right, or that a physician was sent for if he was hurt. It was *her* duty, since she had dragged the enterprising youth from a familiar environment, to secure a place away from the stables for him.

She found her way back into the main part of the house and asked a footman trimming candles in the Great Hall to take her to Mrs. Sutton.

The housekeeper received her graciously and not only provided a vase for the lilacs but nodded in a very encouraging fashion while listening to Meg's troubles with Jigger.

"Leave it to me, Miss Megan. I'll speak with Cook, and when we're done, she'll think 'twas her own notion to have him in her kitchen. What did you say the boy's name is, Miss Megan?"

"Jigger."

Meg smiled. She was Miss Megan now. Mrs. Sutton had obviously accepted her as Sir Richard's daughter.

"Elspeth will take you back to your room, Miss Megan. But if you have the time after lunch, I'd be honored to show you over the house. When you've seen it all—and I'll also let you have a peek at the drawings in the muniment room—you won't no more need a guide than I do."

"Thank you, Mrs. Sutton. I'd enjoy seeing the house."

And thus, by late afternoon, Meg felt fairly certain she would no longer get lost in the dim passages that might take a turn when one least expected it, or end at a set of locked doors. Seeing the old drawings had helped her get an overview of the basically E-shaped house with its two additional tower wings protruding at either end on the back of the building.

Every day, she took time to explore on her own—in the house and outside. She ventured farther and farther in her walks, but always circled back to sit awhile by the brook or in the gazebo before returning indoors.

During one of those long, rambling walks she discovered the small thatched cottage where Nanny Grimshaw lived and, pulse racing, called a greeting to the old woman rocking in her chair just outside the open door. But she received no response and, as she went closer, she realized that the old woman's stare was blank.

Meg spoke to her, explained who she was, but Nanny Grimshaw did not seem to hear. It was quite painfully obvious that she lived in a world of her own, a world no one else had the key to enter.

"And that's why Alvina didn't mind my visiting you," Meg said under her breath.

Finding the old nurse unresponsive had been a blow, and Meg could not quite suppress a sigh of disappointment as she watched the slight figure who kept rocking, rocking. Absently, she noted the neat dress, the soft white hair brushed and pinned in a tidy chignon. From the open cottage door drifted the smell of boiled onions, sage, and chicken. Someone obviously stopped by regularly to look after Nanny.

"Good-bye, Mrs. Grimshaw." Slowly, Meg turned to leave. "I'll visit again some other time. Perhaps," she added with little expectation of seeing it come to pass,

104

"when you're feeling better."

Refusing to give in to discouragement, Meg pinned her hopes on Sir Richard, who was beginning to relax in her presence and to speak of the past. Every morning, she visited with him. She learned during one of their talks that he had met her mother in the glover's shop on one of the rare occasions when Rosemary had been asked to help fit customers. Rosemary's father had been occupied with a hard-to-please gentleman, and she had measured Sir Richard's hands for a pair of riding gauntlets.

It had been love at first sight, Sir Richard admitted. As he told Meg about his courtship of her mother, she could see them clearly—the middle-aged bachelor, self-assured and forceful, and the shy young girl, overwhelmed by the dashing fiery-haired gentleman who swore he loved her and promised marriage.

Of course, Rosemary had fallen in love with Sir Richard, who must have seemed like a demi-god to the tradesman's daughter. And with her father's grudging consent, they had married a month later.

Knowing her mother's marriage had such a fairy-tale beginning only raised more questions for Meg, questions about the time Rosemary had spent at Carswell Hall. But she was reluctant to press Sir Richard. He still tired easily, and often she cut her visit short, promising to return in the evening before dinner, when she would play a rubber of piquet with him, or two-handed whist.

He seemed to enjoy the card games and said once, with a fierce look from beneath bushy brows, that she was a deucedly sharp player. Meg was no longer misled by his gruffness; she was sure she detected a hint of pride in the raspy voice.

Alvina's feelings were more difficult to read than her brother's. She seemed resigned to Meg's visit, showing neither resentment nor pleasure when her niece joined her in the salon after dinner. But every once in a while, when Meg happened to look up from the book or periodical she had chosen to while away the time until the gentlemen finished their port, she would find Alvina's cold eyes resting on her. And she would shiver, even though a fire was kept burning in the salon in case Sir Richard should wish to take tea with the family.

One day flowed into the next, and the only unexpected occurrence was Philip's offer to teach Meg to ride. After some hesitation, she accepted and met him at the stables, early, before breakfast, garbed in a voluminous riding habit of moss-green velvet that smelled of camphor. Mrs. Sutton had unearthed the garment from one of the trunks in the attic and told Meg that it had been worn by her grandmother some forty or fifty years ago. The housekeeper had also found a pair of boots ordered by Alvina, then discarded as too snug.

Somewhat to Meg's surprise, she took to riding as a Dials urchin took to thieving. When, on their third morning out, she said as much to Philip, he gave a shout of laughter.

"My Meg! Have I told you yet that you are a sheer delight?"

"Yes. Or something along those lines," she said drily, and wondered if Miss Evalina Lyndon could make him laugh.

She nudged the mare into a light trot. "Stanbrook, don't you think I'm doing well for a novice?"

He looked her over critically. "Exceptionally so, but I don't see anything amazing in that. All the Carswells have a good seat. Besides, you were a dancer, weren't you? It was to be expected that you'd be supple and graceful and not sit a horse as though you fear to be thrown."

So much for his paying her flattering attention!

Torn between laughter and annoyance, she said, "Thank you—I think. Your manner of bestowing praise leaves much to be desired. But speaking of being thrown—I don't believe that a lump on the head and bruises all over his skinny body have left a lasting impression on Jigger. I've had several talks with him and, like you, threatened to wring his neck, but Mrs. Sutton tells me that he still sneaks off to the stables 'just ter give them 'osses an apple.'"

"I know. I told him if ever I caught him doing anything more than feeding a horse an apple, I'd toss him into the brook."

"Is that threat more effective that wringing his neck?"

"Indeed, it is. Jigger hates water. Didn't you know?"

"I did not." Catching the tip of the peacock feather on her hat which kept tickling her cheek, Meg gave Philip a sidelong look. "You wouldn't consider teaching Jigger to ride?"

"I would *not*."

So much for his charming manner!

For a minute or two, they rode in silence. Meg did not mind. Every day, she was fascinated anew by the beauty of the countryside. It mattered not that she could identify fewer than half the trees and shrubs and plants; she took pleasure in the mere sight of the lush greens, the delicate shapes and colors of the wildflowers.

She had no doubt, however, about the identity of the trees surrounding them. When they had gone out on their first ride, Philip had told her that for a week or so, until she was totally familiar with the mare, they'd keep to the wide paths in the Beech Wood. It stood to reason, therefore, that the sleek, regal trunks and the smooth branches decked with dark-green oval leaves were beech trees, didn't it? Although there were other trees as well, with slim silvery trunks and light-green leaves that looked almost heart-shaped.

She cast a surreptitious look at Philip but refrained from asking botanical questions when she saw the corner of his mouth twitch as though he were suppressing a grin. His eyes met hers, and she could not doubt that he was enjoying some private joke.

"What is it, Stanbrook? Since you praised my seat earlier, it cannot be that I'm a figure of fun on a horse. Are you, perchance, reconsidering my request to teach Jigger?"

He grinned openly. "I did consider it," he admitted, "thinking a few hours of purgatory would be preferable to a murder charge. However, I've since spoken with Stewart's head groom and it seems that your obnoxious young man has made his own arrangements. Beginning tonight, he'll have lessons from one of the grooms, and in return he'll provide delicacies from the kitchen."

"Good for Jigger!"

In her exuberance, Meg bumped her heel into the mare's flank and was thus, inadvertently, introduced to a canter—and to Miss Evalina Lyndon.

If she had not broken into a canter and enjoyed it so much that she kept up the pace, they would not have left the woods and entered the Bluebell Copse—a place she knew because Stewart had shown it off when he had joined her on one of her long walks—just as a young lady accompanied by two gentlemen rode through the clearing. The lady saw them first and brought her mount to a stop.

"Lord Stanbrook!" she cried. "I didn't know you were at Carswell Hall."

Philip doffed his hat to the three riders. "Miss Lyndon, it's a pleasure to see you. Lyndon, Flossingham, your servant."

Evalina, thought Meg. *The future Countess of Stanbrook.* She studied the young lady avidly and found nothing she could dislike in the open countenance and pleasing appearance.

Before Philip could perform the introduction, Mr. Flossingham urged his bay closer. "By Jupiter! If it ain't Miss Fletcher! Ralph," he said excitedly, addressing the second gentleman, who bore a striking resemblance to Miss Lyndon, "d'you see who this is? It's Meg Fletcher from the Drury Lane!"

"'Course I see, you nodcock. I've got eyes in my head, haven't I?"

Ralph Lyndon, who sported, even with his riding coat, shirt points so high and stiff that he could barely turn his

108

head, bowed to Meg. "Pardon my friend, Miss Fletcher. Flossie gets a bit addled when he's excited. We saw you in all of your plays, and we think you're absolutely top of the trees."

Meg flashed her famous smile. "Thank you, gentle-men."

For a moment, she was back in the Green Room where adulation and praise had been her due for the past nine months. Philip's dry voice dispelled the illusion.

"Lyndon, if you're done spouting off, allow me to present you to Miss Megan Carswell, Sir Richard's daughter."

The two young gentlemen were struck dumb, but Miss Lyndon, who had listened to her brother's words with barely concealed boredom, now opened her deep-blue eyes with interest.

"Oh!" she exclaimed. "So that's what Mrs. Goodwyn was talking about. That Sir Richard's daughter is an actress!"

Ralph Lyndon scowled at her. "No one's interested in what Mrs. Goodwyn said. And I'm sure Mama did not invite you to listen to the old gossip, so you must've been eavesdropping again. I was hoping they'd cure you of that disgusting habit at that fancy school in Switzerland."

"Oh, no! You're wrong." Miss Lyndon's pink-and-white complexion turned a shade rosier. "I just happened to be passing the morning room, and I heard Mama say it's a miracle Sir Richard's daughter is alive when she was believed dead these many years, and then Mrs. Goodwyn said it would have been better if—"

Miss Lyndon broke off, her delicate features suffused in red. She threw Meg an agonized look. "I beg your pardon, Miss Carswell. I am a prattlebox, and speaking without thought, not eavesdropping, is my besetting sin."

"I can hardly fault you for something I, too, have been accused of," said Meg. "It comes from having a candid disposition."

Unaccountably, she felt drawn to this blushing young lady who was considered the future Countess of Stanbrook. But whatever had Stewart been thinking of when he described her as "proper and refined"? A diamond of the first water—yes, Miss Lyndon was that and better, with guinea-golden curls framing a heart-shaped face, a figure that bid fair to rival Lady Maryann's daintiness. And, what was more to the point, the young lady was not a simpering miss, but as outspoken as Meg herself.

"Why are you staring at me?" Miss Lyndon asked sotto voce. "It's not my hat, is it?" Anxiously, she touched the piece of headgear that more resembled a hussar's shako than a lady's riding hat and perched at a rather precarious angle atop her golden curls. "Mama warned me, but I fell in love with it on sight. I absolutely had to have it."

"The hat's beautiful, and so is your habit." Meg cast a quick, envious look at the comfortable material and cut of Miss Lyndon's attire, then glanced at the gentlemen, who had moved a little way off and were arguing about the projected outcome of some prize fight that would take place in a fortnight.

She nudged her mare, christened Patches during their first ride, closer to Miss Lyndon's gray.

"To tell the truth, I was staring because you caught me by surprise. When Stewart told me about you I did not expect that I would like you. But I do. Indeed, I believe we could be friends."

Miss Lyndon's eyes shone. "I think so, too. In fact, I was sure of it when you did not fly up into the boughs when I repeated Mrs. Goodwyn's horrid gossip."

"But you did not repeat it," Meg corrected her. "And you don't need to. I know what the lady must have said . . . that it would have been better if Sir Richard's daughter had remained lost rather than turn up like the proverbial bad penny and embarrass him with her scandalous profession."

110

Miss Lyndon sniffed and tossed her head. "I think it's romantic. Both that you returned to Carswell Hall and that you're an actress."

Meg suppressed a smile. Romantic? No, she had a totally different notion of what was romantic.

Patting her mare's neck, Miss Lyndon said, "Let's move on. Pepper doesn't like standing. And besides," she added, looking demure as a nun's hen, "it's about time the gentlemen paid us attention."

Which reminded Meg that Miss Lyndon was expecting a proposal of marriage from Lord Stanbrook. But it did not make her like the young lady one dot less. And it shouldn't, since she had already made up her mind that Stanbrook could be of no possible interest to her.

They rode side by side, and after a moment, Miss Lyndon said, "You mentioned Stewart a while ago. What exactly did he say to you?"

"Nothing outrageous. Only that you were supposed to be very proper and refined."

"Oh."

Miss Lyndon sounded disappointed, and Meg noted with interest that the young lady's color deepened while a militant spark lit in her eyes.

Chapter Nine

The week passed quickly. Friday, the day Meg had originally planned to leave, dawned gray and misty. Moisture settled on her riding habit before she and Philip had been out ten minutes. Halfway through the session, the velvet hung limp and lifeless, while the curl in her hair was more riotous that ever.

By the time Meg had visited with Sir Richard, a fine drizzle netted the air. It was the first rainy day since her arrival, and she had no excuse *not* to stay in the house, *not* to pen a note to Lady Maryann informing her of the change in plans. Meg had definitely decided to prolong her visit at Carswell Hall.

Seated in the morning room where Mrs. Sutton had pointed out the elegant escritoire supplied with pens, paper, inkwell, and wafers of sealing wax, Meg wrote the letter, folded and sealed it. Still, she remained seated at the small desk, not doing anything in particular, just staring at the inscription on the letter.

She wondered if Maryann had started work on the botanical gardens. Her friend had always said the gardens would be in or near Seven Dials, and Meg thought she knew the place Maryann had started to describe: ". . . nothing but rubble now. Collapsed houses, the burnt-out shell of a small church, and heaps of rubbish." Such an area was located not five minutes from the

Fighting Cock.

Meg's eyes started to smart as she thought about the tavern, about Mrs. Bellamy, Sam the tapster . . . and Fletcher, who'd never again drink his mug of ale in the smoke-stained corner by the fireplace.

She blinked, determinedly turning her mind from Seven Dials to Carswell Hall. Despite extensive walks, she had yet to discover a building that might be the dower house, her home the first two weeks of her life. She had been reluctant to ask, wanting to find it herself, but—

The rattle of carriage wheels caught her attention. She rose and went to the window overlooking the front drive in time to see a post chaise draw to a stop. A postilion opened the door and let down the steps for an elderly gentleman who reminded Meg of Sir Nathaniel Conant. But perhaps it was only because she had just been thinking about London and the people she knew there, or mayhap it was the black leather satchel the visitor carried that brought the Bow Street magistrate to mind.

A cloakbag was unloaded and handed to the Carswell footman. Coachman and postilions paid, the dapper gentleman stepped purposefully toward the front door while the post chaise clattered away.

"That, if I'm not mistaken, is Mr. Potter."

Philip's voice made her jump. She had not heard him enter. She turned, then wished she hadn't, for he stood so close she clearly saw the ring of green circling his irises, and smelled the sandalwood scent of his shaving soap.

Meg leaned against the window frame, a movement calculated to give her breathing space, yet subtle enough not to look like a recoil from his overpowering masculinity.

"And who is Mr. Potter?"

"Your father's solicitor."

"Oh." The visitor lost Meg's interest. Stephen Fant was obliged to deal with solicitors, and he had described them as a fusty, pedantic set of elderly men to whom a mild jest was tantamount to blaspheming the king.

114

"Stanbrook, do you suppose it'll stop raining by afternoon?"

Philip narrowed his eyes at her. "Meg, your father's solicitor has arrived, and you ask me about the rain. That's doing it much too brown. After all, it's probably on *your* account that Potter is here."

She had noticed before that her temper showed an alarming tendency to brittleness when Philip was around. Predictably, it flared at his words.

"Just what are you implying?" she asked hotly. "That I demanded Sir Richard send for the solicitor so he could change the will?"

Philip continued to look at her. Finally, he shrugged.

"It'd be no bread and butter of mine if you did," he said mildly.

"Perhaps no bread and butter," she countered haughtily. "But half an estate."

Unexpectedly, he laughed. "Very well, I apologize for thinking you might have an interest in the solicitor's arrival. But pray don't fall into your duchess role. It shakes my self-confidence when you use that tone."

"The only thing shaking about you is your voice. I didn't realize that's where your self-confidence is located."

"There are quite a few things you don't realize about me. Did you know I have a mole about an inch below the collarbone? I'll show you, if you like."

He was outrageous. He deserved a trimming, and it was unfortunate that she couldn't administer it because his very outrageousness made her want to smile.

"No, thank you," she managed to say.

Philip placed a finger under her chin and gently tilted up her face. "*Your* voice is rather unsteady, too. Why don't you give in and laugh with me?"

His touch, the smile in his eyes, melted her bones. Once again, as on that moonlit night a week ago, she had to guard against the singing in her blood and the foolish longing to feel his mouth on hers. But she no longer tried

115

to suppress a responding smile.

"That's better." His thumb briefly touched the corner of her mouth before he dropped his hand. "About the rain, Meg. Can you not survive one day without a walk?"

She blinked at the abrupt change of topic. In fact, she had forgotten she'd asked about the weather.

"Of course I can. It's just that I was looking forward to exploring behind the towers. I've been everywhere else, but I have yet to discover the dower house."

"I'm not aware there is a—" Philip broke off, frowning. "But, yes, of course there is a dower house. Why the interest?"

"Because my mother was banished there after her confinement. It's where she stayed when she decided to run away. Do you know where it is?"

"If I'm not mistaken, the so-called dower house is the east tower—the one that's falling to pieces."

Her first thought was that Sir Richard had not banished her mother from the main house after all. But that discovery paled beside the next realization.

"Then I shan't be able to go into the rooms where she lived? Where I spent the first days of my life?"

After Nanny Grimshaw, this was almost too much disappointment to swallow. Giving Philip no chance to confirm her fears, she said, "But perhaps I can. I'll speak to Sir Richard, find out how badly damaged the tower is."

"You won't see Cousin Richard today. He'll be closeted with Potter." Philip turned to leave. "Ask Stewart. He'll probably know more about it than your father does."

Since Stewart was gone all day on some estate business or other, Meg's earliest opportunity to speak with her cousin was at dinner. At first, though, it looked as if no one would be allowed to say anything at all, for Alvina kept complaining about the difficulties of serving a meal when the more experienced of the footmen had been commandeered to wait on Sir Richard and his guest in the west tower.

116

It was Philip, giving Meg a conspiratorial wink, who finally changed the topic.

"Meg was asking me about the dower house, Stewart. That's the east tower, isn't it?"

"Yes." Stewart looked at Meg. "I understand your interest, but if you're thinking of exploring, please don't. It is not a safe place."

"Why?"

"Cracks the width of a man's fist have appeared in the walls, and once, a footman was hit by a veritable avalanche of crumbling masonry in one of the lower rooms."

"Why don't you have it repaired?"

Alvina said snappishly, "Because my brother has not seen fit to give the necessary orders."

"Uncle Richard," Stewart said with a wary look at his mother, "has not yet decided what's best to be done. We had two architects examine the tower. One recommended tearing the whole thing down; the other said there's a chance of saving it if we filled in the dungeons below. Uncle has written to a third architect, an expert on old buildings, but he won't be able to come until late summer."

"Then I cannot see the tower at all?" Meg asked.

Stewart started to point out that she would be foolish to expose herself to danger, but Philip interrupted him.

"Come now, Stewart! Surely, if you or I were to accompany Meg, she could at least peek into the rooms her mother occupied."

"I still say it's foolhardy. But, very well—if Uncle has no objections. I'll speak to him. Just promise me not to go into the tower alone, Megan."

She promised but resolved to speak to Sir Richard herself. The following morning, however, when she knocked on the big double doors of the west tower wing, Marsden informed her that Sir Richard begged her pardon; he was still engaged with the solicitor. Would she please come to see him before dinner, when he would be happy to introduce her to the chess board.

Since the sun had shown signs of wanting to break through the clouds, Meg had no fault to find with the scheme. She had been indoors most of the previous day, she'd had to forgo her riding lesson with Philip because of the rain, and now she craved physical activity.

"Tell Sir Richard I'm looking forward to a game of chess." A twinkle in her eye, she added, "And thank him for the warning. I ought to be able to find someone who can teach me the basics before evening so our first match won't be a total disaster for me."

"And I'm sure it would do you no harm to lose a game or two, Miss Megan. You have all the luck with the cards, but on the board, I daresay, Sir Richard will rout you."

"I don't doubt it. But you disappoint me, Marsden. How can you refer to my skills as luck?"

A smile deepened the wrinkles around the valet's mouth and eyes. "Could those be the skills Sir Richard refers to as a cardsharper's tricks?"

Chuckling, Meg went on her way. As was her habit, she used the French doors in the music room to step out into the garden. The rain had indeed stopped and pale sunlight reflected on the wet gravel. The lilac hedge drooped with moisture, but to her left, in the formal gardens, the head gardener and his underlings were out in full force staking the plants she had learned to recognize as dahlias. They wouldn't begin to bloom until late summer, the gardener had told her, but they'd be a sight to behold when they were in full flower. She'd like to see them. It was doubtful, though, that she'd extend her visit that long.

Keeping to the graveled walks, Meg strolled toward the rose garden. The roses, too, would need another month at least before they showed their glory, but the flagged paths criss-crossing among the various beds would keep her shoes as dry and clean as possible after twenty-four hours of rain. And, away from the gardeners, she'd be at leisure to let her mind roam into the past, when her mother had walked these paths.

But in this, she was disappointed. As she rounded a corner of meticulously trimmed yew hedge, she saw one of the undergardeners weeding among the roses.

Swallowing her disappointment, she bade him a good morning and would have passed without paying further attention had he not jumped like a pickpocket's apprentice when the bells go off on the practice dummy.

After a startled look at her, he touched his cap, pulling it far down over his eyes, mumbled a greeting, and scuttled off.

Meg stared after him. She had met everyone working on the estate, but she was sure she had never seen this man before.

And yet, as she watched him lope off, something familiar struck her about the cadaverous frame, the furtive movements. If not here at Carswell Hall, *somewhere* she must have encountered him before.

But why would he run off as though she had caught him at some wrongdoing?

Footsteps rang on the flagged path behind her. The by now familiar sound brought a smile to her lips even before she turned, and her puzzlement about the undergardener's strange behavior was forgotten as she watched Philip stride toward her.

"Hello, Stanbrook. You look as though you'd just ridden through a quagmire," she said, with a glance at his mud-spattered boots and buckskin breeches.

"Not a quagmire. Squire Lyndon's turnip field, where one of his heifers decided to calve."

"Oh."

Stupidly, Meg could think of nothing else to say. Philip had been to Lyndon Court, had visited Miss Evalina, the young lady he was expected to make his countess. Perhaps he had already popped the question, as Stewart had phrased it.

119

A look at Philip's face provided no clue, but, then, she had not really expected to see a moonstruck expression if and when the lady of his choice accepted his suit. Lord Stanbrook would not wear his heart on his sleeve.

"What is it?" he asked, narrowing his eyes at her.

"A speck of mud, I thought. On your jaw," she said airily. "But I see I was mistaken."

She started to walk down one of the paths and, when Philip fell into step beside her, asked, "What took you to Lyndon Court?"

"You."

"You're jesting!"

"Not at all. It's about time you were introduced to the neighbors. If we waited for your father to make the first push, we'd still be waiting at Christmastide."

This was quite unexpected, and Meg was aware of a hollow feeling inside.

Of course, she had already met Miss Lyndon and her brother Ralph. She had liked the young people and their friend Mr. Flossingham. But when she had decided to go to Carswell Hall, she had not in her wildest imagination envisioned a presentation to the local gentry—formally, as Megan Carswell. Sir Richard's daughter.

But she *was* Megan Carswell, and Sir Richard *was* her father. She had known him a little over a week, and although they hadn't become close, it no longer seemed strange or wrong to acknowledge him as such—her father.

It was time she faced facts. Acknowledgment took nothing away from Fletcher, who had raised her, loved her, chastised her. Fletcher would always hold that special place in her heart that belonged only to him, to her pa.

She had loved Fletcher, missed him fiercely. But for Sir Richard she was beginning to develop a certain respect. And she did not want the proud old gentleman to be humiliated on her account.

"Meg? Why don't you want to meet your father's friends?"

"It's not a question of what I want."

Philip clasped her wrist. "Stop a moment. You're running as though the devil were after you."

She faced him with a wry little grimace. "Not the devil, Stanbrook. But I fear the Mrs. Goodwyns of the neighborhood will be after me. Or, rather, they will give me the cut direct."

"Surely that does not frighten you?"

"Heavens, no! But how do you think Sir Richard will feel when his neighbors snub me?"

"I told you before, he won't give a straw for anyone's opinion. But what you're not taking into account is your father's position. He is *not* a nobody, my dear Meg. Mrs. Goodwyn may whisper about you, but she wouldn't do or say anything that might jeopardize her next invitation to Carswell Hall."

Meg digested this in silence. She had assumed a baronet would have some local standing, but she had not thought it possible that Sir Richard wielded power enough to still wagging tongues. Her respect rose another notch.

"Let me understand, then. You rode over to Lyndon Court and asked Mrs. Lyndon to call?"

"I did. And normally she would have been delighted to do so. However, she's preparing for a dinner and impromptu dance three days hence, and she asked me to convey her apologies. But we're all invited to the party. A welcome-home party for Evalina."

"A welcome-home? I should have thought preparations would have been under way weeks ago. Or was Miss Lyndon unexpectedly 'sent down' from her school in Switzerland?"

"No." Philip gave a chuckle. "Evalina may be a prattlebox, but I'm sure she wouldn't do anything that warrants a drastic measure such as expulsion. She

121

returned as planned to spend April and May in London."

"So she's had her season. She's officially out," said Meg and thought, *she's ready to become betrothed to the very eligible Lord Stanbrook.*

Evalina and Stanbrook were still on Meg's mind when, responding to Sir Richard's summons, she made her way to the west tower in the late afternoon. Miss Lyndon, she mused, was not much older than Rosemary had been when she married Sir Richard. And although Stanbrook was not thirty years Miss Lyndon's senior, Meg was fairly certain that he was skating dangerously close to his fortieth natal day—in short, he was far too old for a miss barely out of the schoolroom.

What the dickens was it that made a seasoned man look to a very young girl for his bride?

She had spent much of the day pondering the imponderable, and was only too glad when Marsden, opening the door to Sir Richard's suite, gave her thoughts a different direction.

"You're late, Miss Megan. The rest of the family are already gathered in the study."

"The family!" she said astonished. "But am I not to play chess with Sir Richard?"

"Later, perhaps. At present, Sir Richard is waiting to make an announcement."

Meg was aware of a sinking sensation as she walked toward the study. An announcement. It could only have to do with the solicitor's visit, and she feared that the heated reference she had made to Philip about Sir Richard changing his will would come back to haunt her.

In which case, she thought ruefully, being haunted by thoughts of Stanbrook and Evalina would have been the lesser of two evils.

She did not wish to be included in Sir Richard's will— or to receive an allowance, which seemed to her the more likely arrangement he had made with the solicitor. Meg had accepted that Sir Richard was her father and that her name was Megan Carswell. At the same time, she was Meg Fletcher—proud, independent, self-sufficient; she had no need of financial support.

"Marsden, has Mr. Potter left?"

"About an hour ago." The valet threw open the door and announced formally, "Miss Carswell."

"Come in! Come in," Sir Richard said testily, reminding Meg of that first night when Philip had taken her to see the baronet. "You took long enough."

The old gentleman was seated, as usual, in the wing-backed chair, his right leg propped on the footstool and extended toward the fire. Alvina occupied a straight-backed chair on his left, while Stewart, arms crossed over his chest, stood behind his mother.

Meg looked at Philip, lounging against the brick mantel. In contrast to Stewart, whose features this afternoon held something of Alvina's tight-lipped look, Philip seemed totally relaxed and at ease as he stood there, an elbow propped on the shelf above the fireplace and one gleaming Hessian boot crossed over the other.

Their eyes met, and the smile in his warmed her more thoroughly than the crackling fire in the grate.

She heard someone clear his throat—Sir Richard, growing restless—and she swiftly took her place in the chair she had come to consider her own.

Again, Sir Richard cleared his throat. "I'll make this brief. Potter's visit was no secret to any of you, and neither can you be wondering why I sent for him."

"Richard!" Alvina said tensely, but the baronet cut her off with a glare.

"I'll have my say first, if you don't mind." Sir Richard's voice left no doubt that he'd have his say whether anyone minded or not. "*Then*, when I'm finished, you may add your tuppence's worth."

Meg's stomach knotted as it did before a performance, and she wished Sir Richard had spoken to her privately before doing something as drastic as including her in his will—if that was indeed what he had done.

His next words dispelled any vestige of doubt.

"This young woman calling herself Meg Fletcher," he said, looking directly at her, "is my daughter. She is Megan Carswell." His voice rose belligerently. "Anyone with eyes in his head can see that!"

He paused to pick up the cordial glass on the table at his elbow. With a shaking hand, he raised it to his lips.

Philip said softly, "Cousin, no one is contesting that Meg is your daughter."

"And it wouldn't matter if they did!" Sir Richard set the glass down with a snap. "I say she is, and I've changed my will accordingly. The house, the estate, which, I need not remind you, is unentailed, and my fortune—everything will go to Megan."

Chapter Ten

"No!"

For one horrifying instant, Meg wondered if it had been she who had cried out at the startling news. Heiress to all of Carswell Hall! It was utterly ridiculous. Outrageous. She wouldn't accept, of course, but she hadn't shouted the denial. It was Alvina who, pale and trembling, had jumped to her feet to confront her brother with a torrent of recriminations.

"How could you, Richard! I've devoted my life to Carswell Hall. And so has Stewart. How could you do something so unprincipled as giving the estate to . . . to that actress!"

"You forget yourself, ma'am!" With the aid of his cane, Sir Richard heaved himself out of the chair. "*That actress* is my daughter, and you had best remember it."

"Sir." Meg rose as well.

She saw Stewart spin on his heel and stride off, his back and shoulders poker-stiff. She wanted to tell him not to worry. But her cousin must wait.

The door shut behind Stewart, and Meg laid a soothing hand on the baronet's arm. "Sir, none of this is necessary. I can assure both you and my aunt that I have no intention of depriving anyone of his inheritance."

Neither of them paid her the least attention.

"*Your* daughter?" Alvina's voice dripped poison. "She

is also the daughter of that little harlot you married."

Something flared in Meg. Pure rage, wild and hot. Her hand shot out, raised high. But before she could connect with Alvina's distorted face, fingers of iron clamped around her wrist, bore her arm down, and, not content with that, pulled her bodily away from Sir Richard and Alvina.

Meg knew it must be Philip who was manhandling her in this humiliating manner, but, for the moment, she had no strength to fight him. She was shaking and could barely see for a red veil of fury in front of her eyes.

She could, however, hear Sir Richard's roar, "Tare an' 'ounds! Alvina, this time you've gone too far."

And her aunt's high-pitched response, "Have I? Your daughter is an actress, Richard! A flighty bit of muslin and no better than she should be."

Meg heard no more, and after a moment she realized that she was no longer in the study, but that her captor was propelling her will-ye-nill-ye along a short stretch of dim passage within the tower wing. A spiral staircase loomed ahead. Fighting the force of the powerful arm, Meg came to a stop and focused on the Earl of Stanbrook.

"How dare you drag me off!" Deprived of the original object of her wrath, she had no compunction about aiming her fury at him. "Treating me as if I were a mill-ken and you the watch taking me before the magistrate! Dammit, Stanbrook! Let go!"

Philip released her wrist.

"I beg your pardon. But what on earth," he said in a puzzled tone, "is a mill-ken?"

The question disconcerted her. If anything, she would have expected a reminder that a lady did not swear or talk flash, not curiosity.

She snapped, "A housebreaker, of course. Anyone with a particle of wits would know that."

"Then, I suppose, my ignorance of the term proves I'm an absolute numbskull."

His smile did much to dull the edge of her fury, but she

was still angry enough to glare at him.

"Don't try to change the subject. I want to know why you dragged me off. You had no right to interfere, you know."

"No right at all." He sounded quite affable, but his look held a hint of steel. "I could not, however, allow you to strike your aunt."

She did not falter under that implacable gaze.

"No," she said, "I don't suppose you could. But neither could I allow her to malign my mother."

"Meg, a lady does not strike another woman."

"I am no lady, Stanbrook. I am a woman schooled in the back slums of London."

His expression softened, but before he could make what would, no doubt, be a polite disclaimer, she said firmly, "And if Alvina and I were men, I would have called her out."

He was nonplussed. "My Meg," he murmured, shaking his head. "Before long you'll have me doubting the code of honor by which I was raised."

"And would it be such a bad thing if you did? After all, a code of honor that prescribes one set of standards for women and another for men cannot be very desirable, can it?"

He drew in a long breath, then said in a rather unsteady voice, "It quite depends on the point of view."

She saw the tell-tale quirk of his mouth, the laughter in his eyes, and felt her mood lighten miraculously.

"Oh, very well, Stanbrook. I concede the point to you. Now, will you please tell me where you planned to take me in this unorthodox fashion? Where are we? I have not seen these stairs before."

"You're in the west tower proper, and I shall take you up one flight to the gallery."

"I did not realize the gallery was accessible from this part of the house. I saw no door when Mrs. Sutton gave me the guided tour."

"Come on up. It'll be my pleasure to show you one of

Carswell Hall's secrets."

Meg knew the portrait gallery was on the first floor, but, somehow, going up by a spiral stair made the ascent seem longer. By the time they reached a narrow bit of landing, her head was starting to spin.

Philip opened a door deeply recessed in the thick wall between tower and house—a wall, she realized, which must have been removed at least partially on Sir Richard's floor.

"Marsden showed me this way to the gallery when I visited just after your father's first stroke," said Philip. "It's my grandfather, you see, who guards the secret on the other side."

He ushered Meg into the long chamber that occupied all of the western main portion of the house and, according to Mrs. Sutton, had served in the past as the ballroom.

She heard a soft click and spun around, but the aperture was gone. All she saw was the full-length portrait of a young gentleman in a curled and powdered wig and dressed in the silks, satins, and laces of the previous century.

And, of course, she saw Philip, looking as proud as a peacock, as though he himself had designed the invisible door.

"All right, Stanbrook. How do you open the dratted thing from this end?"

"Do you see the ring on my ancestor's hand?"

"I'm not blind. I may not see a door," she said tartly, "but I do see the ring."

"Touch it."

She did, gingerly, as though it might sting.

"Oh!" She snatched back her hand. "It's not painted. It's a real ring!"

"Twist it, and at the same time push it to the right. You'll see a small cavity and inside, the latch that'll open the door."

It was all so simple. Meg raised the latch, opened the secret door, then closed it again.

Laughter tickled her throat. "A set-up straight out of a novel by Mrs. Radcliffe. Are there any more of these neat contraptions?"

"I should think it very likely in a house of this vintage, but I haven't been made privy to their location. Come along, now. I want you to look at your ancestors."

Meg sighed. The interlude was over. Philip was not about to let her forget the happenings in Sir Richard's study.

"Why? If you believe a collection of portraits will make me accept my father's—" Startled, she met Philip's solemn gaze. "I actually called him my father!"

"So you did," he said drily. "And your father wants you to have what is yours by right. Carswell Hall. You're not depriving anyone of anything."

"What about Stewart? And you?"

"Stewart will be no worse off than he is today."

"How can you say so! He was the heir. That is, he was to share with you. But now he has nothing."

Philip shook his head. "That is not true. Alvina didn't give her brother an opportunity to go into the details of the arrangements he made."

"What arrangements? And how do you know about them?"

"Your father acquainted me with the contents of the new will when he asked me if I would serve as executor, along with Mr. Potter. Thus I know that both Elmores will have life tenancy at Carswell Hall, and Stewart will retain the position of estate manager, which pays him thirty thousand pounds annually."

Her eyes widened. Thirty thousand pounds was not an estate manager's salary; it was a fortune. She remembered the night at the Drury Lane when she saw her cousin the first time, remembered how she had noticed his elegant, expensive attire, the ruby on his finger, the sleek carriage. And by now, she knew that twelve of the horses stabled at Carswell Hall were his personal property.

But overseeing an estate was not the same as owning it.

She remembered what Fletcher had said shortly before he died. He had suspected someone had discovered her true identity, and this someone was responsible for the attack on her outside the tavern and the near-accidents that had dodged her steps since her face became as known as that of the old queen.

He was wrong, she thought. Quite wrong. Nothing at all had happened since she came to Carswell Hall, and here *everyone* knew who she was.

Philip's voice cut into her thoughts.

"Meg, before you go to your father and repeat that foolishness about not wanting to be his heir, take another look around you. This is where you should have been raised, here at Carswell Hall. You cannot tell me that you prefer the squalor of Seven Dials to this luxurious setting."

She bristled. "Prefer the slums, the undefeatable filth that breeds fevers and infections? You must be mad! Of course I wouldn't tell you anything so bird-witted."

"Then why make a to-do about being your father's heir? You don't even want to live at Carswell Hall, you told me, and be the daughter Cousin Richard would like to have."

"I am an actress," she snapped. "How can I live away from London?"

"Meg," he said in a tone one would apply to a particularly dense child. "Your father will provide an allowance. You need no longer earn your keep. You can give up acting anytime you like."

"Give up acting? Never! It is my life."

He looked puzzled. "Then why did you bother coming here in the first place? What is it that you want?"

"I came because I wanted to see the place of my birth and to find out why my mother fled from Carswell Hall. Why she was afraid to live here."

"She was afraid? You never mentioned that before."

Meg shrugged. "Mother was afraid of her own shadow.

130

I suspected she was intimidated by Alvina, and all I've seen of my aunt so far has served to confirm my belief."

Philip looked skeptical. "I admit," he said pensively, "at times Alvina has me quaking in my boots—"

"Indeed!" Meg gave him a withering look. "There's no need to poke fun at the situation."

"—but that would hardly be reason enough to run away in the dead of night," he finished, unruffled. "Are you certain nothing else precipitated her flight?"

"I am not certain of anything. Fletcher believed—"

She had been about to tell him of Fletcher's suspicion that someone had recognized her as Megan Carswell when she started to act in leading roles at the Drury Lane—someone who meant her harm. And that Fletcher was convinced the near-accidents and the attack on her were connected to her mother's panicked flight from Carswell Hall. But Fletcher had been wrong. Nothing had happened since, which proved that she was correct: she had simply been in the wrong place at the wrong time. And there was no point in saying anything to Philip and raking up something that would only cloud the issue.

"What did Fletcher believe, Meg?"

Again, she shrugged. "Only that there was more to Mother's story than she ever told him."

"Have you asked your father?"

"Not yet. He is beginning to speak of the past, but slowly, so slowly. It makes him sad, I believe."

"And you're too tenderhearted to press him."

Philip's eyes rested on her for a long moment. He took her hand, raising it, and brushed his mouth across the back. Her skin tingled under his touch, and when he turned her hand over and kissed the throbbing pulse in her wrist, she felt as though she were melting inside. It no longer mattered that he had angered her, exasperated her. It mattered only that he made her feel wonderfully, gloriously alive.

"Meg, my Meg," he said softly. "I always knew you were a woman of feeling."

131

No thought of struggle entered her mind when he released her hand, took hold of her shoulders, and drew her closer. She knew a lady would not permit such intimacy. But, then, she was no lady—or, at best, she was a scandalous lady of the stage.

Forgotten were the admonitions to herself, that she must guard against the singing in her blood, the fire in her veins, that she must keep her distance from the Earl of Stanbrook. She raised her face to his and waited breathlessly while his mouth slowly descended on hers.

And her peace of mind was forever shattered.

There was nothing of the butterfly touch to this kiss. Nothing gentle and brief as it had been that first night in the garden. The kiss touched Meg to the core of her soul. It turned her inside out, sapped her willpower until she was nothing but a whirlpool of intoxicating sensations.

The melting warmth, the liquid glow spreading through her body when Philip's tongue brushed her mouth, when his hands caressed her shoulders and back, were a magical pleasure. Meg understood now why a woman might forget common sense, toss caution to the wind, and give herself to a man without thought of consequences.

When Philip broke the kiss—and Meg was instantly, painfully aware that it should have been *she* who pulled out of the embrace—he smiled at her. It was a nice smile as smiles go, but, for once, it did not reflect in his eyes. His voice, however, was as deep and warm as she could wish.

"My Meg," he murmured, a form of address he had used before, but never, it seemed to her, with such emphasis.

She was disconcerted by the shadowed look, and too shaken by the kiss to say anything. She could only stare at him, a question in her eyes.

He touched a finger to the corner of her mouth. "Kissing you is like drinking nectar while burning at the stake. It is like drowning in a maelstrom while floating on

132

a still lake. You are innocence and seduction. Your touch is torture and delight. And never have I enjoyed a kiss more than yours."

Still far from composed, she blurted out, "Then why do you look as though you've lost something precious?"

He gave a wry laugh. Stepping back, he said, "You're too observant. Someday in the distant future, if we're still on speaking terms, I may tell you why. I may tell you what I lost."

Unbidden, the changed will came to mind. His loss of half the estate. But, surely, *he* would not think of it—not just after a kiss he professed to have enjoyed more than any other.

She glanced at the portrait of Philip's grandfather beside her. It seemed they had spent hours in the gallery, yet they had not moved more than two or three steps away from the secret door.

She reached for the ring. "I believe I shall return to the study. If my father is alone I'd like to speak to him."

If Philip was disappointed at her leaving, he did not show it.

He nodded to her. "Very well. Will you keep in mind what I said about the new will not depriving anyone of anything?"

"I'll keep it in mind."

Meg sighed, hoping her face was as inscrutable as his. She was definitely disappointed that he made no effort to detain her. Not that she would have been persuaded; she knew better than that. But it would help to know that he was as reluctant to part as she was.

Opening the hidden door, she looked at him over her shoulder. "But you cannot tell me that Stewart doesn't feel deprived. Are you certain *you* don't mind losing one half of a prosperous estate?"

"How can you doubt it?" A shadow of annoyance darkened his face but was gone in an instant. He grinned. "After all, I still have the title to look forward to."

She gave him a quick, searching look, then stepped

133

through the door and shut it.

As she started down the spiral staircase, she glanced upward to the second floor, where Stewart occupied the two tower chambers. Was he up there? Was he still angry? Upset?

She would not blame her cousin if he were. He had been raised at Carswell Hall, had considered himself Sir Richard's heir. It must have come as a blow when first the baronet made over one half of the estate to Stanbrook. And now Stewart was to have nothing at all.

Before she reached the ground floor, however, her mind was once again on Philip and the kiss that had revealed her as a weak woman, as vulnerable as any girl she knew. She had believed herself wise to the ways of the world, a knowing one who wouldn't be caught unawares in any situation. And yet, here she was, floundering in a net of her own weaving. She had been aware of the effect Philip had on her, yet she had given in to temptation. She had permitted him, in fact, had invited him, to kiss her.

And—ultimate folly!—she wanted him to kiss her again.

Muttering a Meg Fletcher expletive, she turned into the short passage to her father's study. The door was closed. She heard no voices, which could mean either that Alvina had left and Sir Richard was alone, or that he had retired to rest before dinner.

She knocked and entered.

"Megan!"

She saw Sir Richard's—her father's—eyes light up, and something stirred in her. She could not quite define the feeling, but it was rather like the warmth she felt when Fletcher had smiled at her.

Sir Richard, once again seated in the wing-backed chair by the fire, beckoned her closer.

"Daughter, will you join me in a cognac?"

"With pleasure."

Cognac couldn't make her feel any more light-headed than Philip's kiss had done. And perhaps the drink would

134

help keep her mind on other matters.

She accepted the glass and settled herself in the chair beside the fire screen.

"Alvina will apologize to you," Sir Richard said gruffly.

Her eyes widened. "You must have held a pistol to her head. I cannot imagine my aunt volunteering an apology."

"What I did or said need not concern you. But I want you to know that from now on Alvina will mind her tongue."

"I wish, sir, you had made her mind her tongue twenty-four years ago."

"Aye," Sir Richard said heavily. "So do I."

Heart pounding, Meg asked, "What exactly happened? I know my aunt accused Mother of adultery, and that eventually you came to believe your sister rather than your wife. I also know Mother and I briefly lived in the dower house—the east tower, that is. But why did she run away?"

Sir Richard's fingers tightened on the stem of his glass. "If I knew—"

His gaze met hers, and the pain she saw in his eyes made her want to keep silent. Yet for her sake and, perhaps, for his, she must ask her questions now. It was even possible that speaking about the past would help ease his suffering.

"Did you not see my mother at all after you banished her to the east tower?"

"No." As though the words were torn from his throat, he said, "When I saw the child, the black hair and blue eyes, I could not bear to look at Rosemary again."

"The child—that was I. And now I am red-haired and green-eyed."

"Martha Grimshaw tried to tell me a baby's coloring can change. So did Squire's wife, Mrs. Lyndon."

Incredulous, Meg asked, "And you did not believe them?"

"I did not."

Sir Richard's gaze fixed on the dancing flames in the grate.

"I did not believe them, but being parted from Rosemary was harder and harder to bear." His voice was low, hesitant, as though he were speaking to himself. "I was willing to make any excuse to see her. Three weeks, I said to myself. I'll give the baby three weeks; then I'll see for myself if eyes and hair can change color."

"But before you could do so, Mother took me and left Carswell Hall. Why, if you loved her, could you not trust her, or at least ask her if Alvina's accusations held any truth?"

He frowned and looked confused. He was silent for so long that Meg regretted disrupting the flow of his memories. Perhaps she should have let him tell the story in his own fashion and asked questions later.

Finally, he said, "It was not my way to probe or to beg for explanations."

Meg looked at him, willing him to go on. When he did not speak, she decided to risk another question.

"You were so much older than Mother, more experienced. Did you not see that she was as guideless as a child, and probably as shy? That she didn't possess an iota of the gumption necessary to indulge in affairs?"

He shook his head. "I saw, but I did not understand. Fact is, I did not know much about women. Never had much traffic with them. A misogynist, Alvina used to call me, and matchmaking matrons had given up on me two decades before I ever met your mother."

Silent once again, he stared into the dregs of cognac in his glass.

"But then you fell in love," Meg prompted.

"Aye. But I should never have married. Brought nothing but misery to Rosemary."

"It must have been quite a shock to your friends and neighbors, your sudden marriage."

136

A gleam of humor lit Sir Richard's eyes. "Could have knocked 'em over with a feather! There I'd gone to town to see my bootmaker and my tailor, and a month later, I returned with a bride."

"The bride everyone believed to be a harpy who trapped you into matrimony."

"No! There you're wrong, gal. The neighbors all took to Rosemary. Even the servants liked her. And that," Sir Richard added pensively, "should have given me pause to think when Alvina spoke out against her. Servants are excellent judges of character. Have to be, dependent as they are."

"Yet you listened to Alvina, who, I believe, resented my mother on Stewart's behalf."

Sir Richard swallowed the last of his cognac.

"Alvina's my sister," he said simply. "Knew she could be spiteful, but never thought she'd lie to me."

Meg did not point out that a husband should believe his wife above all others. Any argument or advice would be four-and-twenty years too late.

Instead, she said, "You did not come after my mother and me. Perhaps her running away only confirmed to you what Alvina said about her?"

"Gal, what are you talking about?" Sir Richard sat bolt upright in his chair and glowered at her. "I did go after Rosemary. Ordered my horse saddled, and set out within ten minutes of Nanny Grimshaw telling me that the two of you had gone."

"You did?"

To cover her confusion, Meg drank from her glass, carelessly, as though she were drinking water. Her breath caught as the cognac rolled a fiery trail down her throat into her stomach. But once it settled, she felt only a glowing mellowness.

Mellow or not, her mind still functioned needle-sharp. "Pardon me, Sir Richard. If you had followed my mother, wouldn't you have looked for her at the glover's

137

shop first?"

"Naturally, I would have." He scowled at her. "But I was thrown not a mile from here. Jumping a blasted hedge I had jumped I don't know how many times before! Broke my collarbone, five ribs, and a leg. Old Doc Morrison, that damn quack, kept me in bed the better part of two months."

Chapter Eleven

An accident! Such a simple explanation for Sir Richard's apparent neglect of his wife and daughter.

Meg ventured another mouthful of her drink. And another. The cognac had lost its edge and went down smooth as honey.

"So you never got to London before my grandfather's shop burned down?"

"No, dammit! Had to send Alvina. She saw my wife, but Rosemary told her she wouldn't return to Carswell Hall until I had personally come for her and apologized."

Sir Richard shifted the leg on the hassock, grimaced in pain, and cautiously moved it back to the former position.

He shot Meg a fierce look. "Say what you want about Alvina, but she is a persistent woman. She has no liking for town life but stayed on—well over three weeks— trying to change Rosemary's mind. And then, one curst morning, she arrived in Oxford Street and the shop was cinders and ashes. Old Melton, Rosemary, and you had died in the flames, the neighbors told her."

"But Mother and I did not die."

There were certain aspects of Sir Richard's tale that made no sense, and Meg's head spun with a number of niggling questions.

Or could it be the cognac that made her head spin and

her face burn? She was unused to strong liquor. Fletcher had not approved of females imbibing. Even when she had posed as one of Faro's daughters for the Bow Street magistrate, the tapster at the Fighting Cock had strictly followed Fletcher's orders to serve nothing but colored water or a glass of watered wine.

Fletcher, Meg thought ruefully, would have raked Sir Richard over the coals for offering cognac to a lady. Carefully, she set the almost empty glass on the floor.

"Sir." Fanning herself with her handkerchief, she focused her gaze on the baronet and her attention on the holes she saw in his story. "Why would my grandfather's neighbors lie?"

"I don't know." Sir Richard leaned forward, peering sharply at her. "You don't look right, gal. Shouldn't have given you the cognac, I suspect. Never did know a woman with a head for strong liquor."

Meg directed her best duchess look at him.

"Sir, if you mean that I'm tipsy, you're dead wrong. It's the heat. I'm not accustomed to a fire at the end of May."

The corners of his mouth twitched. "Indeed?"

"Yes, indeed," she replied with dignity. "However, I don't mind admitting that cognac is not a ladies' drink and that, perhaps, I may be just a trifle above par."

He came as close to smiling as Meg had ever seen him, and she promptly responded with a true Meg Fletcher smile.

All too soon, however, Sir Richard grew serious once more. He looked at his glass, saw that it was empty, and reached for the decanter. But he set it down again without pouring.

"So you thought I simply let Rosemary go?" he asked abruptly. "And you?"

She nodded.

"That I left you both to fend for yourselves?"

"Yes."

A fierce frown scored his brow. "That's your reason,

140

then, for rejecting your inheritance?"

"To get back at you? No, I wouldn't be so silly."

"But you don't want Carswell Hall? You didn't come for money?"

Unlike that first night when Sir Richard made a similar remark, Meg did not lose her temper. "I never wanted anything from you save the truth."

"I've tried to give you the truth as I know it. But I owe you more. Much more."

"You don't owe me anything. If it is any consolation to you, I have no regrets about my childhood. . . . I do not feel deprived or bitter because I did not grow up at Carswell Hall."

"You were bitter when you came here."

"That was because you had treated Mother quite shabbily."

His shoulders sagged. "That I did. Should never have let Alvina influence me. In fact, I should have found her a place of her own."

"Why didn't you?"

He took a moment before he answered. "My sister's a damned good housekeeper. I thought she could teach Rosemary. Three rooms above the shop had not prepared her for a household like Carswell Hall."

"No. Mother must have been quite at a loss when she first came here."

"Besides, Alvina's proud. Wouldn't accept charity, from me or anyone. She'd rather work for her keep."

It was a sentiment Meg could identify with. "Did Mr. Elmore leave her nothing, then?"

"Debts," Sir Richard said drily.

He turned stiffly in his chair and peered short-sightedly at the large clock ticking away in the far corner.

"It is almost six o'clock, sir."

"I can see that, gal! I'm not blind yet."

Quite accustomed to his testiness by now, Meg bit down a smile. She studied his face for signs of exhaustion. She'd like to settle the question of the will once and

141

for all, but not at the cost of his health.

The bushy brows met in a scowl. "Can't stand it when people stare at me," he grumbled. "What's the matter? Think I'm about to swoon like some vaporish female?"

"Not at all, sir," she said coolly. "I was merely trying to judge whether you'd snap my nose off if I insisted you change the will again."

With a shaking hand, he reached for the cognac decanter, then pulled back.

"You pour, Megan."

Hiding her astonishment, Meg rose and did as he bade her. Never before had he asked for assistance. He did not look ill, but looks could be deceiving. He must be more tired than she suspected.

"We shall have to continue our discussion after dinner," she said quietly. "If I don't want to incur my aunt's wrath, I must go and change."

He gave her a disconcertingly shrewd look. "And much you care about Alvina's wrath."

"Be that as it may. I certainly don't want to be the cause of a delayed dinner."

"Alvina already saw to that. She was madder than a hornet when she left here. Paid a visit to the kitchen, with the result that Cook had an attack of the vapors and Alvina retired with a migraine. So you may as well sit down again."

Meg decided that further argument would merely bring about the state of exhaustion she was trying to prevent.

Settling herself, she said, "In that case, we can clear up the matter of the will."

"Megan." Sir Richard's voice was unusually gentle. "Like it or not, you *are* my daughter."

"I don't deny that. I merely wish you had not changed your will. It does not seem fair that Stewart should be relegated to a mere caretaker."

"A caretaker with thirty thousand pounds," Sir Richard corrected. A brooding look entered the green

142

eyes that were so like her own. "It was Alvina who hammered into Stewart's head that he was my heir. *I* never told him so, and he took it well enough when, four years ago, I had Potter draw up the will dividing everything equally between him and Philip."

"I understand that the baronetcy will go to Philip, but was there a reason to bequeath him half the estate? He is not, after all, as closely related to you as Stewart is."

"No reason save that I like the cut of his jib."

She smiled. Oh, yes. She, too, liked the cut of Philip's jib.

Sir Richard twirled the stem of his cognac glass.

"There's a provision in the will," he said with an unusual display of diffidence, "that may be of interest to you. If you should die without issue, the estate will be divided between the cousins as in the earlier document."

Meg blinked. To find that suddenly she was heiress to a vast estate was crazy enough. To learn that the displaced heirs would in turn inherit from her, was like reading the lines of a rather bad farce. But perhaps she had misunderstood.

"Did you say that Stewart and Philip are *my* heirs?"

"Aye. Unless you produce an heir yourself."

"For that," she pointed out, "I'd need to be married."

"True. But that should not prove difficult. You may be four-and-twenty, but you're not an ape leader yet."

"No," she said, amusement dancing in her eyes. "Although an uncharitable soul might consider me on the shelf."

"Balderdash! Good-looking gal like you needs only to crook her little finger and every Tom, Dick, and Harry will come flocking around."

The thought darted through her mind that she'd rather have a Philip come flocking.

"So, daughter, tell me," Sir Richard demanded. "Will you accept your inheritance when the time comes?"

She noted that his voice was amazingly loud and strong for a man whose hand was too unsteady to pour a drink.

143

Meg rose. "It would be much better if you let the old will stand."

He glared at her, then, suddenly, seemed to shrink within himself.

"My apologies." His head dropped until his chin rested on the folds of his snowy cravat. "Shouldn't badger you."

"No need to apologize."

Concerned about the sudden change in him, she wondered whether she should ring for the valet when the door opened and Marsden entered carrying the ubiquitous cordial.

"Marsden," Sir Richard muttered, "if you *dare* say I must rest, you may pack your bags and leave. And there won't be a recommendation, either."

Standing just inside the door, the valet looked from Sir Richard to Meg, then stared woodenly at a point above the fireplace.

"Yes, sir. But I wouldn't be worth my salt if I didn't remind you that neither Miss Megan nor you have changed for dinner."

"It's only six o'clock. Surely, life at the theater has taught my daughter to change in less than three hours."

"As you say, sir."

It seemed to Meg that Marsden gave her a wink, but if that was so, she failed to see the significance.

She rose, facing Sir Richard.

"I will take my leave," she said firmly. "*You* may not need a rest, but *I* do. This has been rather an eventful day."

Sir Richard's head sank a little lower. "I want to do right by you, Megan. All I'm asking is that you take some time to consider before you reject your inheritance."

She could not see his features, only the shock of silver-white hair with the thin streak of copper.

"Fair enough. I'll take a week or two to consider the matter," she said, knowing full well she'd never change her mind.

"A month." The baronet's voice grew stronger. "Give it a month. Then we'll discuss the will again."

Meg hesitated. Did she want to spend all of June at Carswell Hall? Possibly witness Philip's betrothal to Miss Evalina?

Dash it! The girl was too young for him. Didn't anyone but she see how glaringly ill-suited they were?

"Very well, sir. We shall let the matter rest for a month."

"Excellent."

Miraculously fortified by her acquiescence, Sir Richard groped for the cane beneath his chair. Before either Meg or Marsden could come to his assistance, he had risen and started for the door.

Meg watched his slow but stately progress through narrowed eyes. There was nothing weak or tired about his step. The sporting of the cane seemed a habit rather than a necessity.

When he had rounded the door post and disappeared into the hallway, she looked at Marsden.

The valet shrugged. "Your father, Miss Megan, has his good days and his bad days. Today is a good day."

"You mean it was all pretense—the shaking hand, the drooping head?"

"No, miss. If that's what he did, it was *acting*." This time, there was no doubt at all that Marsden winked at her. "Sir Richard, you must know, used to dabble in amateur theatricals."

Her father an actor. And he never said a word! She didn't know whether to be indignant or amused.

"The devil! He didn't play fair."

Turning to follow his master, the valet said, "You cannot blame him for playing the trick he had up his sleeve. Got him what he wanted, didn't it?"

"Yes, it did."

And perhaps it had gotten her what she wanted.

Her sense of the ridiculous won the upper hand. Laughing softly, she left the tower wing to change for dinner. Then, if it was not totally dark outside, she'd walk in the garden, perhaps sit in the gazebo awhile, and enjoy the irony of the situation: Sir Richard had gained time to change her mind about the will, something *she* did not want at all to do. And by prolonging her stay at Carswell Hall, she had gained time to change Philip's mind about proposing to Miss Evalina, when undoubtedly *he* did not wish to change his mind, either.

If he didn't hurry, he'd be late for dinner.

An unholy gleam of amusement lit Philip's eyes as he slowed his mount to a walk. Beelzebub snorted and tossed his head indignantly, but, thinking of Alvina and how irritated she'd be, Philip held him to the sedate pace.

After the way she had behaved in the study, it would serve Alvina right to have her timetable upset. And besides, he thought in a surge of protectiveness, it would draw her ire away from Meg.

Prior to Potter's visit, Alvina had been cold and disdainful toward her niece; now, she had unsheathed her claws. He did not doubt that Meg could give as good as she got. In her own words, she was a woman schooled in the back slums of London. Still, her aunt's barbs and the slurs she'd cast on Rosemary would hurt. And above all, Philip did not want to see Meg suffer.

His Meg . . .

Memories of the kiss in the gallery made his blood pump faster. Since he had first set eyes on her, he had wanted to hold her, to kiss her until she was breathless. He had known that once he felt her pliant body against his, she would ignite his passion. But he had not expected the upheaval she had caused within him.

When he tasted the softness of her lips, the sweetness of her response, he had lost the sense of control in which he took such pride. He had no longer been the experienced, clear-thinking seducer, but a man consumed by

146

fire and softened by a totally unexpected tenderness toward the woman in his arms.

And she had asked him why he looked as though he had lost something precious! The question had been a slap in the face. Obviously, she had not been as deeply stirred as he. Obviously, she did not feel as he did—that they had lost the chance for an association more meaningful than a mere business arrangement.

Meg would have been the perfect woman for him. Not only would he have set her up in prime style, in an elegant house with an adequate staff and her own carriage and pair, not only would he have been proud to call her his and to show her off after a performance, but he would have cherished her as no man had cherished a woman before.

But, because of who they were, a relationship was out of the question. Even if she were already pursuing the lifestyle of an ordinary actress with an eye to personal advantage, he could not take her as his mistress. It simply was not done.

And Meg asked what he had lost!

His knees tightened against the gelding, and immediately Beelzebub broke into a canter. Philip allowed him his head for half a mile or so, then reined him in again.

Several hours earlier, when he had realized how deeply *one* paltry embrace, *one* kiss, affected him, he had shoved his feet into riding boots, thrown himself on Beelzebub's back, and galloped off. He now realized with considerable chagrin that he had been in a blind panic. The depth of his feelings for Meg had shaken him to the core, and he had not even noticed the direction of his wild ride until he saw the timbered structure of Lyndon Court ahead.

Lyndon Court, residence of the uncomplicated Miss Evalina, whom he had considered making his wife.

When Evalina first arrived in London, Squire Lyndon, an old acquaintance from the hunting fields, had asked Philip's assistance in launching his daughter into the *ton*. It had been a simple request, easily complied with. A

147

dance every now and then, lending his escort to the Bond Street shops or to the library, an introduction to some eligible young man or two.

Then Mrs. Lyndon had dropped hints that she would welcome him in a far closer relationship. After the initial surprise wore off, Philip had acknowledged that the lady's veiled suggestion was an eminently sensible one.

He was seven-and-thirty years old. If he did not want, like Cousin Richard, to leave his title and estates to some distant relative, it was time that he married and set up his nursery. Miss Evalina Lyndon, refreshingly unspoilt after a long seclusion in a Swiss school, seemed just the right girl to shape into a pleasing wife. Their children, he did not doubt, would adore her. And if she lacked in the dignity expected of a countess, it was not a problem that a few years of matrimony and motherhood would not alleviate.

Thus had been his reasoning in London. He had not immediately made his intentions known to Miss Lyndon or to her parents, but he had not refused any of their many invitations—with the result that the *ton* began to speculate about the Earl of Stanbrook and Miss Evalina Lyndon. He had realized it was time to openly court the young lady.

But then he had seen Meg on the stage of the Drury Lane, and any thought of matrimony had been wiped from his mind. How to capture Meg became his only concern. Meg, who could never be his.

He had believed it would be easy to forget about his plans for Meg Fletcher, especially with Miss Lyndon conveniently close by. There was no reason now to further delay his courtship of the beautiful Evalina—except that her beauty did not touch him, her artlessness exasperated him, and when she smiled he saw in his mind the enticing curve of Meg's mouth. But he must forget Meg. Must ignore the desire that could never be fulfilled.

Seemingly without provocation or purpose, the thought flashed through his mind that Meg possessed more dignity and natural grace than Miss Lyndon and the rest of the season's debutantes combined. And they weren't acquired accomplishments either; grace and dignity were as natural to Meg as frankness and pride.

Beelzebub picked up the pace again, and with a start, Philip realized that he had arrived in the courtyard of Carswell Hall. Suddenly, he could not wait to see Meg again. He wanted to speak with her before dinner, to advise her not to antagonize Alvina further, to—

Hell, he wanted to be with her. Any excuse would do.

Dusk had fallen. The stables beneath the sheltering limbs of gigantic old oak trees lay deep in shadows. Only a narrow beam of lantern light spilled through the open stable door, where he dimly perceived one of the grooms lounging against the wall. Dismounting, Philip tossed him the reins.

"M'lor'? Yer lor'ship!"

On the point of setting out for the manor house, Philip cast an impatient look over his shoulder. The groom moved, and the light from the lantern fell on the sharp features of the hell-born youth from the Fighting Cock.

Philip wheeled. "Jigger, what the devil are you doing here? I thought I made it clear that you're not to lay a finger on one of my horses again."

"Ho!" the boy said indignantly. "An' who was it as threw me t'reins? Did oi ask ter 'old the bloody 'orse?"

Despite himself, Philip grinned. "You didn't. Listen, Jigger. I'm in a hurry. Take Beelzebub into his stall, will you? My groom should be there to look after him."

"Oi'll take Bellsee—what d'ye call 'im?"

"Beelzebub. The prince of devils."

"Aye," Jigger said, looking with awe and admiration at the prancing, snorting chestnut gelding. "That he be, a prince o' devils."

"And he'll nip your backside if you don't do as I bid. Take him into the stall, and, if Harv isn't there, be sure to rub him down before feeding him. I assume you've learned by now how to care for a horse?"

Jigger's foxy face lit up. "Aye, m'lor'. Oi'll take good care o' him."

Philip nodded and strode off.

"Yer lor'ship! Can oi have a word with ye?"

"Not now. I must see your mistress before dinner."

"Dinner's been set back an hour. An' it *be* about Miss Meg that I wants ter talk."

The worried note in the boy's voice stopped Philip in mid-stride. Slowly, he turned.

"What about Miss Meg, Jigger?"

"T'gardener, yer lor'ship. There be a new 'un, an' he ain't no more a gardener than Bellsee—than yer 'orse or me!"

"The *gardener?*"

Philip retraced his steps. Laying a soothing hand on Beelzebub's neck, he asked, "What does a bloody gardener have to do with Miss Meg?"

"Oi've seen 'im spy on Miss Meg, that's what! An' what's more, oi've seen 'im afore. In Lunnon. 'E was there when Miss Meg was set upon outside 'er pa's tavern. An' when Fletcher an' me—"

"What's that?" Philip cut in sharply. "Miss Meg was attacked?"

Chapter Twelve

"That's what oi said, didn't oi?"

The boy's sharp features looked more pinched than ever, and the frustration and anxiety Philip saw in the narrowed eyes made his stomach tighten. Unless she had changed her mind, Meg would be returning to London, to the Drury Lane and to Fletcher's tavern. And hadn't he told her—more than once, he was sure!—that Seven Dials was not a suitable place?

"Somehow," Philip said with a savagery born of deep concern, "I cannot muster any surprise. Why the devil must she live in Seven Dials where assaults are as common as streetwalkers?"

Jigger scowled. "None o' the Dials tenants would 'urt 'er! Without Miss Meg there wouldn't be no free soup an' bread at the Fightin' Cock for those as need it. No, m'lor'! The attack on Miss Meg were a diff'rent kettle o' fish altogether. 'Twere right around Christmastide. An' about a month afore that, 'twas touch 'n go with a carriage bent on runnin' her down in Piccadilly."

"Wait, Jigger! One thing at a time. The assault outside the tavern—you're saying it was a gardener from Carswell Hall who attacked her?"

Looking uncomfortable, the boy humped his shoulders.

"Couldn't tell for sure 'twas him as hit Miss Meg. She were out cold from a knock on 'er noddle. An' this bloke, him as is gardener here, an' another feller stood right by 'er. Not doin' nothin', but not helpin' either. An' when Fletcher an' me come runnin', they made off 's fast 's can say whodunit. Fletcher was mighty worrit, 'e was. Tol' me ter keep me ogles on Miss Meg. That someone 'ated 'er. Someone was tryin' ter kill Miss Meg."

Philip stared at the boy through narrowed eyes. "Do you know what you're saying? You're talking of murder. Why should anyone wish to murder your mistress?"

"Oi didn't ask, but oi tell ye what, m'lor'. Fletcher weren't no flat. Devilish sharp, 'e was! An' if he said—"

"Nonsense!" interrupted Philip. He was aware of a cold, hard knot twisting his insides, and the denial was as much for his own benefit as it was for Jigger's. "Most likely, the thug mistook her for someone else. And the carriage mishap—why, a runaway team was the culprit."

"Aye," the boy said scornfully. "An' t'box of marchpanes sent to the theater an' made 'er sick as sick can be, that were a mistake too, eh?"

"When was that?"

"Febr'y, or p'rhaps March."

Philip stared at the tips of his boots. Someone hated Meg, Fletcher had told the boy. Someone wanted to kill her. But why?

Don't be a dunce, he told himself. *If someone is willing to commit murder, he has expectations of profit . . . a prosperous estate like Carswell Hall . . . a vast fortune like Sir Richard's.*

And Alvina had been aware of Meg's existence since the latter part of September . . . as had Stewart.

Rubbish! It was impossible that the Elmores were in any way involved in the incidents. Stewart's admiration for his cousin was plain to see for anyone with eyes in his head. And although he wouldn't put much past Alvina in the department of vicious verbal attack, he could not believe her capable of physical assault. No. Even Alvina would not sink to such depth. After all, she was a Carswell.

"M'lor'? What'll oi do?"

Philip met the boy's worried gaze. "Do exactly what you have been doing. Keep an eye on Miss Meg, and if you see anything unusual, *anything at all*, come and tell me immediately."

"An' how's oi s'posed ter do that? Go prancin' through the house, pokin' me head in every door lookin' for ye?"

"You know Mr. Hawkins, my valet. Tell him, and he'll give me your message immediately."

Philip's calm instructions had the intended effect on the boy. He looked considerably relieved.

"If ye was wantin' ter see Miss Meg," he offered, "she went to the garden 'ouse."

Without further ado, Philip hurried off across the stableyard. It was going on seven o'clock. Just what the devil did she think she was doing, dancing off to the gazebo at dusk?

As he turned toward the lilac hedge, the knot in his stomach made itself felt again. It was impossible to dismiss Jigger's report from his mind, even though it could have nothing to do with anyone at Carswell Hall. Except, perhaps, a new gardener whom Jigger had seen before in Seven Dials.

Or Stewart, an insidious voice insisted. Stewart, who stood to gain so much from Meg's death.

He remembered Meg's assertion that Rosemary had been afraid at Carswell Hall. That was why she had fled. Rosemary's fear could have been more than a shy, timid woman's reaction to Alvina's spiteful tongue. It could have been fear for her safety. Or her baby's.

Meg could be in danger right now, right here at Carswell Hall.

But, dammit! Any danger to Meg could have nothing to do with Stewart or Alvina. They were not of a class that commonly practiced thuggery—or murder.

Greed, the insidious voice persisted, knows no class distinction.

Philip found a gap in the hedge without difficulty and

153

stepped onto the graveled walk leading from the manor to the gazebo. It was almost dark now, the gardens very quiet and glum-looking. Surely Meg had returned to the house? With any other young lady he would have had no doubt at all, but Meg was unpredictable.

Slowly, he continued down the path until he could see the outline of the gazebo's white structure ahead. The crunch of gravel under his boots covered any other sound nearby, but his sight was quite adjusted to the dark, and he did not miss the slight, shadowy movement in the lilac bushes nearest the gazebo.

He stopped. Before he could decide what it was that he had seen, the tall, narrow shape of a man darted across the clear space in front of the garden house just as a husky female voice rose inside the gazebo and filled the quiet night with the haunting melody and words of *Greensleeves*.

Meg's voice.

And the man? Was he the new gardener Jigger had caught spying on Meg and whom, he swore, he had also noticed near the Fighting Cock?

For an instant, Philip stood quite motionless. It seemed to him that even his heart had ceased its beat. Seeing the tall, narrow-framed figure hurrying off had triggered the fleeting memory of a man skulking in the shadows of the Drury Lane Theatre, then starting after the hackney that had carried Meg to the tavern.

He had believed the man to be an admirer, disappointed that he had missed the actress. But now he wondered if the fellow had hung about the theater side entrance for a different, more nefarious purpose.

The thought had barely crossed his mind before he was chasing after the man. Once more, the gravel crunched beneath his riding boots. Meg in the gazebo faltered on "my lady Greensleeves," then started up again, stronger than before, with "Alas, my love."

With his long stride, Philip gained steadily on the fugitive as he criss-crossed between the flower beds, then

154

fled toward the part of the garden thickly planted with ornamental shrubs and sculpted yew. The man might be light on his feet, but he was in poor condition. Already, Philip could hear the labored breathing, the cough and the wheeze, telltale signs of a diseased lung.

The fellow cast a quick look over his shoulder, but it was too dark to distinguish the features of the narrow face, save for the mouth gaping wide. In a desperate attempt to escape his pursuer, the man increased his speed. Seconds later, he disappeared around a shrub sculpted to resemble an elephant.

Philip turned the same corner and stopped in his tracks. The man was gone. No sound of running feet or wheezing lungs broke the still night—only Philip's own breath and the rapid pumping of his heart.

He spent two or three precious minutes searching the shrubbery. It was not a maze proper, but to Philip it might as well have been. He found nothing and no one at all.

Gritting his teeth in frustration, he stalked toward the gazebo. If he could not get the one, he'd get the other. And Meg better have a damned good explanation why she was out in the gazebo after dark. Singing!

It had been quiet for a minute or two. Uncannily quiet after that sudden flurry of footsteps that had made her hold her breath. Slowly, cautiously, Meg slid the bar aside and edged the gazebo door open. She stared at the dark shadows of shrubs and trees. Was he hiding, the stalker? Or was he gone?

She didn't know how long she had been trapped in the garden house while someone, stealthily, furtively, circled the gazebo again and again. Judging by the increased darkness, she'd venture a guess that close to half an hour had passed since she heard the first sound, a rustling in the shrubbery that was too loud to be caused by a squirrel or some other small animal.

She had stepped into the open doorway and called out. No one answered, but soft, slow footsteps had come closer—which put a stop to the comforting thought that it was one of the servants sneaking off to meet a sweetheart. Or a thief. Anyone out on an illicit errand would take to his heels when he knew someone else was around.

Heart pounding, she had barred the door. Not that the bar would hold if the someone outside were truly determined to enter, but it would give her that split-second advantage she needed to position herself with one of the unwieldy, backbreakingly heavy candlesticks she had admired on previous visits to the gazebo.

Straining her eyes, Meg peered into the gathering dark. If only she could be sure that the stalker was gone. She could run fast and knew how to fight, but hampered by the silken skirts of her dinner gown, she wouldn't care to wager on the outcome of a possible confrontation.

Who could he be? She did not think it was a woman. She had worked too closely with Fletcher not to know that a woman stalking someone would be absolutely quiet to keep the element of surprise on her side. It was the male stalker who terrorized his victim with sound.

Twice now, she had experienced the sickening terror that settled in the pit of the stomach like a lump of lead. The first time, two sets of footsteps had pursued her the night she visited an old, sick woman living not too far from the Fighting Cock. Every time she turned, the alley was empty and quiet. When she continued, the footsteps at her back were there as well. She had walked faster and faster until she was running, but she had not escaped. A blow to the head knocked her unconscious just as the lighted front of the Fighting Cock came in sight.

Getting knocked out was not a fate she'd care to suffer in the deserted gardens of Carswell Hall. Thus, she had stayed in the gazebo, had barred the door and doused the candles, whose soft glow would betray her every movement to the man on the other side of the windows. On previous visits, she had been pleased with the large

156

glass panes that allowed an unobstructed view all around. Now, they made her feel vulnerable.

Meg shivered. Why was she being followed? This time, unlike that night in Seven Dials, she could not believe in coincidence.

And who knew where to find her?

Only Jigger, whom she had caught as he darted around the house on his way to the stables, knew that she planned to visit the gazebo. And the gardener, clipping the ivy around the music room windows. He had not looked at her when she opened the French doors and stepped outside; but he must have noticed her.

She was more than ever convinced that she had seen the fellow before. In London. But when and under what circumstance? Living in the Dials, she had encountered too many starved-looking men to remember one particular face, and she had met more in her work for the Bow Street magistrate.

Well, it was a puzzle that must solve itself—unless the gardener was prepared to talk when questioned.

She opened the door farther, concentrating on the silent garden, but at the back of her mind the question "Why?" once more started niggling, and from that her thoughts jumped to Fletcher's suspicion that someone who had recognized her as Sir Richard's daughter was behind the various incidents of the past six or seven months. Incidents that might well have resulted in her death.

Goose bumps pricked the skin on her arms and neck. If that were indeed the case, she need no longer ask why, nor need she look far to find the culprit. She knew only two people who would benefit from her death. And a third, who would benefit indirectly.

The knowledge was horrifying, and she did not want to think about the implications. Not now when she must have her wits about her for a safe getaway.

Meg's forehead creased as she renewed her efforts to pierce the still shadows. But when she was finally convinced it would be safe to leave, when she was about to step outside, she heard them again. The footsteps.

The stalker was back. As was the sick feeling in her stomach. With bated breath, she listened to the muffled thud-thud of heavy shoes or boots on the flagged pathway.

Meg whisked the door shut but changed her mind about barring it when she heard the grating crunch of gravel near the gazebo. There was something different about those steps. There was no stealth, no effort to make it sound as though he were hiding his approach. This time, he was determined to force a confrontation.

Her spine stiffened in a sudden rush of anger. Devil a bit! She was just as determined to have it over with. She'd put an end to this cat-and-mouse game and face him. With any luck, once he crossed the threshold, he'd be in no position to carry out whatever nefarious plans he had hatched.

Smiling grimly, she started to hum one of her favorite tunes. "Don't ever show fear," Fletcher had told her when he prepared her for the first decoy role she had been hired to play for the Bow Street magistrate. And she wouldn't. She'd show only unconcern and confidence.

Her voice grew huskier as she lifted the two-foot candle holder she had placed nearby. Her arms were not quite steady when she raised it high just as the determined footsteps thumped on the shallow wooden stairs leading up to the door.

The door was pulled open. For an instant, she saw the man's silhouette, tall and wide of shoulder. Impossible to miss with her makeshift weapon.

He rushed inside, shouting in an all-too-familiar voice, "Meg!"

"Oh, blast!"

It was too late to stop the blow; she could only try to aim it away from Philip. But even in that she was unsuccessful. She felt the impact in her hands and wrists as the base of the candle holder struck his arm, or perhaps

158

his hip.

"Blast!" Philip echoed.

She stood motionless, confused. She had expected the stalker. Philip's appearance and the knowledge that she had hurt him threw her off balance. And there was something else that deeply disturbed her—a suspicion dismissed as soon as it crossed her mind—that Philip himself was the stalker. It was too awful a notion to be allowed to take root.

"Dash it, Meg!" he said gruffly. "Why'd you hit me?"

"I am so sorry. I hope you're not badly hurt."

"No," he said, a scathing edge to his voice. "I only lost the use of an arm."

His tone exercised a bracing effect. Lost the use of an arm? Balderdash! Surely she had not hit that hard. Setting down the candlestick, she felt her way to a tiled table on which she had seen a tinderbox. She'd take a good look herself at whatever damage she had wreaked.

"Meg, what are you doing?"

She heard a note of sharpness in his voice, and tension coiled in her again before she remembered that he could not see her. The whisper of her silk gown and the scrabbling noise of her fingernails against the tiles must have sounded quite mysterious in the dark.

Her fingers shook as they closed around the slender metal box she had sought, but she managed to say quite calmly, "What do you think I'm doing? I'm trying to light a candle, of course."

Moments later, the golden glow of several burning candles lit the gazebo and she turned to face Philip.

He was rubbing his left arm above the elbow, but when he noticed her anxious look, he dropped his hand.

"Meg, you're as pale as a ghost. If you're worried that you hurt me, don't be. I cannot even feel it any longer."

It was such an obvious fib.

A sound between a laugh and a sob escaped her, and he came to her instantly. He wrapped his arms around her— he had *not* lost the use of one—and held her close. Not caring that he could hear her sigh, she leaned against him, her cheek resting against the broad shoulder so conveniently offered.

"Stanbrook, I *am* sorry. But it was quite your own fault that you were hit. Why didn't you call out sooner? When you finally spoke and I realized who you were, it was too late to stop the blow. I could only deflect it."

"Thank goodness you did."

His fingers caressed the back of her neck, and she felt her tense muscles relax.

"What did you use?" he asked. "An iron club?"

"It was only one of the candlesticks."

"Not solid iron, then," he said wryly. "We cannot discount the layer of bronze."

Reluctantly, she moved her head to look up at him.

"Pray don't turn it into a jest, or you'll make me wish I had bashed you with all my might. Stanbrook, why did you give me such a scare? When I heard the footsteps, the crunch of gravel— Dash it! Why the dickens didn't you identify yourself?"

He gave her a look that, had it come from a person of less distinction than the Earl of Stanbrook, she would have called sheepish. "I was rehearsing the scold I was about to read you."

She frowned. "Wasn't the reprimand you administered this afternoon sufficient for one day?"

His hold on her tightened. "Had I known then you'd be foolhardy enough to sit in the gazebo after dark, I would have locked you in. Dammit, Meg! It was a blatant invitation to anyone wishing you ill."

Her breath caught. Slowly, she pulled away from him until they stood facing each other.

"What do you know about someone wishing me ill?"

"Obviously not much since *you* did not see fit to tell me. I know only the few facts Jigger could provide. And barely had I digested that *three times* you came close to death in London, when he dropped as casual as can be that you had gone to sit in the gazebo!"

160

"I like it here," she said, and was immediately annoyed that she sounded defensive. She continued in a haughty tone, "It really is none of your concern, Stanbrook. But I do come here quite often to think. And besides, why should it make a difference whether I walk in my father's gardens during the daytime or at night?"

He started to pace, but after a few steps wheeled and faced her again.

One look at the tightly knit dark brows, at the grim set of mouth and jaw, made her say quickly, "Save your breath. I know exactly what you're about to say."

"Then it won't come as a surprise if I call you a little fool to have gone out unescorted. Didn't the attack outside your home in London teach you anything? Someone tried to kill you, Meg! How could you possibly think the Carswell Hall gardens would provide safety?"

Resentment kindled. "Very well, so I was foolish to think that the London incidents were not aimed at me personally, that I was merely in the wrong place at the wrong time, and that nothing would happen here. I learned different this evening, didn't I? But it does not give you the right to speak to me as though I were an imbecile. Especially when *your* actions a few moments ago were anything but laudable."

"If you're still harping on the subject of my unannounced arrival, let me tell you—"

She cut him off. "I daresay I shouldn't be surprised. It is typically man! You know you behaved like a brute when you charged in here, and to redeem yourself you find it necessary to read *me* a scold."

Their eyes met and held. She did not know what he was thinking, but she saw the harshness seep from his face to be replaced by tenderness and concern.

Two long strides brought him back to her side. Gripping her shoulders and giving her a gentle shake, he said, "Meg, my Meg! Don't you realize that I'm worried?"

Her heart beat faster, and if she had resented him, she

161

could not remember why. All she knew was that he had called her *his* Meg again, that his voice held the power to make her believe he cared for her . . . and that she wished he weren't besotted enough to propose to Evalina Lyndon so he could carry her off to Stanbrook Castle, the enchanted castle to which Meg would dearly like to be carried off herself.

"When I approached the gazebo," that deep, vibrant voice continued, "a man darted out of the shrubbery near the door and ran into the gardens. I chased him, but—"

"You *saw* him?"

Philip's besotted state, Miss Evalina, and the enchanted castle were consigned to the back of her mind in her eagerness to learn the identity of the stalker.

"Who was he? Did you recognize him? Or can you at least describe him?"

Philip frowned. "Then you did know that someone was out there, watching you, before I appeared on the scene? I couldn't be certain, and I was most reluctant to frighten you further with a tale of a lurking stranger if my footsteps were the only ones you'd heard."

"Of course I knew," she said impatiently. "That's why I was armed with the candlestick. I thought he was coming back. What did he look like, Stanbrook? Did you know him?"

"No." A frown still darkened his face. "You knew he was there, and yet you sang. What the deuce were you about, Meg?"

"I often sing when I am frightened."

"You *what?*" He stared at her, speechless.

"Not to show fear is one of the first lessons you learn when you work for the Bow Street Court. When I sing, I cannot hear my cowardly, pounding heart and I can at least pretend that I am brave. And as you know from personal experience," she added with a little smile, "singing or humming gives me a definite advantage over someone wishing to surprise me."

162

"Meg, what's this about you working for the Bow Street Court?"

"You know my pa was a runner?"

"Yes. But *you*— Dash it, Meg! I never heard of a female runner."

"Nevertheless, I have worked off and on for the various Bow Street magistrates since I was thirteen years old. And now," she said, determined not to be side-tracked again, "please describe the man you chased."

His facial expression did not change, but there was something about his eyes, a shuttered look, that put her instantly on guard.

"This is turning into a somewhat lengthy session," he said abruptly. "I for one would like to sit down, but I cannot do so as long as you're standing."

This was the third time he had evaded a description of the stalker. Trained by Fletcher to accept nothing and no one at face value, she could not stop herself from asking "Why?" What was it Philip did not want her to know?

That he had recognized the man but did not want to betray him? Or, as she had suspected for that one awful moment, that it had been Philip himself who skulked in the shadows and frightened her?

She could not and would not believe that he would harm her. If it had been Philip creeping around the gazebo, then he had meant only to give her a scare. But with what objective? Did he want to drive her away from Carswell Hall? That would be in direct contradiction to his demand that she reconsider refusing her inheritance.

"Well, Meg?"

She realized that he was watching her as closely as she watched him. He looked pale in the candlelight, and he held his left arm stiffly at his side.

Without a word, she took a seat on one of the cushioned benches lining the circle of the garden house, while Philip pulled up a chair fashioned of wrought iron, painted white. Crossing his long legs, he braced the sore arm against his thigh.

163

"That's better," he said, the corners of his mouth turning down ruefully. "You put a devilish strong kick into that blow, my Meg. Unfortunately, I'm not made of hero material. I find I cannot blithely ignore pain."

"I am sorry."

She hated herself for her doubting nature and the duplicity of using concern to test him. But it seemed so simple. She'd offer him an easy way out, and if he took it . . . well, then she'd know where she stood. Wouldn't she?

"Perhaps you are not up to any more talk, Stanbrook. Perhaps you'd rather go to the house and have your valet apply a poultice to the arm?"

"Devil a bit! I only said I wasn't a hero, not that I'm a milksop."

"I beg your pardon." Hope made her heart beat faster. "Does that mean you'll finally tell me what the stalker looked like?"

Again, she caught the shuttered expression in his eyes.

"Yes, among other things I'll tell you what I know about the stalker."

A wave of relief washed over her, leaving her light-headed. Never before had she been so glad to have her suspicions proved wrong.

"But first, my Meg, contrary to what I recommended this afternoon, you must promise me to go to your father immediately and persuade him to change the will back to the original version. And, for your safety, you must also arrange to leave Carswell Hall immediately."

Chapter Thirteen

Once again, suspicion soared. He wanted her to reject the inheritance! So that he and Stewart would have Carswell Hall?

He wanted her to leave. *For her safety*. Was there a threat implicit in the words?

Meg felt as though she had been pushed off the top of the east tower and was helplessly hurtling through space while the tower walls crumbled about her. She could do nothing but wait for the pain of hitting the ground and the falling brick and mortar crushing her.

"Meg."

Taking a deep breath, she stared at Philip, uncertain whether he had saved her from a nightmare or awakened her to an even more horrifying reality.

"Meg, what did I say to make you look as though you'd seen a ghost?"

She did not reply. Could not reply. She was afraid anything she might say would solidify the ugly thoughts spinning through her mind.

"Less than three hours ago, you *wanted* your father to change the will," Philip said. "And when I tell you that for your safety it *must* be done, you seem . . . devastated. Why?"

"For my safety," she repeated, wondering if in her misery she had imbued the words with a sinister meaning they could not possibly contain.

Before the experience in the gazebo, she would not have questioned Philip's motivation. Even now, she *wanted* to trust him. But it wasn't trust Fletcher had stressed when he trained her to recognize and evade danger. It was caution.

"Why, Meg?" Philip asked again. "Why does my suggestion shock you speechless?"

His eyes searched her face. She saw the dawning of understanding, a flicker of hurt and reproach. The glimpse she had of his feelings was brief; almost immediately he was cool and self-possessed again.

"You don't trust me," he said, his voice as unemotional as that of the footman announcing dinner.

She would have been deceived by his coolness, but she had seen the look in his eyes, and that instant of recognizing pain had been sufficient to show her how utterly wrong she was to doubt him.

Pressing her hands against her burning cheeks, she admitted, "I did think for a moment that you might have been the stalker."

His expression was inscrutable, the features rigid as though hewn in marble or granite.

Meg did not often find it necessary to justify herself, but something about Philip—perhaps the meticulous concealment of emotion, the carefully maintained aloofness—compelled her to explain.

"I was frightened, Stanbrook. It was difficult to know what to believe. Earlier, I suspected Stewart as well. But it was you who came rushing into the gazebo. And then you said I must leave. I—I wondered if it was a threat."

Philip kept looking at her. Gradually, his expression softened.

"I suppose I have only myself to blame if you don't trust me. I should have realized you were frightened and confused and, therefore, suspicious. Anyone would have been."

"It's over now." She took a deep breath. "I'm being

166

quite level-headed again."

"Level-headed enough to see that I have your welfare at heart?"

She met his gaze squarely. "Yes."

"Good."

He leaned against the chair back and crossed his arms. If the left arm was still sore, he did not show it. In a matter-of-fact voice he continued, "According to Jigger, you've had three near brushes with death. Tell me about the first one, the incident with the carriage. What style of carriage was it? And what about the horses? Can you describe them?"

"It was a curricle, I believe." She frowned in concentration. "And the horses—well, they were . . . horses. Four great, big stamping brutes. Dash it, Stanbrook! You know I'm no expert. All I know is that the driver could not control them."

"Or pretended he could not control them. What color were they? Were they a matched team? Thoroughbreds?"

"I suppose they were Thoroughbreds. At least, they looked like the kind of horses Stewart wouldn't be ashamed to have in the stables. And yes, they were matched. All four were a beautiful, glossy chestnut color."

Their eyes met. They both knew that Stewart owned a team of matched chestnuts.

"No!" Meg cried, but, somehow, the pounding of her heart seemed louder than her voice. "You're wrong! I am wrong. For an instant, as I jumped aside, I saw the driver clearly. It was *not* Stewart, or his groom. And you know as well as I do that he wouldn't let anyone else touch that team of chestnuts."

"He lets me handle them."

Her heart drummed faster, then slowed to its normal pace.

"Don't be a nimwit," she said gruffly. "I would have remembered if I had seen you before that night at the Drury Lane."

167

"I should hope so."

She caught a glint of devilment in his eyes, but it was gone in an instant.

"Meg, do you remember anything at all that might help?"

"No. It does no good to harp back to the incidents in London. I do not know who drove the carriage. I do not know who sent the marchpanes which, the physician said, contained a generous dose of arsenic. And I do not know who attacked me in Seven Dials."

"But someone wants you—" He broke off, gritting his teeth.

Dead. The word hung between them, but Meg was glad he had not said it aloud. It was terrifying enough just to think it.

"Someone is out to do you harm," Philip amended. "Admit, Stewart and I make a pair of prime suspects."

Meg mentally added one more name to the list of suspects.

As though he had read her mind, Philip said. "Or Alvina. She'd do anything for Stewart."

"Yes, I suspected her, too. But it's impossible, isn't it? Alvina is a bitter woman. I am certain it was she who frightened my mother away from Carswell Hall. But plotting to harm me . . . to hire a thug? I should think it takes more than bitterness to drive a woman to such desperate measures."

"That's what I assured myself," said Philip, but he looked distracted, as though he were thinking of something else.

"Still," he said after a moment, "we cannot dismiss that the stalker, as you call him, appeared right after your father announced the change in his will. You must ask Cousin Richard *tonight* to change it once more."

"I cannot do that."

With an obvious effort at patience, Philip said, "Meg, it's the only way I know to keep you safe. Then, when I've discovered who is behind the attack and the other incidents, Cousin Richard can reinstate you as the heir."

"You don't understand. I truly don't wish to be the Carswell heir, but I have just promised my father I'd not pester him about the will for another month. I'd have to explain why I cannot keep my word, and I don't want to do that. He'd worry too much."

"Devil a bit! I didn't consider your father's precarious health."

"No, I don't suppose you did. But you can see that it is out of the question to tell him about the stalker. It might precipitate another stroke."

Frowning, Philip stared at the signet ring on his left hand. "Damn," he said softly. "It was a good plan. But I suppose I can think of another."

"Please don't worry too much. Remember, I'm not a pampered and protected young lady. I was taught to take care of myself."

"Don't worry?" Philip laughed, but it was not an altogether mirthful sound. "Surely that should have been my line. I should be the one telling you not to worry, but to leave everything to me. I wonder, did Fletcher in his training of you also stress that there are times when it would be better to let a man take over?"

She could remember several instances when Fletcher or the Bow Street magistrate had forbidden her to continue an investigation because the situation was proving more dangerous than they had anticipated.

"That was different," she said, firmly overriding the timid inner voice that told her it would be a blessed relief to place the burden of protecting her on Philip's broad shoulders.

Philip rose and started to pace.

"Then Fletcher did realize you might get hurt working for the Bow Street court."

"Of course he did," she said quietly. "Just as he knew—and accepted—that *he* could get hurt. Or killed."

Philip stopped, facing her. "Meg, could the attacks on you be acts of revenge?"

She considered the question. Surely, if it were a possibility, it would also have occurred to Fletcher?

"It is possible, Stanbrook. But not very likely. The attack in Seven Dials could easily be the deed of two thugs whose plans I once thwarted, or whose friends I helped send to the gallows. But the criminals I dealt with were not the sort who could afford to buy or hire a carriage-and-four. They probably couldn't even afford the marchpanes sent to the theater."

"No doubt you're correct. I may be clutching at straws to avoid looking for the culprit close to home. But, dash it, Meg! Fletcher should never have allowed you to perform such dangerous work. Why the devil did he?"

Philip sounded angry, but the look he gave her was one of perplexity. She suppressed the stab of irritation that he dared question Fletcher's decision. Once more, she was forcefully reminded of the different circumstances in which they had been raised.

"Did you know that I once had brothers and sisters? Half-brothers and half-sisters," she amended punctiliously. "When I turned thirteen, only one of them was still alive—the youngest boy. But he and my mother were both ill, while I was strong and healthy and already far older than the average Dials child when it is sent out to work. We needed money desperately, but I was too big to be hired out as a climbing girl, and—"

"Meg!" he said, horrified.

She gave him a questioning look.

"No, it's nothing. I apologize for interrupting. Please go on. I want to know. I want to understand."

"I wish more ladies and gentlemen of your position would want to know. Then there'd be hope for the slum dwellers. Lady Maryann—" She shook her head. "I'll tell you about my friends some other time. Now, I'd rather convince you that Fletcher had my interest at heart when he let me work for the Bow Street magistrate."

"I'm half convinced already if the alternative was climbing girl."

She gave Philip a wry half-smile. "What an innocent you are if you believe that was the worst of alternatives. In any case, it was out of the question because I'd have been stuck in the first chimney. And I ruled out crossing sweep, another occupation frequently held by girls, because I didn't want to fight some other sweep for an advantageous position."

"Tenderheart."

The gentleness of his voice drove warmth into her cheeks. To hide her confusion, she told him with some asperity, "I wasn't quite as altruistic as you might think. The most traveled crossings are held by the bigger lads. And they, I assure you, wield a wicked broom. It is no joke fighting one of them."

"I know. I once tried to break up a fight between two sweeps, and I still carry the scars."

Slowly, Philip came closer until he stood directly in front of her.

"Very well, Meg. I accept that you could not have been a climbing girl or a crossing sweep. Without another roundabout line, give me the awful alternative to working for the Bow Street court. That's what you've been leading up to, isn't it? You want to shock me out of what you call my innocence."

She wanted to protest, but the words remained unspoken as she realized that Philip was, at least in part, correct. She did want to shock him. Not because he might have too simple a view of life in the slums and stews, but because he had set himself up to judge the men and women forced to send young children out to work. It had not, however, been a conscious maneuver on her part, merely an instinctive reaction in defense of Fletcher.

Before she could speak, Philip said harshly, "The alternative was to sell you into prostitution, wasn't it?"

"Yes."

Philip drew in his breath sharply. He let loose a string of expletives more colorful than those used by the patrons of the Fighting Cock.

171

Meg listened with interest and, when he paused, congratulated him on his fluency. "Fletcher would have been proud of you, Stanbrook. He always appreciated a man who could express himself."

Even in the weak candlelight, she could see his color deepen.

"Dash it, Meg! There's nothing commendable about my swearing in front of a lady. But when I consider what might have happened to you—and all because your mother was too frightened to live here!—my blood runs cold."

"Nothing did happen," she reminded him. "I never came to harm."

"And I'll make certain you remain unharmed." He gave her a fierce look, as though daring her to contradict him. "Fletcher, I realize, had his ways of protecting you. I have mine. Like it or not, I will not allow you to face danger alone."

Ordinarily, the masterful tone and manner would have set up her back, but, to her astonishment, they delighted her. Not that she intended to let him rule her life, but simply knowing that he was on her side filled her with warmth and serenity.

"Thank you, Stanbrook. I shall be glad of a friend during the next weeks—until I can ask my father to change the will again. I don't mind admitting that I am rather scared."

Once more, she witnessed the transformation of his features as his expression softened.

"Don't be," he said gently. "I'm here to protect you."

She didn't quite know how it happened, whether she had risen or whether Philip had drawn her off the bench, but suddenly she was in his arms and he was holding her in a crushing embrace.

"I'll keep you safe, my Meg." His voice was low, but to her ears the words sounded like a pledge. "I'll find the man who attacked you in London and who stalked you this evening. Trust me."

"I do."

It did not seem worth the effort to tell him she could very well find the stalker herself. Philip's arms tightened around her so that she could scarcely breathe. But she did not mind. Breathing became an unimportant detail when the pressure of his lean body against hers, the warm caress of his hands on her back, created the most delicious sensations to be savored and explored.

Now, if only he'd kiss her as well. Didn't he know she was waiting?

Apparently, he did not. Raising her head, she boldly offered her lips, but Philip did not avail himself of the invitation. He loosened his hold and frowned into her upturned face.

"The man outside the gazebo," he said brusquely. "It could have been one of the gardeners. I cannot be certain, since I never paid much heed the few times I encountered one of them, but Jigger swears there's a new gardener here, a man he saw near the Fighting Cock the night you were attacked."

Meg blinked in confusion. Attackers and stalkers had retreated to the very back of her mind since Philip's arms closed around her. In fact, she was quite piqued. When she had asked him, nay, pleaded with him to describe the man, Philip had evaded her. Now, when all her thoughts were centered on just one goal, to win a kiss, he presented her with a bloody gardener who might or might not have been the stalker.

With an admirable effort, she called herself to order. Just because she was thinking of kisses did not mean that Philip was, too.

"If Jigger says he saw the man at the tavern, then you may safely wager your last groat that it is so. I've never known him to be wrong about a face. But why the dickens did it take you so long to tell me?"

"I couldn't make up my mind whether this bit of speculation would be an unnecessary worry for you, or whether it'd be better if you suspected danger even from a rather unlikely quarter. You did not, perchance, recognize a Carswell Hall gardener as one of the men who attacked you in Seven Dials?"

"How could I? I never even caught a glimpse of the thugs in the Dials." After an instant's hesitation, she added conscientiously, "But I do believe I've seen one of the undergardeners, the tall, cadaverous-looking one, somewhere in London."

"Where? Think, Meg! Could it have been near the theater?"

"Perhaps."

She really did not want to be bothered with further speculation. Or with anything that might recall ugly, frightening memories. She wanted to feel Philip's arms tighten around her once more. She wanted to taste his mouth.

Reaching up, she clasped her hands behind his neck.

"If it was the gardener you saw outside the gazebo, leave him be," she said huskily. "He was probably snatching lilacs for his ailing mother."

Something was happening to Philip's eyes. They were growing darker, more compelling, and his face was coming closer and closer.

"A likely story," he murmured, his mouth almost touching hers. "And then again, the fellow may have a sweetheart who likes lilacs."

Meg was not the young lady to insist on having the last word. She said nothing. In fact, she had no desire to speak at all, or to think of anything that might diminish the pleasure of the moment when Philip's mouth finally closed over hers.

She was still basking in the pleasure of the kiss when she rose the following morning. Elspeth, bringing the morning chocolate, took one look at her face and said, "Why, Miss Megan, you look like you was kissed awake by a prince, or a knight at the very least!"

174

Or by an earl? It was a lovely thought—to be kissed awake in the mornings by Philip. But it was also sheer nonsense. Still, a tiny smile kept tugging at the corners of Meg's mouth as she hurried to the stables for her riding lesson. Properly speaking, it was a lesson no longer; several days ago, Philip had declared her an honors graduate of the Stanbrook Riding School.

The horses were saddled and waiting in the yard, Beelzebub snorting and prancing and struggling against the groom's firm hold on the bridle, while Patches sidled up to Philip to rub her forehead against his shoulder. Philip half turned and stroked the mare's brown-and-white neck, but his gaze remained fixed on Meg as she approached.

Warmth rose in her face under that look, which was as much a caress as though he had touched her. She was glad that the groom was too occupied with Beelzebub even to glance at her while he muttered his good morning—doubly glad when Philip, instead of cupping his hands, clasped her waist and lifted her into the saddle.

He did not let go of her immediately. Staring up into her face, he said softly, "You're a witch, my Meg. You kept me awake all night thinking about you."

"Palaverer," she murmured, convinced her cheeks must by now be a flaming scarlet.

For the first time, she wished she'd had the experience of a "season" among members of the *ton*. Surely, she would have acquired a stock of repartee for occasions such as this. She would have learned and mastered the art of verbal fencing that was so useful when one faced a gentleman with a penchant for flirtation.

"Whether you were awake or not," she said with a cautious look at the groom, "your arm must have had all the rest it needed. Unless I did not hit as hard as you led me to believe?"

"You hit hard all right, my Meg." Philip grinned broadly. "It must be that I am more of a hero than I gave myself credit."

A laugh tickled her throat, but, still very conscious of the groom nearby, she suppressed it. "Shall we ride, Stanbrook? If we delay much longer, Beelzebub may decide to go off on his own."

"You're not tired, then?" Slowly, caressingly, Philip slid his hands off her waist. "No sleepless night for you?"

"Never slept better in my life," she said and added, deliberately misunderstanding him, "It takes more than a little scare in the gazebo to keep me awake."

"That's not what I meant. And you know it."

"I do." She shot him a sidelong look. "But I didn't want to hurt your male pride."

His mouth twitched. "I've changed my mind. You're not a witch. You're a hornet."

He mounted and they left the yard, Beelzebub several impatient steps ahead of Patches. Once they were out in the open country, they broke into a canter. Obviously, Beelzebub was not happy with the pace, but Philip was firm and would no longer let him draw ahead of the mare—a situation that suited Meg perfectly.

She felt close to Philip this morning, not only physically but emotionally as well. They hardly spoke, but the silence between them was a bond, not a separation. The stillness of the early morning surrounding them was an invisible dome that enhanced the illusion of being quite alone with the other.

When they did exchange a word or two, as if by mutual consent, they did not touch upon the disquieting events of the previous night—the kiss, or the stalker. For Meg, it was an added enchantment that Philip seemed to feel exactly as she did. Words would have destroyed the lingering magic of the passionate embrace, and a reminder of danger would have been a jarring intrusion into this enchanted hour.

However, reality would not be banished forever. Meg had not paid close attention to their surroundings, but she was aware that they had been riding in a wide circle on Carswell land. And as they crossed a sun-dappled

176

clearing between two stands of trees, she saw Elspeth hurrying toward them on the path she recognized with a jolt as the one sloping down to Nanny Grimshaw's cottage.

It was impossible, then, to keep up the pretense that she and Philip were alone in the world, that there was no threat hanging over her that might well have its origin in the past. Nanny Grimshaw was a part of the past.

Acting without conscious thought or reason, Meg reined the mare in. Philip shot her a look of surprise, but brought Beelzebub to a stop as well.

When the little maid, red-faced and panting from running up the incline, was within speaking distance, Meg called out, "Elspeth, were you looking for me?"

"Well, no, miss."

Taking the last few steps at a more sedate pace, she reached the top of the slope. "But I was hopin' I'd get back to the Hall before you did, and I'm right sorry I'll be late when I'm sure you'll be wantin' a bath and all."

"That's all right," Meg said absently. "I am perfectly able to take a bath and change without assistance."

Her mind was on the old nurse living in the tiny thatched cottage, but she did not miss the flash of amusement on Philip's face. It was disturbing and not totally welcome that she should be so aware of him even when she was preoccupied with the mystery-shrouded days of her infancy at Carswell Hall.

Turning Patches so that her back was toward Philip, she said, "You must have been visiting Nanny Grimshaw. I did not realize it was part of your duties to look after her."

"It be a duty I asked for." Elspeth looked and sounded defensive. "You see, miss, Nanny Grimshaw's my great-auntie."

Meg smiled reassuringly. "I'm sure she enjoys your visits, Elspeth. You certainly need not hurry off on my account."

The maid gave Meg a strange look, a mixture between

177

gratitude and alarm.

"Thank you, Miss Megan. But Mrs. Elmore don't like it if I'm late. She says Auntie's upper works are gone, and she's been after Sir Richard this past week or more to put Auntie away instead of havin' me waste my time with her."

"Put her away?" Meg asked, startled. "Surely Mrs. Elmore doesn't mean to place her in an almshouse?"

"Aye, miss. That be it. She's sayin' as Sir Richard ought to get Auntie into that place in Ascot."

"Sir Richard would never do that," Meg said soothingly.

"I hope you're right, Miss Megan. Auntie would hate it!" Elspeth's eyes flashed. "She ain't totally gone. She's got her good days and her bad days. And those times when she's sharp and spritely, she'd know she's in the almshouse. She'd die of shame, Miss Megan! She would!"

"Her good days and her bad days," Meg repeated slowly.

Just like Sir Richard. And he even pretended to have a bad day if it suited his purpose.

Chapter Fourteen

Sensing Philip's restlessness but not wanting him to interrupt with questions at this point, Meg said quickly, "And this morning, Elspeth? Would you say Nanny Grimshaw is having one of her good days?"

The girl wrinkled her brow. "Well now, miss, if you'd asked me that just after I first saw her, I'd have said yes. Auntie recognized me and was talkin' as clear as a bell. But then she slipped off, and there was no makin' sense of her at all."

"But she still talked?" Meg remembered the silent old woman whose vacant stare had gone right through her. Even if Nanny Grimshaw spouted nothing but nonsense this morning, it must still be considered one of her better days. "What does she talk about, Elspeth?"

"I don't pay much heed when she's like that, Miss Megan. She just keeps mutterin' about people I don't know. Most of 'em dead, I should think."

"So this morning her mind is wandering in the past?"

"Aye, miss. Matter of fact, Auntie's been goin' on and on about Miss Lydia Carswell, the one that looks like you."

"The lady in the portrait?"

Elspeth nodded vigorously. "And she's been dead I dunno how many years! Mayhap sixty. Mayhap five-and-sixty years. But Auntie's insistin' that Miss Lydia

179

stopped by to see her."

Meg's heart started to beat faster. Turning in the saddle, she said, "Stanbrook, would you mind if I went to see Nanny Grimshaw for a few minutes?"

"Not at all."

He dismounted quickly, and when he stepped around Patches to help her down, she saw a gleam in his eyes—a gleam of excitement, as though he knew that something might be afoot.

Effortlessly, he lifted her from the saddle. "I'll wager a pony that you've already been to visit with Nanny," he said softly. "And I'll offer odds that the Miss Lydia she's talking about is really you."

"Too bad there's no one around to take you up on the wager," Meg replied in equally soft tones so Elspeth wouldn't overhear. "You might have won."

Looking at the maid, she said, "Would you come with me, Elspeth? It may upset your aunt if I'm by myself."

"I dunno, Miss Megan." Elspeth twisted her apron nervously. "I s'pose I could go with you, since you asked and I'm s'posed to be your maid. But I dunno what Mrs. Elmore will do if I'm back late. I don't want her to put Auntie away!"

Meg and Philip exchanged glances.

"Run along, Elspeth," he said. "I'm sure Miss Megan worries unnecessarily. Your aunt probably enjoys visitors."

"Aye, that she does. And I can use the time to get Miss Megan's bath ready."

Not trying to hide her relief, the girl hurried off.

"I could tie the horses," Philip offered, "if you want me to go with you?"

"Truthfully, no," Meg said with her usual candor. "I would have taken Elspeth to put Nanny at ease, but I fear you'd be dreadfully in the way."

Philip grinned. "I hope you'll never marry a diplomat. Our country would be in great trouble."

Marry? A diplomat? Meg slowly descended the sloping

180

path to Nanny Grimshaw's tiny cottage. Surely, Philip was aiming high for an actress?

However, all thought of Philip's rather strange remark faded as soon as she saw the old woman in her rocker by the open cottage door. As on Meg's first visit, Nanny Grimshaw was rocking back and forth with spellbinding monotony. But there all similarity to that other time ended. This morning, the old nurse's dark eyes sparkled with interest as she watched Meg's approach.

"Good morning, Mrs. Grimshaw."

The path had not been steep and she had walked quite slowly, yet Meg felt breathless as she crossed the narrow strip of grass between woodland shrubs and cottage. She was excited and at the same time apprehensive, and it was Nanny Grimshaw's alert appearance that made her feel that way. Anything might happen this morning. Anything at all.

"I hope you don't mind my stopping by without warning, but Elspeth said you might enjoy a visitor."

"Miss Lydia!" A toothless smile accompanied the happy cry. "I knew you'd come today! Felt it in my bones. Come and sit by me. Tell me why it took you so long. I almost started believing that I'm indeed going soft in the head . . . that I'd imagined your visit when I was feeling poorly. But I didn't imagine it, did I?"

Meg sat down on a wooden bench painted a brilliant green. Leaning her back against the cottage wall, she said, "I was here once before. It was about a week ago."

"I remember. You promised to come again when I was better. And you did, Miss Lydia. You did. You always were one to keep your word. Unlike," she added darkly, "some others we know."

Meg took a deep breath. "I am not Miss Lydia. My name is Megan Carswell. I am Sir Richard and Rosemary's daughter."

A change came over Nanny Grimshaw. She frowned, and when she spoke, she sounded decidedly put out. "And what would you be knowing about Sir Richard and

181

Miss Rosemary? "Are you going to act like Alvina, then? Uppity and downright spiteful?"

"No, Mrs. Grimshaw. But I don't think you quite understand."

"Oh, I understand, all right, Miss Lydia!" The rocking ceased abruptly and Nanny drew herself up. She looked younger, stronger, and ready to pull caps. "Now that you're seventeen and are about to have a season in London, you think you know more than I. Well, let me tell you! That Miss Rosemary is a sweet little thing, and she's the best that could have happened to Sir Richard."

Meg stared at the old nurse. Nanny Grimshaw sounded perfectly lucid and rational, yet she consistently called her Miss Lydia—who had been dead sixty or more years, if Elspeth was to be believed. Worse, Nanny seemed to believe that Lydia and Alvina, who could not be much over fifty, knew each other, and that Lydia knew even about Sir Richard's marriage to Rosemary, which had taken place a scarce twenty-five years ago.

Nanny's mind, apparently, had condensed several decades of the past, and to the old woman that time had become the present. It was irrational by anyone's standards, except, perhaps, by Nanny Grimshaw's.

And perhaps this living in the past would enable her to clear up the mystery of Rosemary's flight from Carswell Hall.

"Mrs. Grimshaw." Meg swallowed. Her throat felt dry, as it did before a performance. "Do you remember the night my mother—Miss Rosemary—ran away with her baby?"

Their eyes met. For a moment, the old woman's remained bright and intelligent. She cocked her head in an inquisitive manner, as though she were about to pose a question of her own. Then she seemed to shrink within herself and the brightness of the eyes clouded over. Nanny was once more the feeble old woman with the vacant stare Meg had encountered on her first visit to the cottage.

Anxiously, Meg leaned forward. "Mrs. Grimshaw? Nanny? I am sorry if I upset you, but I hoped you could help me."

"The past is better left alone," the old woman muttered. "Nothing can be changed and nothing can be amended."

"I don't want to change anything, Nanny. I just want to know what happened."

The only response was a resumption of the rocking. Back and forth the old woman rocked, and her wide, unblinking stare was fixed on a vine climbing the cottage wall. Tiny drops of dew still clung to the dark leaves and glittered like diamonds in the pale morning sun, but Meg did not think Nanny Grimshaw saw the vine or that brief flash of beauty before the sun soaked up the water droplets.

She rose, her legs weak and her stomach tight with disappointment. She should have known better than to hope for a miracle. She had been disappointed the last time, but then she had been able to shake off the feeling of defeat because she still had hopes that Sir Richard could tell her what she wanted to know. Now, there was no such anticipation.

"Good-bye, Mrs. Grimshaw," she said softly, and she started back toward the sloping path.

After a few steps, very much against her better judgment, she looked over her shoulder. "I'll come back when you're feeling less poorly, shall I?"

She thought she saw Nanny Grimshaw nod and the rocker move just a little faster, but that was undoubtedly her imagination.

Meg made no attempt to hide her disappointment when she rejoined Philip. Leading the horses, they walked side by side while she recounted the brief, disconcerting conversation with Nanny.

"The more I think about it," Meg concluded, "the more I fear she's completely addled and will never be able to tell me about the last few days before Mother

183

ran away."

"Why?" asked Philip. "I'd say it's remarkable that she remembers so many people from the past."

"The question is, does she truly remember or does she live in a world of fantasy? We cannot be sure that she even *knew* Lydia, except from the portrait. Elspeth could very well have been mistaken in the date of death. Lydia was my father's aunt. She died a young woman. For all we know, she may have been dead before Nanny was born!"

Philip had been listening to her with utter concentration, but at her final exasperated outburst, a glint of amusement lit his eyes.

"My poor Meg. If that's all that's keeping you from putting your trust in Nanny's ability to remember, let's go see your father. He'll know when Lydia died and how long Nanny Grimshaw has been at Carswell Hall."

"Of course." Meg's face flamed. "Believe me, I am not usually such a scatterbrain that I cannot think of the obvious. But since I started to explore why my mother found it intolerable to live here, I have met with one impasse after another. I ask questions, and instead of finding answers and solving the puzzle, I am haunted by more questions than I started with. I suppose," she said with a self-conscious little laugh, "I'm afraid the same will happen if I ask about Lydia or Nanny."

"Hm." Philip's attention was diverted by Beelzebub, who had stopped to sample the shrubs bordering the bridle path. Tightening his grip on the rein, he called the gelding to order. Then he finally looked at Meg.

"Don't you think you had better tell me what new questions you have uncovered?"

"Yes." A sigh of relief escaped her. She hadn't realized until now just how much she longed to confide in someone.

Meg launched into the story of her father and mother as she had pieced it together from the bits of information gleaned first from Fletcher, then from Sir Richard. She ended with Sir Richard's tumble when he set out after her mother, and the fire that destroyed her grandfather's glover shop.

"When Alvina inquired about Mother and me, the neighbors told her we had perished in the flames. They *knew* we didn't. Why on earth did they lie? Or," she said with kindling indignation, "was it Alvina who lied to my father?"

They had reached the meadow at the far end of which lay the chapel ruin, goal of the first walk they had taken together. By mutual if unspoken consent, they both stopped. In a very short while, they'd be back at Carswell Hall. Anything of importance they still had to share must be said now.

Ignoring the impatient nudges Beelzebub directed at his back, Philip faced Meg. "I don't know who lied all those years ago, or for what reason. But I'd certainly like to find out."

"It may not be impossible to find one or two of my grandfather's old neighbors. I know where the glover's shop was located, and I also remember that Mother used to visit one of the women in the building next door. They were childhood friends."

Philip cocked an eyebrow. "How long ago was your mother's last visit?"

It had been eleven, almost twelve years ago, but Meg was in no mood to face doubts.

"I'm not saying that Mrs. Kindred would be the only one to remember my grandfather's shop or the night of the fire. There may be dozens of people who'll remember, and I'm very much inclined to return to London for a few days to make inquiries."

Philip looked as though he were about to protest most strenuously. Then, suddenly, he changed his mind.

"If you're set on going, *I'll* take you," he said in a tone of voice that brooked no objection. "We can leave tomorrow morning, if you like."

More pleased than she cared to admit by the prospect of spending several hours confined in a carriage with

185

Philip, Meg gave him a dazzling smile.

"Splendid. I'll stay with Lady Maryann and Stephen Fant. I've long wanted you to meet them. And besides, they'll want to help."

"Any friends of yours I'd like to meet, too. There's just one thing. What excuse will you give your father for going to London?"

Her smile faded. Not because she could not think of an excuse; there was always theater business she could take care of while in town. But she suddenly remembered other excuses that would have to be made.

"Stanbrook, we cannot go tomorrow. Evalina Lyndon's party is the day after, and I'm sure we'd take longer than that."

"Damn—dash it! I had completely forgotten. There's nothing for it, then, but to postpone the journey."

"I suppose so," Meg said with a sad lack of enthusiasm. She really was not looking forward to being shown off to Sir Richard's neighbors.

As though he read her mind, Philip grinned at her. "Coward," he teased. "Having faced crowds night after night at the Drury Lane, you tremble at the thought of a small gathering?"

"I do not tremble," she said with dignity. "I merely deplore. And I do not believe that's as bad as totally forgetting. Especially when the honoree of the party is one's intended bride."

His eyes narrowed. "Where on earth did you hear that Miss Lyndon is my intended?"

Still very much on her dignity, she replied, "I believe it was Stewart who mentioned that you're about to make an offer for the young lady."

A smile tugged at the corner of his mouth. A *fatuous* smile, Meg thought, then scolded herself for being cattish. Philip could hardly help it, besotted as he was.

But could a man be infatuated with one woman and yet kiss another the way Philip had kissed her? The sad truth was, obviously, that he could.

"Meg, do you think Evalina would make a good countess?"

Ha! Now he wanted her opinion, did he? Well, like it or not, he would have it.

"Yes, she'd make a delightful countess. But she wouldn't make you a good wife. Help me mount, Stanbrook, will you?"

As he had done earlier that morning, he clasped her around the waist and lifted her into the saddle.

"And why wouldn't she make me a good wife?"

"You're too old for Evalina."

It was obvious that he had not expected that particular thrust. Looking considerably taken aback, he said, "Thirty-seven is *not* too old to marry."

"I did not say that you're too old to marry."

No, not a bit too old, she admitted wistfully, but quickly pushed the thought aside before it led to other, even more foolish, notions.

"I merely pointed out that you're *too old for Evalina.*"

"I am, am I?" A dangerous gleam lit in his eyes. "And what put that notion into your head—aside from the example set by your father and mother?"

"Isn't that sufficient reason?"

"I thought that, perhaps, you had someone else in mind for me?"

He stood so close, she only had to move her hand a fraction to touch his face. Instead, she moved Patches, pointing the mare in the direction of the stables.

"Someone else, Stanbrook?" She gave a little laugh, determined to show him that she could enjoy the game of verbal fencing as much as he did. "No, indeed. I'm no matchmaker."

And if she had once in a while imagined herself as his countess, he need never know. In any case, it was merely a private jest she allowed herself on occasion. On the stage, she might be a duchess, a queen, or even a goddess; outside the make-believe world of the theater, her aspirations had better be kept in check.

She directed another dazzling Meg Fletcher smile at Philip. "If you're game, I'll race you to the stables. If I win, I'll get to ride Beelzebub tomorrow."

"And if *I* win? What do I get?"

"Why, you'll get to ride Patches, of course."

The gleam in his eyes had not diminished. "If I win, I'll choose my own reward."

He swung himself into the saddle. Keeping Beelzebub in check, he said, "I'll give you a start of fifty paces. And remember! The mare knows the terrain better than you do. When you get to the brook, let her have her head lest you want to risk taking a bath sooner than you expected."

"I've jumped the brook twice before, and you said I did very well." She gave him a sidelong look. "But if your praise was mere lip service, I can always cross by the bridge and still beat you to the stables."

"No!"

She blinked at the suddenly thunderous expression on his face. "Devil a bit, Stanbrook! There's no need to snap my nose off. I was only jesting. I hope I know better than to cross those flimsy planks at a gallop."

He might have said more, but Meg gave him no opportunity. Touching her heel to the mare's flank and calling out, "Remember! Fifty paces!" she raced off across the meadow.

She could hear no sound above the thunder of Patches's hooves, but when she glanced over her shoulder, she saw Philip—well over fifty paces behind her. She laughed out loud in happiness. It was a moment of sheer pleasure, the exhilarating pace of the gallop, the cool morning air sweeping her face, and Philip's chivalry, which, she hoped, would cost him dearly. She fully intended to win this race.

And so, apparently, did Patches. The mare, indeed, knew the terrain. Sure of foot, she raced over the uneven ground, flew past the chapel ruin, and aimed straight for the spot where the brook was its narrowest and where the opposite bank marked the beginning of a straight path to the stables.

Meg cast another look over her shoulder. Beelzebub had caught up considerably—was, in fact, only about two lengths behind Patches. And he was still gaining ground.

She felt the change in the mare's stride, the powerful muscles bunching beneath her in preparation for the jump, and quickly directed her attention forward.

There was the brook. Patches leaped. They soared across. The mare's front legs came down with beautiful precision right on the narrow path. Next would be the hind legs.

But something was wrong. Terribly wrong. Meg felt a jolt. A sickening lurch. It felt as though Patches were turning a somersault. But the mare was all right. It was she alone who flipped through the air, over the horse's head.

She heard the mare's distraught whinny, a shout—Philip's shout—just as she hit the ground with breathtaking force. Stabs of pain shot through her head, her neck and back, and through the arm that had cushioned the fall.

The saddle, she thought numbly. What the deuce happened to the saddle?

A particularly vicious stab of pain pierced her head, and the world went dark and soundless. If she suffered unconsciousness, it could not have been for long, for the next thing she saw was Patches grazing calmly at her feet and Philip vaulting off his horse.

He dropped to his knees beside her. Cradling her face in his hands, he said hoarsely, "Meg, my Meg! Where are you hurt?"

She saw the beads of perspiration on his forehead, the fear in his eyes. She wanted to assure him that she was in pretty good shape considering the circumstances, but what she did say was, "The saddle, Stanbrook. I do believe the bloody thing came off."

A mixture of emotions crossed his face. She couldn't

be bothered to read them all; it was enough to know that one of them was relief. The few words she had uttered apparently convinced him that she was not lying on her death bed.

"I'll check the saddle in a moment," he said. "First let me make sure that you have broken no bones."

She tried to smile at him. "Remember, I was a dancer once. One of the first lessons we learned for the panto-mime was to take a spill."

He looked doubtful. "Do you think you can sit up if I help you?"

"*After* you've checked the saddle."

"Stubborn wench." A reluctant grin displaced the worry lines on his face. "I guess you are all right. But don't you dare move until I get back."

She was quite content for the moment to lie still and watch him as he examined the saddle lying on the ground halfway between her and the brook.

"Bloody hell!" Holding two separate ends of the cinch between his fingers, Philip turned to look at her. "The damned thing was cut!"

Chapter Fifteen

Despite the throbbing in her head, Meg sat up.

"Bloody hell!" she echoed.

Philip carried the saddle over, and together they studied the broken cinch. The upper sides of the two ends were rough and uneven where the break had occurred. Neglected leather might tear that way, but none of the gear in the Carswell Hall stables was ever neglected. And the undersides told their own blood-chilling tale: the leather had been cut smoothly and expertly within a thumbnail's thickness of the upper surface.

"It held as long as we rode at a sedate pace," Philip said tersely. "Might even have held throughout the gallop if there hadn't been the jump."

Feeling quite ill, Meg clamped her mouth shut. She did not want to ask the question burning on her tongue, but when she looked at Philip, she saw it reflected in his eyes.

Who?

Who was so desperate, so mad, to see her hurt or killed that he would cut her saddle girth? Stewart? Alvina? Someone she had not considered before? It was best not to think about the possibilities right now. Her head ached, and the sick feeling in her stomach was getting worse.

"Let me take you to the house."

Philip's voice might be gruff, but his hands were gentle

when he lifted her as though she were but a child. He set her on Beelzebub's back, then mounted behind her. Gratefully, Meg leaned against his broad chest. For now, she was content to let him take charge.

With Patches following in their wake, they rode into the stableyard. It was empty, save for Philip's groom Harv spreading saddle blankets to air in a sunny corner of the yard. He came running the moment he heard the clatter of Beelzebub's hooves.

"My lord! What happened?"

"We'll talk later, Harv." Philip dismounted and immediately lifted Meg down.

Cradling her in his arms, he said sharply to the groom, who was about to lead Beelzebub off, "Leave him for now. Someone else can look after him and the mare. I need you to go down to the brook to fetch the sidesaddle. And you will not let that saddle out of your sight until I tell you otherwise. Is that understood?"

"Aye, my lord."

When the groom was out of earshot, Meg said, "You had better set me down, Stanbrook. If I'm not mistaken, there's Miss Lyndon and her brother driving up."

Philip gave her a crooked grin. "I probably saw the curricle before you did. But I fail to understand why that should stop me from carrying you to your room."

"Well, because—"

Meg frowned, trying to recapture the logic behind her suggestion, but the fall must have addled her brains. Her head still hurt, and all she could think at the moment was that she did not want to be set down. She felt safe and comfortable within the shelter of his arms.

Two of Stewart's grooms came to lead the horses into their stalls, and Philip started for the house, where the curricle had just rolled to a stop at the front door. He had taken only a few steps when Stewart strode out of the stables and hailed them.

"Philip! Megan!"

He caught up with them in a hurry. "Whatever is the

matter? There's Patches without a saddle, and Megan needing to be carried. Did you take a toss, Megan?"

"You might say so."

She looked at him, at the usually cheerful face taut with concern, the gray-green eyes dark with anxiety. It was ridiculous to suspect him even for an instant.

"With Patches?" he asked in disbelief. "But she's so gentle. How did it happen? And where's your saddle?"

When neither Meg nor Philip answered immediately, Stewart said in some alarm, "Don't tell me you rode her bareback!"

"Harv has gone to fetch the saddle," Philip said curtly. "It came off when Meg jumped the brook. The cinch broke."

Stewart blanched. "But that's impossible! All the gear is carefully inspected every day."

Slowing his pace, Philip gave his cousin a hard look. "I'll tell you what I know after I've taken Meg upstairs. She needs rest."

"And the physician." Stewart was recovering his composure. "He's quite a young chap, but very competent, Squire Lyndon says. I'll send for him."

"Rubbish!" From her secure haven in Philip's arms, Meg found it easy to dismiss the offer of a physician's services. "I suffer from nothing more than a headache and, I don't doubt, assorted bumps and bruises. A hot bath and a cup of tea will do me a lot more good than getting prodded and poked."

"Meg is right," said Philip. "If you want to be of help, you might head Evalina and young Lyndon off when we get to the door."

"Yes. Yes, of course."

Although he seemed much calmer, Stewart was still pale. He wiped his brow with a trembling hand, then reached into his coat pocket.

"If I had known . . . if I'd had the slightest inkling," he stammered, "I would have—oh, never mind! Philip, I wanted to give you this."

He held out a clasp knife, and since Philip's hands were otherwise occupied, Meg took it. She recognized it at once. It was the knife she and Stewart had used to cut lilacs. Philip's knife.

"Gracious," she said. "I'd have thought you'd returned it to Philip ages ago. It's a precious heirloom, isn't it?"

"I did give it back. That same day." Some color was returning to Stewart's face, and his voice was now quite steady. "And I do know that Philip values it highly. That's why I picked it up when I saw it lying on the floor of the harness room. I knew Philip would miss it."

"In the harness room?" Meg and Philip echoed simultaneously.

Philip stopped in his stride. They were about forty or fifty paces from the front door, where Miss Lyndon and her brother appeared to be embroiled in an altercation. Neither Meg nor Philip paid attention to the siblings. Their eyes locked in an intense gaze, as though each wanted to read the other's deepest thoughts.

"Meg!" His hold on her tightened painfully. "Don't—"

"Shh." Pressing a finger to his mouth, she silenced him. "There's no need to say anything. I trust you."

She felt his relief. His grip relaxed, and his heart, which had a moment ago drummed hard and fast against her shoulder, resumed its normal beat.

"Is *that* Evalina Lyndon?" Stewart burst out, his voice a blend of disbelief and awe.

Reluctantly, Meg took her gaze from Philip's face.

"Yes." She looked from the young lady, who left her brother on the door stoop and came rushing toward them, to Stewart. "You haven't seen her since she returned to Lyndon Court?"

"No." Stewart stood spellbound as Evalina tripped toward them. "No, I haven't."

"Miss Carswell, what happened?" Ignoring both gentlemen, Evalina peered anxiously at Meg in Philip's arms. "Ralph says I'm nosey, the old stick. He says I

194

must show decorum and not thrust myself at you. But I was so worried when I saw Lord Stanbrook carrying you. Did you take a tumble?"

"Yes. Isn't it mortifying?"

Evalina nodded, making the blond curls peeking beneath a dashing straw hat bounce. "And such a nuisance. One hurts for days in the most inconvenient spots. I know. I've taken more than my share of tosses."

Philip cleared his throat, a maneuver that gained him Miss Lyndon's attention.

She frowned at him. "Lord Stanbrook, I don't know what you can be thinking of. Miss Carswell needs to soak in hot water immediately. It'll relive the soreness. Why are you keeping her here in the yard instead of taking her up to her chamber?"

A little stiffly, he replied, "My dear Miss Lyndon, I was about to do so when you arrived."

"But you were simply *standing* here," she pointed out. "That's why I didn't stay with Ralph, no matter what he said. I wanted to know what's wrong with Miss Carswell."

Assuming a confidential tone, she said to Meg, "Isn't it just like a man to try to put the blame on someone else when he does something stupid?"

Meg carefully avoided looking at Philip. She was certain he, too, remembered that she had said more or less the same in the gazebo.

"Please take me upstairs now, Stanbrook," she murmured, pretending to a greater weakness than she felt. It was either that or give in to the unseemly giggles rising in her throat. "I'm sure Stewart will look after Miss Lyndon until your return."

If Philip had reservations about the arrangements she made for his intended bride, he did not show it. "Don't forget Ralph," he said dryly. "No doubt, Stewart will be delighted to look after him as well."

"Will he?"

Meg peeked around Philip's shoulder as he carried her swiftly toward the house. Her cousin and Miss Lyndon still stood in the same spot. Tilting her head coquettishly, Evalina was smiling up at Stewart. A breeze ruffled her golden curls and the skirt of her cherry-striped gown. It also blew snatches of conversation across the distance.

"Why, Mr. Elmore! I feared I'd never have the pleasure of seeing you. I've been home for over a week, and not once did you . . ."

". . . heard you've turned into a diamond of the first water. But that, Miss Lyndon, is an understatement. You are more beautiful than . . ."

"Oh, Stewart—I mean, Mr. Elmore. That is the prettiest compliment anyone . . ."

Meg darted a look at Philip. His hearing was excellent, as she well knew. He must have heard the flutter of excitement in Miss Lyndon's voice, and the dark, intense note in Stewart's. But Philip did not seem at all perturbed. Or perhaps it was simply his upbringing and social training that enabled him to greet young Mr. Lyndon with every appearance of pleasure and thank him politely for holding the door, while his intended bride flirted.

They encountered no one when Philip carried her to the second floor, and Meg breathed a sigh of relief. As good an actress as she was, she did not know if she would have been able to face her aunt without showing that she believed her fully capable of sneaking into the stables and sabotaging the saddle.

The door to her chamber stood ajar. Without ceremony, Philip elbowed it open and carried her inside. Only then did he set her on her feet.

He looked toward the dressing room whence came the sound of water being poured. "Good," he said. "Your maid is here. I'll leave you to her ministrations."

Despite the firmly stated intentions, Philip lingered. And Meg, reluctant to see him go, took a step toward him.

"Thank you, Stanbrook. I know I'm no featherweight—"

196

"That you're not." The smile in his eyes contradicted the dryness of his tone. "But you're the most delightful nonfeatherweight it's been my privilege to hold in my arms."

"A compliment?" Meg hoped she didn't look quite as pleased as she felt. "Let me return the favor. I think you are indeed more of a hero than you give yourself credit. You're not even out of breath after carrying me all that distance and up the stairs!"

His expression turned grim. "Much as I enjoyed it, we must make sure that I will not be required to act the hero again. For *your* sake."

She wished he hadn't reminded her. For a few minutes she had been able to forget about her bruised body, but now the aches and pains returned tenfold.

"Believe me," she said with feeling, "I'd like nothing better than to make certain. But how can we do it? We have nothing but speculation to go on."

"Leave it to me. I'll come up with a plan."

It was not her nature to leave matters to someone else, but at the moment she did not quite feel up to an argument. The tub Elspeth was filling and the bed behind her drew her aching body irresistibly.

She held out her hand, showing the clasp knife in her palm. "You had better take this."

"Yes." His eyes did not leave her face as he took the knife from her. "I had better, hadn't I?"

Philip softly closed the door. His Meg was safe. For now.

The knife in his hand burned against his skin, as though he were carrying a live ember. He could not believe it was coincidence or mischance that the knife was found in the harness room on the morning Meg's saddle girth was cut. But if it was purpose, who had used the knife, then left it?

And whose knife was it? Sir Richard's or his own?

Philip did not attempt to examine it in the corridor. It was going on ten o'clock. Most of the lights that illuminated the long passageways of Carswell Hall at night had been extinguished, and two dim oil lamps widely spaced on the walls, and the diffused rays of daylight from the mullioned windows at either end of the corridor, did nothing to brighten the gloom. Philip hurried straight to his chamber at the head of the main staircase.

Hawkins was there, his valet of many years. He was tenderly placing a stack of snowy cloths in the cravat drawer and did not look up from the important task when Philip entered the room.

"Your bath is ready, my lord. And I've set out—"

"Never mind the bath, Hawkins." Philip, standing at his bedside table, stared grimly at the bare surface. "Where's my clasp knife? I know I removed it from my pocket before changing for dinner yesterday. I set it down next to the water jug."

"Yes, my lord. I remember. I put it on the dresser this morning, together with your watch."

Philip strode over to the tall chest of drawers with the ornately framed cheval glass on the polished top. Only when he saw the carved ivory handle with its three razor-sharp blades hidden inside did his tense muscles relax slightly.

He shifted the knife Meg had given him to his left hand and picked up his own in the right hand. As he had expected, they felt exactly the same. He carried them to the window and examined them in the bright light. They looked exactly the same.

And yet they shouldn't look the same. Not exactly.

"Hawkins, would you know where to find a magnifying glass?"

He felt the valet's eyes on his back.

"Yes, my lord. I believe Sir Richard occasionally makes use of a magnifying lens. Shall I inquire of Marsden if we may borrow it?"

Philip's pulse quickened. "By all means, ask him."

He occupied the time until Hawkins's return by fingering the handles and tilting them this way and that in the light to get a sharper image of the carvings. But no matter how hard he peered at the initials hidden in the intricate pattern, they stayed the same. P.C.—Philip Carswell, *his* grandfather—on each knife handle.

Yet one of the knives should be initialed R.C.—Richard Carswell, the baronet's grandfather.

On both knives, the ivory was smooth and slightly yellowed, but that was not surprising after decades of use. Neither was it surprising that the carved patterns were faint and almost impossible to feel. But the lines and curves were all visible—save for the short, slanted line that would change a P into an R on one of the knives.

As though he knew how eagerly he was expected, Hawkins returned a scant ten minutes later, flushed and out of breath from hurried negotiations of stairs and passageways that should have been taken at a sedate pace by a self-respecting, middle-aged valet.

"Thank you, Hawkins."

Philip set the knife he had retrieved from the dresser onto the windowsill. With the valet hovering close, he trained the magnifying lens on the knife Stewart had found in the harness room. He stared at the handle for a long time.

Slowly, he held out knife and glass to the valet. He was as certain as he could be about what he had seen. There was no need to check the ivory handle of the second knife.

"Take a look, Hawkins."

Hawkins made no effort to hide his curiosity and puzzlement, but he knew better than to ask questions before he had complied with the request.

After a thorough study of the handle, he said, carefully choosing his words, "It would appear, my lord, that this is your knife."

"So it would."

The valet's gaze slid to the knife on the windowsill. "But *that*, if I am not mistaken, is the knife you took from the dresser."

"You are not mistaken, Hawkins."

The valet opened his mouth as though to say something else, shook his head, and once more directed his attention to the knife in his hand.

Burning with impatience, Philip watched him. More than once during the next minute or so he was tempted to guide the valet's examination of the carvings. But he resisted. Hawkins's father had valeted for Philip's father *and* grandfather; thus Hawkins was familiar with the history of the twin knives. If there was anything to be discovered on the handle, he would find it unassisted and draw his own conclusion. And it would be the same one Philip had drawn—unless Philip had exaggerated to himself the significance of what he'd seen.

The valet set the knife on a small table nearby. He reached for Philip's on the windowsill.

"With your permission, my lord?"

Philip nodded, bracing himself for another prolonged inspection. But Hawkins was satisfied after one quick look at each side of the handle and carefully put the knife back in the window.

"Someone took great pains to make it look as though that one's yours," he said, pointing his thin, long nose toward the knife on the table.

"What makes you say that, Hawkins?"

"Without a magnifying lens, you'd need the eyes of a lynx to see that the ivory is less yellowed around the base of the P. But with the glass, it's as plain as a missing button on a coat that someone scraped or filed away until the R became a P."

"That's what I thought, too."

Alas, there was no satisfaction in having his observation confirmed. It merely showed up the total senselessness of it all.

As the detection, so the alteration of the initial must

have required the use of a magnifying glass—and a very small blade or file. If the knife had been used to cut the girth of Meg's saddle, then was left in the harness room to cast suspicion on him, it would have been so much simpler to just use *his* knife. There was plenty of opportunity to sneak it from his room. Anyone with a grain of sense must know he wouldn't carry the dratted thing in the pocket of an evening coat, and Hawkins was off duty after Philip had changed for dinner. Anyone could enter the chamber at the head of the main staircase and take the knife, without being observed.

So, why wasn't his clasp knife used? Surely, someone preparing to cause injury or even death would not balk at a bit of petty theft? In fact, he had already engaged in theft when he appropriated Sir Richard's.

"But why, my lord? Makes no sense at all changing the initials," said Hawkins, unwittingly echoing Philip's sentiments. "Who'd do a daft thing like that? And what about Sir Richard? He'll be in a towering rage, I don't doubt, when he finds out."

Sir Richard, indeed. How long before he'd miss the heirloom?

With his long stride, Philip took a quick turn about the room. He would have to talk to Cousin Richard about the bloody knife, assure him that it wasn't lost and find out where it was kept and who had access to the baronet's rooms.

But first things first. Hawkins must be informed about the cut saddle girth. The valet was aware of the danger to Meg, since Philip had already asked him to be available to Jigger when the boy had information, but Philip also wanted Hawkins to listen closely to any gossip below stairs. Maids and footmen saw and heard more than they would ever let on to their masters, and they wouldn't put a lock on their tongues in the servants' hall.

He must see Harv. The groom would keep his eyes and ears open in the stables.

Then he'd try to locate the new gardener. In his

concern about Meg's fall he had almost forgotten the scare she'd had in the gazebo.

And, of course, there was Stewart. How much should he tell him?

Hawkins cleared his throat. "Shall I return the magnifying glass, my lord?"

"Yes. But first listen to me. Listen carefully."

Put in a few bald words, the briefing of Hawkins did not take long, and Philip found himself facing the copper tub filled with water that couldn't be called even tepid any longer.

He didn't like cold baths, not since his early days at Harrow, where cold baths had been the lot of a shy nine-year-old. But this morning, he wasn't prepared to wait for more hot water. He wanted to speak to Stewart, as soon as possible. He wanted to see his reaction when he told him that Meg's tumble was not the result of worn leather and a groom's negligence but a deliberate, malicious attempt to bring her to grief.

Fifteen minutes later, hair still damp against his scalp, he made his way downstairs. He was about to turn into the short passage that would take him to Stewart's office at the back of the house when he heard tinkling laughter from the morning room.

Miss Lyndon! Dash it, if he hadn't forgotten all about Evalina's and Ralph's visit. What a nuisance. Stewart was bound to be wherever Miss Lyndon could be found.

As he was about to open the door to the morning room, he thought of some very pungent comments Meg would make if she knew that he considered Evalina a nuisance. And that he had forgotten she was here.

Thus it was that a wry smile twisted his mouth when he entered the room. Wryness deepened to self-mockery when he saw that his cousin and Miss Lyndon were alone. Sitting side by side on the chaise longue, they were quite unaware of his presence.

Stewart possessed himself of Miss Lyndon's hand. "I *will* call you Lina," he said firmly. "It's what I've called you since you started tagging after me and when you were no more than knee-high."

Miss Lyndon blushed prettily. "But it wouldn't be proper, Mr. Elmore. I am no longer a child. I am a grown woman."

"In that case, you must forget about Mr. Elmore and call me Stewart."

Philip knew he should be incensed. But he wasn't. He'd take up the question of propriety with Stewart some other time, he told himself. Right now, he had a more important matter to settle: Meg's safety.

He cleared his throat.

The couple on the chaise longue jerked apart. Evalina's eyes widened. Not apprehensively, as they should, Philip noted. But rather with expectancy, as though the young lady couldn't wait to see how he would react to her conduct.

Devil a bit! If she was thinking of playing Stewart against him, she had better learn patience as well as decorum. He did not have the interest or the time to deal with her coquettishness.

No longer smiling, Philip looked at Stewart. "Cousin, I'd like a word with you. In private."

Chapter Sixteen

Meg heard of the ensuing fracas between Stewart and Philip from Elspeth, who had heard it from James, the footman stationed in the Great Hall. The maid peeked into Meg's chamber shortly before three that afternoon, ostensibly to check whether Meg was rested enough to take some food.

"Yes, I'll have tea and sandwiches," said Meg, who'd had no breakfast and had refused a lunch tray. Now she was feeling quite peckish.

Uncharacteristically, but perhaps not surprisingly, she had been reluctant to leave the comfort of her bed when she awoke from a long nap. She still felt every bone in her body and a niggling pain in the right shoulder. A tray in bed would suit her very well.

"And perhaps," she added expectantly, "Cook has made some raspberry tarts?"

"Aye, that she has. But they'd be from preserves," Elspeth said disdainfully. "It's too soon for fresh raspberries."

"I like preserves."

"Then I'll bring a tray at once."

But Elspeth made no move to leave. Eyes bright with suppressed excitement, she sidled farther into the room.

"Miss Megan, did ye hear about his lordship and Mr. Stewart? James says 'twas a right fine quarrel they had."

"How could I have heard up here in my room? And no one's been to see me or to tell me anything." That sounded self-pitying. Hurriedly, Meg added, "Besides, I've been asleep."

"Well," Elspeth said, judiciously considering the matter, "you wouldn't have heard anything even if you was awake. They weren't shoutin'. Leastways, his lordship wasn't. Mr. Stewart, now, he did raise his voice once or twice."

Meg pushed herself higher against the pillows. "What the dickens did they quarrel about to cause such excitement among the staff?"

"James, he was in the Great Hall trimming the candles, and he says the two gentlemen was in a rare takin' when they came out of the morning room where Mr. Stewart had been entertainin' Miss Lyndon. *Alone!*"

Meg raised a brow. "Hardly alone. Miss Lyndon was in the company of her brother."

"Not then she weren't. She and Mr. Stewart were *quite* alone when his lordship came downstairs."

The image of Evalina and Stewart in the courtyard flashed through Meg's mind: the breeze ruffling the young lady's curls while she smiled up at Stewart. Philip must have lost his temper when he discovered the couple in the morning room without Ralph. It was not surprising, but for some reason, the thought of Philip in a fit of jealousy made her cross.

"I'm sure I don't care if they came to cuffs," she muttered. "Or if they'll be meeting with pistols at dawn." She gave a little sniff and, with more force than conviction, reiterated, "I don't give a straw!"

Clearly, Elspeth believed this as little as Meg herself did. Giving her a knowing look, the maid giggled and said, "Aye, and that would teach 'em, wouldn't it?"

Meg deemed it prudent to leave well enough alone.

Swallowing her pride, she asked, "Are you going to tell me what happened, or not?"

"I'll tell."

Eagerly and with a great amount of relish, Elspeth retold the tale as she had heard it from James. According to the footman, both gentlemen had come storming out of the morning room. The instant the door closed behind them, Mr. Stewart had rounded on his lordship.

"There's no need to 'have a word with me'!" Mr. Stewart said heatedly. "I'll have you know that Ralph left but a moment ago. He thought one of his horses was casting out a splint, and he went to check on him before starting out for home."

"What the devil are you talking about?" His lordship scowled. "Have I said a word about Ralph? I want to talk to you about Meg."

If Lord Stanbrook thought this would calm Mr. Stewart, he was dead wrong. If anything, it made him look angrier.

"You're *not* taking me to task about Miss Lyndon? About holding her hand? So that's how you value her reputation. You don't care a rush!"

"The devil take you, Elmore! We are talking at cross purposes."

"We are not!" Mr. Stewart's voice rose in outrage. "You want to talk about Megan. That's how it's been from the beginning. You can think and speak of no one but Megan. Don't think I don't know about the designs you had on her! And perhaps still have."

"Elmore, I warn you—"

"And at the same time you're pursuing Lina—Miss Lyndon. But you don't really care about her, do you? Yet you'll marry her because she'd make a good countess, while Megan would not."

"The devil you say!"

His lordship grabbed Mr. Stewart by the lapels of his coat. "How dare you belittle Meg! She has more dignity than Evalina will ever possess."

"Then why don't you marry Megan?"

Lord Stanbrook let go of Mr. Stewart's coat. He said nothing, just stood there with the strangest look on his face.

"Cat got your tongue, Stanbrook?" Mr. Stewart mocked. "Just remember this! Megan is my cousin, and I'll call you out if you dare offer her *carte blanche*."

His lordship stared at him a moment longer. He visibly relaxed, and when he spoke, his voice was so calm it was hard to believe that a moment ago he'd gone for Mr. Stewart as though he were ready to mill him down.

"Now, if only you'd decide which of the two ladies you wish to champion."

Mr. Stewart's face flushed an angry red. "Both, if I must!"

"Come now, Stewart. Enough of this wrangling. We have an important matter to discuss."

"If you don't think Lina's happiness and Megan's virtue important—"

"Cut line! The matter I'm talking about is the saddle that came off when Meg jumped the brook. It was no accident. Some Bedlamite cut the girth."

At this point, according to the footman's report, several things happened all at once.

Mr. Stewart uttered a phrase no one had ever heard from his fastidious tongue before.

Miss Lyndon, opening the morning room door and peeking into the Great Hall, asked, "Is it safe to come out yet?"

Mr. Ralph Lyndon strode in through the front door and, catching sight of the cousins, said cheerfully, "No sign of a splint or anything. So I'll be taking Evalina off your hands."

And James, alas, dropped the scissors he had used to trim the candlewicks, alerting his lordship and Mr. Stewart to the fact that they'd had a witness to their altercation.

Elspeth, carried away by the retelling, sighed dramatically. "And a real shame it was that James made such a clatter. His lordship, he glared at James, then straightaway handed Miss Lyndon over to her brother. And no

208

sooner was the door shut behind 'em than he bundled Mr. Stewart off to his office, and no one knows what happened next."

The maid looked expectantly at Meg, but Meg was too much in a daze to notice.

Philip had *not* quarreled with Stewart in a fit of jealousy. In fact, he had jumped on Stewart for saying she wouldn't make a good countess!

On the other hand, he had not denied that he had designs of an improper nature on her. And when Stewart challenged him to marry her, he had been struck speechless.

What did it all mean? If only she'd been there to see Philip's face.

And what was she to think of Stewart's fierce championship? He was prepared to fight for her virtue, no less.

"Miss Megan."

Reluctantly, Meg focused on the maid.

"Will you be marryin' his lordship, then?"

"No, of course not." Meg raised a brow to counteract the note of regret that had stupidly crept into her voice. "Whatever gave you such a daft notion? I am an actress, remember?"

Elspeth's face fell, but she wasn't one to give in to disappointment easily. "There's been other actresses as married lords. And you're the daughter of a baronet as well!"

Meg was silent. She remembered the excitement, the flash of hope among the dancers and actresses when one of them married above her station. After all, if it happened to one, it could happen to another. A maid would feel the same way.

Neither, Meg noted in a spurt of grim humor, was the daughter of a baronet exempt from foolish dreams.

But miracles happened so rarely. A lord would not only have to be deeply in love with his actress—or seamstress, or maid—to marry her; he'd also need the strength of character to fight for her acceptance by the *ton*. And if not acceptance, then at least tolerance, or the poor woman would find herself sentenced to a solitary life within her own home.

Philip certainly did not lack in strength of character, but Meg did not believe he was the man to take it lightly if his wife were merely tolerated. It would be a severe blow to his pride.

Quite subdued by the prolonged silence, Elspeth asked, "And the saddle girth, Miss Megan? Was it really cut?"

There was no use denying it. Philip had already let the cat out of the bag.

"Yes, Elspeth. I'm afraid so."

"Fie and foul!" the girl cried indignantly. "Who'd do a rotten thing like that?"

"I'd give up a season at the Drury Lane to know the answer to that question."

If Meg had felt neglected earlier, she had no cause for complaint after she had consumed a light repast of watercress sandwiches and raspberry tarts.

The first to pay a visit was her aunt. After the most cursory of knocks, Alvina sailed into the room.

"Megan, my dear!"

Was there concern in Alvina's voice? Meg could hardly believe her ears. None of the previous occasions, least of all the spat after the will change or the brittle apology Alvina had delivered during dinner at Sir Richard's insistence, had led her to believe that her aunt felt anything but acute dislike for her.

Pulling up a chair, the older woman sat down by the bed.

"I did not know you'd had a fall until moments ago, when I returned from Ascot. You did not come to harm?"

"A bruise or two. Nothing worse."

Her aunt's eyes flicked over her, and Meg shivered.

210

Had she actually seen, or had she only imagined, the flash of regret in those cold gray-green eyes?

Alvina said, "I could hardly believe it when Stewart told me you'd taken a tumble! And on that nice little mare—what did you christen her? Patches, I think. But it seems utterly impossible that you should have been thrown. Only yesterday Philip was bragging about your horsemanship."

Meg listened to Alvina in growing astonishment. Such garrulity. Such . . . pleasantness. But it rang false.

And didn't Alvina know about the cut girth? Stewart knew. Hadn't he told his mother?

"I believe the best of riders will take an occasional toss," Meg said cautiously. "But this fall need not have happened. You see, the saddle came off when I jumped the brook."

"Tut, tut." Alvina shook her head sorrowfully. "Such carelessness. It reminds me of the time your father took a fall."

Meg had been prepared for astonishment or shock, pretended or real, but not for a reference to her father.

"Are you talking about the accident when he rode after my mother?"

"Yes, he jumped a hedge he had jumped countless times before. But that time, he came to grief. Broke his collarbone and a leg, I believe."

"Yes, he told me. I was lucky, I suppose. I did not break anything."

"So Stewart assured me, and that wasn't why I said it reminded me. It was the saddle. Your father's came off, too."

"It did? How?"

"The cinch gave out. Tore right in two."

Meg's mind was awhirl. Her father's saddle had come off. A worn cinch? Had her father been a careless master who allowed negligence?

"Rest easy, my dear." Alvina smiled that chilling smile that did not reach her eyes. "Stewart will discover who-

211

ever gave you a defective saddle—if that was what happened. And he'll dismiss the man without a reference."

"I'm sure he will," Meg said absently.

Why was her aunt talking so much, even delving into the past? It was so very unlike her.

"Unless, of course—" Alvina muttered, then, irritatingly, fell silent.

Impatiently, Meg asked, "Unless what?"

"Unless, of course, it was Philip's groom," Alvina said slowly, as though giving the matter deep thought. "Stewart can hardly dismiss a man not in his employ."

Meg bristled. "I don't think you need to worry about Harv. I have always found him to be very conscientious."

Alvina smiled. "I'm sure you have."

As on previous occasions, Meg marveled how anyone could smile while the eyes stayed ice-cold.

An awkward silence fell between them, but Meg made no attempt to break it. She was still thinking about her father's accident. Had it been truly that—an accident? And if not—

Alvina's voice cut into her thoughts.

"Elspeth tells me that you went to see Nanny Grimshaw this morning. How was she, the poor dear?"

"As well as can be expected of a woman her age."

"Did she know who you are?"

Alerted by a tense note in Alvina's voice, Meg chose her words carefully. "I don't believe she did. She seemed to be living totally in the past. Kept talking of Miss Lydia. I wondered, could Nanny even have known her?"

The tenseness left Alvina. "Of course she knew Lydia. They were born the same year. Of different mothers, naturally; but of the same father."

"They were . . . half-sisters?"

"Happens in the best of families," Alvina said dourly. "My grandfather was a virile man. He survived three wives and still had the reputation of a terrible rake even

212

in his seventies. Lydia and Nanny were born when he was five-and-seventy."

So, Alvina's grandfather, who was also, of course, Sir Richard's grandfather, was Nanny's father. Which made Nanny Grimshaw a sort of aunt to Sir Richard and Alvina. Meg groaned inwardly. The whole family situation seemed awfully twisted.

She remembered a remark made by Nanny Grimshaw, that Lydia was getting to be like Alvina, uppity and downright spiteful. It had made no sense then and made none now, since it could only have been Alvina who acted like her Aunt Lydia.

"How old were you when Lydia died?"

Alvina sniffed and gave her a don't-you-know-anything look.

"I wasn't even born when Lydia died—of smallpox, just after her seventeenth birthday. But Richard knew her. He was about seven or eight then."

Which confirmed that Nanny's mind had indeed condensed time and that she imagined generations living side by side when they could not possibly have done so.

"They should never have let the two girls grow up together," said Alvina. "It gave Nanny airs. I was her first nursling here at Carswell Hall—she had several positions before that, but none hereabout—and I remember her as a very uppity young woman."

Uppity, Meg thought wryly. That's what Nanny had called Alvina.

"When I was old enough for a governess," Alvina continued, "Nanny Grimshaw left again. Then, when I was expecting Richard—" She paused, as though she had lost the thread of what she wanted to say. "Richard convinced my husband that Nanny Grimshaw's place was with me."

Wishing her shoulder would stop hurting, Meg moved restlessly. Once again, her aunt was unusually forthcoming. But whatever the reason, Alvina's confiding mood suited Meg very well. She still had more questions about the old nurse.

"And when Mr. Elmore died and you came back to Carswell Hall," Meg prompted, "you brought Nanny as well. How long ago was that?"

"Stewart was two; that would make it thirty years ago." Alvina looked as though she had bitten into a lemon. "And she's been here ever since, in that cottage Richard deeded to her."

Meg felt a rush of warmth for her father. He had made it possible for the woman who but for a slight of nature would have been his aunt, to settle in her birthplace.

"How did she keep busy? There were no more young children to care for after Mother left with me, or am I wrong?"

"There was Ralph Lyndon—he's about your age— and, later, Evalina. But Nanny also knows midwifery. The tenant families still call her when there's a lying-in. But she should be put away," Alvina said tersely. "She's not right in the head—a menace to us all."

"You're exaggerating, surely!"

"I am not. The old woman is quite, quite mad. Your father won't listen to me, but perhaps if *you* spoke to him he'd pay attention. He must send her away!"

So that was the reason for Alvina's readiness to talk. She wanted Meg's help to put Nanny into one of the horrid almshouses.

"Aunt, I would not deliver my worst enemy to a charity home. And neither would you, had you ever visited one. Besides, Nanny is a little mixed-up at times, but she is not mad."

"One visit doesn't qualify you to judge," Alvina said sharply. "I tell you, the old woman is insane. Danger-ously so!"

"Why? What does she do?"

"Twice this past sennight, I've caught her in the east tower, muttering to herself, poking through the rooms as if she's looking for something. And when I asked her

214

what she was doing, she had the impertinence to shake her fist at me and—"

Alvina broke off. She cocked her head, listening.

A moment later, Meg heard it, too: the tap-tap of a cane and the slow, shuffling approach of footsteps in the hallway.

Chapter Seventeen

A flush of pleasure warmed Meg's cheeks. Her father, coming to see her!

Eagerly, she answered the knock and watched as Sir Richard, supported by his cane on one side and Marsden's arm on the other, walked slowly into the room.

He cast a quick, anxious look toward the bed, then turned to Alvina.

"Thank you for keeping my daughter company. I will relieve you now," he said politely but firmly.

Alvina's mouth compressed. Without a word, she rose and sailed out of the room as majestically as she had entered.

Meg was never more glad to see her aunt go. Close relation or not, she could not bring herself to like or even respect the lady. Send Nanny to the almshouse, indeed!

Meg's pawnbroker mentor Mr. Finney had taken her to one of those charity homes where the old, the infirm of body and mind were "looked after." She had been appalled and sickened. Surely, the inhabitants' suffering must equal that of the poor souls condemned to Dante's hell.

When she said as much to Mr. Finney's daughter, a wardress in that horrid place, Miss Finney's face had puckered up. "It's worse, Meg. Much worse. And if anyone offered me another position, I'd grab it with both hands."

"Megan!" Sir Richard's short-sighted eyes peered at her with concern. "You look . . . distressed. Not put out that I routed Alvina, are you?"

Shaking off the memory of almshouses and suffering, she said, "On the contrary. I am grateful. I only hope my aunt won't upset Cook again and delay dinner."

He gave her a crooked grin. "If you believe that, it just shows you don't yet know Alvina. She takes too much pride in her housekeeping to make such a slip twice."

"Please sit down. And, Marsden, pull up a chair for yourself." Meg leaned back against the pillows. "I must say, this is rather more pleasant than I thought it would be. I might stay in bed all afternoon and evening to receive visitors."

"And why shouldn't you?" Bushy white brows drew together in a frown. "You've had a nasty spill. You ought to spoil yourself a little."

This was a novel concept to Meg, but before she could explore it, another thought struck her.

"You don't leave your rooms during the day, so you wouldn't have heard about me at luncheon. Who was the numbskull that went running to you with the tale of my fall, Father?"

"Megan. Daughter." Sir Richard's voice was hoarser than usual. "This is the first time you've called me Father."

She smiled at him, a smile part winsome, part apologetic.

"I've called you Father in my mind. But I suppose I've been rather hardheaded about addressing you as such." Resolution deepened her voice. "No longer, though."

Back in a corner of the room, out of Meg's line of vision, Marsden blew his nose.

Meg's eyes met Sir Richard's, and once more a crooked grin twisted his mouth. "Marsden was always one to get maudlin," he said, then turned serious. "You're a devilish fine woman, Megan. You are like Rosemary,

218

warm-hearted and generous."

"I wish I were," Meg said ruefully. "I have a temper and quite a broad streak of selfishness. If that isn't as obvious as it might be, it's thanks to Fletcher's influence."

"You loved that man, didn't you, daughter?"

"Yes."

"I would have liked to shake his hand for what he did for you and Rosemary. I wish I could have known him."

"So do I."

Meg blinked suspiciously moist eyes. "Like Marsden, I've always been one to get maudlin. But," she said firmly, "that's no reason to forget about immediate matters. And my most immediate concern is the blathering idiot who went running to you to tell you about my tumble. I'll give him a trimming he won't forget."

"You'll get your chance. He asked permission to see you in about half an hour."

"Asked permission? You mean to tell me it was Stewart?"

Her father looked amused. "Can't say I blame you for jumping to a conclusion. Thanks to Alvina, Stewart's a stickler for propriety."

Not, thought Meg, where Miss Evalina Lyndon was concerned.

"But it wasn't Stewart who asked my permission to see you in your chamber."

Her eyes widened. "You cannot mean Stanbrook?"

"Ho! Can I not? You'll find out soon enough."

"But then it was Philip who told you about my fall." Meg frowned. Hadn't they agreed last night that her father must not be worried?

"And what's wrong with that, young lady? Doesn't a father have the right to know when his daughter meets with an accident?"

She managed a light tone. "Since you put it that way, I'd sound churlish if I said no. But I do hope you didn't worry too much."

"Philip said the saddle came off."

The devil take all meddlers! With an effort, she stopped herself from speaking her thoughts aloud. But how dare he approach her father with matters she wished undisclosed!

"He mentioned a worn cinch," said Sir Richard, watching her closely. "Which I find hard to believe. Stewart is a strict taskmaster. He'd summarily dismiss any groom who neglected his duties."

"Did you dismiss the groom who put a saddle with a worn girth on *your* horse that night you went after my mother?"

Sir Richard scowled. "And how did you hear about that? I don't recall giving you details about my accident."

"Alvina told me. She said your saddle came off just like mine when you jumped that hedge."

"The tattler." He looked more confused and perturbed than angry. "But never mind. My mishap is water under the bridge."

A chair scraped against the floorboards somewhere in the back of the chamber. Marsden. Meg had quite forgotten about her father's valet.

"Sir Richard's fall was no accident, Miss Megan." Marsden shuffled toward the bed, his seamed face set in rigid lines, the look in his eyes determined. "His saddle girth was cut."

Saddle girth cut . . . saddle girth cut . . . The words rang in her mind.

"Marsden!" the baronet roared. "You forget your place."

"That may be so, sir, and you can dismiss me if you like. But beating around the bush never did no good, and even though his lordship said nothing to the point, you were fretting that Miss Megan's saddle may have been tampered with as well."

Sir Richard glared at the valet, then slowly turned back to Meg.

220

"Marsden—damn his impudent soul!—is right. I *am* worried. I *am* wondering whether your tumble wasn't an accident, either. Didn't want to say anything to you, though. After all, nothing may be wrong. No need for you to get alarmed if nothing's amiss."

Meg didn't know what to say. She had not meant for her father to know about the ugly incident. But Philip, without consulting her, had visited Sir Richard and had said something to arouse his suspicion.

Meg's hands itched to box his lordship's noble ears. "Father, what exactly did Stanbrook say to start you fretting about my accident?"

"It wasn't anything he said. It was the knife that started me wondering. The clasp knife Stewart found."

"In the harness room," said Marsden.

Meg went cold inside. "But it was Philip's. Father, you cannot possibly believe that he would harm me! Not Philip!"

"So the girth *was* cut."

She saw the look on her father's face—shock, pain, more confusion—and called herself all kinds of fool. In her haste to assure him of Philip's innocence, she had confirmed what had been only a suspicion.

She sighed, "Yes, the girth was cut. But *his* knife or not, Stanbrook had nothing to do with it. I know it as surely as . . . as I know my own two names," she finished on a lighter note.

"Of course he didn't," Sir Richard said testily. "And it isn't his knife. It's mine. The damned thing disappeared the night *my* saddle girth was cut, and I hadn't seen it since."

"*Your* knife! But, of course. Philip mentioned that there were two. One with his grandfather's initials, the other with your grandfather's."

"That's what should have been. Both knives now have the initials P.C. It's natural that the carving has faded after all these years, Philip said. But I wonder."

"You wonder whether someone deliberately changed

221

the initial?"

"Aye."

Her thoughts tumbled. It was quite possible that the person who had tampered with her saddle had wanted it to look as though Philip were the culprit. Quite possible, even probable.

And about one thing there was no doubt at all. The past and the present were inextricably interwoven.

A leaden weight settled in the pit of her stomach. Somehow the knowledge that her father had also been deliberately placed in peril made the danger to herself more real, more immediate.

"Apparently, then," she mused aloud, "someone did not want you to go after Mother and me. And unless you believe it possible that your knife accidentally disappeared at that time and someone just happened to find it and for some reason forgot to return it to you—"

"I don't believe any such rubbish!" Sir Richard glared at her. "And neither do you."

"No," Meg said quietly. "But, in that case, the only alternative is that whoever wanted to stop you from following Mother also wants to—to do what? Hurt me?"

She took a deep breath and, for the first time, put the ugly thought into words. "Kill me?"

Into the silence that followed her terse question, Marsden said, "If you're dead, Miss Megan, you cannot inherit."

Meg saw her father's face turn ashen, and said hastily, "This is all nonsense. Stewart and Philip are the only ones who'd benefit from my death. Father, you already ruled out Philip. Surely you don't believe Stewart, your own nephew, capable of such depravity? Besides, at the time of your accident, he was only eight. Hardly of an age to hatch a sinister plot."

But someone could have put the boy up to it. Someone the young Stewart would obey. Or perhaps it had been presented to him as a prank to play on his uncle.

She said none of this aloud. It was a possibility too

222

horrible to contemplate. But neither was the second possibility any more palatable.

That Alvina might have wanted to prevent a reconciliation between her brother and his detested low-class wife Meg could, if not condone, then understand. But would she do it in a manner that would risk her brother's life?

Meg looked anxiously at her father. He was so quiet. Just what was he thinking?

"Father? You don't believe it was Stewart, do you?"

With an effort, Sir Richard roused himself. He snorted. "No. Stewart's too much of a milksop. But there are others who'd do anything for the boy if they believed him slighted."

Others? Meg knew of only one. But she would not point a finger at her father's sister. And she wondered how well Sir Richard knew his nephew. Stewart was not as masterful as Philip—but a milksop?

"There's Martha Grimshaw," said Sir Richard. "She came to tell me about Rosemary that night. Told me Rosemary had left. But, dammit! She did not want me to go after her."

"Why not?"

"How the deuce should I know?" Increased testiness was a sign that Sir Richard was growing tired. "'Twasn't at all like her to make a fuss, but she made one then. I finally pushed her aside. She screeched at me, said I wouldn't like the consequences if I didn't listen. The child wasn't safe here."

"Why wasn't I safe?" Meg asked urgently. "Did she say?"

"Didn't say a word that made sense, and I wasn't about to waste time with her when I should have been on my way."

The child wasn't safe. A slap in the face just to make certain she knew that the ugliness, the menace, was directed at her alone.

Feeling quite ill, Meg leaned against the pillows.

And her mother must have known it. That was why she had been afraid, why she had been desperate enough to run away to brave the dark night and a long, difficult journey to London with a two-week-old infant.

Again, Meg was roused from her thoughts by Sir Richard's silence. Quite obviously lost in memories, he was staring at a point above her head. She would have liked to ask him whether Nanny Grimshaw could have cut his saddle girth, whether the consequences she had warned about could have been a threat to him.

But it hardly mattered. Meg did not really believe Nanny was the person they sought, even if Alvina said she was dangerously insane. If Nanny poked around in the east tower, she was a danger to herself, not to others.

Marsden shuffled closer and gently touched Sir Richard's arm. "It's time for your cordial and a little rest, sir."

The baronet frowned. "Martha Grimshaw always did have a soft spot for Stewart," he muttered. "But, confound it! She liked Rosemary, too."

He had not addressed anyone in particular, and Meg did not think he expected a reply. In any case, she would not have known what to say.

Sir Richard fumbled for his cane. "Still and all . . . this is a damnable business. I cannot let it go unremarked this time. What a fool I was. What a bloody fool."

"Father?" Meg looked at him in some alarm. "What do you mean, you cannot let it go? What do you plan to do?"

"Summon Potter again. After that—we'll see. Marsden, your arm!"

Deftly, the valet helped him rise. "May I suggest, sir, that you consult with Lord Stanbrook? He'll know what's best to be done. His lordship will be here any moment. Miss Megan can tell him that you wish to see him."

"Aye." Sir Richard's shoulders straightened, as though a weight had been removed. "Philip will know what to do. I can leave matters in his hands."

Meg stared at her father. Leave matters in Philip's

224

hands? This was preposterous! After Philip had made such a mull of it by going to the old man in the first place?

However, when she saw the relief on Sir Richard's face, she swallowed the caustic remark hovering on the tip of her tongue. She wouldn't destroy whatever peace of mind her father had gained—but she would certainly shatter Philip's.

The opportunity arose sooner than expected. She could still hear the tapping of her father's cane in the hallway when a peremptory knock heralded Philip's arrival.

With relish, she bade him enter. She knew the dangerous glitter in her eyes would put him on the alert, but she did not care. Perhaps she even wanted him to notice.

"Stanbrook! Just the man I wanted to see."

He stopped in his stride. A wary look crossed his face, and he closed the door with exaggerated care.

"Why do I get the feeling you should have said *en garde* instead of 'just the man I wanted to see'?"

Her voice was deceptively mild. "Perhaps because you are a man of great perception?"

"Ah, yes. Cousin Richard came to see you." Philip's mouth twitched. "Not that it takes perception on my part to be aware of his visit. I heard his cane as I approached your door."

Her eyes narrowed. "You should have met him in the corridor. Unless—"

"Unless I came from Alvina's room or from the east tower."

Philip strolled toward the bed. Instead of sitting in the chair her father and Alvina had previously occupied, he sat down on the edge of the bed. Instantly, the large chamber seemed much too confining.

He looked at her.

And suddenly, Meg was painfully aware that she was in bed, clad in a nightgown—which, admittedly, concealed more of her than a dinner gown, but was quite definitely an intimate garment. To make matters worse, her hair, relieved of its pins in deference to an aching head, was tumbling in a riotous mass around her shoulders and down her back.

Definitely, she was at a disadvantage opposite the sartorial elegance of immaculate Hessian boots, creaseless pantaloons, and a coat that fit as though it were molded to Philip's broad shoulders. And it didn't matter that he, along with hundreds of spectators, had seen her on the stage in far more scandalous attire.

This was here and now. She had planned to read him a thundering scold, to rake him over the coals—and all she could think of was the bedcover and how nicely it would hide her from head to toe, if only she could pull it a little higher. But Philip was sitting on it.

He smiled that special smile that made her heart turn somersaults. "How do you feel, my Meg? Did the bath and the rest help?"

"Yes, they did. I feel perfectly fine."

She dismissed the notion of hiding under the covers. "*Did* you go into the tower, Philip?"

He nodded absently, as though a visit to the east tower were of no consequence at all. If the look in his eyes, warm with concern and tenderness, had not disarmed her, she would have been very annoyed indeed.

"Why did you go there? Why did you go without me? You *knew* I wanted to see the rooms my mother occupied."

"I'll take you just as soon as you have recovered."

"Tell me what you found. Did you see my mother's rooms?"

"I could hardly miss them." He finally paid her questions due attention. "As in the west tower, there are only two chambers on each floor. The ground floor has a small kitchen and a pantry, the first floor two sitting rooms, and the second floor a bedroom and a dressing room."

"I take it they are furnished?"

"Yes." He hesitated. "There's a bed, a crib, and a rocking chair in the bedchamber. The wardrobe is filled with gowns, and a chest of drawers contains what must be an infant's necessities."

An infant's necessities.

Philip went on to describe the rooms on the third and fourth floors just below the turret, but Meg listened with only half an ear. Her mind was preoccupied with the chamber containing the crib. *Her* crib. *Her* baby garments. Her mother's gowns. She must see them for herself.

Without conscious thought, she shifted her body as though getting ready to leave the bed, and winced when a particularly nasty twinge in her shoulder reminded her to move with caution.

Philip broke off in mid-sentence. "What is it? You're in pain! Dash it! I shouldn't have listened to you but let Stewart send for the physician."

"Nonsense."

Any further protest remained unspoken, for Philip leaned toward her and she was aware of nothing but his nearness, his touch—light and impersonal as he ran his hands down her arms, along her neck and back.

He might have been checking a horse for injuries, she thought dazedly as her skin started to tingle and glow with warmth under his fingers. And that with a long-sleeved, high-necked gown of best Irish linen enveloping her!

She closed her eyes tightly and gripped the bedcover lest she succumb to temptation and fling her arms around him. She wanted to hold him, wanted him to hold and kiss her, wanted—

Why was it that he remained so cool when she responded to him like a moth to the flame? Wanting to get closer and closer despite the danger inherent in such wanton desires.

"Meg." The huskiness of his voice was like a caress. "Where does it hurt?"

"I don't remember."

She raised her face a little and, without looking, she knew that he was very close. She could smell the scent of him, the familiar sandalwood. She heard his breathing—rapid, as though he'd been running—and the warmth of his breath fanned the side of her face and her neck.

Her eyes flew open and met his, dark and unfathomable like a deep well. But for an instant, the fraction of a heartbeat, she also saw the flame of desire.

It was gone immediately and he drew away from her.

Raising a brow, he said severely, "In that case, my Meg, we will definitely ask the physician to call. Not remembering could be a sign of concussion."

She smiled. Exultation flowed through her veins, stirring her blood. He had recovered nicely, but too late. She had seen the flame. He was *not* unaffected.

She became aware of his gaze on her, the beginning of an answering smile. Once more, he leaned close. With an arm on either side of her, he braced himself against the headboard.

"You may be an actress, and a dashed good one to boot, but off the stage you are transparent as glass. Yes, my Meg," he said, gently mocking her and himself, "I would have liked to make love to you. But I am glad to know that there's a shred of decency left in me."

"*Decency?*" And she had none of that commodity, presumably!

Ignoring a bothersome shoulder, Meg thrust her fists against his chest and pushed him away.

"Or was it prudence, my lord, that brought you to your senses?"

"Who can tell?" He gave her an unreadable look. "In the end, there is no difference between the two."

She knew it was prudence that made him draw back. If he'd been caught in a compromising embrace with her, he would have felt *compelled* to marry her. Perish the thought!

He rose. One hand jammed into the pocket of his coat, he took a quick turn about the room. When he stopped by the bed and looked at her again, not a trace of a smile or self-mockery remained on his face.

"I have decided to drive up to town. Tonight."

Chapter Eighteen

"What?" Letting the bedcovers slip where they would, Meg sat bolt upright. "Devil a bit, Stanbrook! *Not* without me!"

"I admit, leaving you worried me at first. But I know exactly how to keep you safe,"

"That's not what I meant!"

He brushed the objection aside. "You *are* still in pain, and I will personally fetch the physician to see you. I'll make certain he orders rest in bed for you and we'll have Elspeth set up a truckle bed here in your room. That way I can be assured of your safety until I return."

Meg had listened with growing indignation. Now she said coldly, "And when, pray tell, will it suit you to return?"

"Before Miss Lyndon's party, I assure you."

As though the party was of concern to her! Did he think she'd be afraid to attend the bloody gathering without him?

The chill in her voice dropped another degree. "And I am to stay in bed until the day after tomorrow?"

The expressive dark brows rose a fraction. So he had finally realized that his plan did not have her unqualified approval, the slowtop.

Sitting down on the edge of the bed again, he said coaxingly, "Meg, be sensible. After what happened this morning, we cannot wait. We must discover what we can about the early attacks. And the place to ask questions about those is London."

If only he didn't sound so dashed reasonable. Well, she could be logical and sensible, too.

"I see your point, Stanbrook. But you must admit that I would know better than you where to start looking and whom to question. Besides, I wanted to call on my mother's old friends, the ones she visited even after she became 'Mrs. Fletcher' and lived in Seven Dials."

"Meg, I will not take you along. You *are* hurt. You'd be very uncomfortable in the curricle, especially since I don't intend to stop except for a change of horses."

"I am *not* hurt." She held her temper on a tight rein. "I have a twinge of pain now and then because I strained a muscle when I used my arm to cushion the fall. It is nothing that would make me a poor traveler."

He ignored her. "You furnish me with the necessary directions, and I'll enlist the help of your friends the Fants and that of the Bow Street magistrate you've been talking about. With their assistance, I'm bound to get some answers fast. I'll return with as much information as can possibly be uncovered about the attempts on your life and even about the fire—why your grandfather's neighbors lied to Alvina."

"Which will be scant information at best," she said bitterly. "Storekeepers and the Dials tenants do not confide in the law or in the nobility. But you'll go ahead anyway, won't you? Whether I agree to the scheme or not."

He looked amused. "Yes. And I don't believe you'd expect it any other way."

A part of her agreed with him, but the other part—the independent, stubborn Meg Fletcher side of her—bristled at the hint that she might welcome his masterful ways.

"Well, you're wrong! I can look after myself and I prefer to make my own decisions."

"Then we are in perfect accord. I want you to look after yourself—by staying in bed. And you can make any decision you want—as long as it's a reasonable one."

Her temper flared. "I would, for example, have preferred not to worry my father with tales of my accident. But *you* took matters into your own hands. *You* told him the saddle came off, and if that's not bad enough, you also showed him the bloody knife that was in all likelihood used to cut the girth!"

"I admit I blundered there. In more ways than one. But if he hadn't learned of your accident from me, he'd have heard it sooner or later from one of the servants."

"*Accident!*" Her voice dripped scorn. "That was not what you proclaimed in the Great Hall. 'Some Bedlamite cut the girth,' is what James heard you say. Dash it, Stanbrook! You might as well have told the town crier."

"I know," he said quietly. "I lost my head for a moment."

His eyes were watchful, guarded. But if he wondered how much more she had learned about his altercation with Stewart, he did not ask.

And she was not about to enlighten him.

"In any case, I would have spoken with your father sometime today. I felt I had to tell him about the knife. I feared he'd miss it and get upset. I know I'd be if I thought I had mislaid my grandfather's knife."

Meg's bursts of anger never lasted long. She darted one more dagger-look at Philip, then settled back to mull over his words. Did he not know, even now, that her father's knife had disappeared twenty-four years ago?

"I suppose no harm was done," she conceded. "On the contrary. If you hadn't told him, I might never have learned that my father's saddle girth was cut as well. Quite likely, with the same knife."

She met his startled look. "You were not aware of that?"

"No. I sure as hell was not. But it makes sense. It certainly explains his apprehension when he asked where the knife was found. What else did he tell you?"

While she filled Philip in on the details she had learned about the night her mother fled, it occurred to her that Philip's decision to drive up to town might not be a bad one after all. She could use his absence to do a bit of sleuthing on her own.

There was no reason, however, for bringing her intentions to Philip's notice. She did not doubt he'd object to her plans—just as she did not doubt she'd go ahead, no matter what he said. After all, *he* had paid no heed when she asked to go to London with him.

Only one more point must be raised between them: her father's decision to send for Potter.

"I would like you to dissuade Father," she told Philip. "If the will is changed now, the attempts on my life might cease and we'll never catch whoever is behind the attacks."

Philip's brows drew together in a deep frown. "If I were convinced the attempts would stop as soon as the will is changed, I'd personally fetch Potter. But I am not. I believe we are dealing with a madman. Or a madwoman. Until we know who it is, I'd always fear for your safety."

Meg shivered. "Neither would I feel easy. So you'll speak with Father?"

Philip hesitated. "I wish I knew what's best."

"Father thinks you know. He wants to leave the matter in your capable hands."

The frown did not lift.

"Isn't it much better that I am the intended victim than have the lunatic suddenly turn against Father for fear that he might change his mind yet again?"

She saw the struggle of emotions on Philip's face— apprehension, a desire to tell her not to talk nonsense, even a flash of admiration, and, finally, resignation.

"That's my Meg." The merest hint of regret crept into his voice. "Trained to take care of herself and determined to protect others."

"Does that mean you'll speak with Father?"

"Yes, my skeptical lady. I'll speak with him. I am just as determined as you are to put a stop to the madman."

Philip had left shortly after the promise he had been so reluctant to give, carrying with him a list of names and addresses in London. At the top of the list, Meg had written *Lady Maryann and Stephen Fant, Fant House, Curzon Street*. Philip had been confident—cocksure—of success, but Meg did not hold out much hope that he would discover anything.

Without his disturbing presence, she should have been able to sit back and assess the bits and pieces she had gathered from her aunt and her father. Instead, she mulled over certain aspects of the altercation between Philip and Stewart—a fruitless effort, one that had her mind going in circles before long.

She could quite easily picture Philip clutching Stewart by the lapels of his coat, but she could not come up with a reason for this show of temper. Dignity or not, youthfulness or not, Miss Lyndon *was* better suited than Meg to become the Countess of Stanbrook.

More difficult to picture was Philip standing speechless, "with the strangest look on his face," when Stewart asked cynically why, then, he didn't marry Meg. She wouldn't have expected Philip to laugh outright—he was, after all, a gentleman—but he was quite an expert at indicating disdain by the mere lift of a dark brow or a sardonic twist of his mouth. Yet he had done nothing of the kind.

Meg did not doubt that Philip desired her. She'd even state with some authority that he liked and admired her. But, dash it! What idiocy to suppose that Stanbrook would allow admiration and desire to interfere with his marriage plans!

Her hand balled into a fist and smacked the bedcovers, an ill-advised move, punished immediately by stabs of pain in her shoulder. Who was to say that the strange expression on Philip's face had *not* been disdain? She hadn't been present in the Great Hall. She hadn't witnessed the confrontation. She had only the footman's interpretation of what transpired, or rather Elspeth's interpretation of the footman's tale.

And besides, Philip's sentiments were of no concern to her. She was not interested in marriage, no matter how much she might be attracted to a certain gentleman. She was committed to the stage.

Wasn't she?

Bah! Feeling thoroughly disgusted with herself, Meg slid out of bed. No matter what Philip had said about staying safely in her room, she would brush her hair, don the green silk gown, and go downstairs to the salon for the ritual of sherry drinking. And for good measure she'd have dinner downstairs as well.

Furthermore, she wouldn't waste another thought on the aggravating, high-and-mighty Earl of Stanbrook.

The clock on the mantel showed it was past six, and she wondered if he had left yet. If he wanted to reach London—

The deuce! She was thinking about him again. Why couldn't it be out of sight, out of mind?

With an air of grim resolution, Meg lit the lamps, then sat down in front of the dressing table and picked up a hairbrush. She had never given much thought to the fact that she was right-handed—until she tried to brush her hair with the left hand. It simply did not feel right. She was pulling a face at the tangled mane reflected in the large mirror when Elspeth peeked into the room and asked if she was ready to receive the physician.

Meg compressed her mouth. Confound it! Why couldn't Philip leave well enough alone? But, she thought irrelevantly, at least she knew that he had indeed left.

"Tell the physician I'm asleep, Elspeth. No, wait! Better tell him it was a misunderstanding, that I don't need his services."

Elspeth grimaced in the most disconcerting manner and shook her head.

"Run along," Meg said impatiently. "Tell him—"

A male voice interrupted her. "Come, now, Miss Carswell. You wouldn't want the poor girl to get into trouble, would you?"

A stoutish man of about Stewart's age, a twinkle in his eye and an untidy thatch of sandy hair standing on end above a ruddy face, pushed past the maid. In his hand, he carried the ubiquitous black bag that was part and parcel of every physician Meg had known.

Favoring her with a friendly grin, he stepped purposefully closer. "Simon Meade at your service, Miss Carswell."

Meg liked him immediately. "I wish Lord Stanbrook hadn't imposed on you. It was he, wasn't it, who sent you to see me?"

"Yes." The twinkle deepened. "And he warned me I wouldn't be welcome."

Against her will, Meg chuckled. "The wretch! I *told* him it's merely a strained muscle."

"I don't doubt it. But since I'm here I may as well take a look."

With Elspeth hovering at his elbow, Dr. Meade examined Meg's shoulder and promptly confirmed her own diagnosis.

"Nothing that a bit of rest won't cure," he said cheerfully.

"Rest, Dr. Meade? Are you advising rest in bed?"

"Simplest way I know to keep a strained muscle still." He set the black bag on the dressing table. "I'll leave you a liniment and some laudanum for tonight, if you like."

"Keep the laudanum. I never touch the stuff." Meg gave the physician a challenging look. "And just whose notion is the prescription for rest in bed? Yours or Lord Stanbrook's?"

Dr. Meade lost none of his cheerfulness, but there was a hint of reproof in his look. "Miss Carswell, I write my own prescriptions."

"I apologize. I shouldn't have said that. It's just—You said Stanbrook warned you that I didn't want to see a physician, and then you came anyway because that's what he ordered. And on top of it, you prescribe rest in bed, which is exactly what he—"

He interrupted. "I did not come here because Lord Stanbrook ordered it. I *wanted* to see you."

Her eyes widened. "You did? But why?"

"I was curious."

Under Meg's incredulous look, the ruddy face turned a little ruddier.

"It's no secret in the surrounding country that Sir Richard's long-lost daughter is Meg Fletcher. I saw you as Rosalind, was one of the hundreds who cheered you from the pit, and I thought this would be as good a time as any to make your acquaintance."

Elspeth gasped and pressed both hands to her mouth, but whether to stifle giggles or a protest Meg could not tell.

"Why didn't you come to the Green Room to meet me, Dr. Meade?"

He gave her a rather sheepish grin. "I didn't have the nerve."

"And I am supposed to swallow that plumper? You did not lack pluck or resourcefulness this evening, my good sir."

"Aye, and a little show of backbone finally got me my reward, too."

Meg felt at ease with him, just as she had been comfortable with the gentlemen in the Green Room. Why the deuce did composure desert her when she faced Philip?

"And what reward is that, Dr. Meade?"

"I wanted to see your eyes. And today, I did."

She blinked in astonishment, but made no comment.

"I was in town for a few days only," he explained. "To attend some lectures at the Royal College of Surgeons. And all the fellows were in alt over the actress who had taken the town by storm. Her hair was like burnished copper, they said. And her eyes had the color and brightness of emeralds."

Meg suppressed a smile. "But you did not believe them and, therefore, attended the play to see for yourself?"

"Exactly. And I did see the hair. But as for the eyes—I might as well have stayed in my lodgings." He looked aggrieved, and yet the twinkle in his own eyes was unmistakable. "You see, I had neglected to equip myself with an opera glass."

Meg no longer tried to hide her amusement. "An unforgivable oversight. I cannot help thinking you do not deserve your reward this evening."

"I hope that's mischief speaking, for I'm about to claim another reward for my courage."

"Indeed?"

He put a hand to his hair and raked his fingers through the untidy thatch, with the result that it looked worse than before. But apparently the gesture gave him confidence.

"Miss Carswell, I take it that like everyone else in the neighborhood you will attend Miss Lyndon's party, and I would greatly appreciate it if you would favor me with a dance."

"Well, now, Dr. Meade, that quite depends on how strictly you mean to enforce that prescription of rest in bed, doesn't it?"

He chuckled. "Trying your hand at a bit of blackmail? Might have saved yourself the trouble. As long as you stay in bed for the rest of the evening and don't try to ride in the steeplechase tomorrow, I'll be satisfied."

"In that case you may have as many dances as you like."

"Thank you, Miss Carswell."

He closed the black bag with a decisive snap. Looking at the mantel clock which lacked but a few minutes till seven, he grimaced and executed a hurried bow.

"If you'll excuse me? I have an appointment with yet

another great lady, and I'm already late."

"Fie! And I thought you were a respectable country doctor."

Before Simon Meade could make a retort, Elspeth cried, "Oh, but he is, Miss Megan. The doctor's only goin' to a birthin'. Phyllis Hogden's first. Ain't that so, Dr. Meade?"

Carefully avoiding Meg's dancing eyes, he patted the little maid's arm. "Yes, that is correct, Elspeth. And even though it's a first child and may take hours yet, I had better make haste or your aunt will never ask me to assist again."

"You are assisting Elspeth's aunt?" Meg tried in vain to hide her astonishment. "Nanny Grimshaw?"

Simon Meade cocked a brow. "Do I detect doubt? Censure? To tell the truth, Miss Carswell, I am not so much assisting as *learning*. Nanny Grimshaw is teaching me the art of midwifery."

"But do you find Nanny reliable? My aunt believes she's . . ."

Meg did not finish the sentence, but Dr. Meade did so without hesitation.

"Mad? Yes, Miss Carswell, I'm well aware of Mrs. Elmore's opinion. But she's wrong. Mrs. Grimshaw may confuse yesterday and today, but she's as sane as you or I. And she's an excellent midwife. She could teach those chaps at the Royal College of Surgeons a thing or two."

"There!" Elspeth muttered. "Didn't I say so all along?"

"You did," Meg replied absently. "Dr. Meade—I have spoken with Mrs. Grimshaw twice. You see, she looked after Mother and me after I was born. But each time I ask her about those days, she just gives me this vacant stare and . . ."

"And she looks as though she'd lost her upper works? Yes, I, too, have seen her like that. It does not mean she's mad, Miss Carswell. I believe at times Mrs. Grimshaw is troubled about something that happened in the past and

238

she does not wish to think about it. So she lets her mind wander. That's all."

"But isn't that a dangerous trait in a midwife?"

"She's never done it while she delivers a baby. And I don't think she will. It's not the birthing process that troubles her, or guilt that she failed as a midwife in the past. No, it's not that. I've seen her at work. I know."

Simon Meade strode off, but his exit was prevented by the housekeeper, who stood pale and trembling, hand raised to knock, just outside the door.

"Dr. Meade, can you come quick? One of the under-gardeners—" A shudder ran through Mrs. Sutton's plump form. "We found him dead."

Chapter Nineteen

One of the undergardeners dead?

Numb with shock, Meg stared at the door closing behind Simon Meade's husky frame.

Which one? She must know.

Brushing aside Elspeth's protest, she thrust her feet into slippers, drew a wrap around her shoulders, and fastened after the physician and the housekeeper.

It was a good thing that she'd hurried. The two were out of sight already and only the unusual shrillness of Mrs. Sutton's voice guided her to the back stairs concealed in a narrow passage that led off the main corridor near Alvina's rooms.

She followed them down the stairs, through the pantry and kitchen and out into the yard, which was quite dark, and learned from Mrs. Sutton's disjointed account to the doctor that the dead man's name was Will Fratt. He hadn't shown up for work in the morning and had been found a short while ago by one of the Carswell Hall tenants, who had been out searching for a runaway hog.

Meg hadn't consciously tried for stealth, but neither had she made a sound or called out to alert the physician and the housekeeper to her presence. She was, therefore, surprised when Dr. Meade turned suddenly.

"Miss Carswell! You shouldn't be out here. Death is not a pleasant sight."

"I know," she said simply.

How well she knew. In the dank alleys of Seven Dials she had seen too many deaths—men and women, starved and disease-riddled, who collapsed suddenly and never got up again.

Falling into step beside them, she said, "I need to see the man—Will Fratt, is that what you called him, Mrs. Sutton?"

"Aye, Miss Megan. But the doctor's right. A corpse is not a sight for a young lady. You go on back to the house."

"As soon as I've seen him. I want to know if he's the new man I recognized as someone I met in London."

"Why didn't ye *ask?*" The housekeeper huffed indignantly. "Will Fratt is—was the one as looked like a bag o' bones. He came from London just about a sennight after you and Mr. Stewart arrived. Will was the only one of the staff not from hereabouts. So, you see, Miss Megan, there's no need to come all the way to the coach house and look at him. *I* ain't settin' foot inside. Farmer Weller said he's dead, and that's good enough for me."

Meg, however, could not be satisfied with Mrs. Sutton's description of the undergardener. Not that she doubted he was the fellow who had worked near the music room and watched her go to the gazebo, the man Philip suspected as the stalker. But she simply must see his face once more and hope that the sight would trigger a memory. She needed to know *where* in London she had met him before.

He was laid out on boards set atop trestles, and he looked even more emaciated in death than he had in life. Meg stared at the face illuminated by the light of three carriage lanterns—not in sudden recognition but in dawning horror.

News of his death had shocked her—for selfish reasons she admitted, because he would never answer her questions now. But she had not wondered about the cause of

242

his death.

And then she saw Will Fratt's contorted features. Pity, horror, and shame at her indifference filled her. She looked away quickly and met Simon Meade's eyes.

"He did not die," she said hoarsely. "He was killed."

The physician placed a hand under her elbow as though he feared she would swoon. "Please, Miss Carswell, come away. You ought to be in bed."

"Dr. Meade." Her voice was sharp and clear now. "I was raised in the back alleys of London. I've seen worse than this, so don't patronize me, please. Just tell me. Was he killed?"

He said nothing, but she noted that his gaze strayed to the dead man.

"Dr. Meade, could he have been poisoned?"

He let go of her arm. Raking through his hair with both hands, he said, "Without an examination, I cannot confirm or deny anything, Miss Carswell. But there are certain . . . signs I'll have to report to the justice of the peace. And Squire Lyndon, no doubt, will ask me to perform a postmortem examination."

"Signs that point to death by poison?"

"Signs that *could* mean poison," he corrected gently.

But Meg was satisfied. Feeling exhausted all of a sudden, she wanted nothing more than to return to her room.

"Please let me know the results of the examination, Dr. Meade. It is very important to me."

"Miss Carswell—"

But she had turned away and was walking toward the wide coach house door, toward crisp, cool night air.

Making use of the back stairs once more, she returned to her chamber. As she opened the door, she stopped in mid-stride.

Just where was Stewart all this time? Shouldn't he have been the one to fetch Dr. Meade, or, at least, to meet him in the coach house?

Elspeth gave her no time for further thought but, with

243

a look of concern, drew her into the room and to the bed.

"Come now, Miss Megan. I've put a warmin' pan in your bed. It's time you was restin' like the doctor said."

Meg allowed her to pull off the wrap and slippers. She might as well rest. There was nothing she could do this evening.

Sitting on the edge of the bed, she said, "It's Will Fratt they found dead. Did you know him, Elspeth?"

"Aye. Cook told me when I was heatin' the water." Elspeth sniffed. "I don't like to speak ill o' the dead, but he was a nasty piece o' goods if ever I saw one. And Mr. Soames—he's the head gardener—he said Will's no more a gardener than a violet is an orchid. He only kept him on because Mrs. Elmore 'specially recommended him."

"Mrs. Elmore did?"

"Aye. But this mornin' Mr. Soames was ready to dismiss him, Mrs. Elmore or no Mrs. Elmore. I heard him tell his lordship."

"His lordship?" Meg said weakly. "Lord Stanbrook asked about Will Fratt?"

"Aye, that he did. His lordship came into the kitchen this mornin' when Mr. Soames was havin' his cup o' tea. And I was havin' mine, so I heard it all. That Will had wrecked the ivy alongside the music room winders and Mr. Soames was goin' to dismiss him without a reference. But Will must've known he was in trouble, 'cause he didn't show up for work this mornin'."

"Maybe he was already dead."

"Maybe so." Elspeth shrugged. A moment later, her eyes widened and her mouth fell open.

"Miss Megan, do you think his lordship killed him? He might have discovered it was Will as cut your saddle girth."

"Of course not," Meg said sharply. "But why would you think Will Fratt tampered with the saddle?"

"I dunno. Can't think of anyone else who'd do a rotten

ning like that. But don't you think if his lordship believed—"

Meg shook her head. "When Dr. Meade has examined he body, I think he will confirm that Will Fratt was oisoned." The ghost of a smile touched her mouth. "I an see Lord Stanbrook milling the wretched man down, erhaps even wringing his neck. But poison him?"

"No," Elspeth said regretfully. "I don't s'pose he'd go or poison."

Busying herself at the dressing table, the maid ontinued to speculate about the undergardener's death. Meg did not listen. All the talk about his lordship had eminded her that Philip had known of Fratt's disappearance and hadn't told her.

Gingerly, she settled against the pillows. A pox on her houlder and on Stanbrook as well for keeping things om her. He should have told her that the undergardener had disappeared!

In retrospect, Fratt's absence would explain the udden decision to drive to London immediately. She hould have been suspicious. Should have realized that he undergardener, whom Philip suspected as the stalker, as no longer around. More than once she'd had reason o complain about Philip's overprotectiveness. Was it kely he'd have left her with the stalker on the loose?

Of course he had tried to make sure she'd be in bed ntil his return. . . .

As though in confirmation of that last thought, there as a knock on the door and, when Elspeth opened it, two ootmen carried in a truckle bed.

Exhaustion, unease over Fratt's death, all her pent-up motions turned into irritation.

"For goodness' sake, don't set the bed down in here! ake it into the dressing room!"

"But, Miss Megan," Elspeth protested. "His lordship ft orders for me to sleep right here with you."

"To the devil with his lordship." Meg's tone was awe-inspiring in its quietness. "Take the bloody thing into the dressing room."

There was a moment of absolute stillness, then a flurry of activity as Elspeth hurried to open the dressing room door and the footmen lugged the bed through Meg's chamber.

It was a hollow victory at best.

Meg awoke to the jiggle of curtain rings sliding on the rod. She had not heard Elspeth rise and leave, but with the aromatic smell of hot chocolate teasing her nose, she could not doubt that the maid had been up for some time.

Something else teased her nose—the sweet, familiar scent of white lilacs.

Her eyes flew open, widening at the sight of a gigantic bouquet of her favorite blooms on the night table.

"Aren't they loverley?" Carrying a cup of chocolate, Elspeth approached the bed.

"Very lovely."

The maid sighed. "But they're the last, exceptin' those two little bushes behind the gazebo. They's always late and are only just startin' to set bloom."

Meg settled herself against the pillows. Taking the cup from Elspeth, she said, "Then I'm especially grateful that you cut these for me. Thank you very much."

"You're welcome, I'm sure. But the orders to cut 'em came from his lordship."

"Stanbrook!" A drop of hot chocolate splashed on Meg's nightgown. Hastily, she righted the cup. "He told you to put lilacs in my room?"

"Yes, Miss Megan. Quite set on it he were. *White* lilacs, he told me. As many as I could find."

"Indeed."

She had not forgotten her irritation with Philip for going to London without her, for keeping things from her. Neither had she forgotten Fratt's death. But she could not stop a very wide, very happy smile curving her

outh. To hide it, she quickly took a sip of the choco-
te.

How silly she was to let a small gesture touch her. But
e could not help it; she felt ridiculously pleased.

Fussing with the bedcover, Elspeth shot Meg a side-
ng look.

"First, his lordship said to take the flowers up at bed-
me, but then he changed his mind. He gave me this look,
 did, and a grin made his eyes dance. An' his whole face
nd o' lit up, if you know what I mean, Miss Megan?"

Meg did know. Only too well.

"And he told you to wait until morning to cut the
acs?"

"Said if I took 'em up when there was a chance the
ctor or the truckle bed would arrive at the same time,
u'd likely hurl 'em in my face."

Meg laughed, letting the sound fill the room.

"But he's wrong, Elspeth. His lordship may think he
ows me, but I would never have hurled the lilacs at
u. I'd have waited until *he* showed his face again."

"Aye, an' I suspicion that's what he meant, Miss
egan."

Arms crossed over the bib of her apron, an expectant
ok on her face, Elspeth stood by the bed. Clearly, she
as prepared—and eager—to expound on her theory at
e slightest sign of encouragement.

But Meg did not give that sign. Elspeth, as she had seen
e day before, was a romantic. Asking if Meg would
arry his lordship, forsooth! There was no telling what
e girl would read into the metaphorical hurling of
acs.

Thus, instead of further commenting on the aggravat-
g Earl of Stanbrook, Meg went immediately through
e routine motions of rising and dressing. At eight
clock, an hour later than she would have left her room
she had gone riding with Philip, she opened her door
d stepped out into the corridor.

"Megan!"

At the far end of the east wing, her aunt was leaving her chambers. Gowned in long-sleeved, high-necked pale lavender poplin, gray hair meticulously coiffed, Alvina Elmore sailed toward Meg, who waited for her reluctantly.

"Should you be up and about?" Alvina asked.

"Why not? I am feeling perfectly fine."

As, indeed, she was. Her shoulder was a little stiff, but hardly sore.

"Philip said—" Alvina gave her an unreadable look. "Well, perhaps the least attention paid to what Philip says, the better. I am glad, though, that he won't be here for a day or so to lure you into more ill-advised equestrian feats."

The implication of her aunt's words left Meg speechless.

"And yet, my dear," said Alvina, placing a hand on Meg's arm, "if Philip is correct and you are hurt worse than you let on, you should be in bed."

"I'm not hurt at all." Meg did not think she was the fanciful type, but there was no denying that her skin crawled under her aunt's touch. If only she hadn't chosen the sprigged muslin with the short, puffed sleeves.

She hugged her arms to her chest and started walking toward the stairs. "How cold the house gets overnight!"

"Yes, it does, doesn't it?" Alvina hurried to keep up with Meg's longer stride. "But the breakfast room will be pleasant with the sun coming in through the terrace doors. And if you're still cold, I'll send James to fetch your shawl."

Meg lengthened her stride. Alvina's solicitude rang as false as it had the day before, and she couldn't get away from her aunt soon enough.

Several paces ahead of Alvina, she hastened down the stairs. "I'm going for a walk before breakfast. That'll warm me more than anything."

"Megan, wait! You shouldn't be out alone."

"Why not? I'm only going into the garden."

Breathing just a little faster than usual, Alvina reached the first-floor landing right behind Meg. Again, she placed a hand on her niece's arm.

"Take Stewart with you." For once, her eyes showed not coldness but a good deal of anxiety. "He is worried about you. And so am I."

"You are?" Meg stared at the hand on her arm until Alvina, her mouth tightening, removed it.

"Pardon me, Aunt," Meg said quietly. "But this sudden concern rather unnerves me."

Spots of bright red flamed high on Alvina's cheekbones. Whether from embarrassment or anger, Meg could not tell; her aunt was careful not to look at her.

"I don't blame you. I—I am rather set in my ways, and I'm afraid you caught me by surprise when you arrived so suddenly on our doorstep. You see, I do not like surprises."

"Yes, I believe I do see. My mother was a surprise, too."

"She was, indeed."

Alvina finally met Meg's eyes, and the bitterness and hatred in that look made a lie of her words.

"I should have learned from my mistake then. But again I let irritation rule me when Stewart brought you, for which I beg your pardon, because it was not your fault but my son's. He should have warned me."

"As my father should have warned you of his marriage?" Meg asked tartly.

Again, Alvina's mouth tightened. "Richard should not have married at all. He was not meant to be a husband. However, that's neither here nor there. We cannot change what's in the past. But we can change the future."

Meg looked at her aunt. Conviction shone from the gray-green eyes, and something else—a spark of fervor or urgency.

"I never had a daughter," Alvina said in a low voice. "But I remember when you were born, Stewart clamored to have you for his little sister. He couldn't have his wish then, but now . . . perhaps now we can live as a family after all?"

Never! hovered on Meg's tongue, but she merely looked at Alvina. She believed her no more than she believed Philip would return from London with any real discoveries. And what her aunt meant to accomplish with this show of friendliness, she had not the slightest notion.

"I shall do my best," she said. "And now, if you'll excuse me, I'd like to go for a walk."

Alvina followed her down the next flight of stairs. "Won't you wait for Stewart? He does want to speak to you, Megan. But yesterday afternoon you were inundated with visitors, and he feared you'd be too exhausted to see him."

"I thought Stewart must have been out, since he did not meet Dr. Meade in the coach house."

"The coach house!" Alvina's voice was shrill. "What do you know about that? And why would you think Stewart wasn't there? Were you snooping?"

Meg stopped and turned to face her aunt. "Snooping? You seem to forget that Will Fratt died while in *my father's* employ." Then, deliberately, she added, "Besides, I have reason to believe that the man, like me, came from Seven Dials."

Alvina's face turned a ghastly shade of gray. She reached for Meg, whether to steady herself or for a more sinister purpose, Meg did not know, but she quickly clutched the banister.

Her aunt never touched her, though. She dropped her hand and said in an unnaturally high and shaking voice, "Stewart did go to see Dr. Meade. And if you know what's good for you, don't pry into matters that don't concern you."

"I did not think I was prying. Carswell Hall is my home, is it not?"

Alvina's eyes narrowed. "You are as stupid as your

mother was. Stewart is doing his best—"

Meg was not destined to know how or for what purpose Stewart was doing his best. As if she recognized that she had said far too much, Alvina clamped her mouth shut.

They stood staring at each other, Alvina two steps above Meg. Alvina's look was venomous, and after a moment Meg could bear it no longer. She turned and flew down the last steps, her goal the front door, wide open to admit the warm, scented air of a bright summer morning.

She had planned to visit the stables first to question the grooms about the night of her father's accident, but just in case Alvina was watching, she turned left toward the gardens. Once she was out of sight, she could always squeeze through the lilac hedge to get into the stable-yard.

However, when she reached the gardens proper, her attention was caught by the all-too-familiar sound of Jigger's strident voice somewhere in the direction of the sculpted yews. Quite obviously, he was embroiled in an argument of sorts. Also quite obviously, it behooved Meg to settle the matter and to send the boy back to the kitchens where he was supposed to be helping the cook.

Stifling a sigh, she approached the path winding through the sculpted yews. She passed a shrub shaped to resemble some wildcat or other on the pounce, one that looked like a giraffe, and was approaching an elephant when an especially violent outburst from Jigger made her prick up her ears.

"Gorblimey, Mr. Soames! Didn't oi tell ye that oi've come 'ere on 'is lor'ship's orders? An' look what oi found. A grave!"

Chapter Twenty

Meg was well aware of Jigger's propensity for exaggeration. Yet her stomach knotted as her imagination conjured a grave filled—with what? A rotting coffin? Nonsense. The stalker's lifeless body? But that lay in the coach house, or had been taken away by Dr. Meade for a postmortem examination.

Or had Will Fratt not been the stalker?

She stumbled and almost missed the head gardener's response to Jigger.

"Loose-screw! Be gone with ye!" Mr. Soames clapped his hands as he would at a bird or a squirrel threatening his plants. "A grave, indeed, ye silly blighter! It's one of me exp'rimental bulb an' root c'llectors ye've uncovered."

"Root c'llector be damned! Didn't ye pay no heed to what oi tol' ye? His lor'ship said—"

Jigger broke off, his sharp, foxy face turning red at the sight of Meg rounding the elephant-shaped shrub. But she paid him no heed.

She came to an abrupt stop and stared at the hole in the ground immediately beneath the huge green head and the upward-pointed tusks and trunk—a two-foot-deep trench in the shape of a grave, albeit a rather short one. And it was empty.

"Miss Megan." The head gardener respectfully pulled

off his cap. "A very good morn to ye."

"Good morning, Mr. Soames." Meg dragged her gaze away from the trench and smiled at the head gardener. "I take it Jigger is once again making a nuisance of himself?"

"Oi's not!" the boy protested, but Meg silenced him with a look.

"Well, now, Miss Megan. I wouldn't go so far 's to say he's a nuisance. Some cock-'n-bull story he cooked up about his lordship tellin' him to look for some hidey-hole, but I ain't fallin' for it."

Keeping a quelling eye on Jigger, Meg said, "Very wise of you, Mr. Soames. Boys have such vivid imaginations."

The head gardener nodded. "He were in the kitchen yesterday when his lordship asked about Will Fratt, and now Will's dead. Any lad worth his salt would have his imag'nation goin' at full tilt. I suspicion he's lookin' for a bit o' excitement, too."

"I'll deal with Jigger, Mr. Soames. After all, *I* inflicted him on this household, and I'm sure you have more pressing matters to attend."

"Aye, Miss Megan." Turning to leave, the gardener chuckled. "A rare handful he is, but I doubt there's any harm in him. Just natcheral high spirits, I'd say."

Jigger barely waited until Mr. Soames was out of earshot before he burst out, "Ain't no cock-'n-bull story, Miss Meg, an' don't ye believe it! His lor'ship tol' me that bloke 'e chased t'other night, 'e disappeared right about where the elliphant shrub is. An' that's *'ere!* An' 'e tol' me ter look for a place ter 'ide."

"Draw bridle, Jigger. I believe you, but there's no need for the whole household to know. And neither," she added sternly, "is there a need to drop all the aitches I spent months adding to your speech."

"Aye, Miss Meg." The boy gave her an impudent grin. "As long 's ye'll listen to me, oi'll say me aitches."

Meg nodded. "So Lord Stanbrook suspects that this is where the stalker hid when he chased him?"

"Aye."

She looked doubtfully at the oblong trench. It hardly seemed large enough to accommodate a man.

Or a woman? The thought occurred to her that the stalker might have wanted to hide *her* if his scheme had worked out.

Hastily averting her eyes from the gravelike hole, she said, "It was quite dark that night, but not dark enough that Lord Stanbrook wouldn't have noticed a hole in the ground or a man lying in it."

"But ye haven't seen all, Miss Meg!"

Jigger darted behind the large shrub and returned almost instantly, dragging a dirt-stained wooden plank. He laid the plank down, hopped into the trench and, lying down, pulled the board across the cavity.

"Ye see, Miss Meg?" His voice sounded eerie beneath the wooden cover. "When oi found this place, the plank was piled with dirt. If the bloke hid in 'ere, he'd 'ave covered hisself careful-like, an' the dirt would 'ave stayed on the wood."

Yes, Meg could see it clearly. The man running and Philip close behind. The trench uncovered—to receive the inert body of the intended victim?

But he didn't have her body, so the stalker himself squeezed into the convenient hideout. In the dark, an earth-covered board would not be visible. The pursuer would have to step right on it to know it was there. But since it was located beneath the thick foliage of the elephant's head, even an accidental discovery was unlikely at night.

If Philip hadn't come that evening, she might have ended up in the trench. Unconscious? Dead?

She shivered. Perhaps her body wouldn't have been found until Mr. Soames wanted to use the place to store his precious bulbs and roots for the winter.

Feeling as if winter's cold blast had touched her even on this hot morning, she rubbed her arms until her skin grew warm. But nothing could take the chill off her soul.

"Come on out, Jigger," she said sharply. "I'm quite convinced that this is where the stalker hid."

But afterward, when Philip had left and Fratt believed himself safe, where had he gone then?

Who had given him poison—if, indeed, Will Fratt and the stalker were one and the same person?

And suddenly, she remembered where she had seen the undergardener before. It was when she had left the Drury Lane with Stewart. The man had jostled her and quickly retreated into the shadows near the theater door. She had wanted to give him a coin because he'd looked half starved, but Stewart had pulled her away.

Another memory flashed through her mind—a coachman shouting and swearing at an unruly team of chestnuts. She'd had only a glimpse of the man driving the carriage that almost ran her down in Piccadilly. She was certain that it wasn't Stewart or his groom—or Philip. But, thinking back on the occasion, she believed it quite possible that the caped driving coat and the tall coachman's hat had disguised the narrow frame of the undergardener Will Fratt.

Almost an hour later, having dispatched Jigger to the kitchen and after a visit to the stables, Meg was sitting on the white-painted steps of the gazebo, wondering what Fletcher would have made of the situation.

Or Philip, who, most of the time—when he wasn't plagued by his over-nice sense of honor—showed almost as much common sense as Fletcher. But Philip, typically male!—was gallivanting about London when he was most needed at Carswell Hall.

Meg carefully skirted the question why Philip should be needed, or who needed him. She didn't like to lie to herself, and even without probing too deeply, she knew she wouldn't be too happy with the answer. Instead, she put her mind to the conversation she'd just had with Phelps, the Carswell Hall head groom.

According to Phelps, who had been a junior stable lad at the time of her mother's flight, Stewart, as well as Alvina and Nanny Grimshaw, had been in the stables *after* Sir Richard ordered his horse saddled and *before* he set out on the wild ride across country to catch up with his runaway wife.

Alvina and Nanny had both pleaded with Phelps's father, the head groom then, to persuade Sir Richard not to ride after his wife. Both had claimed Sir Richard was too shaken and upset to ride at all. But, naturally, once Sir Richard made up his mind, no one could sway him from the course he intended to take, least of all a groom.

Stewart's purpose for visiting the stables at that particular time was unclear. He had been a boy of eight then, and he often sought the grooms' company. But not, of course, at night. Phelps remembered that his father had told Stewart several times to return to the house, but had not wanted to bodily evict the boy, since he looked quite confused and upset. Neither had Alvina made an effort to coax or order her son out of the stables.

One other bit of news Meg had gleaned from Phelps— that she was not the first to question him about that night twenty-four years ago. His lordship, the Earl of Stanbrook, had been there before her.

And wasn't it strange, the groom had mused, that Miss Megan should have suffered a fate similar to that of her father? Only difference was, this time no one tried to pull the wool over his eyes by insisting that the severed saddle girth was a mere accident.

Or, if it wasn't an accident, that a gypsy must have sneaked into the stables and damaged the leather in revenge for some slight or other—which was what Sir Richard had told everyone the moment he opened his eyes and was shown his saddle.

The baronet had fiercely clung to his conviction, even when Squire Lyndon, the justice of the peace, wanted to investigate the accident. And it hadn't made a whit of difference that for several years no gypsies had been seen in the neighborhood at all.

Meg had thanked the groom for his time and turned to leave. And then, without looking back at him, she had asked casually, "Phelps, do you remember who was in the stables yesterday morning?"

Phelps was a blunt man. "When *you* took a toss, Miss Megan? That would have been Harv, his lordship's groom that is, and the two lads who was muckin' out. But I wouldn't know if anyone else was here, on account of Mrs. Elmore wantin' me to drive her to Ascot."

"Did you pick Mrs. Elmore up at the house, or did she come to the stables?"

"She came here. Said she'd ordered the carriage for six an' why wasn't I ready? It weren't true. She'd wanted to leave at six-thirty, but o' course I didn't say nothing, just went off to change into me livery."

Meg had faced the groom then. "And no one else was in the stables earlier? Not even Mr. Stewart?"

"Aye, Mr. Stewart was here. Rode out at six o'clock sharp, just as he always does."

"Did he see his mother in the stables, or had he already left when she arrived?"

"He must've seen her. Like I told his lordship, last thing I heard when I run off to get me livery was Mr. Stewart and Mrs. Elmore havin' words. They wasn't shoutin' or anything, and I didn't hear what they was sayin'. But I could tell they wasn't complimentin' each other."

Phelps, looking self-conscious and uncomfortable, had asked if there was anything else Miss Megan wanted to know. She had shaken her head. None of the many remaining questions could be answered by the groom.

Leaning her back against the rail of the gazebo stairs, her feet on the same step that served her as seat, she hugged her knees.

She was consumed with curiosity about Stewart and Alvina's quarrel—in the stables, of all places. Had one surprised the other with the knife on her saddle? Or was

t about the previous night, the stalker's failure to get to
her?

She even wondered whether she had been too hasty in
her conclusion that Will Fratt was the stalker; whether
Stewart, who wasn't as broad shouldered as Philip, would
look tall, thin, narrow-framed in the dark.

Half ashamed of her suspicious mind, she reminded
herself that Fletcher would have told her never to rule
out a suspect until she was damned sure he wouldn't stab
her in the back while she looked the other way.

A shadow fell across her, and she hugged her knees
more tightly.

"Hello, Megan."

She looked up, startled, and saw Stewart standing at
the gazebo stairs. Setting one foot on the bottom step, he
gave her a crooked grin.

At first glance, everything about him was as usual—
the immaculate appearance of his riding coat, breeches,
and boots; the boyish grin that never failed to draw an
answering smile from her and did not fail this morning in
spite of the start he had given her with his sudden
appearance.

Even the look he gave her, half admiring, half scan-
dalized that she should be sitting outside, not on a chair
but on the steps, with her knees drawn up to her chin and
an inch or two of leg exposed below the ruffled hem of her
gown, was no different from many a look he had given her
before.

Upon closer scrutiny, however, Meg saw that the
reddish-blond hair was not brushed quite as meticulously
as was Stewart's wont. Or mayhap he had adopted Dr.
Meade's habit of raking his fingers through it—although
Stewart's hair did not stand on end as the physician's did.
She also noted a certain dullness of eye, a pinched look
round the mouth, and a deep groove on the usually
smooth forehead.

She had not seen him since the morning of her tumble.
He had been openly worried and concerned then; now he

looked like a man plagued by troubles he wanted to keep hidden.

"Stewart?" she said hesitantly. "Whatever is the matter? Can I help?"

His smile faded. She thought he turned pale, but she must have been mistaken, because the next moment his face flushed with the dull red of embarrassment.

"Nothing is the matter," he said far too quickly and with too much emphasis.

Watching him, Meg remembered the quarrel he'd had with Philip. She breathed a sigh of relief. What a dunce she was! There was nothing sinister behind his haggard appearance. Her cousin Stewart had committed the ultimate folly. He had fallen in love with Miss Lyndon even though he knew the young lady was as good as promised to Stanbrook. And of course he didn't want anyone to know.

"I'd like a word with you, Megan." Stewart held out his hand. "Will you walk with me?"

"Gladly."

If Stewart wanted to speak with her, he was in no hurry to do so. In silence, they strolled toward the rose garden which lay just to the south of the sculpted yews.

Meg did not even glance at the elephant. If it wasn' Miss Lyndon, then something momentous must be on Stewart's mind. It was quite out of character, but he had even forgotten about such niceties as offering conversation and an arm to the lady he had invited for a walk. No doubt, he was marshaling his thoughts. Stewart, unless roused to anger or taken off guard, would no speak impulsively.

Entering the rose garden proper, she noted the swelling buds pushing proudly through the foliage. If the warm weather continued, the roses would be in bloom before the end of the month—before she'd leave. Four weeks, she had promised her father.

With a pang of regret, she realized that she need no longer hold herself bound by the promise, since he ather himself had proposed to change the will once more. Philip was supposed to have talked him out of it. But had he? Perhaps he'd been too busy interrogating gardeners and grooms to see Sir Richard.

Meg kicked a piece of gravel that had somehow strayed into the flagged walk, and the small gesture of annoyance caught Stewart's attention. He came to a stop.

"Megan, I apologize." He looked contrite and even more troubled than before. "I've been rotten company, and I don't have an excuse for my boorishness, except preoccupation with—well, with the matter I wish to discuss."

Compassion stirred in her, but she did not disabuse him of the notion that she was irritated with him. It would have been too difficult to explain that the kick was directed—metaphorically, of course—at the shin of a man who'd been absent from Carswell Hall since the previous afternoon.

She flashed Stewart her brightest smile.

"Never mind. Just tell me what this is all about. It must be important. Even your mother warned me that you wished to speak with me."

A shadow crossed his face. "When did you see my mother?"

"An hour ago. No. More likely it's been two hours. Why?"

"Never mind."

He echoed her words, but his smile was not half as bright as hers had been. Taking both her hands in his, Stewart drew her close.

"Megan, will you marry me?"

Chapter Twenty-One

Marry Stewart? Good heavens, what next?

Meg was about to make some teasing reply about the unexpectedness of the offer, perhaps even, if he seemed responsive, the absurdity of it, when she was struck by a most unsettling thought.

Like Alvina with her desperate attempt at friendliness, Stewart was pursuing a definite purpose by offering for her.

The ground beneath her feet seemed to shift, and without quite understanding why or how, she felt as though she stood on the edge of a precipice. Even if she could have explained or analyzed the sensation, she doubted she would have remembered the light response she had planned.

"No."

She tried to free her hands, but Stewart's clasp was firm.

"Again, I must apologize. I did not mean to blurt out my proposal like a callow youth and catch you unprepared. Please, Megan, hear me out."

"What difference does it make *how* you propose?" she said, still in the throes of that inexplicable feeling of panic. "I cannot marry you."

"Why? You must know that I've admired you from the moment we met."

263

"You may admire me, Stewart. But more than that you deplore my conduct and my profession. Especially my profession."

"Since you won't be acting once we're married, your profession will no longer worry me. And I'm sure you'll soon learn—"

"Stewart," she interrupted, "I have no intention of giving up acting. And all this is beside the point. For heaven's sake! We're first cousins!"

"It is not unusual for cousins to marry," he pointed out stiffly.

She wanted to shout, "No!" and be done with it. But for some reason, it was important to her that he should see the impossibility of their marriage, perhaps even withdraw his offer.

"But it is unusual to propose marriage to one woman when you love another."

Again, the color fluctuated in his face. "I don't know what you're talking about, Megan."

"Don't you, Stewart? Do you deny that you're in love with Evalina Lyndon?"

He dropped her hands. "We'll leave Miss Lyndon out of the conversation, if you please. This concerns only you and me."

There was a look of resolve about him that, under different circumstances, she would have applauded. At the moment, it was difficult, even impossible, to understand. She had told him no. That should be sufficient to cool the most ardent of suitors. And Stewart's ardor was directed at Miss Lyndon. Meg was prepared to wager on it.

And then she understood. Sadness filled her. If she had given him reassurance when her father disclosed the contents of the new will, Stewart need never have made the absurd proposal. But she had not. She had totally ignored her cousin's disappointment.

"Poor Stewart. Do you want the house and land so badly that you'd take me into the bargain?"

She thought Stewart would choke, but whether or

anger or on embarrassment and chagrin, she could not tell.

"Stop it!" There was no doubt about his anger now. "I like you, Megan. Like you very much. You *cannot* doubt that."

"No. I—"

"Dash it! Don't interrupt. I don't want to lose my thread."

With swift, long strides, he started to walk farther into the rose garden. Before she had quite caught up with him, he whirled and faced her.

"It's not so much your calling me 'poor Stewart' in that patronizing manner that made my blood boil, but what you said afterward—that I want Carswell Hall so badly I'd *take you into the bargain*. It's an insult! A slap in the face."

"Stewart—"

"But we'll forget about the insult to me. You insult yourself, Megan! That's what I cannot stomach."

"No, Stewart. *I* am proud of being an actress. *You* feel it is scandalous. It is something you'd never be able to forget. I grant you that you like me. I never doubted it. But liking, especially when accompanied by disapproval, is not enough to make a man like you propose marriage."

Stewart's open countenance had always betrayed him, and it was no different this time. Meg knew she had scored a hit before he opened his mouth and tried to cover his discomfiture with bluster.

"I suppose you wouldn't have batted an eye if I'd made you an *improper* proposal—like Stanbrook!"

"How dare you! Philip has nothing to do with this, and don't try to tell me otherwise."

"Then I shan't," he said almost sulkily.

They were of near enough the same height that she did not have to crane her neck to meet his eyes. She looked at him sternly.

"Stewart, if it is not for Carswell Hall, why do you want to marry me?"

"Because I don't want you hurt!" he burst out. "Or killed."

She drew in her breath sharply as the sensation of teetering on the edge of a precipice returned.

"Dash it, Megan! You must know that your tumble wasn't an accident. Marry me, and I can promise that you'll be safe!"

"How can you promise?"

Her voice was low and hoarse; she wondered if he could understand her.

"How, Stewart? Unless it was *you* who cut the cinch."

He had understood. His mouth contorted into an angry, tight slash, and the look he shot her was one of ice-cold fury. He looked so much like Alvina when she learned about the changed will that Meg took an instinctive step backward.

"You accuse *me?*"

His hands shot out, clamping around her upper arms in such a painful grip that she was hard-pressed not to cry out. She tried to tear away, but he was much stronger than she had believed possible, and she could not pull free.

"Didn't I drive to London to fetch you?" He shook her until she felt like a rag doll. "Didn't I do everything possible to reconcile you with your father? And yet you accuse me of wanting to kill you!"

Anger flared, hot and sharp. But she was also aware of fear clawing at her. At fear that, if she did not nip it in the bud, would equal the terror she had experienced in the gazebo. Only this time, Philip would not be there to chase away the danger.

"Dammit, Stewart! Let go! Or do you want to snap my neck and kill me right here and now?"

He blinked as though to clear his vision, and stopped shaking her. But he did not loosen the grip on her arms.

Meg shifted her weight to the left foot, prepared, if necessary, to apply the swift knee kick Fletcher had taught her, when Miss Lyndon's voice, high and rather

266

breathless, broke the tense silence in the rose garden.

"Miss Carswell! Stewart!"

Stewart gave a start and dropped his hands. He swung around, and the look on his face as he watched Evalina hurrying along the flagged path almost compensated Meg for the discomfort she had suffered. But uppermost was a sense of great relief that she need not continue the argument with her cousin.

She believed she had wronged him. He was not a good enough actor to pretend an outrage such as he had shown. And yet, the fact remained that for no plausible reason that she could see, he had proposed marriage. For her protection.

"Lina," Stewart croaked; then, apparently, he was struck speechless at the sight of Miss Lyndon.

And, indeed, Evalina presented a picture that would have affected most gentlemen in a similar manner. Twirling the handle of a parasol tilted at such an angle that the blue-and-white striped silk was a backdrop rather than a source of shade for her face, Evalina looked young and artless, and yet utterly devastating, with a mass of curls gleaming golden in the sun, cheeks tinted a delicate rose, and the deep blue of her gown mirrored in her eyes.

A tiny frown marred the smoothness of her forehead as she faced the cousins. "Are you two quarreling?"

Meg darted a look at Stewart, but he still seemed incapable of speech and devoured Evalina with eyes that showed as much hunger as despair.

"You might say we're having a cousinly tiff, Miss Lyndon. Nothing that time, common sense, and perhaps your influence won't resolve."

"*My* influence? Miss Carswell, are you funning with me? I didn't realize I had any influence over you!"

"Not over me," Meg corrected gently. "Over Stewart."

"Oh."

Evalina peeked at Stewart. Her eyes widened under his intense stare, and the pink in her cheeks deepened. But she was not the type of young lady who swooned merely because a man looked at her a certain way.

She tipped the parasol back a little farther. "Mr. Elmore . . . Stewart, just what have you done to make Miss Carswell quarrel with you?"

Meg's sense of humor overcame the last shred of uneasiness. Laughter tickled her throat as she waited for Stewart's reply. How absurd this was! Miss Evalina was unwittingly turning a tense situation into a farce.

"Lina, my dear." Stewart tugged at his cravat as though it had become too tight. And it might have. His color was alarmingly high.

"My dear," he repeated, "if you've come to see Stanbrook, I'm afraid you'll be disappointed. He drove up to London last night."

"I'm sure I don't care." Miss Lyndon scowled. "Except that now he won't know I planned to give him the cut direct. How typical of him! He insults me, and he doesn't have the decency to stick around so I can pay him back."

"That is too bad of him," said Meg, her voice unsteady. "But, pardon me, Miss Lyndon. I know Stanbrook has a few rough edges, and yet I cannot believe that he would deal an insult. What on earth did he say to you?"

"*Say?*" Evalina placed a fist on her hip and drew herself up. "He said nothing at all. He put his hands on my waist, the . . . ruffian! He snatched me up bodily and thrust me into my brother's arms. Just because I happened to peek into the Great Hall while he and Stewart were having a brawl."

"Indeed."

Meg was aware of the inadequacy of her reply, but she did not trust herself to say another word without bursting into laughter. Elspeth had meant it quite literally when she said that his lordship "handed" Miss Lyndon over to her brother. If only she'd known yesterday. How she would have teased Philip!

As she remembered their last meeting, something happened inside her—a slow, wrenching pain in her chest that had nothing to do with a physical ailment.

She missed Philip. Perish the thought!

He had been gone less than twenty-four hours, and she missed him—the deep voice, the smile that softened his features and lit his eyes. She even missed the moments when she would have been annoyed with him, when he raised a sardonic brow or exhibited that lamentable streak of arrogance and cocksureness.

An evening and a morning without Philip, and she felt wretched. How the dickens would she feel when he returned to his castle in Wiltshire and she to the Drury Lane?

Growing aware that Stewart and Evalina were embroiled in a debate that was fast assuming the proportions of an argument, she gave herself a brisk mental shake. She could count herself lucky they were intent on each other and had not tried to draw her into the conversation. She would have looked a complete fool, staring into space and mooning over the loss of something she had never held and would never have.

"Hush, Stewart! I will *not* let you take me home." Evalina's chin lifted mutinously. "I drove myself in the gig, and I will leave the same way. And if you're turning as stuffy as Ralph, I shan't dance with you at my party."

"Lina," Stewart said coaxingly, "it would give me great pleasure if you allowed me to accompany you."

Miss Lyndon's face softened and it looked as though he'd have his way. But, unwisely, he added a rider.

"Your papa would not like it if he knew you did not take a groom. And Stanbrook, no doubt, would call me out if I allowed you to leave without protection."

"*Stanbrook!*"

Evalina closed her sunshade with a snap. Much in the manner of a fencer wielding his foil, she thrust the point of the parasol against Stewart's chest.

"I don't want to hear that name again. Never was I so deceived in anyone! And you, Stewart! You still have not told me what you said or did to Miss Carswell to make her upset. I think you're no better than Stanbrook."

Stewart turned pale. "Lina, I cannot tell you until Megan and I—"

"But if you want to prove me wrong," Evalina cut in ruthlessly, "all you need to do is leave. I did not come to see Stanbrook *or* you. I came to visit with Miss Carswell."

"How kind of you," Meg said quickly. It was time someone put a stop to the squabble. Stewart, if given the chance to say anything else, would only make matters worse by uttering unwise protestations. "I was hoping for an opportunity to get to know you better, but I feared you'd be too busy before the party."

"Oh, no," Evalina said airily. "Mama takes care of everything. Would you like to know what my gown looks like? Madame Frenault made it while I was in London, and it is absolutely stunning."

"Lina. Megan." Stewart sketched a bow. "Will you excuse me, please?"

Evalina inclined her head regally, but Meg gave him a smile. Poor Stewart. If he were just a bit more like Philip, he'd deal much better with Miss Lyndon.

Stewart did not respond to her smile. Looking harassed, almost desperate, he said, "Megan, won't you please consider what we discussed?"

She had believed that Evalina's appearance had driven the proposal out of his mind or, at least, made him think better of it. Apparently, she was wrong.

"There is nothing to consider, Stewart."

His hands clenched as though in anticipation of another shaking, but he turned on his heel and stalked off.

Miss Lyndon watched until he disappeared behind some shrubbery. She turned to Meg with suspiciously bright eyes and a mouth that trembled just the tiniest bit.

"There!" she said. "Now we can be comfortable."

"Yes, indeed." Meg started walking in the direction of the house. Stewart and Evalina at odds did not suit her purpose at all.

"Miss Lyndon, was it quite wise to dismiss Stewart so summarily?"

Evalina looked defiant, then uncertain. "Why do you say that, Miss Carswell?"

"I had the impression that you quite liked my cousin. But now he's left, believing that you cannot bear his company. And that is not true, is it?"

"No."

Swinging her parasol, Evalina walked in pensive silence.

"And you plan to give Lord Stanbrook the cut direct, which," Meg pointed out, "might deprive you of *two* gentlemen if there's to be dancing at your party."

"Oh, yes, there will be dancing." Evalina looked subdued. "I did not tell Stewart that I *never* wanted his company again. Do you think . . . ?" Her voice trailed. "I'd be stuck with Ralph and Flossie. And Dr. Meade. . . ."

Meg hoped she had made her point. She bypassed the French doors of the music room and continued along the front of the house.

"So Mr. Flossingham is still with you? I am looking forward to getting better acquainted with him. He seems to be a very nice young man."

"Yes," Evalina said absently. "Flossie can be fun. More than Ralph." She took a deep breath. "Miss Carswell, before I leave I'll speak with Stewart. I don't want him to think he cannot ask me to dance tomorrow night."

Meg's smile flashed. "Good. And now, will you join me in a cup of tea and some scones or whatever I can coax out of Mrs. Sutton at this time of day? I am famished. You see, I missed breakfast this morning."

"I'll join you. Your cook makes the best scones in all of Berkshire."

"They are very good, although—" She had been about to praise Mrs. Bellamy, the cook at the Fighting Cock, whose scones were light as air. But a tavern in Seven

271

Dials was hardly a subject to broach with the squire's young daughter.

As casually as possible, Meg asked, "What about Lord Stanbrook? Do you still plan to snub him?"

They were mounting the steps to the front door. Evalina came to a stop and turned wide, questioning eyes on Meg.

"Do you think I should not?"

Meg shook her head. "It is never wise to alienate a gentleman. Especially when one is as good as promised to him."

"*Promised* to him?" Evalina blinked up at Meg. "Oh, no! It is Mama who wants me to marry Lord Stanbrook. And I suppose Papa does, too. And perhaps for just a little while in London I also thought it might be very agreeable to be a countess. But nothing was ever settled and Lord Stanbrook never said anything the least bit lover-like. And, of course, now it is quite out of the question."

"Of course," said Meg, whose heart had begun to flutter quite alarmingly. "Because of the way he treated you yesterday?"

Evalina giggled. "I'm not quite as silly as you think me, Miss Carswell. Actually, that was merely the crowning insult. I have been disenchanted with him ever since I came home."

"But perhaps he is not disenchanted with you. Have you told him how you feel?"

"There's no need, is there? We did not have an understanding, and when he called at Lyndon Court, he hardly noticed me. He talked to Ralph and Flossie about you and the theater. Or, more often, he was closeted with Papa and asked him about things that happened ages ago—like when your mother still lived here. So, you see, he never behaved like a suitor, and I believe he's really more interested in you than he is in me."

"Rubbish."

Even to her own ears, Meg sounded less than convincing. But it did not matter. Miss Lyndon had lost interest in the subject and was staring down the long, tree-shaded drive.

"I hear a carriage," she said. "If it does not turn in at the gates here, then it's probably Grandmama and I must go."

And if it did make the turn, thought Meg, could it possibly be Philip already?

Then she laughed at herself. The only way Philip could have accomplished that feat was by starting on the return journey a few hours after he arrived in London.

"It's not Grandmama," said Miss Lyndon. "It's company for you. Whoever it is, please bring him to my party."

Meg distinguished two large trunks strapped atop the traveling coach. Did a gentleman require two trunks for a visit?

"What if it is a lady?"

"You may bring her, too," Evalina conceded generously. "Do you know who it is?"

Meg frowned at the coachman pulling on the reins. He looked familiar. The carriage came to a stop just as the two Carswell Hall footmen hurried out of the house. The second footman opened the door and let down the steps while James, fully aware of his position as first footman, stood by to help the traveler alight.

Meg first saw a dashing black velvet hat as the lady inside the coach bent her head to accommodate the tall peacock feather. Once the feather was safely out the door, she looked up. Honey-brown curls framed a pixyish face. A generous mouth curved in a wide smile, and dancing gray eyes looked straight at Meg.

"Maryann!"

Chapter Twenty-Two

Meg's pleasure could have been surpassed only if Philip had followed Lady Maryann out of the coach. But that would have been expecting too much. It was going on eleven-thirty, and he could hardly have started his investigations before eight or nine that morning.

After Meg had hugged and kissed her friend, introduced Miss Lyndon, and sent Maryann's maid with the housekeeper to ready the chamber next to her own, she whisked Evalina and Maryann into the salon for refreshments.

Evalina, indeed a very well-brought-up young lady, excused herself after one cup of tea.

"You will have lots to tell each other," she said, giving Meg and Maryann a dimpled smile. "And I really don't dare stay much longer on account of Grandmama. She doesn't like travel, but she's braving the roads to attend my party tomorrow. You'll come, too, Lady Maryann, won't you?"

"She will," said Meg. "Did you want to see Stewart before you leave, Miss Lyndon?"

Evalina blushed. "Yes. I daresay the footman will know where he can be found."

As the salon door closed behind Miss Lyndon, the clock in the Great Hall struck the noon hour.

Meg poured more tea. "Gracious, Maryann, I just

275

realized that you must have left town in the middle of the night. Are you tired?"

"Not a bit. I slept in the carriage."

"Did Stanbrook tell you—I assume it was Lord Stanbrook who sent you?"

"You might say so. He arrived at about eleven last night, and when he'd told his tale, Stephen rang for Jane and asked her to pack my trunks immediately."

At eleven! Philip must have driven as though he'd been racing for a wager.

Aloud, she said, "Then Stanbrook told you everything?"

"Everything?" Maryann gave Meg a sidelong look. "I wonder. But he did tell us about the will and the stalker and the toss you took. And about your father's fall and the knife with the switched initials that may have caused both."

"Well, that *is* everything."

"Nonsense. But if you like, we can talk about the unsaid things later."

Surely Philip had made no mention of certain private matters! After all, he was a gentleman.

"There's nothing to talk about," Meg said firmly.

Maryann only smiled and picked up her tea cup. "Stanbrook also said I'd find you laid up in bed."

"And did you believe him?"

Maryann chuckled. "I told him not to count on it, but he was quite sure of himself. Wagered a guinea, poor man."

"Poor man, indeed! That cocksureness is going to be his downfall yet. I wish he'd placed a monkey on the bet. Or better still, a plum!"

"I know a monkey is five hundred pounds. But what on earth is a plum?"

"A hundred thousand pounds."

Maryann raised a brow but made no comment.

While they finished their tea, Meg briefly told Maryann of the undergardener's death, Alvina's strange

276

ehavior, and Stewart's unexpected proposal of marriage.

"Meg, this is worse than I thought! No wonder Stanrook was worried."

"But I can deal with it. I only hope that Stanbrook can ositively link Will Fratt to one or more of the incidents n London and that he can find out who engaged the nan's services."

"Wouldn't it be easier from this end?"

"No. Everything that happened here points equally to lvina or Stewart. Or," Meg added judiciously, "to Janny Grimshaw. Did Stanbrook tell you about her?"

"That, but for being born on the wrong side of the lanket, she would have been a Carswell, your father's unt? Yes, Stanbrook told me."

"She tried to stop my father from going after Mother nd me."

Maryann reached for Meg's hand. "I know how vearying this is for you."

Meg returned the pressure of her friend's hand. Marynn was the one person who could truly understand her ilemma. She had been betrothed to Lord Tammadge, vhom society regarded as an upstanding, respectable nan. But he was a black-hearted scoundrel. When Marynn learned of his nefarious deeds, she had been torn etween duty to her father, who expected her to honor he betrothal, and her conscience, which demanded that ammadge be brought to justice.

"I don't want to suspect anyone," Meg said. "And I nd up suspecting each one in turn. It is really quite a orrid feeling."

"The sooner we find the culprit, the better," Maryann aid briskly. "When Stanbrook arrives tomorrow, we'll ave the answers we need."

Meg raised a brow. "I am not one to deny credit where redit is due, but I doubt Philip can solve the puzzle in 1st one day."

"Philip?"

277

Meg's mouth twitched. "Don't try to tell me you didn't learn Stanbrook's first name within the first half hour of your meeting, for I shan't believe you."

"Very well, I won't try. But Stanbrook is not working alone. Stephen is helping, and when I left town, they were on their way to Sir Nathaniel's home."

A day in Maryann's lively company always passed quickly, but especially this one. Lady Maryann had to be introduced to Alvina and Stewart at luncheon, and, of course, to Sir Richard when he emerged from his afternoon rest.

Alvina was gracious—she would be toward an earl's daughter. Stewart was polite but rather distant, as if his mind were on other, more weighty matters. And Sir Richard was pathetically pleased to meet a friend of Meg's.

Mostly though, Meg and Maryann talked. Meg wanted to know about the progress of the botanical gardens Maryann was designing in London and how Stephen fared with the solicitors and executors of Lord Tammadge's estate. She was overjoyed to learn that Fant Court, which Tammadge had wrested from Stephen's brother in a crooked card game, had already been restored to Richard Fant's widow, and that the only matter still unresolved was the restitution of funds Lord Tammadge had illicitly won.

Dinner put an end to their tête-à-têtes, and after the meal, Maryann declared that she couldn't keep her eyes open another minute.

She smiled apologetically at the assembled company. "Forgive me, but I did start from London shortly after four o'clock this morning. I'm afraid a nap in the carriage does not make up for a night's sleep."

Meg accompanied her friend upstairs and left her in the capable hands of her maid. Closing the door to Maryann's chamber, she stood irresolute. She did not want to turn to the salon and Alvina's company, but neither did he feel like sleeping.

The corridor stretched before her. Just a few steps away was the door to her own room. Farther down, near Alvina's chambers, the narrow passageway concealing the back stairs branched off to the left. It was also the way to the east tower.

Without hesitation, Meg passed her room and entered the tunnel-like opening on the left. For a while, the dim light from the main corridor guided her; then she found herself in darkness. Feeling her way along the wall, she kept going, irresistibly drawn toward the rooms in the east tower where she had spent the first two weeks of her life—and where her mother made the decision to run away.

Meg reached the tower without mishap—only to find her purpose thwarted by a locked door. Muttering imprecations that would rouse the envy of a Seven Dials dweller, she turned and retraced her steps.

She did not like to admit defeat, but there was nothing she could do at the moment. The housekeeper, who carried the keys to all the doors on her chatelaine, would have retired by now. And before she'd ask Alvina or Stewart for a key, she'd climb the tower walls and crawl through a window.

Reluctantly, Meg retired to her room. The lamp on the night table was lit and the bedcovers were turned down. From the dressing room came the sound of soft breathing, for she had told Elspeth from the beginning that, unless specifically asked to do so, she was not to wait up.

Meg did not think she'd be able to sleep, but the next sound she heard were five soft chimes from the clock on the mantel. Still too early to see Mrs. Sutton.

But as she was about to draw the covers over her head, she remembered the secret door from the gallery to the west tower. What if there were such a door from the opposite part of the house into the east tower?

She had never dressed so quickly and so quietly. Collecting a candle and the tinderbox, she tiptoed from the room, down the corridor and the back stairs to the first floor.

Alas, a thorough inspection of the two unused salons adjoining the east tower proved fruitless. No full-length portrait hid a secret door latch; in fact, the walls in those two rooms were conspicuously bare of paintings, and the furniture was shrouded in Holland covers.

Nurturing a feeling of ill-usage, Meg gave up the search for a secret door and went to look for the housekeeper instead. It was just like a man, she thought, that Philip had not inquired about other secret doors when Marsden showed him the one in the gallery. Any self-respecting woman would have.

At five-thirty, Meg faced the housekeeper in the kitchen.

"Aye," said Mrs. Sutton. "I did have a key, Miss Megan. But just yesterday Mr. Stewart asked for it. He said the man that's supposed to look at the tower may come sooner than expected."

Meg could not believe her ill fortune. "You gave the key to Mr. Stewart? Doesn't he have his own?"

"Not Mr. Stewart. Mrs. Elmore, now, she does have her own key. But the third one's been gone many years. I thought mayhap Miss Rosemary took it with her?"

Meg shrugged. "I don't know, Mrs. Sutton. But if my mother took the key she must have thrown it away, else I would have found it after her death."

She turned to leave, determined to get one of the keys if she had to steal it.

"Miss Meg!" Jigger, his sharp features softened by a look of great importance, stood at the stove and stirred something in a huge copper kettle.

Jigger, who had been a pickpocket before Fletcher took him in charge. And if Stewart expected the architect, wouldn't he carry the key with him?

"Miss Meg, oi's almost done wi' the porridge here. It's

280

fer the stable lads, ye see." He lowered an eyelid in an exaggerated wink. "An' oi'll be seein' Mr. Stewart real soon. He always goes fer a ride at six."

Meg scanned the kitchen. Mrs. Sutton could be heard muttering in the storage room, Cook was occupied with bread dough, and the kitchen maid was scraping ashes from the old-fashioned brick oven.

"I don't want Mr. Stewart to know about the key, or he'll want to go with me. Jigger, can you—"

"Watch yerself, Miss Meg," Jigger interrupted sternly. "Oi don't hold kindly with insults."

"Sorry, lad." Meg gave him an apologetic smile. "I'll be waiting in my room, then."

She felt just a little guilty when she climbed back into bed, and wondered if Fletcher would have approved. But when, an hour later, Elspeth brought along with the hot chocolate a large key, slightly rusted at the wards, she could not help but feel elated.

"From Jigger, Miss Megan," Elspeth announced unnecessarily.

Meg pounced on the key, almost oversetting pot and cup as the maid placed the tray in her lap. She had no desire for hot chocolate, but took a sip anyway, then quickly dressed a second time. Snatching up the candle once more, and patting the pocket of her gown for assurance that the tinderbox was still there, she sped away without a word to Elspeth, who stood gaping after her.

With a key and a light, everything was ridiculously simple, and in less than five minutes she stood inside the tower bedchamber. The room looked exactly as Philip had described it, and yet it did not. Meg had not expected it to look as though her mother had only just left.

Neither had she expected to see the old woman asleep in the rocking chair by the crib. Martha Grimshaw. Nanny.

Heart beating a rapid tattoo, Meg stood motionless, her

eyes on the slight figure in a full-skirted black gown, a ruffled cap askew on wispy gray hair.

Alvina had told her that Nanny had taken to visiting the tower, but how had she gotten in?

Careful not to startle the sleeper, Meg tiptoed across the room until she stood on the rug covering the wooden floor by the bed, the crib, and the rocker. She wanted to speak with Martha Grimshaw, but she'd have better results if she waited for her to awaken naturally.

Meg looked around, wondering at the immaculate condition of the chamber. There wasn't a speck of dust anywhere, the bed was made up with crisp linen, the blankets in the crib were fleecy white.

Four narrow windows allowed pale morning light to filter into the room. Meg blew out the candle and set it atop the chest of drawers near the crib. Noiselessly, she pulled the drawers open one by one, touching with amazement the tiny garments, the swaddling cloths, all smelling of sunshine and fresh air.

After twenty-four years, everything should smell musty. Meg cast a look at the sleeping woman. Could Nanny . . . ? But why?

When she turned to the armoire that took up the better part of one wall, she caught her breath. There, next to the richly gleaming wood, was one of the fissures Stewart had mentioned. The crack as wide as her hand ran in a zig-zag line from ceiling to floor.

She stepped close to the wall and peeked through the crack into the adjoining dressing room. But the hip bath and curtained closet held no interest for her. The armoire did.

Meg swung the doors open, releasing a cloud of camphor and potpourri. The hinges creaked a little, but she was no longer concerned about waking Nanny. She had seen the gowns. Her mother's gowns.

What a contrast to the cheap cottons—very often patched or remade from dresses bought at a second-hand store—that Rosemary had worn in London. Here were silks and satins, dainty muslins, all in the delicate pastels that would have been flattering to Rosemary's pale-blond beauty.

Meg stretched out a hand to touch a long-sleeved velvet gown of soft blue. It would have matched the color of her mother's eyes.

"Lydia!"

Meg whirled.

"Mrs. Grimshaw. Goodness, how you startled me!" She gave a shaky laugh. "I feel as if you had caught me doing something forbidden."

"And so you should. You're snooping, Lydia!" Perched on the very edge of the rocking chair, Nanny looked as though she were about to get up and administer appropriate chastisement.

"I am not Lydia. I am Megan, Sir Richard and Rosemary's daughter. And you can hardly call it snooping if I want to see the things my mother left when she ran away."

Nanny gave her a hard stare.

Slowly, Meg walked toward the old woman. "You do remember that Rosemary ran away, don't you, Mrs. Grimshaw?"

Nanny slumped againt the back of the chair, setting it to rock ever so gently.

"Megan," she muttered. "I *told* Sir Richard she'd end up having the Carswell red hair."

Excitement welled in Meg. She dropped to her knees beside the small figure in the rocking chair.

"But he did not believe you. And Alvina did her best to convince him that I was not his daughter. Yet that was hardly reason enough for my mother to run away. What happened, Mrs. Grimshaw? Why was my mother so frightened that she took me and fled?"

Nanny's back stiffened. "Does no good raking up the past! If I had spoken up then, it would be different. But I

283

didn't, and I must live with it."

"What was it that you kept to yourself all these years?"

But Martha Grimshaw only shook her head. She put a hand to her cap and with a quick shove and a tug set it straight.

Meg tried a different approach. "Why did you not speak up? Were you afraid, like my mother?"

"If I was, it was for a different reason. I knew it was best if Rosemary took the baby away. It was the baby that caused the trouble. Little Megan. Such a beautiful baby."

"Mrs. Grimshaw, *I* was that baby."

Dark, bird-like eyes rested on Meg's face. "And now you're a beautiful woman. Like Lydia. But you're still causing trouble. Go away, child. Go back where you came from."

Feeling frustrated and disappointed, Meg rose to her feet. Once more, she looked about the room.

"Is it you who keeps everything neat and fresh in here?"

"Aye. It's what Sir Richard told me to do."

Meg swallowed, but the lump in her throat was not easily dislodged. Her voice was husky when she asked, "Does Alvina not mind?"

"Alvina?" The gentle rocking of the chair stopped abruptly as Nanny sat up, both feet planted firmly on the floor. "She didn't know. Never set foot in the tower until a week or two ago. Said she was looking for Rosemary's journal. Wants to give it to you."

"A journal? Did Alvina find it?"

"Of course not. Rosemary wouldn't leave it behind, would she?"

"I shouldn't think so."

But if her mother had brought the journal to London, it must have been destroyed when the glover's shop burned.

"Mrs. Grimshaw, how do you get into the tower? Isn't it kept locked because of the danger?"

284

"What danger?" Nanny gave a snort. "A bit of stone and mortar crumbling? But that's mainly in the lower rooms, and Sir Richard's going to have it fixed. And until Alvina saw me, none of the doors were ever locked."

"You have a key, then?"

"Yes, I have a key," the old woman said tartly. "It was Miss Rosemary's, and if you take it, I'll still have ways of getting where I want to go."

"I shan't take it away from you. But I would like to know why my mother ran away with me. You told Sir Richard I wasn't safe here. Why, Mrs. Grimshaw? Why was I not safe?"

"I'm leaving. Must check on Phyllis Hogden's baby. 'Twas her first, and a breech."

As Nanny Grimshaw rose, a small, tissue-wrapped box that had been hidden in the folds of her voluminous gown fell to the floor. Meg picked it up and held it out to Nanny.

"No, you keep it, child. I brought it for you. It's marchpanes."

Marchpanes.

Meg felt as though she had received a vicious blow. She could neither speak nor breathe, and she stared numbly after the old nurse as she hobbled out the door.

When the slow footsteps receded down the tower stairs, Meg let out a shuddering breath. The box she had received at the Drury Lane had been wrapped in pink tissue paper. This one was wrapped in white. The piece of marchpane she had started to eat at the theater had contained poison. Arsenic, the physician said. There were ways of determining whether something was poisoned and what kind of poison it was.

Slowly, she pushed the box into the deep pocket of her gown, where, together with the tinderbox, it knocked uncomfortably against her thigh. She closed the armoire—it would be a pity if after all these years dust were allowed to spoil the gowns—and quickly, without bothering to retrieve the candle, left the tower.

Darkness engulfed her as soon as she closed the door. She was tempted to pick up her skirts and run. But the key must be returned to Stewart. She snatched it from the lock, then gave in to the panicked voice in her mind that urged her to hurry and deliver the marchpanes to Dr. Meade.

Perhaps if she had not run in the narrow passage, or if at least she had not hummed *Greensleeves* to drown the sound of her rapid heartbeat, she would have heard the approaching footsteps or the voice softly calling her name. But when she crashed into a rock-solid body, she was taken totally by surprise.

She screamed. Her lungs were strong, and her voice had been trained to carry. But none of those attributes were of benefit when a large hand pressed her face against the rough fabric of a man's coat and an iron arm caught her around the waist so that she could not pull away.

With the key clutched in her fist, she aimed a blow where she believed the attacker's head must be. But either her aim was poor, or he was very tall.

"Dash it, Meg!" a familiar voice grumbled. "Must you always be hitting at me?"

Chapter Twenty-Three

Philip!

Relief and a blazing joy filled her, but she could not speak, for he still held her face crushed to his chest. She pounded his back—to no avail—and finally let herself relax against that lean, hard body.

Immediately the hand pressing the back of her head was removed.

"What are you trying to do, Stanbrook?" Torn between laughter and irritation, Meg looked up at him. But of course she could see nothing in the stygian darkness. "Suffocate me?"

"What I *should* do is box your ears for going into the tower. Are you all right?" he asked, his voice thick with concern.

"I am. Truly," she assured him. "Except for a crushed nose."

"Goose." The tenderness was a caress. "Should I have allowed you to scream when we're practically outside Alvina's door?"

"No, but your method of silencing me leaves much to be desired."

"Let me try a different method, then. Perhaps this would be more to your liking?"

The arm around her waist tightened. His free hand unerringly found her chin, tilting it up, and his mouth closed over hers.

This was much more to her liking, a kiss perfectly designed to keep her quiet for as long as he wished. She had no desire to speak, let alone scream; she wanted only for time to stand still so she could savor the taste of his mouth, the feel of his hard, lean body against hers.

The heavy tower key dropped on her foot. She was scarcely aware of it as she reached up to touch Philip's face, his hair. She moved a little, wanting only to get closer to him, but the slight shift brought the pocket in the skirt of her gown between them—and with it the instinctive horror of Nanny's gift.

Philip released her. "What the dickens are you carrying in your gown?"

"It's a tinderbox and—and a box of marchpanes Nanny Grimshaw gave me in the tower."

For a moment, Philip said nothing.

He felt for her hand and clasped it tightly. "Let's go outside to talk. I don't suppose you carry a candle as well?"

"I did, but I left it in the tower room."

"Never mind."

He guided her back toward the tower. Opening the door—she must have left it unlocked!—he pulled her inside. On the narrow landing, which gave access to the bedroom, the dressing room, and the spiral stairway with its slitlike windows in the outer wall, she had her first look at Philip.

The sight was not reassuring. His features had always been harsh, but never before had she seen such a hard look in his eyes or the grim lines etched around the mouth.

Without speaking, they went down the stairs Nanny must have descended a short while ago. As they approached the ground floor, Philip's grip on her hand tightened.

"Careful, now. This is where part of the ceiling cracked. Most of the rubble was cleared away, but every

288

now and again bits of mortar still fall."

She was glad to take her mind off Philip's grim face and the marchpanes in her pocket, if only for a moment.

"I believe the architect will arrive much sooner than expected. Do you suppose the tower can be saved?"

"Very likely. I'm no expert, but the damage doesn't look too bad to me."

"The house would look very strange with only one tower."

Philip said nothing, but opened a door heavily reinforced with iron. Then they stood outside in a tiny plot of walled garden with a fountain in the center, and a marble statue. To their left, the early morning sun just touched a wooden bench beneath a canopy of willow branches.

"Meg, look at me." Clasping both her hands, Philip searched her face. Slowly, some of the grimness left him. "I believe you really are all right. When Elspeth told me you had gone into the tower, I—"

"Elspeth! Why, the little tattletale! And I didn't even tell her where I planned to go."

"Which made her curious enough to peek out the door. But she should have gone with you," he said sternly. "She was too scared, the silly chit. Just stayed in the main corridor waiting for you. By the time I got there, she was shaking like a blancmange."

"Speaking of you getting here—I believed you still in London."

"Did you, now?"

Her face grew warm under his look. But she had not promised to sit and meekly wait for his return. So why should she feel guilty that he had surprised her in the tower?

Adroitly, she changed the subject. "It hardly seems possible that you should have discovered anything in such a short time. But Maryann said Stephen was helping and both of you went to call on Sir Nathaniel in the middle of the night."

His mouth twitched, and she knew he had seen

through her ploy. Perhaps she had been flattering herself, and she was not a good actress after all. But she had no time to let the lowering reflection bother her.

"And a good thing it was we went straight to the Bow Street magistrate," said Philip. Touching her arm, he ushered her to the bench. "He already had some of the information we sought. In fact, he was on the point of dispatching a runner to Carswell Hall."

"How could he know what we're looking for? Dash it, Philip! Tell me everything. From the beginning."

She would have sat on the dew-moistened slats of the bench, but Philip stopped her. Removing his coat, he spread it over the damp wood before allowing her to sit down.

"Sir Nathaniel was there when Fletcher told you about Carswell Hall, wasn't he?"

"Yes, of course! That's how he knew." The tinderbox and the box of marchpanes in her skirt pocket came to rest against her thigh as she arranged the folds of her gown. "Because Fletcher also talked about the attempts on my life."

Philip remained standing. "You made light of the incidents, but Sir Nathaniel had come to trust Fletcher's instinct. He set two runners to investigate—"

"On second thought," she interrupted, "don't tell me everything. Just *what* Sir Nathaniel discovered."

"As you wish. One of the runners tracked down a man named Tom Easterwood, who six or seven years ago had been very much enamored of a young dancer named Meg Fletcher."

She gave him a startled look, but hastily averted her eyes when she encountered the gleam of amusement in his. He might speak as if he'd never heard the name Tom Easterwood before, but she was not misled.

"Tom married some other girl," he said blandly. "However, when Meg became a famous actress, he took to hanging around the theater side entrance and back stage."

Once again, a treacherous warmth stung Meg's cheeks. Not because of Tom's childish behavior, of which she had been unaware, but because she remembered how Philip had teased her about him that first evening at Carswell Hall when she had foolishly admitted to having held hands with Tom.

Apparently oblivious to her embarrassment, Philip continued his report.

"This Tom Easterwood, after prolonged questioning and a solemn oath that his wife would not be told of his habit, finally admitted to having seen a tall, very thin man take a small box wrapped in pink tissue paper into Meg Fletcher's dressing room on the night a physician had to be summoned for the actress."

"Pink wrapping. Yes, that was the box. But there are hundreds, maybe thousands of tall, very thin men in London," Meg pointed out. "This doesn't help us at all. And I wish you wouldn't talk as though you were a barrister before the King's Bench. Just get to the point."

For the first time that morning, Philip's face relaxed into a wide grin that obliterated the worry lines around his mouth.

"Certainly, your grace."

She wanted to smile back at him, but that wouldn't do at all.

"Stanbrook!" she said warningly.

"Yes. To the point. This particular tall, thin man was dressed in rags, and Easterwood believed he was a beggar earning a penny by making a delivery. Now, I admit that most beggars are thin, but they are also undersized. Only one of the beggars who had been hanging around the Drury Lane Theatre for the past several months was also very tall. He was known as Will the Wheezer. Did I tell you that the man I chased from the gazebo wheezed?"

Her breath caught. Will the Wheezer. Will Fratt?

"No, Stanbrook, you did not. But then, that doesn't surprise me. I've since learned several things you did not tell me."

291

Aside from a quick, searching look, he gave no sign of being affected by the implied accusation.

"The runners also discovered a young woman who witnessed from her window the attack on you outside the Fighting Cock. Fletcher questioned her at the time, but she did not dare tell him what she saw, because one of the men was her . . ."

Philip seemed at a loss for words. Meg was not.

"He was her pimp? Sally Biggum is the only *young woman* whose window faces the spot where I was attacked. Her husband disappeared two years ago, and the only way she can feed and clothe her children is by selling herself."

To her surprise, Philip reached out and touched a finger to her cheek.

"I should have known better than to think you were unaware of the young woman's profession. No doubt she is one of the many you've given soup and bread at the tavern."

"And I patched her up when her 'protector' beat her," Meg said quietly. "Since she was willing to talk now, I assume she had not seen the cad for some time and believed he had abandoned her. Was he Will the Wheezer—Will Fratt?"

"Those are the two names Sally gave the Bow Street runners." Philip's face was inscrutable. "You *have* been busy since I left. Since you know of Will Fratt, I assume you know also that he had disappeared?"

"He is dead."

Philip stood motionless while she told him what little she knew about the undergardener's death.

"And even if Dr. Meade confirms that he was killed with the same poison that made me ill," she concluded, "we'll never know now who engaged Fratt's services."

"I have a fairly shrewd notion who did."

"So do I. But we cannot act on a notion."

Philip sat down beside her and took her hand in his. It was not the touch of a lover or seducer, but that of a friend. It was infinitely soothing.

"There's still the carriage incident," he said.

As once before, a picture of the driver flashed through Meg's mind—the tall coachman's hat and upstanding collar obscuring the face, the flapping capes of the driving coat that would disguise a hollow chest and narrow shoulders.

"A man of many talents, this Will Fratt," she said musingly. "Beggar, pimp, thug, coachman, not to forget gardener. I wouldn't have trusted him with the money to hire a carriage and four. I would have hired it myself."

"Exactly. And the runners have heard of a flower girl who occupied a spot in Piccadilly for over a year. If she remembers the incident, she may also remember the insignia of the livery stable on the carriage. And livery stables, especially those with horses of the quality you described, keep logs."

"The team of matched chestnuts," she murmured. "But something tells me the flower girl is no longer in Piccadilly?"

"The crossing sweep said she has opened a stall in Covent Garden. The runners are looking for her."

Meg said nothing. She had every confidence in the Bow Street runners. If the girl was in Covent Garden, they'd find her. But the odds were that she had simply disappeared.

Odds were, too, that whoever hired the carriage had given a false name at the livery stable. But why disillusion Philip at this point?

"I went to the corner of Oxford and North Audley Streets," he said.

"Yes?" Meg sat up and half turned to have a better look at him. "Did you find anyone who still remembers my grandfather's shop and Mother?"

"More than I hoped to find." He gave her a rueful look. "But you were correct. They did not care to confide in someone of my class—until I got to Mrs. Kindred."

"Mother's close friend! What did she say?"

"Plenty." Philip chuckled in reminiscence.

Meg snatched her hand away. "Stanbrook, this is not the time to tease me."

"No. I beg your pardon, Meg. It is just that I have never met anyone quite like Mrs. Kindred. At first, thinking I had overawed the other neighbors with my title, I did not tell her who I was. But that did not get me anywhere. Then I handed her my card, asking her to let me know if she remembered anything of consequence, and suddenly she wouldn't stop talking. She was *impressed* by the title."

"You were lucky, then, that she could read. What did she tell you?"

"Mrs. Kindred said that after the fire, before Fletcher took you and your mother away, Rosemary went from neighbor to neighbor begging them to tell anyone who came asking that she and the child had died."

"Why?" Meg dreaded the answer, and yet she had to know.

"Because her sister-in-law, Alvina Elmore, swore to kill the baby."

Meg expelled her breath in a rush. The answer was not unexpected.

And yet—

"Stanbrook," she said, placing her hand on the two boxes in her pocket, "the marchpanes Nanny Grimshaw gave me—"

"Yes. It gave me quite a turn when you told me. But there's no point worrying about that—not until we find out that the marchpanes are indeed poisoned."

"I was about to take them to Dr. Meade. He is doing the postmortem examination on Fratt, so I know he does have the equipment to check for poison."

"Give them to me. I'll send Harv into the village."

The small box was barely visible when he closed his hand over it. "There cannot be many pieces of confection inside. But, then, I don't suppose it would take more than one to kill a person."

"It's the same size as the box I received at the theater, and it contained four pieces. I took only one small bite; then I was distracted by my dresser, who had found a tear in the gown I planned to wear for my visit to the Green Room."

"Admirable woman, your dresser! I'll buy her a diamond necklace. And a bracelet, too."

"I'm sure she'll appreciate that." Meg wondered if he was serious. And if so, didn't that mean he truly cared? She pushed the thought away.

"I doubt, however, that I would have taken a second bite. The marchpane had a disgustingly bitter after-taste."

"Then, supposing Fratt was killed with arsenic, and supposing it was given to him in food, he'd have had to be quite greedy to ingest a quantity of poison large enough to kill him."

Meg remembered the starved appearance of the under-gardener.

"He would have been greedy."

Beside her, Philip moved restlessly. The bench was hard, though not totally uncomfortable. But of course he had just spent hours sitting on the box of his curricle.

Meg was about to suggest that he get some rest, when he said, "Phelps told me that you visited him in the stables yesterday morning."

"Yes, I needed to find out who could have sabotaged my father's saddle. Do you object?"

From the corner of her eye, she caught the slight upward curl of his mouth.

"Much good would it do me. No, my Meg. I do not like that you go sleuthing on your own, but I shan't make the mistake of telling you that you mustn't."

"Thank you." She was oddly touched by his admission. "And really, Stanbrook, there is no need for you to worry about me. I can take care of myself."

"So you keep assuring me." He sounded tired. "Is there anything else that happened yesterday and might

295

be of interest to me?"

Once again, Meg shifted on the bench to look fully at him. The sun had moved while they were talking. It touched his dark hair with golden lights, but it also showed the grim, tight grooves near his mouth which she had believed gone, and the shadows of exhaustion beneath his eyes.

She could not possibly tell him now about Stewart's strange proposal of marriage.

"But Meg," said Maryann, holding the coffee cup suspended between her mouth and the tray on her lap. "It never does any good to keep important things from the man you love."

Curled up in a comfortable armchair by Maryann's bed, Meg stared at her friend. When she and Philip had parted, she had immediately gone to Maryann's room. While they shared breakfast, she had recounted every thing that had happened . . . everything except the brief kiss.

In fact, she had never, not the day before or this morning, touched upon those private moments between her and Philip. Now that Maryann had brought the matter up, however, she would not deny the existence of contradictory and often stormy emotions.

"The man I love? Maryann, how can you say that with such sureness, such authority, when I never mentioned my feelings? I'm not even certain I know what my feelings are!"

"Aren't you?" Maryann laughed softly. "How strange Two years ago you were such an authority on love that you told me how I felt about Stephen before I recognized it myself. And now the roles are reversed."

"Yes, but—"

"And don't think for a moment that you had to tell me anything. It's what you *didn't* say about Stanbrook that makes me sure you're in love with him."

"I am attracted to him." Meg toyed with the fabric of her skirt, pleating it, smoothing it, then pleating it again. "I never denied that. I come alive when he touches me, and when we kiss—"

"Something stirs deep inside you," Maryann said calmly. "Something that makes you want to give yourself to him."

"Something that makes me want to disregard principles and pride," Meg said dryly. "And that, my dear, is lust, not love."

"Only if you're otherwise quite indifferent to him. If you do not care whether he is with you or not."

Oh, but she cared!

"If you never wish you could share his life."

"Well, that settles it." Meg felt strangely deflated. "How can I wish to share his life? Stanbrook is looking for a countess. I am an actress."

Maryann gave a peal of laughter. "Oh, Meg! I don't believe what I am hearing."

"And I don't see anything funny in what I said."

"You will. Just let me get my breath."

Stifling a giggle, Maryann pushed the breakfast tray off her lap, then, curling her legs beneath her, turned to face Meg more directly.

"When I first met Stephen, he kept calling me an innocent. I was deeply insulted even though I realized that there was some truth to it. And I always wished I were as sophisticated as you seemed to be. But, by George, you're even more of an innocent than I ever was!"

"I've been called many things, but never an innocent. Maryann, I must have roused you too soon. Your brains are still addled."

Looking very superior, Maryann said, "It's you who got up too early. Stanbrook, you little peagoose, is *not* looking for a countess. If he wanted a social ornament for a wife, he could have married anytime these past ten years or more. No, Meg. Whether he knows it or not, he is looking for a *woman* to share his life."

"Whether he knows it or not . . ."

Their eyes met, Maryann's dancing with laughter and Meg's quite solemn, even a little doubtful.

Meg took a deep breath.

"Well, then," she said resolutely. "I suppose it behooves me to make certain he *does* know what he wants."

Chapter Twenty-Four

She was in love with Philip. Not merely attracted to him, but in love.

Meg had not felt so lighthearted since her father announced the content of the new will. True, that was only three days ago, but it seemed like eons.

How could she have been so blind, so utterly foolish to think she had succumbed to physical desire alone? Perhaps she must blame the foolishness on her concern that she might follow the path of easy virtue so many of her fellow actresses had taken.

She knew Philip would never have offered *carte blanche*; his sense of honor would not allow it. But she had not been certain of herself, the strength of her pride. There was a slight but definite possibility that, if Philip at some point had called on her again at the theater, she might have succumbed to temptation and made *him* an improper offer—whether he was married to Evalina or not!

Now she need not even worry about Miss Lyndon. Playing "the other woman" was not a role Meg would have enjoyed, but Evalina was clearly interested in Stewart. Meg could concentrate on convincing Philip that his heart's desire was to marry London's foremost actress.

Throughout the morning, she hugged these thoughts

to herself. Beside them, everything else lost importance.

Of course, she still wanted to know who had tried to kill her. Alvina or Nanny? One of the two women was quite mad, and something must be done about it.

Or were they conspirators?

She meant to put the question to Philip, but did not see him until luncheon, when Alvina and Stewart were also present.

It was a strange meal—solely designed, she thought, to snuff her happy mood. On the surface, everything appeared normal. The conventions were observed with a flow of light conversation and polite exchanges. But underneath, Meg was aware of tension, thick and palpable. And it wasn't merely her own rising tension that she felt.

She sat beside Stewart, opposite Maryann and Philip. Every time Alvina, at the foot of the table, started to speak, she saw the tips of Stewart's fingers turn white as his grip tightened on the cutlery.

Maryann was outgoing and vivacious, but Meg was aware of a brittle note in her friend's voice.

Philip seemed relaxed and ate with a hearty appetite. However, his attention was not on the food. He was watching Stewart and Alvina, as though he were trying to catch some silent communication between the two.

But Alvina hardly looked at her son. Most of her conversation was with Maryann, whom she quizzed about the doings of the *ton*. Only once did Meg notice her aunt's gaze on herself. The cold glitter in Alvina's eyes was nothing new, but with the knowledge that twenty-four years ago she had sworn to kill her niece, it became oppressive.

Yet there was no proof that it was Alvina who was trying to kill her now. Only suspicion, that slow poison that destroyed impartiality and common sense.

After the meal, Alvina invited Maryann into the morning room to look at the tapestry she was working. Meg could not, in good conscience, abandon her friend, and she watched with envy as Philip and Stewart escaped through the front door.

She paced near the morning room windows while her aunt explained how she planned to depict various scenes representing a Berkshire family's activities in the country. Alvina grew quite animated as she talked of hunting, house parties, and the Ascot races.

Meg had never seen that side of her aunt, and she wondered if those were memories of Alvina's youth. Surely she had not known much frivolity while living with a husband who had accumulated debts, or later, at Carswell Hall, keeping house for her brother. Meg doubted Sir Richard had entertained much even before his health failed.

Were they part of Alvina's bitterness, those pleasures she'd had to forgo, the missed opportunities?

Meg realized how little she knew about the woman who, next to Sir Richard, was her closest relative. And it was quite useless to speculate.

"Now I understand what my mother suffered," said Maryann, looking at Meg across the expanse of the morning room. "I used to pace when I was restless or troubled, and I'd give Mama the most terrible headaches with my fidgeting."

Meg's eyes widened as she looked toward her friend. "Where is Alvina? I thought you were still discussing the races."

"Mrs. Elmore went to look for some thread she is sure she bought in Ascot yesterday. But now she cannot find it."

"How fortuitous. I was waiting for a chance to lure you away. Come, let me show you the gardens.

Maryann rose with alacrity, and within moments the two young ladies turned into the corridor leading to the music room.

"Don't you get lost in this ramble of passages?" asked Maryann. "I thought our house in Cornwall was confusing in its design, but this is a veritable rabbit warren."

301

"It's not so bad. The front of the house is E-shaped, and then there are the tower wings in the back. What makes it just a little confusing are the short passages leading to rooms that were added to the original structure over the years."

"Thank you." Maryann gave her a withering look. "Your explanation is *very* helpful."

Chuckling, Meg opened the French doors—and came face-to-face with Philip. Their eyes met, and she knew immediately that he had unpleasant news.

"What is it?" Drawing Maryann with her, she stepped outside. "Did you hear from Sir Nathaniel?"

"No, it's Dr. Meade. He has finished his examinations. I took him to the gazebo where we can be undisturbed."

Philip offered no further explanation and Meg did not ask for one. Let the physician be the one to explain his findings.

Simon Meade sat on the gazebo steps where Meg had sat the previous day when Stewart found her. She shot a quick look at Philip. Would there ever be a time—the right time—to tell him about Stewart's proposal? Not that it mattered, since she had no intention of accepting. And yet, she suspected, Philip would not be best pleased if she kept it from him.

The physician rose and Philip briefly introduced him to Lady Maryann. Then, without further ado and without a sign of the joviality that had endeared him to Meg on their first meeting, Dr. Meade made his report.

"The four pieces of confection sent to my office this morning contained arsenic." He gave Meg a troubled look. "And the postmortem examination on Will Fratt established he died from a dose of that same poison."

Meg nodded. She had not doubted that the under gardener was poisoned, but it did not make acceptance any easier. Will Fratt, or Will the Wheezer, had been "a nasty piece o' goods," as Elspeth had put it so succinctly, but he had been murdered.

Because he had failed once too often?

Dr. Meade cleared his throat. "Yesterday, as soon as it was light, Farmer Weller returned to the spot where he discovered the body. He found Fratt's belongings—a bundle of clothing and some foodstuff wrapped in a napkin."

"A napkin, Dr. Meade?" Meg pounced on the irregularity. "Surely you mean a kerchief. Fratt would not have had access to table linen."

She felt Philip's eyes on her and looked at him.

"My Meg," he murmured. "The Bow Street sleuth."

Dr. Meade frowned at them. "No, Miss Carswell. It was a napkin, all right. White damask with the initial *C* stitched in a corner."

"Like those we used at luncheon," said Maryann.

"And wrapped in the napkin was half a sandwich, an apple, and two pieces of marchpane. Poisoned marchpane."

"Thank you, Dr. Meade," said Meg. "Thank you for letting me know so promptly."

There was nothing else to say.

Meg and Maryann followed Dr. Meade and Philip into the stableyard, where an old cob stood patiently waiting between the shafts of the doctor's gig.

"Good day." Simon Meade flicked the whip. "I suppose I'll see you tonight at the Lyndons'."

The two ladies, accompanied by Philip, returned to the morning room. The thought of walking in the gardens had quite slipped their minds.

Meg leaned against the cold fireplace. "So it is Nanny after all."

"It looks that way." Philip started pacing, much as Meg had done earlier. "And yet I cannot shake this odd feeling . . ."

"What feeling?"

"It doesn't fit. Can you see Nanny Grimshaw driving up to London and hiring a thug from the back slums?"

Maryann, seated in front of Alvina's tapestry frame, said, "Neither can I picture Mrs. Elmore in such an

303

environment. And how would she know where to find a desperate character, as this Fratt obviously was?"

"If anyone knows, it's Alvina."

"Why, Philip?" Meg joined Maryann, who had started sorting strands of Alvina's tapestry wool. "Stewart told me she hardly ever goes up to town."

"She lived in London after her marriage. Her husband lost every penny he had in rash speculations and at the gaming tables. Just after Stewart was born, Elmore took rooms in Pye Street, and that's where they lived for two years—until Elmore died in a drunken brawl."

"Pye Street." Meg dropped moss-green tapestry wool atop strands of brown Maryann had set aside. "But that is part of the Westminster rookeries. It is an awful place."

"Yes. It is exactly the place where one would find a man like Fratt." Philip stepped closer. "So you see, Nanny's involvement does not make sense."

"I was thinking earlier that Nanny and Alvina could be in league."

"Possibly." Philip's gaze fell on the worktable where Alvina's materials were spread out. An arrested look crossed his face.

"Meg, hand me that magnifying glass, will you?"

He pulled his clasp knife from a pocket of his coat and trained the lens onto the ivory handle.

"Of course!" said Meg, watching him. "The changed initial! One would need a magnifying glass and a small tool to do such fine work."

Philip looked at her with a faint smile. "My Meg. I'm surprised Sir Nathaniel didn't make you his top runner. How did you find out about the initial?"

"The merest chance. Something my father said."

Maryann asked, "Well? Would Alvina have a small tool such as you mentioned?"

Meg opened her aunt's workbasket and, after some rummaging, extracted a slim, pointed knife, no wider than a blade of grass, with a silver handle.

"This is used to unpick seams," she said. "And,

suppose, the fine stitches on a tapestry. Would it have worked to change an R into a P?"

"Yes, it would. Pray excuse me, ladies."

Philip pocketed his own knife and Alvina's and the magnifying lens as well. Without another word, he strode from the room.

Meg frowned. "I don't like this. You don't suppose he'd confront Alvina, do you?"

"What would that accomplish?" Rising, Maryann shook out her skirts and took a tentative step toward the door. "No, Meg. Your Philip is far too clever to make a move that will not get him anywhere."

Her Philip. The thought made her heart beat faster. She saw Maryann leave. "And where are you going?"

Maryann looked over her shoulder. "Upstairs to rest before Miss Lyndon's party."

"Since when—"

Narrowing her eyes, Meg studied her friend's glowing countenance, the dancing eyes.

"You're increasing! Devil a bit, Maryann! Why didn't you tell me? Up you go, and don't you dare rise until it's time to dress. At six, I'll bring up a tray and—"

"And you ask me why I didn't tell you! Not even Stephen would make me stay in bed the *whole* afternoon."

"That may be so. But Stephen would wring my neck if you wore yourself out while in my care."

"And what will *you* do while I'm safely out of the way?"

"Find out where Philip has gone."

It did not take extraordinary powers of deduction to figure that Philip must have gone to see her father.

Marsden made no demur when she said she'd announce herself. For a moment, she stood in the study door, simply looking at the two gentlemen by the fire. Her father—and the man she wanted to marry.

305

Would marry.

She pushed the thought away. There'd be time enough to anticipate marriage when she had made sure she'd be alive for that event.

Philip turned his head and saw her. He rose.

"Meg, will you join us?"

A certain light in his eyes assured her that he was not displeased. She remembered Maryann's words, "He is *not* looking for a countess. . . . Whether he knows it or not, he is looking for a *woman* to share his life."

Well, *she* was that woman. Meg knew it as surely as she knew that there'd never be a world without the theater.

She took her usual seat in the chair beside the fire screen. On the table, next to a glass of her father's cordial, she saw the two knives and Alvina's magnifying lens. Obviously, Philip had already explained.

"I am sorry, Father. It looks rather bad for Alvina, doesn't it?"

"Yes, especially if that neighbor of Rosemary's didn't lie."

If he was shaken, Sir Richard concealed it well. There was an air of purpose about him, a look of resolution, that made him look younger and stronger than Meg had seen him.

"I had my suspicions when my saddle was tampered with," he said. "But I didn't realize Alvina had threatened Rosemary and the child. If I had known, I wouldn't have sent her to London. I believed her spite and anger were directed only at me."

Meg tried to understand. "You believed Alvina's anger over the marriage was directed at you rather than the wife she disliked and considered ineligible for the position of Lady Carswell?"

"Aye, that I did. Alvina can be very spiteful and she had stored up anger and resentment against me since her own marriage. *My* marriage added fuel to her bitterness, but it was not the cause."

"What does her marriage have to do with anything?"

"Alvina was ambitious, you see. Always wanted to shine in society. After her season in London, she had two suitors: the younger son of the Marquess of Tavistock, who had position but no money, and Elmore. Roger Elmore didn't have a title, but he was as rich as Golden Ball. I warned her against marrying him, but she wanted the fortune."

"I think I'm beginning to understand," said Meg. "Philip told me that Mr. Elmore gambled away everything he owned."

"Aye, Philip knows some of the story." Sir Richard shifted the bandaged leg he kept elevated on the footstool. "Alvina starved herself rather than accept assistance from me, or let the servants go, or stop entertaining. Appearances, you know. As long as nobody knew she was poor, she could bear it."

Philip resumed his seat. "And, no doubt, the debts mounted."

"That they did. And then she found herself expecting. She wrote to me, a bitter, angry letter. This time I offered no money. I sent Martha Grimshaw, who had been Alvina's nurse. An early christening gift, I told her, for the child."

Philip leaned forward. "Then Mrs. Grimshaw was with Alvina when Elmore gambled away the house? I didn't realize that. Living together in Pye Street would form quite a bond between a young mother and her former nurse."

Meg knew he was thinking of the marchpanes and the possibility that Nanny and Alvina were in league to kill her. She'd had the same thought, except—

"Alvina doesn't allow herself to get attached to anyone," Sir Richard said tartly.

"And she doesn't like Nanny Grimshaw." Meg looked at Philip. "She wants to have her put away in a charity home. I think she hates it that Nanny knows so much about her."

Sir Richard nodded. "When Elmore lost the house,

Alvina was stripped of the last tool to help her pretend everything was all right. She tried to cut her wrists, but Nanny stopped her."

"She tried to kill herself?" said Meg, incredulous. "Because she lost the house? What of Stewart? Didn't she think about the child she'd leave behind?"

"I don't know whether Alvina could think rationally at the time. According to Martha Grimshaw, she took it as a personal affront that she must suffer through childbirth to give her husband an heir, and then there wasn't anything to inherit. Not even a bloody house in London."

"She must be mad," said Meg.

It was the only explanation. And wouldn't it in a way be easier to bear if madness lay at the roots of Alvina's wickedness, rather than greed and cold-blooded, evil scheming?

She looked at her father. "At least Alvina had sense enough to return to Carswell Hall after Mr. Elmore's death."

"She had no choice. When I got to London to fetch them, she and Stewart were both ill with some fever they'd picked up in the slums. The boy soon recovered but Alvina lay at death's door for nigh on two months."

Sir Richard took a sip of his cordial. "She never forgave me for being right about Elmore," he muttered. "And when I married, she probably believed I did it merely to aggravate her, to show that I had chosen better than she."

"Why, then, did you believe her when she told lies about my mother?"

"Because I closed my eyes to her wickedness and did not let myself see her true character until now. Much of what I'm saying about Alvina is hindsight." Sir Richard's gaze dropped. "I finally had to face the evil in her—and my cowardice—if I didn't want to lose you. Again."

Meg stared at her father. What he had just said made him look a coward indeed. She almost wished she had one upstairs with Maryann and had never learned Alvina's pathetic story or discovered her father's weakness.

She became aware of Philip's eyes on her. He rose and walked around her father's chair to stand behind her.

Placing a hand on her shoulder, he said, "Cousin Richard, we must decide what to do to keep Meg safe."

"Aye." The air of resolve was still there, but the strength was gone and Sir Richard looked every one of his seventy-two years. "What do you want me to do? Shall I lock Alvina in the tower?"

Chapter Twenty-Five

Of course they could not lock Alvina up!

Seated in front of the dressing table in her chamber, Meg still remembered the warm pressure of Philip's hand on her shoulder when she had stiffened at her father's suggestion—as though Philip had known exactly what she was thinking.

Sir Richard had made it clear that he believed Alvina was evil, not mad. Meg had grown up believing in law and justice. Well, perhaps not so much in justice. But definitely in the law.

She had worked for the law. Like Fletcher when he took Jigger under his wing instead of turning him over to the magistrate, she had more than once protected a child or woman who stole out of desperation. But never had there been a question of turning a murderer or murderess over to the family to be locked in a tower or garret room.

Could Philip have known her thoughts? It was entirely possible. He knew of her involvement with the Bow Street court. He'd understand that she would want to send Alvina over to the justice of the peace. On the other hand, he was a part of that section of society who sent their black sheep to the Continent or the United States rather than face a trial and the ensuing scandal.

Of course he would not want to send Alvina abroad for

fear that she'd return. But, quite likely, he was in agreement with her father, that Alvina should be locked up

Once again, the gulf of their disparate upbringing
gaped before her. And yet, she was glad of the hand o
her shoulder that had made her think before speaking
She had started to consider her father and what the tria
of his sister would do to him.

And to Stewart. The trial of a gentlewoman woul
cause a stir that affected those concerned for years after
ward. If Alvina were convicted, Stewart would suffer a
his life.

Of course, at the moment there was no question of
trial or even an arrest. So far, there wasn't a shred c
evidence linking Alvina to Fratt.

Meg picked up the hairbrush and slowly, methodicall
smoothed the long, tangled strands. She must sto
thinking about Alvina. Must believe that everythin
would work out in the end—without anyone else gettin
hurt, physically or emotionally.

She twisted her hair into loose curls, pinning them t
the crown of her head and letting several dangle a
shoulder length. It was a style that flattered her, and sh
wanted to look her best for Evalina's party.

The party, she had decided, would be the perfec
setting for the seduction of Philip Rutland, Earl of Stan
brook . . . if only she had the slightest notion how to g
about seducing a man into a proposal of marriage
Especially when the man did not consider her a suitabl
bride and planned to wed another.

She'd think of something . . . perhaps during a waltz . .
or outside on the moonlit terrace. If the Lyndons had
terrace.

Yes, this evening she'd make Philip change his view c
her. Perhaps he'd even propose this night and they coul
be married before the start of the theater season i
September.

She'd be Megan Rutland, Countess of Stanbrook. Th
name had dignity.

It occurred to her that maybe Alvina would be satisfied once her niece was married to Philip and Stewart had been made Sir Richard's sole heir.

But she wasn't going to think about Alvina anymore. Not this night.

Rising from the dressing table, she was struck by a realization that made her stand stock-still. If she was willing, nay eager, to put Alvina from her mind in order to enjoy a social gathering, then she had moved closer to Philip's way of thinking than she'd have thought possible. Duty had always come before pleasure, but not once had she considered forgoing the party. It would have looked odd and given rise to undesirable speculation if she did not attend.

She was about to don her gown when Elspeth rushed in.

"Sorry, Miss Megan. I didn't mean to be late, but there was such a to-do! An' Mrs. Sutton said we'd best all help clean up before Sir Richard hears of it."

"Before Sir Richard hears of what?" asked Meg, her voice muffled by the gown Elspeth was slipping over her head.

"Somebody got into the east tower, miss, and wrecked Miss Rosemary's bedchamber. And you know that the tower was locked 'cause—"

Elspeth was doing up the tiny buttons on the back of the gown, and Meg could not see her face but, after a moment of fumbling, the maid resumed both the buttoning and her speech.

"'Cause I myself brung the key to you, didn't I? The one Jigger gave me."

"Yes, that was the tower key." Meg kept her voice steady. "How was the bedroom wrecked, Elspeth?"

"Well, the crib and the rocker was overturned. An' everything was pulled out o' the bed and the drawers. An' Miss Rosemary's gowns, they was all over the floor."

It didn't matter, Meg told herself. It couldn't hurt her. It couldn't hurt her mother, and it couldn't hurt her. But it did, nonetheless.

313

"An' the tower key, Miss Megan, it were lyin' right in the middle o' the passage outside the tower. Somebody must have stolen it from you!"

With a pang of guilt, Meg remembered that she had dropped the key when Philip kissed her. And then she had forgotten about it.

The long row of tiny, cloth-covered buttons was finally done. Meg turned to face the maid.

"Where is the key now? I believe it was Mr. Stewart's."

"Aye, Mr. Stewart has it back."

"Good," Meg said absently.

Was it Alvina who had wrecked the tower room out of spite? Or Nanny, in a misguided effort to obscure the past even more?

She saw Elspeth looking at her with awe, her eyes as wide as the day she had arrived and the maid had seen the resemblance to Lydia Carswell. Determinedly, she put Alvina and Nanny from her mind.

"Do I look all right, Elspeth? Fit to grace Squire Lyndon's drawing room?"

"You look a treat, Miss Megan. Just like a . . . a duchess!"

Philip saw her come down the stairs. His Meg.

He heard Stewart address him and ask something about a hunter they had discussed before he left for London, but he could no more take his eyes off Meg than Stewart could have if the woman had been Evalina Lyndon.

Meg was stunning with the copper glow of her beautiful hair against the creaminess of bare shoulders. Some soft, flowing material hugged her curves and swirled around her ankles in waves of palest gray and silver. The bright emerald eyes rested on him as she descended step by step—every inch the duchess he so frequently called her.

314

He had never believed that his title was of consequence. It was simply a part of himself, a part of his
name. But this evening, he found himself wishing he
could make his Meg a true duchess.

He grinned at the notion and at himself, for he did not
usually chase after foolish dreams. And after all, the
position of countess was not to be sneezed at.

Megan Rutland, Countess of Stanbrook. She'd make a
delightful peeress, his Meg, with her natural grace and
dignity. He remembered when the thought had first
occurred to him—he had compared her to Evalina, who
was quite charming in her own way but did not possess an
iota of dignity.

Yes, he had known Meg would make a wonderful
countess since that wild ride back from Lyndon Court,
where he had fled after kissing Meg—a kiss that had left
him in turmoil. But he had not considered marriage until
Stewart facetiously asked, "Then why don't you marry
Megan?"

He had been stunned. But not for long. Of course he'd
marry her. If he hadn't been so bloody preoccupied
mourning the loss of a mistress, he'd have come to the
decision without Stewart's unwitting aid.

But he must not propose until something could be
done about Alvina. If he announced his engagement to
Meg, Alvina would immediately assume he was trying to
get Carswell Hall through marriage, and she'd lose whatever feeble link to sanity she still possessed.

And a secret engagement? It would be a disaster. Meg
was a damned fine actress; he'd seen her. But—again his
mouth stretched in a grin—she couldn't hide her feelings. At times, she might try to hide them from herself,
but she had never fooled him yet. Only a numbskull
would fail to recognize the signs of a woman in love. A
cowtop he might be, but never a numbskull.

She had reached the foot of the stairs and stood before
him.

"And what is it that you find so amusing about

315

me, Stanbrook?"

He wanted to kiss those curving lips, but had to content himself with a decorous bow over the gloved hand she held out.

"I wasn't laughing at you, my Meg, but at myself. And I do wish you'd call me Philip."

"But that would be quite improper," she said, looking demure as a nun's hen.

He was aware of Stewart standing nearby, and Lady Maryann tripping down the stairs to join them in the Great Hall.

Quickly, he leaned toward Meg. "What do you wager," he said softly, "that before the night is out you'll have called me Philip?"

Her eyes widened, and he saw the mischief lurking in their depth.

"Oh, no, Stanbrook. I never bet against a certainty."

And just what the devil did she mean by that? He could not ask her. Maryann was upon them and, a moment later, Stewart. Then Sir Richard, resplendent in silk knee breeches and blue velvet coat, entered the Great Hall.

Meg hurried toward him. "Father, I did not know you planned to attend the party."

"Did not know it myself," he grumbled. "But Philip seems to believe you need my support. Do you?"

Philip expected a look from her that would scorch his ears; instead, she gave him a strange little smile.

"I may not need support, but I greatly appreciate having it. I can feel easy facing your neighbors with you at my side."

Sir Richard harrumphed, then shouted for Marsden who stood right behind him.

"Yes, sir. You'll be wanting the necklace, I daresay."

"Of course I do."

Holding his walking stick under one arm, Sir Richard fumbled with the clasp of a long, flat box. Removing a diamond choker, he said gruffly, "There you are, Megan lope it's something that'll go with your gown."

Philip couldn't say what made him look up the stairs at his very moment, when he'd rather have watched Meg's elight in the piece of jewelry—he might even have laced it around her neck if he had hurried—but he did ook up, and he saw Alvina.

One foot poised above the next step, her hands clutching the banister, she stood staring at Sir Richard and Meg. A look of such fury distorted her face that Philip ook an instinctive step toward Meg. He would not let lvina near her.

Alvina must have noticed the movement, for she esumed her descent. Her features were smooth, with ven a hint of a smile on the thin lips. But Philip could ot forget that earlier look.

He swore not to let Meg out of his sight for an instant ntil Alvina was locked up—which, if Sir Nathaniel und what they were looking for, could be within a day r two.

Both wings of the wide, arched door connecting the ownstairs drawing rooms at Lyndon Court had been rown open to accommodate some three dozen guests. luch of the furniture had been removed, and in the naller of the two chambers the rugs had been rolled up provide a dance floor. A punch bowl and cups were vailable in both rooms, and the Lyndons' only footman, sisted by the parlor maid, made the rounds offering asses of champagne and lemonade.

Meg followed the footman's progress with a keen eye. nce the end of dinner, she had been surrounded by dies who pelted her with questions about the theater, er mother, and every aspect of her life, and she knew if e were asked just once more about the Green Room, e'd say something utterly unsuitable for the ears of ese gently reared gossips.

Maryann might have rescued her, but an earl's daugh-

ter was almost as much of a rarity as an actress, and she
too, had been captured by a group of ladies, including
Alvina, who wouldn't let go of their prey. And Sir
Richard, who had valiantly supported her before dinner
and throughout the meal, had disappeared with Squire
Lyndon.

When the footman finally reached Meg's circle and
stopped to offer refreshments, she instantly took
advantage of the distraction and slipped away. She had
been aware of Philip always close by, but he had made no
move to extract her from her plight. Fighting a sense of
ill-usage, she slowly walked toward him.

From the corner of her eye, she saw Evalina waltzing
with Stewart in the adjoining room. This, on the one
hand, lifted her spirits, because they had obviously made
up; but, on the other hand, the sight served to sharpen
her irritation. Philip should have interrupted the garru-
lous ladies and asked her to dance.

Then she was close enough to see the warmth and the
smile in his eyes. Only about five or six paces separated
them, and with each step she took, her mood lightened.
This was *her* night, after all.

She dropped into a curtsy just as the music stopped.
"My lord, may I have the pleasure of the next dance?"

He bowed with exquisite grace. "I only hope the next
dance is another waltz. I do not care to share you with
any of the gentlemen."

"Then I fear you're doomed to disappointment. Mr.
Lyndon would not allow such decadence as two waltzes in
a row."

The musicians, three energetic fiddlers, struck up a
Scottish reel.

"There! What did I tell you? Dash it, Stanbrook! I
wish you had asked me to dance much sooner."

"Or *you* had asked me sooner," he murmured, a
wicked gleam in his eye.

Meg deemed it prudent to ignore the interjection.
Giving him a reproachful look, she said, "Believe me,

as most tedious answering the ladies' questions—or
ading them."

"My poor Meg. That's country life for you. Did you
te it very much?"

"I did. But I suppose the next time I meet them, the
dies will not be half as curious. I'll still be Sir Richard's
andalous daughter, but the novelty and titillation will
ve worn off."

Philip offered his arm. "Would you care to step out
to the terrace?"

"A moonlit terrace?"

Skirting the dance floor, they approached the open
rrace doors.

"I don't believe there is a moon tonight," he said. "But
iss Lyndon once mentioned paper lanterns."

"She would." Meg laughed softly. "I did not see her
ncing just now. We'll probably find her out there."

"With Stewart, I imagine."

Her eyes flew to his face. "Do you mind?"

"On the contrary. I believe they're well suited."

A swath of light spilled from the drawing room onto
e flagstones outside, and to either side of that bright
th, paper lanterns shed a soft glow. Inside Meg,
other kind of glow spread its warmth.

Philip's infatuation with Evalina was the one thing she
d not allowed herself to think about when she made up
r mind to marry him. But now it was clear that he was
finitely not enamored of the lovely young girl. That
dn't mean, though, that he did not still intend to offer
r her. A man could take the strangest notions into his
ad.

She looked around the terrace, but if Evalina and
ewart had slipped outside, they had gone into the
rden. She and Philip were quite alone.

Walking around small tables and a number of chairs,
ey stopped at the low stone wall bordering the terrace.
eg took her hand off Philip's arm.

"You don't intend to make Miss Lyndon an offer?"

319

"No. You were quite right. She would not make me suitable wife at all."

She turned away a little, pretending to look beyond the wall into the garden.

"What sort of woman do you suppose *would* make you a suitable wife?"

He did not hesitate. "A woman I can admire, not only for beauty of face and figure, but for courage, honesty, indomitable spirit, even a certain amount of boldness.

"It seems to me those are trends you'd most deplore.

"Why?" He chuckled softly. "Does it rankle that said I ought to box your ears when I discovered you in the tower?"

Slowly, she turned and faced him again.

"Meg," he said gently, "it doesn't mean I don't admire your spirit and courage. Just that, at times, you are led astray by them."

Her heart pounded. She swallowed, convinced her throat was too dry to speak.

"Philip, am *I* the woman you'd want for your wife

They stared at each other. In the dim light of the lanterns she could not see his face clearly, but the tightening of his mouth, the grimness of expression was unmistakable.

And then, just when she thought the silence, the very stillness of his body would break her heart, he moved and lightly touched her arm.

"You called me Philip. I'm deeply honored. But I afraid this is not the time to discuss your or my marriage plans."

Chapter Twenty-Six

Had he slapped her, it would have hurt less.

I'm deeply honored . . . The echo of his voice mocked her. Weren't those the words generally used by a lady refusing an offer of marriage? How fitting! After she had practically proposed to him.

Once more, Philip reached out, but withdrew his hand as though afraid he'd get burnt if he touched her again.

"Meg, don't you see? It's the very worst I could do—ask you to marry me."

"I'm not a dull-wit, Philip." He had rejected her, but he'd be dashed if she reverted to Stanbrook! "I understood you perfectly the first time."

"I wonder."

His voice was so low that she barely heard him. And perhaps she had only imagined the note of regret.

He leaned against the wall. "I do believe we've caught the truants. Isn't that Miss Lyndon's pink gown in the garden?"

Her throat seemed too tight for speech, but, "Yes," Meg heard herself say, "it is Stewart and Evalina."

The two came quickly closer.

"Miss Carswell, isn't it a lovely party?"

The garden was darker than the terrace, and Meg saw only the pale blur of Evalina's face, but she knew it would be flushed with excitement and the blue eyes would be sparkling. Meg wondered if *her* voice would give away her feelings the way Evalina's had betrayed the young girl.

By jove, it better not! Or she'd give up her career immediately.

She raised her chin. "It is the most delightful party ever attended. And if there is a way onto the terrace without climbing over the wall, why don't you and Stewart join us?"

Miss Lyndon giggled. "There is a step and a break in the wall just a little way farther down. But I wanted to show Stewart my kittens. Our cook is keeping them for me tonight, and the kitchen door is just around the corner."

"Megan." Stewart placed an arm around Evalina's shoulders. "Have you discussed my proposal with Stanbrook?"

Meg stared at him. Didn't he see the incongruity of his behavior? Embracing one woman and speaking of his proposal to another?

Beside her, Philip stirred with interest.

"It is none of Philip's business," she said sharply. "And if you want to see the kittens, you'd best hurry. Else they'll be asleep."

"What proposal is that?" drawled Philip.

"For goodness' sake, Stewart!" Placing both hands atop the low wall, Meg leaned forward in a most precarious manner. "Consider Miss Lyndon's feelings!"

"Oh, I know all about it, Miss Carswell. And I think it is so very clever of Stewart to have thought of it. Only—" Evalina's voice broke. "Only it is so very awful, isn't it?"

"Will somebody kindly tell me what this is all about?" Philip said in a deceptively soft voice.

"To protect her, I offered marriage to Megan." Stewart held himself stiffly; the tone of his voice was aggrieved. "She refused, accusing me first of trying to get Carswell Hall through her, then of wanting to kill her."

"I'm surprised you expected otherwise," Philip said

322

lmly. "But, like Miss Lyndon, I must congratulate you
n your cleverness. I wish *I* had thought of it."

Meg glared at him. "Indeed!"

"It would only be pretense, Miss Carswell," Evalina
id shyly. "Just for a little while."

"That's not how Stewart presented it to me."

"No." Stewart tugged at his cravat. "That was
valina's notion. I was too overset at the time to think
early."

"It makes no difference whatsoever." Meg knew she
ouldn't give in to temper, but all this was just too much
bear after Philip had turned her down. "I won't agree
marry you, pretense or otherwise."

She faced Philip. "In fact, I have no intention of
arrying anyone!"

"Meg—"

She thought she saw pain in the look he gave her, but
en he turned to Stewart, and she could not be certain.

"What have you learned, Stewart? From whom do you
ant to protect Meg with a proposal of marriage?"

Meg caught her breath. In her distress, she had over-
oked the obvious. "Stewart, if you know something,
ll us!"

"Yes, please tell." Evalina moved closer to Stewart
d leaned her head against his shoulder. "You shouldn't
ve to bear the responsibility alone, and Lord Stanbrook
ay know what to do."

"It's Alvina, isn't it?" Philip said softly.

With a groan, Stewart removed his arm from Evalina's
ist. Alone, he stepped close to the terrace wall.

"Yes, it's my mother who wants Megan dead."

Meg felt no shock or surprise; Alvina had been the
ajor suspect for what seemed a very long time. But the
ld confirmation made her shiver.

In a harried voice, Stewart explained that he had paid a
sit to Alvina when she was laid low with a severe head-
he after the announcement of the new will.

Alvina had alternately cried and raged. She swore

she'd never give up Carswell Hall to Megan, and promise to be rid of her and of Stanbrook as well, so that her son would be reinstated as the heir.

Stewart, his brow glistening with perspiration, gave Meg an anguished look. "I did not then think she'd try to kill you. You must believe that, Megan!"

Meg nodded. "You believed she wanted to make me run away, as she'd done with my mother."

"I tried to soothe her, Megan. But I doubt she ever heard me. I talked with her again the next morning before she left for Ascot."

"Was that in the stables?" asked Meg, remembering what Phelps had told her about Stewart and Alvina having words.

"Yes. I reminded her that Carswell Hall will always be our home, even when you become the mistress, and she got quite angry again. Said she didn't want charity, and if I didn't know the difference between the caretaker of an estate and the master, *she* did. And . . . and she had seen to it that I'd be the master of Carswell Hall."

"Indeed," Philip said coldly. "She cut the saddle girth."

Even in the dim light of the lanterns, Meg saw Stewart blanch.

"Philip, I swear I did not understand what she meant until I saw you carry Megan from the stableyard and you told me the saddle had come off."

"Dammit!" Philip's voice was taut with suppressed anger. "Why didn't you say something then?"

"Say what?" Stewart asked defensively. "That my mother lost her wits—and should be sent to Bedlam?"

Evalina stepped closer to him. She did not speak, but her presence had a soothing effect on Stewart.

"When Mother returned from Ascot, I told her of Megan's tumble. I did not accuse her. I could not! But I said I'd marry Megan to keep her safe from further mishaps. Mother was furious . . . something in her face . . .

Stewart shook his head as though to shake off the

324

emory. 'Then she laughed and said I might as well
arry the heiress. It'd be as good a way as any to secure
rswell Hall."

"Ha!" said Meg. "That explains the change in her."

Philip's face remained grim. "Just so. What else was
e to do after her scheme to kill you in a riding accident
sfired!"

Stewart leaned against the wall. It almost reached his
ist since the garden lay several inches lower than the
rrace.

"Uncle Richard summoned me late that night—after
ilip had left for London. Uncle worried about the knife
found in the harness room and he told me about the
anged initial. That's when I realized what Mother
eant when she talked of getting rid of Philip as well. She
nted Megan's death blamed on him."

"You're not telling me anything new." Philip's tone
s cutting. "Only thing I cannot figure out is why she
dn't simply use *my* knife."

"Because she already had Uncle Richard's."

Again, Meg shivered. She felt Philip's hand, warm and
mforting, close around her own. Instinctively, she
asped it tightly. She needed the closeness, his support.
e needed Philip, who was attuned to her every mood,
r needs . . . and yet had struck her a harsh blow.

Stewart wiped his forehead. "For years I fought the
ghtmare. Nanny told me that I must forget, that I had
eamed it all because I was so upset the night Rosemary
ok Megan away. But when Uncle Richard had me look
the knife handle through his magnifying glass and I
alized it was *his* knife I'd found in the harness room, I
membered—"

His voice shook. He drew breath in a ragged gasp.

Evalina briefly touched her palm to his face. "Go on,
ewart," she urged softly. "They must be told."

"Yes," Stewart said dully.

His eyes met Meg's. "I remembered seeing my mother
the harness room the night Rosemary ran away. I had

325

followed Mother because she'd had the most awful ro
with Uncle. And I saw her with the knife in her hand.
saw her cut his saddle girth."

For Meg, the rest of the night was a blur of impre
sions—Squire Lyndon telling her that her father an
Alvina had pleaded fatigue and left; a buffet supper;
dance or two with Mr. Flossingham and Dr. Meade an
with a young gentleman whose name she had forgotten
soon as the music stopped.

The only part of the evening she remembered wit
clarity during the drive home was the waltz she ha
danced with Philip shortly before they took their leav
from the Lyndons.

She remembered Philip holding her far too close fo
propriety, but she had made no attempt to reprimar
him. Despite everything, she wanted to be held in h
arms and to whirl around the small dance floor in time
the intoxicating music. All she asked at that point was
be allowed a moment of pleasure, a moment for dream
where Evalina's party had not disintegrated into disaste

Philip had pulled her even closer. "I wish you ha
accepted Stewart's proposal."

Her dream world shattered.

"Do you?" She looked straight at him. "In pretense?"

"Meg." His voice was rough, as though her name wa
torn from his mouth. "I love you more than my life.

For an instant, time stood still. A glow of happine:
started deep inside her, spreading slowly.

"But that's precisely why I *cannot* ask you to marı
me."

She stared at him. After the first moment of shoc
her heart began to race.

"You cannot ask me now? Or ever?"

He did not reply, but she had read his answer in tl
look he gave her.

She prayed she had not misunderstood.

With a weary sigh, Meg leaned her head against the
abs of the carriage seat. Beside her, Maryann was
er quiet, and Meg hoped her friend had not exerted
self. But even concern for Maryann's condition could
 long keep her mind off Philip.

No one had thought to light the interior lantern for the
rt drive, and she could barely discern Philip's and
wart's shapes on the opposite seat. What was Philip
king?

They knew so much about Alvina now. Surely it
ldn't be necessary to go through a sham engagement
 Stewart? Surely they had sufficient evidence that
ina was insane?

When they pulled up at the lighted front door of
swell Hall, James came running down the stairs. He
ned the carriage door to let down the steps, and deftly
ed her and Maryann alight.

"Sir Richard would like to see you, my lord," the
man said when Philip stepped down.

"My lord," Phelps called from the coachman's perch.
iss Megan, might I have a word with you?"

"Go to bed, Maryann." Meg gave her friend an encour-
ig pat on the arm. "You're worn out. I'll talk to you in
 morning."

"I am a little tired," Maryann admitted; she followed
wart into the house while Meg and Philip approached
 groom.

"What is it, Phelps?" asked Philip.

"I heard talk at Squire Lyndon's that Will Fratt died of
on."

"That is correct," said Meg. "He ate some confections
d with arsenic."

helps shifted nervously on the box. "The poison was
oodstuff wrapped in a napkin, they said."

"Yes."

hilip said impatiently, "Come, Phelps! Open your
get. Don't keep Miss Meg standing all night."

"No, my lord." The groom cleared his throat. "I didn't

think nothin' of it at the time, but Mrs. Elmore had ▪
stop near the village the mornin' we was drivin'
Ascot."

"Yes?" Meg prompted. "What does that have to
with Will Fratt?"

"Shortly after we stopped, Will came lopin' across t
meadow. He came up to the carriage an' Mrs. Elmo
talked with him. She gave him a purse an' said she hop
he hadn't bungled his job like he did the night before. S
told him to go back to Lunnon."

Meg and Philip exchanged glances.

"Did she mention anything about the jobs?" ask
Philip. "What they were?"

"Sounded like they was talkin' about his gardenir
Mrs. Elmore asked Will if he'd put the tool where she t(
him to."

Meg frowned. "She specifically said tool?"

"Aye, Miss Megan. I r'member 'cause I kind
wondered if it was a spade or a rake she was talkin' abo▪
and why she didn't say outright."

"A tool," murmured Philip, his mouth close to Me₂
ear. "I'll wager a pony that was the knife in the harn▪
room. Alvina had Will Fratt cut the girth long bef▪
even the grooms were up and around."

She nodded, unable to speak. Now that they had pr◦
of a connection between Alvina and Fratt, the ugliness
her aunt's scheming made her stomach churn.

"And then," said Phelps, gulping noisily, "M
Elmore gave Will some food wrapped in a white napkir

Meg tasted bile.

As on the Lyndon terrace, Philip's hand found h
and held it firmly.

"Thank you, Phelps." Philip nodded reassuringly
the groom. "You did right by telling us. I may have to ₂
you to repeat it to Sir Richard."

"I'll be in the stables, my lord, or in me room in t
coach house loft."

Her mind and emotions in turmoil, Meg watched ▪

carriage as it rumbled away. Then, heart beating in her throat, she faced Philip.

"The link, Philip. We've got the link to Fratt!"

"Yes." He snatched her up in his arms and whirled her around. "We have indeed."

He set her on her feet by the front steps. "Do you know what this means?"

"Yes." She thought of the painful decisions her father and Stewart would have to make.

"It means that I can court you now."

Her eyes flew to his face. Gone was the grim look, replaced by the smile that reflected in his eyes and never failed to make her pulse race. She pushed away the dark thoughts about Alvina, letting hope and happiness fill her mind.

"Does it, Philip?" she asked huskily.

"Indeed, Miss Carswell." His arm was suddenly round her waist. His head bent toward hers. "I already have your father's permission."

More than anything in the world did she want his kiss, the solidity of his strong body close to hers. His voice, his touch made her forget the ugliness of the past days and assured her that the future would be bright. But she felt obliged to issue a caution.

"Philip, have you considered the consequences? You wouldn't be courting only Megan Carswell of Carswell Hall but also Meg Fletcher of Drury Lane."

The arm tightened.

"My Meg."

His mouth touched her forehead, brushed butterfly kisses on her temples, her eyelids. By the time he kissed her mouth, she was dizzy with delight. There was no room in her mind for doubts.

A beam of light fell upon them as the front door opened wide. Someone cleared his throat.

"Begging your pardon, my lord," said James as Philip slowly released her, "but Sir Richard's waiting. He has something urgent to discuss with you and he said to be

329

sure to tell you as soon 's you return from Squire Lyndon's."

"Yes," Philip said cheerfully. "And you did tell me before I quite left the carriage. But Sir Richard, I don't doubt, won't mind the waiting when I explain that *I* had something important to discuss with his daughter."

James allowed himself a smile. "Quite, my lord."

Entering the Great Hall at Philip's side, Meg said, "I take it, James, that my presence is not desired?"

"I don't know, Miss Megan." The footman cast a helpless look at Philip.

"Always desired. But mayhap not advisable this time." Philip's eyes locked with hers. "Consider your father's position in the matter I must discuss with him. He'll find it easier to make a decision if you're not present."

Meg was relieved she didn't have to decide Alvina's fate. She felt certain her aunt was mad. At some point between the disastrous marriage and her return to Carswell Hall, something had snapped in Alvina's mind. And by the time she discovered that her niece was alive after all, she could no longer discern between right and wrong, good and evil. She saw only that Meg stood between her and Carswell Hall.

"What about Stewart?" she asked. "Shouldn't he be present?"

"James will fetch him."

Philip's look turned into a caress. "Good night, my Meg. Will you meet me in the morning to finish our discussion?"

As so many times before, she could do nothing about the blush warming her face. Very much aware of the footman's interested gaze, she said as casually as possible, "At eight o'clock. In the gazebo."

On winged feet, she hurried upstairs. She paused briefly at Maryann's door, then continued to her own room. If she stopped to talk with Maryann, they'd be up half the night, which would not benefit either of them. It was much better to see Maryann *after* she'd met with

330

hilip in the gazebo.

Smiling to herself, Meg opened her door. To her surprise, Elspeth was not asleep in the dressing room but drooped, still gowned and aproned, in one of the chairs.

"Oh, Miss Megan!" Rubbing her eyes, the maid stumbled to her feet. "I was waitin' up for you."

"So I see. But surely you know by now that I am perfectly able to disrobe and get into bed by myself."

"Aye, that I know. But Auntie came looking for you and when I told her you'd gone to the Lyndons' party, she left a message."

"And what is the message?" Meg asked warily.

"Auntie's worried about some marchpanes she gave you. She said not to let you eat them, but I told her I hadn't seen no marchpanes and I didn't think you had any. But she still fretted an' asked if you'd meet her in Miss Rosemary's room."

Chapter Twenty-Seven

"She's waiting for me now? In the tower?"

"Aye, miss."

Meg thought of the wreckage Elspeth had reported earlier. But it had been put to rights by Mrs. Sutton and the maids; there was no reason for gooseflesh.

"Shall I go with you, miss?"

Mechanically, Meg accepted the woolen shawl Elspeth handed her. She noted the droop of the thin shoulders, the sleepy eyes. It was well past midnight, and for Elspeth the day began at five-thirty.

"I appreciate the offer, but you had better go to bed, Elspeth. In fact, after tonight you can move back into your own room."

"Thank you, Miss Megan." The girl scuttled toward the dressing room. "And I hope Auntie won't keep you up too late. If she starts ramblin', just interrupt her an' tell her you're tired. She's always considerate, is Auntie."

Meg lit a candle and slowly walked out into the corridor. She was reluctant to go into the tower. In fact, she wanted to go downstairs and ask Philip to accompany her.

Always follow your instinct, Fletcher had impressed upon her. But, surely, her desire for Philip's company was nothing but selfishness?

She stood in the corridor, first looking to the right past Maryann's chamber toward the main staircase. At the top of the stairs was Philip's room. Perhaps she should send his valet to fetch him, even if it meant interrupting the meeting with her father.

She thought she saw a shadow move in the dim light shed by wall sconces outside Philip's chamber; she gave a start, spilling hot wax onto her hand.

Dash it! If she jumped at shadows, she had come a long way from Bow Street and Seven Dials. It was time she pulled herself together.

Resolutely, Meg turned left toward Alvina's chambers then left again into the dark passageway to the tower. As so often when she felt apprehensive, she sang very softly.

The tower door was unlocked and as soon as she stepped inside she saw the light in her mother's bedroom. She stopped singing and entered.

Nanny Grimshaw sat in the rocking chair, but Meg only glanced at her, then looked around the room. Mrs. Sutton and the maids had done excellent work. The bed was as crisp and neat as Meg remembered it, the crib with its tiny blankets stood in the same spot it had occupied when she had seen it the first time.

"Miss Megan."

Nanny Grimshaw rose. This time, there was nothing vague about the old woman. She walked toward Meg with brisk steps.

"Thank you for seeing me, Miss Megan. I shan't keep you long. All I want are the marchpanes I gave you."

"It's too late, Mrs. Grimshaw."

Nanny faltered, her face as white as the starched cap on her wispy hair. "What did you do with them?"

"I sent them to Dr. Meade to be examined."

"Thank God!"

Martha Grimshaw's relief and gratitude could not be doubted. Meg walked to the chest of drawers and put down her candle, then sat on the edge of the bed.

"Mrs. Grimshaw, did Alvina give you the marchpanes?"

For a moment it seemed as though Nanny would not reply. Then she nodded.

"For my eighty-first birthday a sennight ago. Alvina makes them herself. She has given me marchpanes for my birthday every year since we moved back to Carswell Hall, but I never was keen on sweets. I—I thought you might enjoy them, Miss Megan."

The two women stared at each other.

"Were they poisoned?" Nanny asked.

"Yes." Meg's gaze did not waver. "Mrs. Grimshaw, when did you suspect something was wrong with them?"

"Not until this evening when I heard in the village that the gardener died because he ate poisoned marchpanes." Nanny pressed a hand to her breast. "Alvina . . . I cannot believe it . . ."

"What can you not believe? That Alvina would try to kill you, too?"

Shrill laughter from the doorway made them both jump and turn toward the chilling sound.

Alvina stood there, hair hanging in a loose braid down her back and her bony figure shrouded in a voluminous nightgown. Her right hand clutched the folds of her gown, raising the hem off the floor, and in the left she carried a large oil lamp.

"So I find you both," Alvina said gleefully.

"Alvina, behave yourself." Nanny spoke quite sharply. "You're overwrought again, and you should be in bed."

Alvina ignored her. She looked straight at Megan.

"Did you think I wouldn't find out that you turned Stewart down? You're stupid, Megan! As stupid as your mother was. She thought she was clever. Left her journal—so Richard would read it, no doubt. But she sewed it into the mattress, the silly chit! I found it this afternoon."

Meg's fingers dug into the counterpane. "What did you do with it?"

"Burned it." Alvina's eyes glowed with malicious pleasure. "All the lies she told about me went up in smoke."

335

"Oh dear!" said Nanny Grimshaw. "I wish I'd known I could have asked Mrs. Sutton to help me turn the mattress. It always was too heavy for me, but I thought it didn't matter."

Again, Alvina ignored the old nurse and spoke directly to Meg.

"You shouldn't have refused Stewart. I might have let you live until you'd given him an heir. But you hankered after Philip, don't you? Dear Cousin Philip, who has so much and still wants Carswell Hall!"

Meg rose. There was nothing Alvina could do, and yet Meg felt terror reaching for her, threatening to paralyze her.

Concealing her fear behind an outward calm, she said, "Aunt, don't you know that Stewart wants to marry Miss Lyndon? He'd be miserable married to me."

"Miserable with Carswell Hall?" Again Alvina broke into that shrill, grating laugh.

"Alvina!" Nanny started for the woman who had once been her nursling. "Come to bed immediately, or I'll have to tell Sir Richard about you."

"Stop!"

Alvina dropped the folds of her nightgown and raised a small pistol that had been hidden in the depth of the white linen.

"You wicked old woman. You have threatened me and ordered me around for the last time. Get back! Stand beside Megan."

Martha Grimshaw did not hesitate. She scurried around the rocking chair and stood close to Meg.

"Don't," she hissed when Meg made a move toward her aunt. "She's stark, raving mad, but she's a good shot. It's the only thing that no-good husband taught her."

"Stop whispering," Alvina said sharply.

She took a few steps into the room, then stopped to turn up the wick of the lamp. Looking once more at Meg, she smiled.

"A fire seems like just retribution," she said pleasantly. "The fire at the glover's shop should have killed you twenty-four years ago, but I hired someone to set it. He bungled. Everyone I hired, bungled. This time, I'll do it myself."

The fire at the glover's shop . . . Alvina had killed Grandfather Melton!

Before Meg could fully absorb the horrible truth, Alvina whisked the glass dome off the lamp and hurled the base with its cache of oil and the burning wick onto the bed. Within seconds, flames licked along the path soaked by the oil.

"Good riddance, Megan Carswell!"

Alvina's laughter rang in her ears as Meg snatched up a pillow and started to beat out the flames—with no noticeable result.

Nanny touched her arm. "Leave it. The covers are new but the ticking is older than you or I. It'll burn like tinder and there's nothing to be done about it."

Meg looked up. "Where's Alvina?"

"Gone. And she locked us in."

"Then help me beat out the flames," Meg said tersely as she renewed her desperate efforts. "I have no desire to suffocate or burn to death."

"Neither have I."

Again, Nanny Grimshaw touched her arm. "I must see Sir Richard, must tell him about Alvina. Should have told him years ago. I was wrong to keep quiet, but I thought it was better if Sir Richard didn't know."

"Nanny!" Meg gasped for breath. Her arms and shoulders ached. "Talk later. Right now, help me!"

"It's no use, Miss Megan. Come with me. I'll get us out."

"How? You said Alvina locked the door."

"Hurry, Miss Megan!" Martha Grimshaw pressed a handkerchief to her nose and mouth. "Don't you remember? I told you I know ways to come and go without a key."

Meg cast a frantic look from the burning, evil-smelling bedcover to Nanny. She was making no headway fighting the smoldering fire. But could she put her trust in an old

337

woman whose habit it was to retreat into the past at critical moments?

Beckoning her, Nanny hurried to the armoire. She pulled the doors open and thrust aside the gowns hanging in the right-hand corner. Before Meg's astonished eyes, an opening into the dressing room appeared, a hidden door set cunningly into a panel at the back of the wardrobe and the brick wall behind it.

Meg coughed as the smoke grew thicker and the flames burned higher. Sparks flew. She felt a sting like a pinprick on her arm and jumped back. Once more she swung the pillow at the flames, but only stirred up another shower of sparks. She hated to admit defeat, but without water it was hopeless. The thick walls of the tower would contain the fire, but she could not save her mother's furnishings.

Without a backward look—much better not to carry a picture of the destruction—she followed Nanny into the dressing room. She hurried to the door leading to the tower landing and stairway, but found it locked.

What now? She shouldn't have given up so easily, shouldn't have believed the old woman who had disappointed her every time they met.

She needed to close the panel in the armoire! Meg pushed and shoved, but it would not budge.

"Nanny, help me!"

If they could keep out the smoke . . . But even if the panel closed, there'd still be the wide crack in the wall.

"Miss Megan!" A clatter and banging accompanied Nanny's impatient call. "Come this way."

Meg turned to see that Martha Grimshaw had pulled aside the closet curtains and was pulling and tugging at a long, rusted zinc tub that lay on its side behind the close-stool and a clutter of buckets, basins and jugs. And behind the rusted old tub hung the full-size portrait of an Elizabethan lady.

Meg remembered the Georgian gentleman who guarded the secret door in the gallery, and immediately rushed to

338

anny's aid. Together, they shifted the tub just as a
ound like a soft explosion came from the bedroom. A
ick cloud of acrid smoke pushed through the opening
the armoire and cut off their source of light.

"Those old feather ticks," gasped Nanny. "I knew
ere was no saving them." Her voice grew weaker.
Miss Megan. Look for the ring."

Meg did not bother saying that she knew the trick.
oughing and gagging, she ran her hands over the
ainting where moments ago she had seen several orna-
ents on the lady's slender fingers. She found the ring
at opened the cavity concealing the lever to the hidden
oor, and within seconds she had pulled the trembling
d nurse into a dark chamber.

Meg carefully closed the door on the smoke, then
aned against the solid wooden panel. Her hands and
ees shook and her heart hammered in her throat. What
e dickens was the matter with her? The danger was
ver. She could relax.

Drawing a ragged breath, she clutched at something
at felt like a shelf. She could see nothing in the stygian
ark.

"Where are we, Nanny? Can we get out?"

"It's a storage room."

Nanny's voice was thin and feeble, and it came from
w down, near the ground. With an effort, Meg bent
er until her hand touched the old woman's shoulder.
She dropped to her knees. "Nanny, are you all right?
ou didn't fall, did you?"

"Just sitting down a moment, catching my breath."

After some hesitation, Meg sat down beside her. For
e moment, they were safe enough. The air in the
orage room was a little musty, but smoke-free. The fire
ould be contained in the bedroom, and even if it spread
rough the opening in the armoire into the dressing
om, it would take a while before it reached the thick
or she had just closed. They could afford to rest a
inute or two before giving the alarm.

She breathed deeply, feeling strength return to he legs. Thank goodness. She might have to carry Nanny Grimshaw.

Muffled sounds in the tower rooms made her sit up in alarm. She put an ear to the door, but it was so solid, she could not make out what the noise was.

"Nanny, we must go." She groped for the old woman' hands. "Come, let me help you up."

"Not just yet." As weak as she sounded, Nanny had some strength left, and she pulled out of Meg's clasp "Want to tell you about Alvina."

"Later. We must rouse the household. I fear the fire i spreading more quickly than I believed possible. And al those doors—"

"Miss Megan, listen! Alvina never quite recovered from the shock of living in Pye Street. Sir Richard know only the half of it, but it was unbearable for a woman lik Alvina. And then she caught that fever—"

"Yes," said Meg. "I know about fever and what it can do to the brain when the temperature rises too high o lasts too long."

"Alvina always did have a nasty streak in her. She wa uppity and spiteful, but after the fever her mind wa twisted." Nanny's voice was barely audible. "I shoul have warned Sir Richard that she was mad."

"Didn't he realize it himself?"

"She is crafty, is Alvina. And Sir Richard does no know her as I do. There's more than a dozen year between them, and in any case, he never did know wha to make of a woman."

Again, Meg heard a noise in the tower rooms. She rose "Nanny, we must go."

Meg heard the rustle of fabric and put out a hand t help the old woman to her feet.

"I was suspicious when Alvina returned from Londo and told Sir Richard that you and Rosemary died in th fire," said Nanny Grimshaw, her voice high and bri tle. "But Sir Richard was in bad shape from the fall, so

340

id nothing."

Meg heard a sound like a sob and put a hand on the old oman's shoulder. "I doubt my father would have elieved you at the time."

"He might have! And Alvina would have been locked her rooms when you arrived." Nanny's frail body ook. "I've been plagued by guilt until I was driven nigh ut of my mind. And now it's just too much. I cannot be lent any longer. Not for Stewart's sake, and not for the ke of the Carswell name. Alvina must be locked up."

There was a tightness in Meg's throat that made speech fficult.

"Alvina is responsible for my grandfather's death and r the death of Will Fratt. You don't think she ought to punished?"

"You don't mean—" Nanny Grimshaw faltered. "You n't mean hanged?"

"I mean taken before the justice of the peace to termine whether she ought to be tried."

"But she's your aunt. She's a Carswell."

Nanny sounded bewildered, and Meg wished there ere just a glimmer of light so she could see her face.

"None of the Carswells ever had anything to do with e courts," said Nanny. "Think of the scandal, Miss egan!"

"Will there be no scandal if she's pronounced mad and cked up?"

"Only the family will know, and Dr. Meade. To the rest the world she'll be in poor health, too weak to be ceiving or to go out into society."

"Very neat and tidy."

"Yes, it is." Nanny seemed oblivious to the bitterness Meg's voice. "I feel stout enough now, Miss Megan. If u take my hand, I'll guide you out of here."

In the dark, it seemed like a long walk between metal cks and shelves that stuck out and bumped sharp rners against Meg's arms and hips. Finally, Nanny opped and opened a door.

Lanterns sat on the stone floor of the passagewa
outside, and Meg blinked against the sudden brightnes
She smelled smoke and saw servants hurrying past wit
buckets of water.

"Good," said Nanny. "We don't need to give th
alarm. If you'll be all right on your own, Miss Megan, I'
see if I can find Sir Richard."

"Yes, I'll be fine."

Meg stepped out into the passage and watched Nann
Grimshaw as she hobbled toward the main corridor o
the left. Slowly, Meg turned to her right. To the towe

Without conscious thought she started toward i
keeping well out of the way of footmen, stable lads, an
gardeners armed with water buckets. And then she sa
Philip.

He stood just outside the tower door, his shoulde
propped against the wall and his breath coming in ragge
gasps. Her eyes widened at the tears and singes on h
clothing, the sweaty and soot-stained face.

"Get me another blanket!" he shouted to a servan
"I'm going back in."

"Philip."

Her voice was hoarse and his name came out as a wea
croak that did not carry the short distance separatin
them. She wanted to run but, maddeningly, her leg
would not obey her.

"My lord." A man whom Meg recognized as Philip
valet clutched a dripping blanket. "You're exhauste
Please wait until there's less smoke."

"Don't be daft!"

Philip snatched the blanket. As he threw it around h
shoulders, his eyes fell on Meg.

He moved so fast, she had no time to blink before h
was upon her. Soot, wet blanket and all, he crushed her t
his breast.

It was a most satisfying embrace, and Meg, who was n
watering pot, felt tears sting her eyes.

Chapter Twenty-Eight

'You were looking for me," Meg said stupidly, but she
uldn't think of anything else to say that would express
e wonder, the gratitude, the love she felt. Philip had
ked his life in that smoke-filled tower. For her.

His arms tightened. "You're shaking. Were you badly
ghtened?"

'I don't think I had time to be frightened. At least not
til Nanny and I got out of the room. Then my knees
rted to shake like a blancmange."

She noticed that the servants were no longer rushing
ut with buckets of water and, a moment later, she saw
wart leave the tower and come toward them.

"The fire is out." He wiped a sleeve across his perspir-
, soot-blackened face. "I'm sorry, Megan. Rosemary's
niture, the rugs—everything's gone."

'It doesn't matter any longer, Stewart. I'll have the
mories of my first visit to the rooms."

She freed herself from Philip's tight clasp, but stayed
se to him.

'What about Alvina?" Bitterness threatened to suffo-
e her. "Have you seen her, Stewart?"

'She's in her room. Uncle Richard and Marsden are
ing with her until Dr. Meade gets here."

'Two feeble old men with that raging madwoman!"

She would have run pell-mell to Alvina's room, but

Philip, reading her mind as he did so often, caught h
around the waist and held her close.

"Easy, my Meg. Alvina is mad, but she's not ragin
Not anymore. We don't know exactly what happene
but a maid who had decided to fetch water from t
fountain instead of running all the way to the ma
kitchen found her unconscious at the foot of the tow
stairs. There was fresh debris on the floor, and we belie
she was hit by falling stone. In any case, she has a brui
just above her right temple, and a lump on the top of h
head."

Struck by falling stone. . . . Mayhap Alvina had n
totally escaped justice after all.

"Is she still unconscious?" Meg asked.

"No." A shadow crossed Stewart's face. "But wh
she came to, she did not recognize anyone. Moth
believes her night rail is her wedding gown. She believ
she is about to marry Lord Frederick Woofington, t
younger son of the Marquess of Tavistock."

His eyes met Meg's. "Lord Frederick has been de
five or six years."

She saw the look of defeat and pain in her cousir
eyes, and suddenly it was not difficult to swallow her b
terness.

There was nothing she could say or wanted to say, b
she held out a hand. Stewart took it and pressed it brief

He straightened his shoulders. "The architect
coming tomorrow—no, later today. If the tower is saf
Uncle Richard will have the rooms refurbished f
Mother. We'll need someone—an attendant or a nurse

"Those decisions can wait," said Philip.

"Yes." Again, Stewart's eyes found Meg's. "I dor
know what to say, except I'm sorry. I wish I had—"

"Don't, Stewart. I doubt there's anything you cou
have done. It's best to forget the past."

"You're very kind and generous. Thank you, Megan
He turned on his heel and walked off.

Poor Stewart.

As though he'd read her thoughts, Philip said, "He'll be all right. He'll face a few rough days with Squire Lyndon—"

"About Fratt?"

"Yes. There'll be an inquest. Since Phelps saw Alvina hand Fratt the napkin-wrapped food, she may even be charged. But there won't be a trial. Squire Lyndon will release Alvina into the custody of her brother and her son."

Meg thought of her grandfather, killed twenty-four years ago. And of her mother, fleeing in fear first from Carswell Hall, then from the ruins of the glover's shop to hide herself and her child in the squalor of Seven Dials.

But she said nothing. Keeping Alvina at Carswell Hall, locked in her rooms or in the tower, was for all concerned the best solution. She'd ask her father to send immediately for Mr. Potter to change the will once again, with Stewart as the beneficiary. Stewart could keep his mother at Carswell House as long as she lived, but Meg would never have to see her again.

"By the time Stewart has found a caretaker or a nurse," said Philip, "he'll have come to grips with the situation."

A caretaker. Of course.

"Miss Finney," murmured Meg, remembering the sad, kind face of the wardress at the Litchfield Home that took in the infirm of body or mind. Her mood lightened. To engage Miss Finney as nurse for Alvina would be the ideal solution for both Miss Finney and Stewart.

"Meg?" Philip touched her arm. "What was that you muttered? You have that certain look on your face that tells me you're hatching some new plot."

"No plot," she assured him. "It was just a thought I had about Alvina and the care she'll need. But, as you said, these decisions can wait."

"Why do I have the feeling those wide, innocent eyes are meant to throw me off the scent?"

"Because you believe that only you can come up with

345

the solution to a problem?"

"Indeed?"

She was aware of the stillness around them. The servants had disappeared; only she and Philip still stood in the tower passage. She smelled the lingering smoke, the biting odor of charred wood and fabrics. And as she looked at Philip in the lanternlight and saw the quizzingly raised brow in the sooty face, the wet blanket flopping around a once-elegant evening coat and pantaloons, she felt laughter bubbling inside her.

She did nothing to stop it, but let it build until it rang out and filled the glum passage. It was wonderful to laugh, to know she hadn't forgotten how during the past dismal days.

After one rather startled look at her, Philip grinned, his teeth very white in the smudged face.

He touched a finger to her chin. "Don't think *you* look any better. Your hair is powdered with ashes, there's a daub of soot on the tip of your nose, and even though the dampening of a gown was once the rage, you may have carried the custom a bit too far, my scandalous lady."

She looked down at herself, the silk of her evening gown clinging to her bosom and hips. And she had nothing to cover herself with. Somewhere in the tower, she had lost her shawl.

Hoping he couldn't see the blush that warmed her face, she said, "That'll teach me. I'll never again allow a gentleman to hug me when he's been playing fireman."

"You'll allow *no* gentleman to hug you at *any* time," he corrected.

He shrugged off the blanket, and once more she found herself crushed to his breast.

"This, my Meg, is a privilege *I* reserve."

"Indeed! I don't recall—"

His mouth covered hers and she could say no more. She had no desire to speak or think. It was so much better to shut out everything so she could feel the liquid warmth spreading through her body, could hear the sing-

346

ng in her blood.

But then she heard something else, a voice she'd heard many times before, in London at the Bow Street court. Much as she tried, she could not shut it out.

"Meg, my dear. If you'll give me your attention for just moment, I'll be happy to offer you my felicitations."

Philip would not let her go. All she could do was turn n his arms to face the Bow Street magistrate, who had, pparently, just come out of the tower.

"Sir Nathaniel! What are you doing here?"

A smile softened the magistrate's stern features. Keeping my promise to Fletcher that I'd give you proection if need be. I'm glad to know you'll be taken care f. Fletcher would be pleased with your choice."

"But, Sir Nathaniel," she said, trying in vain to put ome distance between her and Philip, "nothing has been ettled yet."

Philip gave her a stern look, but she did not miss a ertain gleam in those hazel eyes.

"Meg, if you mean to turn me down after all that's appened between us, I'll—"

"How can I turn you down?" She was torn between aughter and annoyance. "You haven't proposed! I did. And *you* turned me down."

"I'm sure you'll settle it in time," Sir Nathaniel said astily. "I felicitate you, Meg, and to Lord Stanbrook I ffer my congratulations. You've made an excellent hoice, sir."

The magistrate bowed and would have hurried off. But Meg, finally gathering her wits, stayed him.

"Sir Nathaniel, I'm sure your promise to Fletcher is ot the only reason that brought you here. You have ews as well, don't you?"

Philip said, "I should have told you, I daresay. Sir Nathaniel drove down to tell us that it was indeed Alvina who hired the carriage and the team of chestnuts that ried to run you down in Piccadilly."

"Yes," she said, giving him a speaking look. "I daresay you should have told me."

Sir Nathaniel edged past them. "I understand I might have spared myself the trouble of the journey. And save for the fact that I'd see you, I wish I hadn't come. The less I know about this affair, the better."

"Will you need to take action?"

"Not unless you file a complaint against your aunt about the incidents in London."

Meg felt Philip's eyes on her.

"I shan't do that, Sir Nathaniel."

Did she see a flicker of relief in the magistrate's eyes? She could not be certain.

He nodded. "We'll talk in the morning if you like Meg. I'm rather fatigued, and Sir Richard was kind enough to offer me a room. Good night."

"Good night, Sir Nathaniel."

Philip did not take his eyes off her. "My little Bow Street runner, are you sure? You're not going to insist that Alvina stand trial?"

"Quite sure. But don't let my decision deceive you into believing that I have accepted the strange code of honor governing the *ton*. And now, Lord Stanbrook—' She gave him a stern look. "Back to the subject of Sir Nathaniel's presence."

"It slipped my mind," he said quietly. "I was too concerned about you."

She suppressed a smile. Of course there hadn't been time to tell her anything, just as she'd had no chance to repeat what Alvina had confessed before she set fire to the tower room. But Philip had a habit of not telling her things. It wouldn't hurt to let him know she would not put up with secrecy.

"Be that as it may. You also haven't said why you were in the tower just after the fire started."

"Hawkins saw you leave your room and he came to fetch me."

She remembered the shadow she'd seen near Philip' chamber. "I suppose you set him to spy on me."

"Meg, I knew you were in danger. I could not keep an eye on you all the time, so I enlisted Hawkins, Elspeth, Harv, and Jigger."

She could not keep up the facade of sternness. Her mouth twitched. "I always knew you were toplofty, high-and-mighty, and overbearing."

Once more his arm tightened around her. "Then you won't say any longer that nothing is settled between us?"

"And too cocksure by half!"

She raised herself on tiptoes and brushed her mouth against his.

"My lord, we have an assignation in the gazebo at eight o'clock. We'll settle matters then."

The morning sun just touched the front of the east tower and the east wing of the main house. Light and shadow fought on the stone walls and the thick creepers. And as brightness won supremacy over darkness, the house looked less like a gothic mansion where unspeakable horrors might take place.

Meg stood at one of the open gazebo windows, her eyes alternately on the graveled path leading to the house and on the battle between light and dark. She wondered what might have happened if her mother had not run away—but it was useless speculation. A question without an answer.

A movement on the path caught her attention. Eagerly, she leaned out the low window—as though that would make Philip reach her any faster. She saw him stop and examine the lilac hedge. He reached up, grasped one of the branches, and broke off a bloom.

Smiling, Meg retreated from the window. She sat down on one of the cushioned benches lining the gazebo walls and carefully smoothed the skirts of her gown—a green silk gown, perhaps too elegant for general morning wear but not too pretentious for a woman about to accept a proposal of marriage.

Philip entered, his step jaunty, the smile she had never learned to resist curving his mouth and dancing in his eyes.

"Meg, my love."

There was no question as to how she'd respond. She rose and stepped into his arms, feeling them close around her and knowing that this was where she wanted to be. Always.

His kiss was feather-light, and almost immediately he released her, ushering her to the seat she had previously occupied. Sitting down beside her, he offered the sprig of lilac.

"It's a little past its prime, I'm afraid. But I hoped it would pave the path to a happy conclusion of our negotiations."

"Thank you." She bent her face over the tiny white blossoms. "Then you do admit that we have not quite settled the matter of . . . of our marriage?"

"I admit nothing of the kind. But then I'm too cocksure by half."

She gave him a startled look, saw the devilish light in his eyes, and had to force herself to stay serious.

"Philip, in all fairness I must caution you that I do not intend to give up acting."

"Did I ask you to do that?" He frowned. "Strange. My memory at thirty-seven, apparently, leaves much to be desired. Perhaps I ought to caution you that you'll be marrying a man approaching the doddering age?"

She bit her lip.

"You are outrageous! But I refuse to be drawn off the scent, as you phrased it last night."

"This morning," he corrected.

"Philip, be serious!"

"How can I when your eyes are laughing at me?"

"*You* will not be laughing when your friends close their doors to you and your actress wife."

He took her hands and one by one raised them to his mouth.

"They are not my friends if they close their doors to ..."

"But your pride—"

He interrupted. "My pride will be in your success. I ...ll adore my actress wife."

"Don't stop. Tell me more."

"And you call me outrageous!" He frowned, giving her ... disconcerted look. "Meg, will you promise me one ...ing?"

"What?"

"Not to give birth to our children while on the stage as, ... was told, Mrs. Siddons did more than once."

Meg could not help it. Her laughter rang out, filling the ...zebo and drifting through the open windows.

"She never did! Whoever told you such a bouncer?"

"Well, I don't recall precisely, but—"

"But nothing! Mrs. Siddons gave birth to one of her ...ildren right after a performance, but she was *not* on ...age. And besides, I decided that one play a season will ... just the thing to keep my audience on tenterhooks. ...'hat do you wager that next year I'll be proclaimed the ...st, the most famous actress England ever boasted?"

"My Meg, I never bet on certainties."

"And the rest of the time I can devote to being the ...untess of Stanbrook. Philip, what are the duties of a ...untess?"

"To be an obedient wife and a doting mother. But ...pecially to be an obedient, compliant wife."

She primmed her mouth. "Impossible."

"I'll teach you, my Meg."

The look in his eyes made her pulse race and drove ...armth into her cheeks. His arms closed around her. His ...outh came closer and closer.

Suddenly, he cocked an eyebrow at her. "Elspeth tells ... there'll be more white lilacs in a week or ten days. ...ey'd make a lovely bridal bouquet, if you could bring ...urself to say yes."

"Devil a bit, Stanbrook! How can I say yes when you

never get around to popping the question?"

"It's your own fault. You bewitch me. No ration
thought stays in my mind, save that I love you."

"And I love you, Philip."

"Will you do me the honor, the very great honor,
taking me to husband?"

"Yes."

He caught her to his breast, and when he kissed he
Meg thought her heart would burst with love and jo
Whatever role she'd play on stage, she knew in life she
play no other than leading lady to Philip's leading ma